In the World of the Outcasts

In the World of the Outcasts

Notes of a Former Penal Laborer

Volume I

By Pëtr Filippovich Iakubovich

Translated with an Introduction by
Andrew A. Gentes

ANTHEM PRESS
LONDON · NEW YORK · DELHI

Anthem Press
An imprint of Wimbledon Publishing Company
www.anthempress.com

This edition first published in UK and USA 2015
by ANTHEM PRESS
75–76 Blackfriars Road, London SE1 8HA, UK
or PO Box 9779, London SW19 7ZG, UK
and
244 Madison Ave #116, New York, NY 10016, USA

First published in hardback by Anthem Press in 2014

Translation, Introduction and editorial matter copyright © Andrew A. Gentes 2015

The author asserts the moral right to be identified as the author of this work.

Cover image: 'Appearances and types [of inhabitants] on Sakhalin island'
by Innokentii Ignat'evich Pavlovskii

British Library Cataloguing-in-Publication Data
A catalogue record for this book is available from the British Library.

Library of Congress Cataloging-in-Publication Data
The Library of Congress has cataloged the hardcover edition as follows:
P. IA. (Petr IAkubovich), 1860–1911, author.
[V mire otverzhennykh. English]
In the world of the outcasts : notes of a former penal laborer / by Pëtr Filippovich Iakubovich;
translated with an introduction by Andrew A. Gentes.
volumes ; cm. – (Anthem series on Russian, East European and Eurasian studies)
Includes bibliographical references.
ISBN 978-1-78308-111-0 (hardcover : alk. paper)
1. P. IA. (Petr IAkubovich), 1860–1911–Exile. 2. Exiles–Russia (Federation) –Siberia–Biography.
3. Prisoners–Russia (Federation) –Siberia–History–19th century. 4. Prisons–Russia
(Federation) –Siberia–History–19th century. I. Gentes, Andrew Armand, 1964–translator, writer of
added commentary. II. P. IA. (Petr IAkubovich), 1860–1911. V mire otverzhennykh. Translation of: III.
Title. IV. Series: Anthem series on Russian, East European
and Eurasian studies.
DK770.I2313 2013
957'.07092–dc23
[B]
2013043691

ISBN-13: 978 1 78308 417 3 (Pbk)
ISBN-10: 1 78308 417 0 (Pbk)

This title is also available as an ebook.

CONTENTS

VOLUME I

IN THE WORLD OF THE OUTCASTS (Vol. I)

VOLUME II

IN THE WORLD OF THE OUTCASTS (Vol. II)

ACKNOWLEDGMENTS

This project began around five years ago as I was completing my first translation, *Russia's Penal Colony in the East: A Translation of Vlas Doroshevich's "Sakhalin"* (Anthem, 2009). As with that translation, I wish to thank Tej P. S. Sood for accepting this one for publication. Thanks as well to my editor Brian Stone and the rest of the staff at Anthem. Nadia Golenkova and Auken Tungatorova helped with some particularly difficult passages. I also appreciate the services of my proofreader Alexey Golubev. I am grateful for the support of my colleagues, in particular Sarah Badcock, whose consistent enthusiasm for this project has been warmly appreciated, and Chris Eley, who was similarly enthusiastic and who helped sharpen my Introduction. I remain responsible for any errors or mistranslations.

Pëtr Filippovich Iakubovich

INTRODUCTION

Pëtr Filippovich Iakubovich was born on 22 October (3 November, new style) 1860, in Novgorod Province, in western Russia, to a family that had acquired noble status in the mid-seventeenth century. In 1882, he completed a degree in philology at Saint Petersburg University. He had by this time already published several poems, and would go on to publish many more under both his given name and pseudonyms.

Like many young men and women of the so-called intelligentsia, Iakubovich was swept up by the heady political events of his day. Tsar Alexander II abolished serfdom—that scourge of old Russia—in 1861; and the next two decades witnessed a number of modifications to the empire's laws and institutions that were collectively known as the Great Reforms.

Despite the rapid change sweeping Russia, conservative and reactionary forces fought tooth and nail to preserve what they could of the old order by countering and stymieing these reforms. Moreover, many reforms enacted by Alexander II were primarily designed to strengthen the government and not to establish any sort of liberal, Western-style democracy.

Accordingly, serf emancipation was accompanied by an exponential expansion of the Siberian exile system, which was disproportionately populated by peasants and poor townspeople. Russia's subjects were first exiled to Siberia in the late sixteenth century, correspondent to Moscow's conquest of Siberia. In addition to ridding the motherland of criminals and other deviants, exile was used to colonize this enormous landmass with thousands of involuntary settlers. Few exiles were ever permitted to return to Russia, and many were forced to bring their families with them.

Siberian exile also had a third major function, which was to rid the Crown of political opponents. In fact, the first exiles sent beyond the Urals in 1590 by Tsar Boris Godunov, came from a town that rioted after learning of the probable murder of Tsarevich Dmitrii, the original heir to the throne.

Following an attempted assassination of Alexander II in 1866 by a deranged young man, the government increasingly relied upon exile to deal with a growing number of political activists and pamphleteers, impatient at what they saw as the slow progress of the reforms. Prior to the Revolution of 1905, these "political exiles" (*politicheskie ssyl'nye*) never amounted to more than one or two percent of Siberia's total exile population. Nonetheless, both Petersburg and Siberian officials considered them to be of the utmost importance. Whereas the criminal exiles who routinely escaped their lightly guarded confines and terrorized Siberia's inhabitants were seen as a nuisance, the "politicals" were seen as a dire threat (quite rightly, as it turned out, given the activities of those later politicals Lenin, Trotsky, and Stalin).

The origins of the Crown's fear of the intelligentsia, itself made up almost entirely of noblemen and noblewomen, lay in the Decembrist Revolt of 1825, when a conspiracy of young officers from some of Russia's leading families hoped to overthrow and murder Tsar Nicholas I. The Decembrists' exile and imprisonment in Siberia were followed by that of the Polish revolutionaries of 1830–31 and 1863 and members of the Petrashevskii Circle in 1848. Among the latter group was the young writer Fëdor Dostoevskii, who spent five years in Omsk's fortress prison, alongside criminal penal laborers.

Like his fellow inmates, Dostoevskii was sentenced to *katorga*. Russia's version of penal labor, *katorga* originated during the reign of Peter the Great (1689–1725). The mercurial tsar used tens of thousands of convicts to construct numerous ports, fortresses, metallurgical works, and even his new capital Petersburg. Penal laborers' lives were cruelly wasted in conditions that left dark stains on some of Russia's greatest monuments.

Though traumatized by his imprisonment, Dostoevskii survived his penal experience and, thanks to Alexander II's relaxation of censorship laws, wrote and published the first full-length account of *katorga* in the Russian language. His *roman à clef*, entitled *Notes from a Dead House*,[1] caused a small sensation among Russia's reading public. For the first time, Russia's penal population was portrayed (mostly) sympathetically, and for the first time, the exile system's probity and efficacy were openly questioned.

With its intimate portrayal of sadistic guards and dehumanized prisoners, Dostoevskii's *Dead House* created a template for subsequent Russian authors. Given the great writer's skill, it was a hard act to follow, as Iakubovich acknowledges more than once in *World of the Outcasts*. Nonetheless, Iakubovich believed that the story he had to tell—and which was based, like Dostoevskii's, on his own prison experience—could be more than just an homage to *Dead House*. In the end, Iakubovich would add to a growing literary canon that was documenting a sore in the body politic still oozing years after the Great Reforms.

In 1882 Iakubovich, still a university student, fell in with a circle of young intellectuals opposed to the prevailing ruling order. Whereas Dostoevskii's Petrashevskii Circle had been little more than an evening roundtable, the group to which Iakubovich allied himself was far more serious. It called itself "People's Will" (*Narodnaia volia*), and took as its mission nothing less than the overthrow of the old order and the establishment of a utopian society to be based on the traditional Russian peasant commune.

As it turned out, People's Will's only major accomplishment was its spectacular assassination of Alexander II, in March 1881. For years, the regime had been turning in an increasingly reactionary direction, imprisoning and exiling by the dozens even those merely suspected of political untrustworthiness. But the shock wave of the tsar's assassination hardened the ruling apparatus still more, for the Decembrist specter had returned to haunt the Romanovs; and the fact that People's Will and other activists were stirring up trouble in the countryside only added to the phantasmagoria of a popular uprising. Alexander II's son and successor Alexander III therefore quickly imposed martial law and set about nullifying many of his father's liberal reforms. The reactionary nature of his reign helps explain Iakubovich's fate.

In 1884, police arrested People's Will member German A. Lopatin (1845–1918). Inside Lopatin's pocket was a list of contacts including Iakubovich, who was immediately arrested along with others and confined deep inside the infamous Peter-Paul Fortress.

Following three years' solitary confinement in a dank cell, Iakubovich was tried in what is called "The Lopatin Case" or "The Trial of the Twenty-One." A closed military tribunal sentenced him to death. But, as was common at that time, his punishment was commuted by imperial decree to eighteen years of *katorga* labor.

Iakubovich spent the first three years of his sentence in the special political prison at Kara, in central Transbaikalia. In 1890, he was transferred to a criminal *katorga* prison in Transbaikalia called Akatui. Politicals (most notably the Decembrist Mikhail S. Lunin, who died there) had been sent to Akatui before him, but Iakubovich was among the first group of prisoners assigned to a prison that had been newly built there. Influenced by penology in Western Europe and the United Sates, Russian officials deliberated throughout the nineteenth century over different ideas to improve their penal system. Yet despite the many articles, books, and debates on this topic that emerged both inside and outside government, the treatment of Russia's prisoners continued along traditional lines: convicts were confined together in large wards and assigned to work in state industries, or else banished to settlements in Siberia and northern Russia where most either survived through beggary or thievery or simply escaped. To this day there remains no real effort to rehabilitate criminals in Russia. Rather, the emphasis is on isolation, retribution, and exploitation.

For most of those sentenced to *katorga* during the tsarist era, exploitation meant laboring in the iron, silver, and lead mines of Transbaikalia. Mining prisons and labor camps were first established there in the early eighteenth century and quickly expanded under Catherine the Great (1762–1796). By the mid-nineteenth century, Transbaikalia's mines were largely exhausted and its prisons dilapidated, and the regime was casting about for new solutions to deal with its growing penal population.

Although focused like its predecessor on mining, the new prison to which Iakubovich was assigned at Akatui (which he renames "Shelai" in *World of the Outcasts*) was meant to serve as a model, indeed, a showcase, for future prisons in Russia. Iakubovich's descriptions of this model prison's features and the extent to which they functioned as intended form a major part of his book, and serve to critique late nineteenth-century Russia's penal system every bit as incisively as Dostoevskii did decades earlier.

In 1895, one year after Nicholas II succeeded his father Alexander III to the throne, an imperial manifesto reduced the sentences of many penal laborers. Iakubovich graduated from penal laborer to "exile-settler" (*ssyl'no-poselenets*), and left prison to move to Kurgan, a large town in Tobolsk Province, Western Siberia. In 1899, afflicted by nerve problems that originated during his work in the Akatui mines (herein described), he received permission to leave Siberia. He settled first in Kazan, and was later allowed to return to Petersburg.

In the World of the Outcasts was first published while Iakubovich was still in Kurgan. Iakubovich had kept notebooks during his time in prison, and he based his novelized account on these. In large part because he was still a convict, Iakubovich used the pseudonym "Dr. L. Melshin." Actually, as he asserts here in "In Place of a Foreword," he (Melshin) is merely publishing the manuscripts of a deceased neighbor whom he identifies only with the initial "D." In adopting this facetious ruse, Iakubovich borrows from Dostoevskii, who similarly disguised the provenance of *Dead House*. Whereas readers surely knew that Dostoevskii had authored the latter work, it is not clear how many of Melshin's readers knew about Iakubovich.

Like those of Dostoevskii and many other tsarist-era writers, Iakubovich's novel was first serialized in one of the era's so-called "thick" journals—periodicals combining prose, poetry, essays, history, criticism, and commentary. The liberal journal *Russkoe bogatstvo* (Russian Wealth) serialized *World of the Outcasts* in seventeen issues between September 1895 and July 1898.

The novel was popular, and along with Anton Chekhov's book on the Sakhalin penal colony that was serialized during this same period, it added to a growing public interest in, and a concern for, Siberia's exiles. What became a burgeoning human rights issue would inspire the founding of aid societies for exiles' families and efforts to abolish the exile system once and for all.[2]

Volume I of *World of the Outcasts* appeared in book form in 1896 and went through three editions prior to 1917; Volume II went through two editions. The work was soon translated into French and German. In 1933, the All-Union Society of Political Exiles and Penal Laborers, a Soviet organization comprising veterans of the tsarist exile system, sponsored an edition. However, this would mark the last appearance of the book for several decades. The transmogrification of the exile system into the GULag and Iosif Stalin's establishment of a police state rendered accounts of the previous regime's penal system damning by comparison. A book like *World of the Outcasts* could not be allowed in a state that was essentially an outgrowth of its penal structure.

The situation changed briefly under Nikita Khrushchev's premiership, during the brief period known as the "thaw." An easing of censorship and Khrushchev's personal intervention had allowed for Aleksandr Solzhenitsyn's *One Day in the Life of Ivan Denisovich* to be published, and the appearance of this novella detailing a GULag prisoner's quotidian existence was as important to civil society as *Dead House* had been a century earlier. *Denisovich* seems to have paved the way, for in 1964 (the same year Khrushchev was deposed by neo-Stalinists) a two-volume edition of *World of the Outcasts* appeared. For the first time it identified Iakubovich, not L. Melshin, as author. The present translation is based on this edition and marks the book's first appearance in English.[3] It is also the first new edition of this book in any language in nearly half a century.

In the World of the Outcasts can be read on a number of levels, at least two of which are literary and historical. In terms of the former, we have here the story of the protagonist Ivan Nikolaevich that begins with his journey to a prison in Siberia for an unspecified crime. Ivan Nikolaevich is clearly Iakubovich's stand-in. Although we do not ever learn the reason for his punishment, the rest of the book is largely concerned with him and his inner world. To this extent, *World of the Outcasts* is much more autobiographical than is *Dead House*, in which Dostoevskii tends to favor the third person and the perspective of the omniscient novelist over that of the first-person, confessional style preferred by Iakubovich.

Volume I consists of two large sections entitled "Shelai Mine" and "Solitude." In-between these is a digression entitled "The Little Eagle of Fergana." In "Little Eagle," Iakubovich undertakes an effort notable for its time to humanize a particular Muslim prisoner in much the same way as he does the other prisoners he writes about.

Within Imperial Russia Muslims were second-class subjects. Their homelands in the Caucasus and Central Asia were conquered by Russia during the nineteenth century; and inhabitants from these regions figured disproportionately among Siberia's exiles. Iakubovich's empathy for and portrayal of the "Little Eagle" Marazgali is a highlight of the book.

"Shelai Mine" and "Solitude" deal with Shelai Prison's many other residents more broadly and episodically. Almost without exception, these colorful characters hail from Russia's lower classes, as Iakubovich demonstrates in a number of vignettes and by reproducing their ungrammatical speech. Additionally, much of "Shelai Prison" concerns Ivan Nikolaevich's efforts to live alongside these people he would otherwise have had almost no contact with in freedom. This draws attention to the fact that the class system in Imperial Russia was even more rigid than that in contemporaneous England, and was even perhaps most similar to India's caste system. As historians have correctly observed, two worlds existed in Russia. Ivan Nikolaevich belonged to the privileged but far smaller of these worlds; in Shelai, he must cohabitate with those he regards as his social inferiors.

It is this canyon between the educated and cultivated nobleman Ivan Nikolaevich and the uncouth and ignorant common prisoners that gives the section "Solitude" its title. Ivan Nikolaevich's real punishment is not so much his labor in the mine or smithy or even the restrictions on his freedom of movement, as it is the humiliation of being treated like every other prisoner and the absence of a boon companion. No one around him speaks French, understands his allusions to Classical antiquity, or can even maintain a logical debate. Psychically, he is at the bottom of a deep well, gradually being driven to despair and thoughts of suicide.

However, it is not fair to say that Iakubovich is treated entirely like the other prisoners. In contrast to the treatment of intellectuals and the privileged in Stalin's GULag, such persons generally received favorable treatment in exile until the very end of the tsarist era. Ivan Nikolaevich is no exception. He is permitted ready access to Captain Luchezarov, Shelai Prison's occasionally avuncular commandant, and talks to Luchezarov as an equal—something common prisoners would never think or be allowed to do. Throughout the story, Ivan Nikolaevich uses his noble status to wrest numerous concessions from Luchezarov, or "Six-Eyes," as the prisoners soon dub him.

Despite the respite of his meetings with Luchezarov, Ivan Nikolaevich is overjoyed when two other intellectuals (by implication, both politicals like he) arrive at Shelai Prison. This encounter occurs at the beginning of Volume II, in the section appropriately entitled "With Comrades." The presence of Dmitrii Shteinhart and Valerian Bashurov render much of Volume II a different kind of account than Volume I. True to their populist convictions, the trio set out to improve and educate the prison population— or *katorga*, as it is sometimes called. They also strive to protect their dignity against Luchezarov and a penal system that is becoming increasingly bureaucratized and, hence, dehumanized. Their campaign leads to a stand-off with Second Lieutenant Lomov, a character Iakubovich seems at least partly to intend to be comical but who, given Russia's subsequent penal history, is actually a harbinger of far more grotesque and dangerous yes-men to come.

Following Ivan Nikolaevich's release from prison, Iakubovich interpolates a section called "Mare on the Road" ("mare" being prison slang for the prison population). Iakubovich narrates this portion in the third person—a narrative switch that is at first jarring. But the characters in this section are among the best realized in the book. Iakubovich is particularly adept at portraying a veteran exile named Old Man Pavel Nikolaev as well as one of the prison "Ivans" called Chinaman.

Iakubovich returns to the first person in the section entitled "Among the Hills," which describes part of his time in settlement. Here again the characters are well-drawn. Iakubovich is especially acute in his description of, first, Ivan Nikolaevich's post-incarceration anguish and, later, his joy at being joined in settlement by his devoted sister (in real life, Iakubovich was joined by his fiancée R. F. Frank). "Among the Hills" also includes a romantic tragedy that is every bit at moving as "The Little Eagle of Fergana."

A second level on which this book is valuable is as an historical document. As a record of late imperial Siberian exile, it is every bit as valuable as *Dead House* and Chekhov's *Sakhalin Island* (large parts of which were fictionalized and dramatized). In fact, given that comparatively fewer exiles were assigned to fortresses or the island penal colony, the settings for Iakubovich's story—a march route, a prison, a mine, and a settlement, all in Transbaikalia—were more typical of Russia's penal laborers.

The verisimilitude of all *World of the Outcast*'s characters allows them to serve as representatives of particular mindsets and classes associated with the late imperial period. For one thing, Iakubovich is known to have based nearly all his characters on real human beings. But he is also a master of insight and nuance, with an ability to empathize with characters quite outside his social sphere, such as the young Jewish homosexual, Shuster, whose lengthy story is related in an autobiographical essay. As a result, we gain insight not just into the lives of Jews in Russia during this time, but also into Iakubovich's effort to combat through literature the Judeophobia so prevalent among his contemporaries.

Yet, at the same time, if *World of the Outcasts* is to be regarded as an historical document, it must be borne in mind that it was written by a privileged member of the nobility who had an agenda of his own. For example, by never stating why Ivan Nikolaevich (or, for that matter, Dmitrii Shteinhart or Valerian Bashurov) has been exiled, Iakubovich leaves a void that may perplex today's readers. Writing when he did, Iakubovich could trust in his readership's familiarity with recent political events to deduce that all three characters have been exiled for political activities. And it may be that, even had Iakubovich wanted to reveal this, he could not because of the censorship reintroduced after 1881. Also unmentioned is the fact that whereas many young activists were banished for little more than publishing socialist pamphlets, others were cold-blooded killers who randomly murdered street cops on the basis of dimly understood socialist slogans. Iakubovich portrays Ivan Nikolaevich and his comrades as do-gooders whose sole concern is the benefit of "the people" and who even manage to carry out their mission within the confines of Shelai's stone walls. But he never hints at the dark side of the motivation that drove People's Will and other populists, that their political ends justified the use of violent means.

Perhaps more than anything, Iakubovich's *World of the Outcasts* testifies to the gap that separated him and other self-appointed social activists from the people on whose behalf they were supposedly acting. At no time do Ivan Nikolaevich or his comrades question their *modus vivendi* of enlightening the "dark people." Their every attempt to better feed and tutor Nogaitsev, Lunkov, Chirok, and other common prisoners is presented as an unalloyed good stemming from the purest and most selfless intentions. The only time Ivan Nikolaevich questions himself is when he feels that his charges have failed him, when, as he explicitly states, he feels he is wasting his gifts and energy to no effect. His is a purely selfish attitude.

Herein lay the Russian intelligentsia's greatest failing as well as the origins of the danger they posed to Russia's other (much larger) half of society. Iakubovich unwittingly demonstrates that he and other politicals would never be content until commoners progressed to share what they saw as their superior level of existence—a level marked by the prim avoidance of vulgarity, sublime appreciation of Pushkin, and a thoroughly Romantic conceptualization of love and nature. Though a young man, Iakubovich's Ivan Nikolaevich is utterly content with himself and his knowledge of the world, to the extent that he feels within his rights not only to lecture other prisoners but the commandant himself. He is even self-righteous toward his comrade Valerian Bashurov, and entertains no doubt that the privileges he demands from Luchezarov are his due. Ultimately, Ivan Nikolaevich demonstrates a myopia every bit as profound (or shallow) as that of the most ignorant and cretinous prisoners he disdains.

It is therefore all the more remarkable that Iakubovich, in speaking through the voices of Semënov, Goncharov, Iukhorev, and other hardened prisoners, is able, if not always to empathize with these men's worldviews, at least to account for them and, for the most part, to present them impartially, appreciating as he does that these embittered, wayward souls are products of their environment, of their own traumatic upbringings, or simply, as he has Ivan Nikolaevich often say, of simple misfortune.

Indeed, when assailed by critics Iakubovich sought to convey this perspective in particular. Later editions of his book included a response to one critic who especially got his goat, and it is included here.[4] "From the Author (*Postcriptum*)" is Iakubovich's strenuous response to what he sees as professor of psychiatry P. Kovalevskii's misuse of his and Dostoevskii's books to support his characterization of the "natural-born criminal." As Michel Foucault has shown,[5] this monster was constructed by a number of late nineteenth-century European and American writers, largely on the basis of Lombrosianism.[6] Iakubovich rather easily dismantles his antagonist's argument; yet, in the process, he reveals through selective self-referencing and gymnastic ratiocination his conflicted attitude toward those prisoners he lived with for so long but failed to reform. A victim of "white knight syndrome," whereby a self-proclaimed altruist is in fact a solipsist whose disappointment with his charges' failings fuels his resentment toward them, Iakubovich simply doth protest too much.

After returning to Petersburg, Iakubovich continued his writing career. He apparently took no active part in the growing oppositionist movement, but wrote poems (many published pseudonymously) of a revolutionary/Romantic bent. Iakubovich died in Petersburg on 17 March (30 March, new style) 1911. He remained blissfully unaware of the devastation that a one-dimensional devotion to *noblesse oblige* (a construction favored by Ivan Nikolaevich and his comrades) would cause in the years ahead, when educated noblemen who had formed the Russian Communist Party would slaughter peasants for not appreciating what they were trying to do for them. Despite some renown as a poet, it is *In the World of the Outcasts* that remains Iakubovich's lasting achievement.[7]

Andrew A. Gentes
Newport, New Hampshire
January 2013

A NOTE ON TRANSLITERATION

Transliteration is according to the Library of Congress system, with the exception that Russian diacritical marks have been removed from the main text to facilitate reading and use of the possessive *s*. Diacritical marks have been preserved in the notes for scholarly purposes.

CHARACTERS

Political Prisoners

Dmitrii Petrovich Shteinhart (Shtengor, Shteingor, Mitrii Petrovich)
Ivan Nikolaevich D. (Nikolaich, Mikolaich)
Valerian Mikhailovich Bashurov

Criminal Prisoners and Exiles

Andrei Busov (Andriushenka)
Andriushka Povar
Andriushka Vodianin ("Iron Cat")
"The Angry Cockroach"
Aziadinov
Bulanov
Bykov
Chinaman
Dasher (real name: Ibrahim Nureddin Sarafetdinov)
Diudin
Dubasov
Egor Rakitin
Evgraf Efimov (Egrashka, Egraf)
Gandorin
Goncharov
Gribskii ("The Amateur")
Iasha (Iashka) Pervanov ("Marmot")
Iukhorev

Karpushka Lipatov
Kolpakov
Komlëv
Koshkin
Krasnoperov
Kuzma Chirok
Letunov
Lunkov
Malaika Kantaurov
Mikhail Ivanovich Nogaitsev ("Bruin," Mikhailo Ivanych [Ivanovich], Mishenka)
Mikhaila Burenkov
Mishka Birkin ("Astrologer," "Postal Hound")
Mishka Shuster
Moisha Borukhovich ("Vorukhovich") and his wife Entale (Enta)
Nikifor Burenkov (Mikishka)
Ogurtsov
Osip (Oska) Nepomniashchii
Palchikov
Paramon Malakhov
Pavel (Old Man) Nikolaev
Penkin
Perminov
Petin ("Elk")
Petrushka Semënov (Petka, Petkin, Petia, Penkin)
Ravilov
Roman (Romashka) Pestrov
Shah Lamas
Shemelin
Shmatov ("Buzzy")
Shooter
Skoropadov
Tiupkin
Tropin
Usanbai Marazgali (Usan, Usanka, Usankin)
Vaska Kos
Vladimirov ("Bear's Ears")
Zhebreek (Zhebreik, Zhebreichik, Zhebrei, "Prickly Weed")
Zvonarenko ("Leather Tack")

Officials, Administrators, and Guards

Andrei Semënovich (Semënych) Monakhov (mine superintendent)
Bezymënnykh (guard)
Kostrov (warden of Kadaia Prison)

Luchezarov ("Six-Eyes," commandant of Shelai Prison)
Pëtr Petrovich (Petrukha, duty officer at Shelai mine)
Petushkov (Ilich) (guard; later, mine duty officer at Shelai)
Prokofii Filippovich (Prokopii, Pron, Pronia, Pronia-the-Living-Dead, guard at Shelai)
Second Lieutenant Lomov (Luchezarov's assistant)
Sholsein ("The Finn")
Snake Head (Vasilii Andreevich) (a guard at Shelai)
Zemlianskii (Shelai's medic)

Female Characters

Anna Arkadevna (Cossack officer's wife and helper to the political prisoners)
Avdotia Finogenovna (Duniashka, Duniakha, Dunka)
Poduzdova (Poduzdikha)
Tania (Ivan Nikolaevich's sister)

IN THE WORLD OF THE OUTCASTS

NOTES OF A FORMER PENAL LABORER

VOLUME I

IN PLACE OF A FOREWORD

I hasten to immediately forewarn the reader that the essays proffered for his attention are by no means attributable to the below assignee, who is nothing other than their publisher. They fell into my hands completely by accident. Due to the constant travel associated with my work, I'm rarely home in the little city in Transbaikalia that serves as my family's residence; for this reason, I encounter my neighbors only very rarely. Indeed, know that few interest me. In my rare leisurely moments I prefer to devote my attention to a newspaper or a new literary journal rather than to sit at a game of vint, which in Siberia is inevitably accompanied by a carafe of vodka. Such behavior, it's true, has not given me a completely favorable reputation among the inhabitants, who call me ursine and arrogant; but I don't aspire to be so, and was neither startled nor pained in the least when, upon return from one of my trips, a new resident, having installed himself next door to my apartment, outdid even myself with his strange behavior. This was a middle-aged gentleman, rather handsome and with prominent streaks of gray in his hair and beard, an exile-settler from the nobility, with a not unknown name. A much discussed rumor had related all the sentimental details of his commission of a murder out of jealousy and it found him to be suffering innocently. At D.'s disposal were an apparently healthy constitution, cultivated manners, a quiet disposition, and an imposing exterior; but from his first moment in the new place he revealed not only a reluctance to become friends but that he had no intention of getting acquainted with anyone. Shortly before his arrival in our city he'd obtained the right to travel throughout Siberia, but he had no wish to go anywhere. The locals complained, judged, and scratched their heads trying to make sense of the newcomer's lifestyle, then just threw up their hands. I, too, was interested by the fact that D. ordered in the new year a bunch of newspapers and journals, not only in Russian but other languages (to that point I'd had no rivals in this regard); but my curiosity was of a purely passive character: I made not the slightest effort to become acquainted, and, though living several yards apart, we remained perfect mysteries to each other. I knew one thing about D.'s life: that he wrote a lot, that whole reams of manuscripts were in his work baskets and desk drawers. I knew this from his landlady, though the contents of the manuscripts remained *terra incognita* to me.

On the 19th of May this present year, having returned from a two-week trip, I learned to my surprise that D. was no longer among the living: the day after I'd left on my trip he'd been found dead, pen in hand, slumped over his writing desk. Death had come instantaneously from heart attack. The deceased's effects were surveyed and recorded, their subsequent fate being unknown to me; also, the landlady took his basket of manuscripts into her apartment. Like nearly all Siberians this kind woman was distinguished by excessive curiosity, and it had long been her desire to learn what her tenant was always writing about. Several days after D.'s death she brought these manuscripts to my wife, with whom she'd developed a deep friendship, and both were impatiently awaiting my return. I myself pored over these manuscripts with great interest, and from the first pages realized they were not just for idle curiosity. Here was a detailed account of the deceased's life in *katorga*… Following Dostoevskii's *Notes from a Dead House*, I'd not encountered any similar literary effort. True, there exist many stories about vagabonds,[1] penal laborers, and exile-settlers, and essays on the way-stations and prisons, but a single, large publication devoted to this "world of the outcasts" and written by a man who'd lived and was a fellow member in it for several years—I knew of no such other collection in the new Russian literature. In many places in the essays the author even draws a comparison (purely superficial, of course: he's always modest) between himself as a writer and Dostoevskii. Completely fairly, it seems to me, he points out that several decades separate his memoirs from *Notes from a Dead House*, and that this period has witnessed such enormous changes in all the structures of Russian activity that the topics could not remain completely the same as they were during Dostoevskii's time, nor could the inner or outer appearance of the Dead House.

These observations give cause to imagine the author had several goals for his work and obviously intended it for publication. In his papers there is even a draft of a letter to an editor of one of the thick journals, albeit apparently unsent at the time of his death.

These are the considerations that have led me to publish these essays. I'm now publishing only the first part, which I managed to sort through and edit. It became apparent during my editing that the writing was obviously rough: the style was uneven in places; boring repetitions were encountered; in certain places the lyrical effusions had to be limited or expanded to acceptable boundaries. But I emphasize one thing: I inserted none of my own opinions into these essays, and the reader should regard me merely as their editor/publisher. In my personal view, they are distinguished by candor and veraciousness; but I do not wish, however, to take it upon myself to answer for the facts presented. I don't even know whether this is literally a composite reality or facts that have passed through a prism of artistic analysis and generalization…

Let critics and individuals more competent and knowledgeable than I of the prisoner's world and his customs judge all this.

—Dr. L. Melshin
June 1894

ON THE THRESHOLD

Pallid darkness! Terrible darkness!
Malice, madness, love…
We're walking, old chap, on our knees through blood!
"Enough—there's the dust, and no blood…"

—N. Nekrasov[1]

For many years I happened to live in a world of outcasts, and to live not in the capacity of an observer, but participating directly in all the minutiae of their existence, lying beside them on plank beds, slurping the same disgusting skilly, performing the same labor, and partially engaging in the same intellectual and customary interests. I often desired to put my impressions down on paper, to communicate them to the world.

True, it's terrible to take on the task that a great artist already brilliantly accomplished at one time. Nevertheless, the goals I've set for myself are very modest, and I'm utterly devoid of a pretense toward artistic letters. I'm anyway seized by fear when I remember the existence of *Notes from a Dead House*: such is the charm of genius…

I hesitated for a very long time… Only the notion that Dostoevskii's epoch is already several decades separated from ours, that since his time so much has altered in that gloomy world that multitudinous changes are reflected in all areas and phenomena of Russian life, and that, anyway, it does not happen too often in history that such writers as Dostoevskii enter *katorga*—this single notion alone finally made me take up the quill and set all doubts aside. I'm fulfilling this task as my powers allow, without standing on stilts and aspiring for just a single reward—an acknowledgement of sincerity.

For a start, I'll try to portray the path along the way-stations into Siberia, comprising as it does the threshold of the outcasts' world. As far as I know, no one in our literature has yet drawn a just portrait of all the splendors and fascinations in this compulsory voyage—now fortunately consigned to history by the laying of the Siberian railroad.[2] At the same time, I add a quick proviso: the reader will not find in this section of my essays a complete representation of the prisoner's world. Being a "political criminal," I entered *katorga* in relative comfort—in the stations I had a room separate from the criminal party, I rode in a cart, etc. In a word, I was still a dilettante convict at that time, only just beginning to familiarize myself with my new status; my observations were therefore unavoidably characterized by a certain superficiality and, occasionally, sheer nervousness. Nonetheless, I hope I can say something interesting and unfamiliar here to the broader public.

I.

The beginning of my own convict life—this is in no way strange—I remember only vaguely. Many things appear to me as if in a dream, and certain occurrences I won't even vouch for—that is, as to whether they happened or I just dreamt them. This is of course because I was physically and morally ill, although none of the doctors who examined me ever thought so. For investigatory purposes I was confined for a long time in extreme solitary confinement under soul-destroying conditions, without books and receiving government rations only.[3] My final weeks of confinement were especially difficult, when from out of a distant provincial backwoods my old mother came to the capital (some friendly soul "brought a hillside down on her chest" and told her everything). She'd become stooped and completely gray from grief, though just some three years earlier I'd seen her a hearty, dark-haired woman—no one had thought her older than forty. During our meetings she at first tried to appear hearty and cheerful: the simple soul, she was seeking to reassure me! But I couldn't see her through eyes swollen with tears, couldn't sense in those moments the deep, deep sadness in her affectionate gaze, couldn't guess that she was tirelessly petitioning, knocking on every door, humiliating herself, praying, weeping…

Akh, those accursed, accursed days!… How much blood can be got from a heart, how much poison can the heart take, how much of one's best strengths can be exhausted… Leave, leave! I don't want to remember… I will say one thing: the final meeting with my mother was terrible. I often had nightmares in prison, but none compare with the pain and horror of our parting!…

We were separated at three o'clock, and at six, as the warden told me, I would be shackled and shaved. I remember now what I experienced then. To that point I'd not seen fetters, nor had I seen shaven heads; I'd also been able to glean but a dim understanding from booklet writings, but for that matter had had no need or inclination to learn more about them. Everything I imagined, I must confess, was far worse than it was. For example, for some reason I thought that when they put me in chains it would be impossible to move about freely, and so I hastened to enjoy my last minutes of freedom by hurriedly pacing about my little cell, which allowed me all of three steps in one direction. Then came the fateful moment; they brought me to the bathhouse where I was defamed: they ever so smoothly shaved precisely half my scalp (the right half, lengthwise) and fettered me ever so securely in ten-pound chains with iron rings, so tight against my ankles that my underwear barely fit between them and my skin. My legs were swollen for several days, such that my constraints had to be re-forged into wider and lighter chains. Later, in Siberia, especially Eastern Siberia, I was pleased that the administration was lenient in this regard: both fetters and shaving were seen as obsolete there and not as indispensable formalities. More often than not, parties went about without fetters, carrying them along with their other regulation items in small lockers; the shaving of heads was also done without especial pedantry, and in the *katorga* prisons there was often no shaving at all. Not so in Russia and Western Siberia. It seems it will be a long time before it's understood that chains or the shaving of heads will never prevent anyone from escaping and concealing himself: a naked scalp can easily be topped by a wig or simply even a cap; any fetters can be broken in five minutes if well smashed along a door-hinge or by a log with rivets; sometimes, simply flattening a ring so that a foot can pass through it is sufficient. Only prison walls and guards can seriously obstruct escapes.

Fetters and shaved heads undoubtedly have but one goal—to humiliate a man deprived of rights. In the not-so-distant past, criminals were branded on the face and shoulders with a special iron stamp, and it's still possible to encounter in convict almshouses and old-timers' settlements those with these terrible stigmata. But modern-day enlightenment forbids such barbarity, seeing in it a form of medieval torture; and so only fetters and shaved heads are left… Is it necessary that these punishments remain? Is it not a shame, when the thinking on this issue occasionally achieves reactionary extremes, that circulars are published on the strict and rigorous application of the law and, as in the past, they once more begin shaving heads and fettering ankles? In recalling my own experience I may furthermore say I'm far more reconciled to the latter practice than to shaving: to a large extent, chains are poeticized by legend and folksong, and in the eyes of prisoners are a kind of honor and not a desecration… You experience a completely different emotion looking at a military barber preparing to do his disgusting business. Shaving, besides being a mental torture, typically causes purely physical pain: clumsy hands and dull razors cut the skin, slice open pimples, and cause abrasions on the naturally uneven scalp… Blood, mixing with the abundantly flowing dirty foam on the head, completes the mute and indifferent executioner's operation,[4] and there are the grimaces and cries of the victim being operated on—all this transforms into a veritable ordeal those minutes when one is awaiting his turn, so that it's both an humiliation and a torture. I won't even mention the freezing of the now naked scalp during Siberia's terrible cold spells and, at the same time thanks to this, the contracting of chills and coughs.

Not once have fetters been accurately described in Russian literature. Smithies tightly rivet a large iron ring around each leg, loose enough so that the underwear can fit between it and the skin, tight enough so that it won't slide off the foot. From these rings extend two chains consisting of small rings; they meet at the single largest ring, to which is attached a strap that substitutes for the prisoner's belt. As such the chains hang downward and during movement slap against the legs and knock each other—"clatter, clank." The rings on the ankles spin and cause sores, for the prevention of which there are leather "under-chains" and "under-strains." In Eastern Siberia, where the administration isn't so pedantic as in Russia and prisoners wear fetters only as a formality, the rings are fixed directly to boots so that under-chains and under-strains are never needed. I've not worn fetters for a long time, and so probably cannot describe how prisoners take off their underwear and trousers when their fetters can't be removed; however, I well remember I perfectly accomplished this necessity without anyone's help. Necessity is the mother…

I remember well the day of my departure or, better to say, the agonizing scene accompanying this departure. That day, my mother wasn't allowed to meet with me (as I've said, our farewell took place the day before, when I was shackled). Early in the morning, I was put in a closed carriage and rushed to the train station, during which I saw something unusual that absolutely tore my heart in two. Beneath the window of the hastily darkened coach I noticed a friendly face, distorted by inhuman efforts to appear cheerful; at first I thought I was delirious, hallucinating… I peered through the window—and what did I see? My mother—a pathetic, sick, and elderly woman—running alongside the carriage, with a flushed and swollen face and stringy locks of hair white as snow falling from beneath her hat; running without noticing her fatigue, apparently saying something that was inaudible beneath the hoof-beats, and blowing kisses… Poor woman! Trying earlier that morning to arrange a meeting with me (she'd been unable to do so the day before), she'd been delayed while I was being put into the carriage, and here she was at pains to amend her mistake ("I'm late!") and to again bid her son farewell with endless love. I waved at her through the window (and my angry guard waved at her), mutely signaling for her to stop, to torment neither herself nor me; but she ran for a long time, until at last her strength ran out and the carriage sped away forever! Then, I remember, I leaned back in the carriage and bitterly sobbed. I didn't see my mother again, and will never see her in this lifetime, for she has long been in eternal rest in one of the unfilled cemeteries of a soulless city. But after I arrived in Siberia I received from her a letter, part of which has been chiseled into my memory and still burns my heart as brightly as any fire, as painfully as any tears.

> Following our encounter at the carriage window [she wrote], I hired a cabbie and hurried to the railroad. But I arrived after you did, of course, because that hateful cabbie refused to hurry his team, and so I didn't see you when you left the carriage. No matter how I begged and pleaded, the gendarmes wouldn't let me onto the platform. Nor could I sneak onto it, since they were following me. What could I do? I came up with a new strategy. Having reconciled myself with fate I was leaving the station, but instead of going home I walked slowly a few steps then suddenly changed direction and ran into the field along a railing, reasoning that the train would pass by and I'd be able to see your dear face once more… I did indeed manage to deceive those vigilant Arguses; but I had to go far into the field, and the train was hurtling by at such terrific speed that I couldn't distinguish one face from another. But I was clinging to the idea that perhaps you'd see me… I stood on a rise, on a small rock, and waved my kerchief back and forth until that black monster passed completely by.

Alas! I never saw her… At that moment I wasn't looking out the window. There was nothing I wanted to see, even inside my soul, where it was so barren, so dark…

Further along, everything appeared to me in a kind of blurry, disordered vision of dissociated pieces. Fortunately—as I've said—I was given special arrangements separate from the criminal party, and in the way-stations up to Irkutsk I stayed in a separate room with my political comrades. Were it not for this, I don't know how I could have endured all the difficulties of that road in so sickened a condition as I was at the time. On the barge,[5] we had a special room in the cabin-house and a special tiny compartment on deck (behind bars, of course), where it was possible to breathe fresh air. It was separated from the general prisoners' deck by a simple canvass partition. I remember I loved to sit on deck, especially at night, gazing for hours at the Volga's and Kama's dark shorelines passing by. I remember the shores disappearing behind me seemed like my own past, the irretrievable years of my youth, and often, gazing into the black distance left behind,

I would shudder at the idea that they would never return! The tarpaulin moved only slightly with the barge's forward motion and concealed the edges of the shoreline; my sick imagination identified these edges with the future in that it, too, was unknown. During the day, I usually lay curled up somewhere in a corner in the cabin-house and only rarely went on deck. This is why I lack clear memories of the Volga's and Kama's luxurious and charming landscapes that so inspire all voluntary and involuntary tourists. I admired them only at night, beneath the fantastic illumination of moon and stars.

Among fellow intellectuals entering administrative exile, I was alone in having been sentenced to penal labor; this is why I was comparatively uninterested in them, well understanding that among them I was merely a temporary guest. Their world understood me far better than that concealed behind the tarpaulin and which would soon become my home... I well recall that for a long time, I idealized the criminal prisoners with their labor collectives' values and customs. They all seemed to me Stenka Razins,[6] a people of great daring and a sort of cheerful despondency... Among the small claque of intellectuals the chains' clinking sounded thin and prosaic; but behind the canvass partition where hundreds of feet were shifting this sound was musical, powerful, enchanting... For centuries, Mother Volga had heard this sound, in which an ingenuous poetry and song was passed from generation to generation... There they were, suffering without malice, without complaints or aspirations, knowing it could not be otherwise: "My mother wouldn't accept me—well then, beat me; but should I fall again, don't you complain!..."

These homeless masses of prisoners elicited such feelings from me especially in the evenings, when their mighty choir would form and a wild melody resounded from beneath their chains' music far up the Volga, where infinite melancholy and reckless courage and bravery could suddenly be heard once more.

> With gusto, you fellow,
> You're not some girl,
> Sing, sing with melancholy![7]

However, I'd barely had my first intimate encounter with this poetic world when—what do you think, readers? —You'll see!... Going on deck one night, I approached the tarpaulin and began listening to the scattered whispers and talk coming from the main section. Suddenly, I noticed a small opening in the partition, through which I peered to learn about this mysterious world. But someone's crude hand prevented me from seeing clearly into the ocean of these modern-day Stenka Razins' shaved heads and varied physiques, and when he poked his fingers through my improvisatory window I moved just quick enough to save my favorite sensory organ. I dared not approach the aperture again. This was my first disappointment with these people among whom I lived so many years—the first evidence that, as a hell of outer darkness and unaccountable evil, this secret world offered an inexplicable cruelty so alien and I, sharing in its existence, would have to suffer so much from it...

In Tiumen,[8] after having entered the prison courtyard for roll call, I saw face-to-face for the first time the huge party of prisoners. Lord! What visages weren't there, from the most kindly and thoughtful to the most repulsive and bestial; what nationalities, what names weren't there! Particularly unique were the names of the vagabonds who accounted for half the party. Ivan-the-Suffering, Pëtr-the-Enduring, Semën-Many-Grievances-Seen, Hightail-it-to-the-Hill, Beaten-to-Pieces, I'm-Following-Him, Thirty-Two-Years-Lost,[9] and so forth and so on in that vein. The following surnames were also favored: Diamond, Gem, Lion, Eagle, Falcon, Stormy, Windy, Adze, Georgian,[10] and similar fine-sounding and boastful names.

But, strictly speaking, it is only from Tomsk onwards that I sufficiently start recalling vividly and distinctly the route and all my impressions. However, I hasten to remind the reader once more that although I was traveling with the party, I lived separately from its existence. I had my own cart and a separate "nobleman's room," outfitted comparatively pleasantly and comfortably. Convoy officers treated me and my comrades courteously throughout our deportation. I repeat that I was just a dilettante convict at that time, and whereas the entirety of the deportation was a constant nightmare for me, I'm afraid even to think what would have become of me had I been in the general prisoners' section.

II.

First of all—what is this way-station route like?

Imagine that the entire length of this endless Siberian trail, which extends from Tomsk to Sretensk (centering on Nerchinsk *katorga*)—that is, stretches three thousand versts—is divided into twenty forty-verst segments culminating in huge, gloomy buildings with barred windows—for the most part tumble-down, withered, and battered by cold—standing beside the road somewhere alone in a field or village outskirts. These are the so-called way-stations—roadside prisons in which exhausted parties rest and spend the night. Speaking more precisely, of two such prisons the smaller is called a semi-station and only the other, larger and better, is the way-station. Inside the latter are barracks for the local military unit that convoys prisoners and an apartment for the officer—unlimited master over an expanse of two or even four such prisons. A party spends just one night at a semi-station, starting along the road again next morning; arriving at a way-station it stops to rest for a day, which is thus called a "day-off." As such, every third day passes without activity, and because of this the party proceeds terribly slowly. It's fair to say that it takes a month to travel the distance (500 versts) from Tomsk to Krasnoiarsk, and two months from Krasnoiarsk to Irkutsk (1,000 versts)!... But, given the conditions, it's generally unthinkable to abolish the days off and proceed faster.

It must be remembered that except for the sick and crippled all prisoners, weakened by long incarceration in prisons and burdened with chains, in heavy boots and wind-tattered sheepskin jackets, travel approximately thirty versts a day on foot with only every third day off, and would prefer to avoid these conditions.

I'll say only a few words about prisoners' clothes. The Siberian administration, intimately familiar with climatic and other local conditions, shuts its eyes at prisoners bringing their own things along the journey. I'm talking about nothing other than a practical consideration, as simple fairness requires a less rigid and formal attitude towards prisoners who find themselves on the road, just beginning their much-suffering convict existence with all possible discomforts and deprivations; it's another matter after arriving in the assigned location, where the lifestyle has solid foundations and settles into a monotonous rut. In Russia, unfortunately, bureaucrats are guided by neither abstract nor practical considerations but strictly follow instructions to the letter. In Moscow, they took *everything of mine* and sent me on the journey with a single regulation outfit, having taken away even my needle and thread. I ended up terribly cold, sick, and unnecessarily enduring much deprivation and suffering. Regulation clothing is suitable neither for the changing weather and climate nor for the peculiarities of invalids' limbs. Everyone's subjected to the same mold—size, fitness, habits—in both body and soul. For example, the regulation hat's so-called ear flaps were sewn in such a way that they laid against my back and I resembled precisely a rabbit, but not a human; my feet, wrapped in thin bast, were as if sunk into fathomless barrels in a pair of boots so enormous I couldn't even walk like a human being; contrarily, my narrow trousers had with difficulty been tugged onto my legs and were with the least incautious movement mercilessly splitting and coming apart at the seams…

Normally, in a party of 400 people, you have many poods of baggage and a sufficient number of elderly and sick so as to require thirty to forty wagons, half of which are loaded with baggage ("junk") and sent off early in the morning before the rest of the party. Around fifteen wagons remain for the sick and frail. The drivers allow only four people in each wagon, five after a big argument. Most spots are taken by the sick, whose right to the seats no one disputes, and only a few spots remain for the weak—those unable to walk all the twenty-five to forty versts along the way. These spots are literally seized by force, and you often see some helpless, pitiful individual running behind a telega, vainly pleading "give me a seat," while in the telega there stands above the rest the insolent physique of a strapping fellow, large-fisted and thick-necked, by the name of vagabond. It should be added that the assignment of spots in the wagons constitutes one of the sources of income for the prison collective's headman.

Vagabonds generally carry out the real punishments in any party. These people are for the most part depraved, having what is called *ni foi, ni loi*[11] for a soul, though they are tight with one another and comprise within the party the actual state within the state. "Vagabond," in their opinion, is the highest title for a prisoner. It signifies a person for whom nothing is more valuable in the world than personal volition, who is cunning and able to avoid any punishment. Such is this inscribed on a vagabond's roguish eyes that he'll say he's a fellow without identity! More than once, he'll tell you, he's been "beyond the sea," that is, in *katorga* beyond Baikal, and didn't want to resign himself to it, so he left!… Moreover, he loudly proclaims the same thing in front of officials.

"How many is this one, old man?" an officer asks with a friendly and familiar smile.

"Fifth time, your honor," answers an old man standing in a soldier's pose. "Twice I went beyond the sea, twice to Irkutsk, 'n' this time I'm goin' to Eniseisk."

"Mind that when I catch you, you scoundrel, you'll be going a sixth time!"

"I'll be happy to try, your honor," whispers the rogue. "Perhaps by then you'll 'ave been promoted 'n' assigned to Iakutsk."[12]

The party laughs and the officer walks off in embarrassment.

"What're you sly ones up to?" he turns to the intellectuals.

Especially in Western Siberia, the portion of a party sentenced to *katorga* in which vagabonds constitute the majority is typically held in check; the minority is more deprived of rights and broken-down, as if most had been branded outcasts even in the prisoner's eyes: "I say, I couldn't get outta this one! 'N' what's worse, I sold myself for a crust!..." Esteem is expressed only for the "die-hards" and those for whom it's certain this isn't their first trip and who will be able "to break away" again. Yet, in general, the *katorga* portion of the party is chiefly known by the contemptuous names *kobylka* (the mare[13]) and *shpanka* (herd of sheep). What is said in prisons and on the road about vagabonds' antics is at times absolutely beyond belief, but among their own it's impossible not to accept it as the unvarnished truth. Vagabonds are the little tsars in the prisoner's world, directing the collective as they please because they act in concert. They occupy all the lucrative, bribe-collecting positions: they are the headmen and junior headmen, the cooks, bakers, medical personnel, and *maidanshchiki*[14]—they are everything and everywhere. In the capacity of headman they distribute the foraging stipend[15] and sell spots in the wagons; in the capacity of cooks they steal portions of the meat ration and distribute them amongst their gang, whereas they give to the wretched mare slops no swine would eat; vagabond medical personnel starve and rob their patients and often dispatch them straight to Heaven if convenient. If one among the mare is known to have money concealed in a "pouch" (in the belt), he's ambushed off the trail and strangled and robbed in broad daylight. The impudent things do even worse. In front of hundreds of prisoners an "Ivan," dressed in a red shirt and rattling a few pieces of silver in his bottomless trouser pocket, sits down next to another man's wife and begins hugging and kissing her on the eyes. If the husband objects, his comrades will beat him half to death and the conqueror will assume rights to his wife. The well-organized "vagabond society" is always well-placed on the sleeping platforms. The vagabond headman is typically given the level highest above everyone, and will save the best places for his comrades just before final roll call. And for the most part, the *katorga* mare huddles on the bare floor beneath the platforms, in filth, darkness, and cold. However, it's said the vagabonds have recently been brought to their knees. Sakhalin, having swallowed in its depths thousands of people who could not produce internal passports, has done more than anything to cut them down to size;[16] and stricter statutes overall have played a role concerning vagabondage. Initially, vagabonds were sentenced to settlements, where they weren't forced to stay; but since 1878, only those arrested in the Russian provinces are sent to settlements, whereas all the rest go to *katorga*.[17] Hundreds and thousands have been resettled from *katorga* to Sakhalin. The vagabonds' ranks have greatly thinned, especially those of the old vagabond, brands on their cheeks, for whom new prison regulations strictly specified continuous surveillance. It's necessary to add that prison conditions have changed: the administration intervenes from the start in prisoners' collective arrangements, in their intimate, internal life, all the time resolutely siding with the penal laborers; in many prisons, vagabonds are totally prevented from occupying the collective positions they would previously have had. The *katorga* mare has raised its head. In the Tomsk forwarding prison, where there are sometimes as many as three thousand prisoners, there were several terrible massacres of vagabonds. In one such battle (in the mid-1880s) it's said up to fifty men were murdered or wounded. The new spirit percolating through the prison world is producing a general breakdown and collapse of old prisoners' habits and customs. Many of the likeable ones are disappearing, but still more the disagreeable ones. Earlier, the husk (exchanger), who'd been tricked into trading sentences, was "nailed" without fail, if not in one then another prison; and those who "squealed" (told) on a comrade in some affair would be murdered just like all "little tongues" (informers). In previous years in that same Tomsk prison hardly a night would pass without a murder, and corpses were often pulled out of the prison well. "Notes," as it were, detailing some prisoner's violation of general standards and exposing his "covers" were passed throughout the entire prison world, from Kiev on to Vladivostok. There even existed a prisoner's law, condemning a "little tongue" to death upon receipt of *seven* such notes about him...

Now, vagabonds are beginning to be more submissive, and when they notice a weakness in a penal laborer's argument they simply grit their teeth and back off, saying: "Them was the ol' days... It's a new generation!"

I return to my depiction of the march route.

We politicals, as I said above, had our own separate room, though it was often provided very grudgingly. The way-stations are not all built to a single plan, and anytime we'd arrive at a place to rest we were uneasy and guessing at what we would encounter during the day off. If given a separate little room, well-heated with a separate corridor, we'd say we landed in Paradise that day. But the combination of that and the other virtue was met with quite rarely. We were sometimes given a room with a separate entrance, but then it was so cold your teeth chattered; another time we'd be given a warm room but without a separate corridor, and outside our threshold the many-throated herd would roar and howl, sounding like a raging blizzard, a hellish concerto of coarsened throats belonging to those whose nerves were frayed by their chains. Malevolent people with shaved heads would peep through the door at us; and if one of us went out for fresh air he had to pass through several wards of prisoners lolling about the pathway and directly on the filthy floor beneath the sleeping platforms, so that their bags and legs had to be stepped over. Women and young girls were there... Even when one happened to spend the night in a room with his male comrades, there were many and all types of torments and difficulties. To clean oneself well, one had to take off one's underclothes (this was absolutely necessary during a several months' journey through filthy, disgusting way-stations), but there was no private corner where one could hide from strangers' eyes. The regular older comrades were able to improvise curtains and screens, though of course this only smoothed over and lightened a little bit the difficulties of the situation. Here I approach a point in my memories that still freezes my soul. I'm speaking of those prostrate spaces, about their terrible filth—and what filth was allowed! It goes without saying that, in principle, the full weight of those inexpressibly licentious conditions would fall mainly on the females. The local administration apparently views all criminal female penal laborers as lost causes and therefore worries over them no more than it does the men. How fair this point-of-view is, I don't know. Personally—and this is the truth—I did not meet a single female convict who did not possess either an Ivan or several prisoners at the same time. But the question is, do not the prisons' and march route's very conditions bring a woman to such a level? Are all women who end up in *katorga* already lost causes? Of course, we'll remember that along with the female convicts entering *katorga* there are many free wives, sisters, mothers, and daughters about whose earlier debauchery, who can say? All must live in the same loathsome conditions… I'm told that the married men and their families travel separately from the bachelors. But this only provides an excuse. To wit, the married men's parties present a continuous organized debauch. Of whom do these parties consist? Of several "bachelorette" women and several dozen families—that is, men, women, juveniles, and children. They all sleep side-by-side in a single ward. In the corridor outside the ward's doors stands a large vat called a Siberian crapper, around which men and women crowd, with a wall providing a natural division. To all this must be added the debauched and debauching soldiers who, just after roll call, when prisoners should be locked in their room, sneak by the dozens into the ward, where an unimaginable orgy lasts all night. Cries, screams, laughter, shameless deal-making, kissing, crass jokes are all on view, out in the open… And so it goes from day to day, station to station, sometimes for as long as a whole year or more, and under these conditions these men dare ruin with stony contempt a girl or a woman without any regard for her chastity!…

Among the prisoners, the convoy's soldiers become especially terribly debauched; they spread all possible physical infections. The Siberian soldier assigned "to convoy" single women views this circumstance as a happy picnic with intriguing diversions. He has no discipline, no concern for others whatsoever! He sits in a wagon, lays down his rifle, embraces convict beauties, sings at the top of his lungs, talks shamelessly, and doesn't want to know anything else! At night, the drinking bouts and debaucheries carry on, and then, with poisoned head and empty pockets, he returns to his post barracks until another such procession… This is his life. Can it be imagined that out of such a warrior an exemplary family man could emerge upon conclusion of his service in a convoy command? By the same token, several of the convoy officers were no better in my day: at least more than once I heard about cases in which they purchased convict father's virgin daughters and about other no less flattering activities.

In my day, because they had separate rooms, female politicals could choose to travel with the bachelor criminals' party, but in recent years it's said they're being assigned to the families' party exclusively (probably as a result of considerations of a moral character!). I'll merely say that in the bachelors' parties there are not the formless ghosts of unconcealed cynicism and debauchery such as I happened to observe in the families' parties… I can imagine nothing more terrible for an educated woman than to be in such circumstances. It goes without saying that debauchery's unclean hands do not touch her lightly, and having to see and hear all that is happening makes her a martyr indeed! Perhaps an even heavier cross is borne by the loving man, suitor, or brother who vigilantly monitors the pests swirling round her, trying with all his might to lessen the suffocating atmosphere, to create more or less humane conditions, and who often sees and feels that whatever he does is ineffectual and weak! I had no relative or dear one within that circle, no single woman who was close to me, yet I nevertheless experienced all these emotions passed on by all these martyrdoms…

Evening arrives. Soldiers take roll call and order the crapper brought into the ward. We protest, saying there are women among us. After a long discussion, the officer decides at last to leave the ward unlocked and the crapper in the corridor. I recall that in one of the way-stations a story was going round that the officer, having agreed to the crapper's placement in the corridor, nonetheless wanted to post a guard next to it… It's hard to say if this was more from naïvety or cruelty! Such problems arose in the way-stations at night, though daylight was little better. There existed only one private spot, covered for the most part in indescribable filth and vileness, in the midst of several hundred people among whom were educated women and all kinds of sick and injured persons… But enough of this. The rest may be left to the imagination. I'll just add a few words concerning prisoners' swearing. Nowhere have I heard such foul, such offensive, beast-like cursing as during my first moments in Siberia among prisoners, soldiers, and free residents (the drivers). It's unknown who borrowed from whom, though it is plausible that this truly artistic form of language could only have been created in prison. I repeat: I've never heard anything like it from any peasant in Russia… There really flourished an exquisitely three-story cursing. The satirist throughout all the Russian lands moans "Mother! Mother!" But only in prison, only in Siberia, does this oath achieve the most precise and appropriate virtuosity. In Russia, the unfortunate "mother" entirely serves everyone as an object for the venting of filthy language; in Siberia, she is broken down to her frills and corset bones, and every tiny piece individually blackened and exposed for defamation: the liver, eyeball, heart, blood, rib, soul, existence—all become objects of vicious cruelty and the most callous hatred! And this isn't enough: true artists of cursing will go further and, utterly without making sense, drag into "mother" words like "law," "faith," and even "God"—curses that for all their senselessness sound no less vile and disgusting.

I positively shuddered the first time I heard these terrible blasphemies; the words literally injured me, as if I'd been stabbed or lashed. Today, of course, I regard them indifferently, though I cannot recall without horror how young girls, educated, with refined sensibilities, nervous constitutions, and delicate and sensitive souls, heard all of it, absolutely everything…

Can anyone who does not understand me really mock my words?

III.

The majority of prisoners for whom there are no special papers or instructions are incarcerated in the central way-stations (in Tomsk, Krasnoiarsk, and Irkutsk), sometimes for six months or even a year or longer, until they're assigned to a party. As a result, the journey to an assigned location frequently lasts from one to three years. Of course, the married men and craftsmen have an advantage, since life on the road is incomparably more carefree than in *katorga*: such men seize every opportunity to prolong the journey, and often, when their assigned place appears, they have already received the right to enter the free command, and so that they don't spend a day in the *katorga* prisons.[18] It's a different thing with regard to those undifferentiated prisoners who possess no profitable trade whatever: they tire of the journey and beseech the administration to assign them to a party quickly. But most excruciating of all is the journey for so-called "returnees," that is, those who've completed their *katorga* terms and are entering a settlement. They proceed most slowly: in those places where a party stops to rest for a day, a returnee sometimes remains for an entire week.

Since the first parties depart Russia no earlier than mid-May, the journey along the Siberian way-stations mostly happens during autumn and winter, when all other travails and deprivations are accompanied by dirt, cold, rain, blizzards, and frosts. I will try to describe a typical day:[19]

Early in the morning (when it's barely light in the yard), the mare is already on its feet; the walls resound with rumbling, clanking, and squabbling. Prisoners go to bed early, but awaken even earlier; some, having slept during the day, don't sleep at all and spend the whole night playing cards. You ask them: why are they hurrying to the next station? They don't know themselves. They just say about themselves: "The mare always hurries, as if mother 'n' father's awaitin' us."

We often avoided the annoyances. Officers and guards for the most part treated us politely and even courteously: we had our own wagons and could separate from the main party with part of the guard and follow after it. We'd catch up to it, pass it, and be first to arrive at the next station. But it sometimes happened that an officer who'd had a previous run-in with a political from another party would order us not to take one step away from the other prisoners, and we'd travel with them simultaneously and arrive at the station simultaneously. If, the day before, we'd not apprised ourselves of the officer's disposition and had stayed up long into the evening talking and reading, then next morning would bring unpleasant scenes. The herd would have already formed itself and be ready to be move out to the road, but we'd still be waking up, hurrying to collect our thoughts and get dressed and grab our things… The herd would rage, curse, and complain they were getting cold because of the "rotten nobles"… A large, rough-hewn horse-stall would indeed be welcoming us when we arrived at a place, preferably before dusk. But there was often no basis whatsoever for any of this to happen: a stall could be a mere sixteen to twenty versts away, yet the mare would hurry along just the same!…

All arguments ended there. The mare tore along at breakneck speed. The only sound along the way was the sledges with their sick and enfeebled, who were barely able to travel. Were there any possibility of it, those true virtuosos of the road, especially among the vagabonds, who in principle always travel by foot, would be sitting in them. Such always go ahead of the parties: it's easier and "more convenient" to go first.

The soldiers run along barely pausing for breath, so habituated are they to moving, and the sledges barely keep pace. We arrived at a place very early.

Then we'd remain a certain distance from the way-station or semi-station, arranged in two ranks in anticipation of roll call. Guards stood around the prison. A sergeant-major would count the prisoners, and following this they immediately fly through the open gates with a wild shout of "hurray!" to secure spots on the sleeping platforms. A terrible crush and scuffle ensue. The weakest fall and are crushed underfoot by the stampeding throng, sometimes receiving serious injury; the sturdiest and most agile, zealously working their elbows and even fists, surge forward and stretch themselves out full-length across the platforms, trying to secure with their bodies as much space as possible, even stretching out their cassocks, sashes, and caps. In this manner one such trickster can occupy several yards of space; once even a small string is cast onto a platform that space is regarded as inviolable. All battles end there, such is the common law. An unaccustomed and nervous persons would be unable, I think, to endure the overwhelming terror of standing somewhere in a corner of the corridor, outside the doors leading into the common wards, and hearing the gradually approaching rumble of frenzied voices, the bellowing, cursing, and fighting, the mad clanking of chains, the tread of rushing feet: a perfectly colossal horde of barbarians coming to assault and tear you apart, smash you into little pieces, completely crush and annihilate you! They're all coming closer and closer… This terrible avalanche has at last now turned into the corridor: savage faces distorted by horror and the last efforts of strength, the gleaming whites of their eyes, clenched fists, the deafening rattle of chains, furious cursing—everything, it seems, is aimed directly at you. You wince in terror… But now the throng's mad flood turns to the right, through the ward's doorway, and merges into an undifferentiated, deafening howl in which nothing can be understood. Following the first breaker comes a second and third, then almost all of the most delinquent, shuffling their feet, cursing and swearing and having despaired of securing places on top of the platforms and now forced to crawl beneath… We, too, trudge along to our side compartment, preoccupied and filled with gloomy presentiments…

We enter a ward dimly illuminated by latticed windows, and gaze cheerlessly at elevated sleeping platforms onto which we climb with difficulty: it's warmer under a roof, but there's no firewood in the timber-box. Br-r-r! So cold… Our breaths form a cloud of steam in the ward. We rush to the little stove in the corner—it's unlit; there's not even any wood in it. We search for the guard (the so-called warder) responsible for stoking the stove for incoming parties.

He's a morose, unfriendly old man.

"Weren't 'spectin' a party t'day," he protests. He's lying, of course.

Someone unburdens his soul by quarreling with him; the more prudent unconcernedly go to find wood. None among them has a fur coat; everyone's trying to warm himself by striding about the ward or stamping his feet. At last, some wood arrives—it's thick, knotty, damp… And needs to be split. The prisoners are already using the axe to split firewood for themselves,[20] so we have to wait a while. But here comes the salvatory axe, and now the wood is split, put in the stove, and lit… Oh, hell! A new, more searing ordeal: the cast-iron stove is terribly smoky… Smoke fills the entire ward, mercilessly stings our eyes so that we can't see, think, or decide what to do… This experience lasted one, two, three hours until the damp wood finally flamed, the smoke cleared, and it became warm and possible to breathe freely. Tea and some kind of simple soup or gruel were prepared. Almost everywhere in Siberia the foraging stipend is ten kopeks per day, fifteen for the privileged. In Western Siberia, where everything's so cheap, where a loaf of wheat bread costs five kopeks, a pitcher of milk three kopeks, these allowances are just right and prisoners do well. Many have never eaten so well in freedom. But with the passage across the borders of Eniseisk and especially Irkutsk provinces, provisions become more and more expensive: a pound of meat costs ten kopeks, a pound of black bread three to four kopeks, and I remember one station where it was impossible to get bread for less than six kopeks a pound, but you had to eat four pounds to feel full!… True starvation afflicts the parties, all the more because of the despair caused by gambling. The almost entirely emaciated "*zhigany*"[21] offer astounding evidence of the terrible squandering of government provisions.

They say that was an exceptional year, when everything was very expensive, but that in general the foraging stipend is sufficient, especially when several prisoners combine to eat collectively. For one thing, not every person can join a group; but, primarily, distribution of the stipend is so uneven, without taking into account local prices of goods,[22] that prisoners are never guaranteed protection against market fluctuations. It seems that if it wanted, the administration could easily quickly adjust the stipend in every given location, correspondent to prices. Unfortunately, at that time, there was no consideration in this regard whatsoever. If sometimes there was a change in the stipend, this was due to red tape, and it was just laughable: in a hungry year the stipend was less, in a good year—more… But it would be even better if, instead of handing out money, a party was given hot soup and government bread at every station. This wouldn't be difficult. Prisoner cooks could go on ahead; and bread could be purchased beforehand from market women at strictly regulated government prices. The worse half of prisoners, consisting of card-sharps and tight-fisted *maidanshchiki*, would of course be terribly chagrined by such a reform, but at the same time there wouldn't be starving prisoners trading away regulation items and other outrages; who knows?—maybe there would be a reduction of this contingent of prisoners, among whom many are now drawn to the prison *maidany*,[23] card game, and other fascinations. But the reform I'm proposing would possibly improve most of all the morals of those very bureaucrats exercising authority over prisoners…

Unfortunately, these morals leave very, very much to be desired. Hence, one station's commander had the laudable habit of not heating the wards ahead of time while the party was in the darkened yard, under the pretext that he feared a fire… We were told that several prisoners suffered frostbite because of this gentleman; I'm amazed that those of us who stayed at his station remained healthy… Our party was put in a huge, damp cellar that had been left unheated for at least ten days (during a terrible frost). We demanded an explanation from the officer in charge, but he just laughed dismissively.

"This couldn't be worse," my companions tried to persuade him. "Report it to the commander. It's good many of us have warm clothes, but what about the other prisoners who'll be sleeping in this cold?"

"He-he!" laughed the officer. "You don't know them… They've some tricks…"

"What kind of tricks?"

"They keep spare wood-chips or coal in their mess-tins…"

Did it matter to continue arguing with this incorrigible optimist? He himself was hurrying to leave. The waste vat was dragged into the room, the door quickly slammed, the key thundered in the heavy lock, and we found ourselves alone. Because we couldn't sleep we drank tea all night and ran about the room playing leap-frog and doing other floor exercises… During this time I remembered the cheerful sergeant-major's consolation: "They've some tricks!" Indeed, a tough and hardy Russian fellow adapts to many situations and possesses many survival "tricks"!

The station commander of whom I'm writing was, among things, reputedly an educated and even liberal man; he sometimes came into the politicals' ward, spoke informally with us and expressed the most progressive and, at times, even audacious views…

The way-stations were in most cases very old and dilapidated; several had even been built in the 1830s, and although (one would think) money for repairs was budgeted at specified intervals, for some reason serious repairs and remodeling were not in evidence. It could be imagined these structures were for rats rather than people, such were the numbers of these loathsome creatures, scurrying at night among the bodies of prisoners and granting no peace with their loud fighting and repulsive squeaking. I remember once a huge rat drew blood from the finger of a person sleeping next to me…

Among other things to be found are gutted way-stations, in place of which they've been "unable" to build new ones for more than ten years. In such places parties either move on to the next station or stay in a private residence, a typical peasant hut in which the windows have been fitted with iron grilles and there aren't even sleeping platforms— nothing except the inevitable waste vat. Everyone in the party sleeps side-by-side on the bare floor. It's no wonder that in such situations, during times of poor and insufficient provisions, continuous marches through terrible Siberian frosts, and life amid filth and cold, prisoners' organisms, even without emaciation from previous years of prison incarceration, often don't hold up and succumb to a mix of typhus, fever, and other epidemic illnesses. The sick are left by the dozens in hospitals and by the dozens separate to rest on the nearest hillsides, where even a broken-down cross doesn't mark their final resting places… Yet entering a hospital isn't so easy. Only big cities and towns have hospitals, and I vividly remember several instances when upon arrival to a station with an infirmary only cold corpses were delivered… And how the wretch suffers before dying! He's laid like a log in a wagon, covered with his cassock and carried from station to station. Upon delivery he's similarly laid somewhere on the floor in the filth and cold. If he has no relative or close comrade then no one troubles over him, gets him water or food, or asks how his pain can be lessened. What happens in this case? Each looks after himself, is afraid to make a misstep and fall victim in this every given day's vicious struggle for survival. Everyone's heart has hardened, fossilized… I witnessed terrible scenes such as, for example, prisoners stumbling over such a sick person and responding to his groan with the vilest obscenities and wishes for his speedy departure to the other world—and no one interceded for these wretches!… Is this not barbaric behavior, reader? And we intellectuals, I recall, were indignant. But were we any better and kinder than the prisoners? Why did we not take these sick into the more salubrious quarters with us, not tend to them, not be there during their final moments? Why? Because charity really does begin at home, and because it was not an easy thing to live with the criminal party.

The year of my deportation a strange sickness resembling neither typhus nor nervous fever raged through the way-stations and took many people to their graves. This sickness began with severe stomach pangs and scythed down especially the educated and those weaker and less habituated to deprivation, and before my eyes several young people, dearly beloved by all my comrades, died.

On a cold autumn day, when snow already lay on the ground but the rivers weren't yet frozen, we sailed across the Biriusa River[24] in a small bark that could barely stay afloat under the weight of the wagons, soldiers, and prisoners, and found ourselves not far from a village of the same name with a station in its midst. We'd been numbed by the cold and were very hungry, and impatiently expected to rest in a warm and cozy room (the next day was a day off). A soldier had cheered us with news that the station was large and clean and there were separate quarters not only for our group but for our women. Everyone especially welcomed the latter. The station turned out to be a truly spacious and comparatively new building, completely unlike those rat holes most Siberian prisons presented us with. Overjoyed and smiling, we ran noisily into the entryway. Meeting us and smiling at our universal happiness, a junior officer from the local command presented a choice of three whole wards.

"This would be best of all," he said, opening one of the doors, "L. left here just three days ago."

"Just three days ago?" My companions were astonished. "But he was in the earlier party that left two weeks ago."

"Indeed, but he asked to be allowed to stay with the sick S. He buried him, then stayed here another two days and left with a guard to catch up to his party."

"He buried S.?! S. died?…"

Like thunder, this news shocked everyone… S. was a young Polish poet whose charming translations of Nadson[25] and original verses even I, who poorly understood Polish, enjoyed, and whom months earlier we'd all seen healthy, strong, and full of cheer and energy. The station building suddenly darkened before our eyes and turned melancholy, cold, and bleak; and when, unsteady and pale, we entered one of the wards and saw the empty sleeping platforms rising oppressively in the dusk, we suddenly caught the cold whiff of death. Here he'd suffered, here he'd died, practically alone, helpless, far from friends and relatives!… True, the kind junior officer, now visibly regretting that he'd blurted out S.'s death, insisted that he hadn't died here but in a neighboring ward, into which we therefore refused to go, but this was small consolation. There was a huge crack in the wall of our terrible ward, and I remember how with agonizing curiosity I looked through it, peering into the murky vacuum where, it seemed to me, the poet's soul had fled. And how the wind whistling occasionally through the tunnel seemed to me to be his cries…

Yet, even more painful than this news about an already accomplished fact was, owing to him, anxiety for the comrades and acquaintances behind and ahead of us. And what about us? Would merciless death once again take away someone close and dear? Indeed, that year death did not pity the most delicate loved ones, striking friends, sweethearts, brothers…

Our mood was of course utterly poisoned, and the whole day off spoiled. Anyone's slightest indisposition seemed a harbinger of a terrible disease; and in actual fact, the very next day one of the convoy soldiers took seriously ill, a very friendly youth who suddenly developed a powerful fever and delirium; despite all efforts by our homespun physicians to get the patient onto his feet, he had to be left in Biriusa. Whether he recovered or died we never learned.

Not a single one of my companions had seriously studied medicine, but sick prisoners, convoy soldiers, and even local residents nonetheless flocked to us at the station, giving us no peace day or night. Rumor of our ability to heal had spread in all directions. And what illness, what malaise didn't we see! What plague didn't visit our room! There came the typhic, the consumptive, the syphilitic. Breast-feeding babies were brought in with swollen necks, faces turned blue, eyes rolling; we were shown horrible sores and putrefying wounds, one variety of which inspired horror and banished the most ravenous appetite… Given our lack of medicines and sufficient knowledge it was so painful to see all these aspirants before us, filled with prayers and naïve beliefs, and to feel ourselves helpless to do anything, to provide any kind of help!

IV.

In Irkutsk Prison, where I happened to separate from the administratively exiled politicals, I became ill and was confined for several months.

Further along the journey, and taking advantage as earlier of significant privileges in comparison to other prisoners, I, due to my habit for solitude, often found them burdensome and brutally tedious. Maybe it was expressly because of this that I turned my attention to the beauty and grandeur of the Transbaikal countryside. I was especially struck by the sudden appearance of Baikal, across which we sailed on one of the first steamers. As if it were today I see this awesome, boiling, roiling iron monster. Behind its furious billows huge yellow cliffs are visible in the distance, close enough to touch, as in a dream, though they are twenty to thirty versts away!

Having remained behind alone, with just my own concerns, I rather involuntarily began devoting greater attention to the prisoners' world around me, then as earlier nearly always failing to notice what was going on. Previously, separate individuals somehow blurred together in my perception; I saw before me only a huge mass possessing, from my perspective, a single face, character, and will. Now, specific individuals began to emerge from this heap and to attract my curiosity. On the other hand, it need be said that for a long time I'd not exactly been idealizing the prisoners: I well knew to regard with skepticism their stories about themselves, and that they always exaggerated, etc.

As a sample, I'll write about certain characters I've remembered.

First of all, I remember a strange Greek subject with penetrating black eyes, terribly thin, with numerous bayonet and bullet wounds on his body that he received during escapes. He was very sullen and uncommunicative, but for some reason liked to approach me, especially when no other prisoner was near me. At times, I expected he'd ask for money; but he never once did. Once, I asked him what he was going to *katorga* for. With the most cynical (albeit simply expressed) candor, he explained that this latest time he and a comrade had murdered an entire family. I was truly terrified…

"Why did you do this?" I couldn't refrain from asking.

"For money, o' course," my interlocutor quietly laughed.

"Yes, but why murder them?… Moreover, why all of them, even the children?"

"Don't matter. Another time, we murdered two families."

I shuddered, at a loss to understand what he was saying.

"But what about God?" I asked. "Aren't you afraid?"

"What God?" the Greek asked in return, lowering his voice slightly as though with a certain sadness. "There was no one there but us, in those faraway places where even carrion crows don't bring their bones or animals go. We saw neither God nor the Devil!"

"And were you in solitary confinement?" I further asked him and, having received an answer in the negative, tried to sketch for my interlocutor a picture of the inner torments that seize many of even the famous brigands and eventually drive them to madness and suicide. He listened for a couple minutes, said nothing, and went away under some pretext.

Soon afterward, he disappeared from sight: he likely remained in hospital somewhere.

I was also approached by a foppish youth from the servant class, in the inevitable gaudy cravat and with refined—according to his understanding—mannerisms. This shallow person recalled all his beautiful "purchases" in Petersburg during public executions in Semënovskii Square: in his language, "to purchase" meant to pick someone's pocket. In the end, I noticed that during his visits he "purchased" something of mine…

On the other hand, I cannot recall without smiling the dear Tiupkin, a military deserter who, after missing for two years, had turned himself in to the authorities and was now marching to the courthouse in Chita. He was a kind hearted chap of twenty-six, physically underdeveloped, beardless, depressed, and always melancholy. He tended after me, prepared my dinner and tea, and lived in my "noble" room. We chatted through the long winter evenings, and I learned all his ins and outs. He was a fearsome gambler, and whenever I gave him a little money he disappeared and played *shtos*[26] all night. In the morning, a prisoner would inform me that Tiupkin had lost everything down to the last kopek.

"A good turn shouldn't cost a cow," the informant philosophized. "Wouldn't someone else be able to light your samovar 'n' get you what you need? E'en if you're feelin' grateful… Who's *he*? He was a spook [the prisoners' word for "soldier"], 'n' a spook he'll be till he's in the grave!"

Whereas Tiupkin appeared gloomy, especially at night, he was quite active in my ward: he'd beat the dust out of my things and move chests and bags from place to place without apparent reason; his incessantly tramping boots, accompanied by his deep, deep breathing, resounded throughout the ward.

"Tiupkin, are you not feeling well?"

Silence.

"Or perhaps you've lost something. Maybe you gambled it away?"

"No-o!" and, following this answer, my Tiupkin would instantly disappear in embarrassment.

One evening, he was again staying in my ward. We slaked our hunger with thin gruel and drank tea; we were very happy to warm ourselves before the coals cheerfully crackling in the burning stove. My Tiupkin completely softened up. He wanted to talk, talk without end, to complain ceaselessly about his fate.

"Akh, I'm woeful, bitter! Why'd my mother bring me into the world!"

"But are you exceptionally more unfortunate than others, Tiupkin? Others are going to *katorga*, but you—at worst—will be transferred to a penal unit. True, you'll be punished…"

Tiupkin attended to my consolations in silence.

"Is it true?" I said. "You really turned yourself in to the authorities and weren't captured? They'll take this into consideration, of course. They'll show lenience."

In place of an answer he suddenly began tugging his hair savagely.

"Okh, I'm woeful, bitter!…"

"Maybe you're covering up? Maybe you escaped after some crime?"

But Tiupkin began vowing and swearing he turned himself in voluntarily, and had fled the military simply out of longing…

"Longing for what?"

"Drinkin' 'n' cards."

"Where did you spend those two years?"

He gently told me how he'd lived in Bichursk canton, with the Seedlings (schismatics),[27] did the simple work of a peasant, lived heart to heart like man and wife with a sweetheart, and had a daughter with her.

"The livin' was good! Th-they made it good!…"

"So, why turn yourself in? You should have lived that way as long as possible."

"Impossible."

"Why was it impossible?"

"Jus' was."

However, with great effort he made me to understand that the reasons were wine and cards.

Swept away by his longing, he'd gambled himself into ruin: he ran away and turned himself in.

"But didn't you tell your wife?"

"Why tell her!"

I relate the details of this night in the confidence that I was nevertheless able to console this little wretch, to calm his worries of impending fate. But next evening, if again there were no money or card game and we were warming ourselves before the stove and chatting, my Tiupkin would once more begin his old tune:

"Okh, poor unlucky me! Why'd my mother bring me into the world?"

I finally couldn't put up with it, and cursed him for his womanly cowardice and whining. He defended himself, and then my Sancho Panza managed to let on that he, in essence, had already been in a penal unit before his escape.

"What for?"

"I was on guard duty… Got drunk 'n' left my post, 'n' was rude to an officer as well."

"That's it! Well, just the same, that's nothing to snivel over. You still won't get sentenced to *katorga*."

"But my little heart won't forget 'bout *katorga*, okh, it won't!… If only you knew ever'thin', yes, knew… Okh, I'm an unlucky little orphan!"

"What's this everything? Tell me now, since you've begun. What else did you get up to? Were you already in a penal battalion?" I asked half-jokingly, half-seriously.

Silence. Labored breathing. I finally began having suspicions.

"So, then, the truth? What happened?"

"Okh, woeful, bitter me! My little uncovered head!"

"What's this for? What did you do then?"

"I let a prisoner go."

"For money?"

"We was both drunk… I took him to the bathhouse… Well… 'Ivan,' I said, 'go off to the four winds.' I just lay down 'n' went to sleep. He left."

"How long did you spend in the penal battalion?"

"Three years. No, I've already been in *katorga*, already been! My heart feels… But e'en worse: I'll kill someone, for God's sake, I'll kill someone. They drunk all my blood, the bloodsuckers!"

"Tiupkin, you've the most guilt of all, so don't reproach people for anything. Get yourself in hand, stop playing cards and drinking—become human once again, now."

But Tiupkin didn't answer me and gloomily went off to sleep. In the morning he'd once more ask for a little money and, if I gave it, that night would again lose it in the common prisoners' ward.

Nearing Chita, he grew noticeably more and more agitated and sweaty; at times he even seemed to be contemplating escaping (the guards, knowing he'd turned himself in, weren't closely watching him); but Tiupkin was a spineless man in the full sense of the word and could never summon up the courage to escape. Thus he arrived at Chita safe and sound. He parted from me rather coldly, without even really saying goodbye. He was preoccupied with other thoughts at that moment…

In most cases, it's difficult to get to know for certain a prisoner during life on the road, when there are no solidly established conditions, nothing is consistent, everything is rapidly changing, and there's no sort of permanent escape from either an invisible enemy or this endlessly protracted, ugly holiday. This is more difficult for the "lord" riding in a separate wagon and living in a separate room for nobles. The prisoner cannot even open his "self " up to all the shifting and nightmarish things in his inner world; given these restraints, upon entering *katorga* he will appear the "lord," albeit in a privileged position. Absolute scrutiny, an ability to analyze the faintest impressionistic shades and most insignificant facts, are needed to distinguish truth from lies in prisoners' tales, the real character from that which is a put-on and for show.

This is why I will not be presenting the reader a large number of portraits or characteristics for this traveling period during my life in the world of outcasts. I still have enough time and opportunities for this. I'll simply note several principal tendencies in prisoners' characters and physiognomies, as they seemed to me *at that time*. The first category is that of the "quiet ones," for the most part old men playing the role of innocent victims and expressing hatred for even their brothers in the mare. In most cases, this is one of the most antipathetic. Moralizingly callous egoism, miserly hypocritical sanctimoniousness—these are these people's principal traits. These traits frequently blend with incorruptible honesty (in the official sense of the word), but a sort of heartlessness always emanates from this honesty, and these moralizing old men are never burdened by extending you sympathy. Another type is also middle-aged, though sometimes they're fully aged prisoners, who won't hide that they're forgers and bandits but carry themselves with a certain honor and nobility: "Well, I do say that in freedom I'm a thief 'n' a bandit, but in prison, 'mong me own, I'm an honest fellow, a tough ol' prisoner." They also have no reservations about loudly complaining about the decline of old prisoners' ways and beliefs, and ticking off the "new generation." The third, of whom there is a majority, forms the herd's heart and soul: it consists of gamblers, *zhigany*, husks, and executioners ready to turn into victims, and victims who will tomorrow become executioners; people whom nature seems to have purposely created for life in *katorga* and the "marching line" especially. Even they know it's a lie that they could live a different, better life than this inferno. They find themselves eternally carried away and intoxicated without wine, always agitated and troubled, even if the object of trouble isn't worth a brass farthing: the greatest agitation is their primary necessity. This is *katorga*'s most impassioned and animated element. You ask, Why is this young sandy-haired chap—with a gaunt, pale face and feverishly burning gray eyes, practically unable to gamble and always getting the birch rod for pilfering regulation items, forever starving and, moreover, the object of universal ridicule—gambling day and night? You look at his perpetually worried face, at his similarly melancholic eyes, and you get your answer. Without cards or vodka, and maybe… even without the birch rod… without something heady and intoxicating, life wouldn't be life for this wayward man! From such fast-lived lives come the so-called "husks" and "eternal prison residents."

"Husk" is the name given to persons deprived of their rights or with brief *katorga* sentences who, for shallow reward, several rubles, or a red shirt (or, as prisoners mockingly say, for a husk), agree to exchange names and futures with a long-termer or even a "lifer."

I cannot but remember, by the way, a special type of exchange, the significance of which I was long unable to comprehend but which nevertheless has a profound and extremely acute meaning. A *lifer* will exchange names with another *lifer*. A certain Belonosov manages, instead of a Dolgoshein, whose features his very little resemble, to leave, while Dolgoshein remains lying in hospital or with the subsequent party. It goes without saying that a "mistake" concerning lengths of sentences turns up here and there. In one or another place, administrators question Belonosov and Dolgoshein.

"Ah! You're a husk?"

"Not at all," answer Belonosov and Dolgoshein, regardless of their words' blatant falsity, and stubbornly continue to insist they are precisely those very persons who appear in the roll call lists and have been sentenced to life terms of *katorga*. Of course, if this pair goes to one and the same prison the authorities will immediately see through the muddle; but let's say a fitting distance has already separated the exchangers and so to follow the real trail isn't so easy. Local authorities celebrate the capture of the husks and reward themselves with a red shirt… Belonosov and Dolgoshein are put on trial (again, let's say in different places) and, as exchangers, are each sentenced to three years' *katorga* with corporal punishment. But such was only a necessity for them… *Se non e vero, e ben trovato*,[28] the reader's probably saying; but let him remember that in the past, and even not so comparatively long ago, cleverer schemes were hatched in the prison world. Since the reform, of course, similar tricks have all become more and more difficult.

Income-generating prisoners whom the collective grants a monopoly for a specified period over the trade in sugar, tea, tobacco, and other items, but most especially over control of gambling and sometimes darker pursuits, are called *maidanshchiki*. I witnessed, for example, how one *maidanshchik* in essence made a whore out of the young woman who'd voluntarily followed him. She was of course traveling separately from the single men's party in which proceed the "suitors," but in those stations where the supervisor can be bribed or deceived with a story about the imminent separation of the loving couple, the "fiancée" is taken at night to her fictional suitor and what then takes place can be imagined.

On the other hand, it must be said that only in rare cases are *maidany* controlled by tight-fisted exploiters who, having enriched themselves, begin living a sober and prudent life (in which case prisoners probably won't sell the *maidan*); usually, all that's needed for this "arrangement" are those same gamblers and *zhigany* who in several days will blow all their earnings on vodka and cards.

V.

In August, I entered the Nerchinsk *katorga* region. A new kind of atmosphere could be sensed: routines became stricter, the commander's and guards' manner harsher, the mood of the prisoners themselves more despondent. They were talking about the imminent searches in Nerchinsk, Sretensk, and Ust-Kara, saying that every last thread would be picked over. They were deciding how to hide even the random kopek in their hands. Soldiers were warning them with tales of how one old man was found with a hundred rubles hidden in his sugar, and how the officer distributed them among the guards. Because of my then naïvety, I couldn't understand for a long time why, disregarding such horrors, my companions nevertheless intended to hide their money. Why not, I asked, just give it to the authorities before the search? It would be safe all the same: registered and enumerated in a ledger, and so on. Prisoners responded by either scratching their heads or saying some nonsense that they themselves clearly hardly believed, such as that the authorities very often didn't return the money. Only in *katorga*, in prison, did I understand the real reason why a prisoner never exchanges illegal for legal money. He sees it as the last vestige, a kind of symbol, of the freedom he's lost. Apart from the card games and purchasing of vodka, most penal laborers won't give authorities all their money out of purely platonic considerations: they'll try to hold onto even a couple kopeks… "Better to lose what I know was mine than have it be theirs." Thus frequently say and do the most well-behaved and honest old men in whose hands there's never a card! During the search of one such old man an empty, dirty tobacco pouch was found and about to be tossed into the oven, when he tearfully explained that it still held three rubles.

"But, where?" asked the astonished officer, poking once again into the pouch and turning it inside out. It so happened that the note was very well concealed, almost artistically hidden in the slender draw-string.

Inching forward at prisoner convoys' usual turtle's pace, we finally reached that point on the Transbaikal road from which penal laborers are convoyed not by soldiers, but Cossacks. Recently, where there have appeared prospects of possible complications in the east,[29] Cossacks have reportedly been "called up"; but at the time, it was being said this part of the Siberian host (and, all the more, the convoy commands) was lacking almost any military discipline and, needless to say, behaved atrociously. I'll never forget a certain terrible scene, in which I was a witness and partially a participant, that took place following the party's transfer to the Cossacks. We'd been provided very few wagons but had a fair quantity of the sick and weak. To top off the misfortune the guards, as usual, were sitting in the wagons. Several of the sick prisoners therefore had to walk, and one began collapsing after his first steps. Not having the fortitude to bear such "disorder," the youngest of the Cossacks suddenly broke away from a telega, ran over to the stumbling prisoner, and began savagely beating him with his rifle butt. The party halted.

"What're ya thrashin' 'im for, Vaska?" the senior officer, picking his nose and sitting with the most impassive look in the baggage cart, asked his subordinate.

"Why won't he move like ever'one else?" Vaska, a rank-and-file Cossack without any stripes, in every way still a boy without any hair on his rather pretty little face, screamed at the top of his lungs.

"Ivan Egorovich," he beseeched the non-commissioned officer, "I gotta worry 'bout the carts. That's why, God knows, I'll really finish him off if he's gonna go on like this!..."

As if to confirm these words, the Cossack began telling the sick wretch that if he got to his feet he'd knock him to the ground again. Still not satisfied with this, Vaska began stomping on his victim. The party began protesting and causing an uproar... This was sufficient so that the sloppy and apathetic senior officer, who seemed at first to be interceding on behalf of the sick man, suddenly roused himself and went at the prisoners as well.

"What's this?! A riot?!" he screamed, brandishing his rifle and fists at those in front of him he took for rabble-rousers. Then, something interesting was to be observed. Those prisoners whom I thought most courageous and decisive suddenly turned silent and hid behind their comrades' backs. I was particularly struck by a certain Levshin, an old vagabond-philosopher, a man of athletic build with an already grizzled beard and savage gray eyes in which figured a tempered will and bold courage. Soon after this, he actually proved himself so, by escaping in broad daylight under the guards' eyes, into which he'd thrown tobacco... But that happened later, in *katorga*, and now, he was hanging his head and being stubbornly silent.

"Levshin, why aren't you saying anything?" I whispered to him. "This can't be allowed. We're not that far from where the authorities are. We should turn back and lodge a complaint... It's no problem if we get a few rifle-butts."

"Give it up, lord," the old man, looking around timidly, whispered to me in turn, "ain't nuthin' you can do... You should complain only for yourself."

"How is this for myself?"

"Just so. You need to remember this. If you're free, you can think like that... But that's 'cause you got the power to!"

Perhaps what Levshin recommended is correct, but at the time, I remember, I couldn't understand what he was saying, and I suddenly cooled toward my recently assumed favorite. But I was nearly more struck by the Pole Matskevich, better known among the mare as Kozhevnikov.[30] Regarding his past, he was an awful liar and blowhard whose innumerable romantic adventure stories were impossible to take seriously. I don't know for certain that he'd lived better in the past, but now, having been completely Russianized and made into a part of the herd thanks to a twenty-year adventure in Siberia and *katorga*, he was a pristine representative of the mare—today a *zhigan*, tomorrow a *maidanshchik*, today a collective headman, tomorrow a candidate for the husks. The prisoners weren't especially fond of Matskevich, considering him a vain "wagger," and those such as Levshin even thought him a "tongue."[31] However, in the abovementioned skirmish with the Cossacks he suddenly displayed a character such as I confess I'd not expected from him. Alone of the entire group, he had the courage to approach the soldier and loudly tell him "that's not supposed to be done." In response to this declaration, the soldier punched Matskevich as hard as he could in the face, so that blood spurted from his nose... Matskevich, however, was not afraid.

"Alright," he said philosophically, wiping his bloody face with the edge of his cassock, "hit me as you will… But all the same, it's not allowed to kick a sick man with your boots."

But the soldier didn't do anymore hitting; having exhausted his energy, it was left for him to pass on his flabby indifference to everyone in the world. The "little Cossacks" were still shouting, running around, making threats… They threatened me with their rifle butts when I, too, opened my mouth and began "clucking," but they refrained from doing anymore hitting… Of course, having put the sick man in a wagon anyway, we set off down the road. And, strange affair, these same Cossacks, having just made such a bestial and scandalous scene, then revealed themselves to be kind-hearted and sweet lads further along the way! Over the next couple of hours they managed to travel alongside and practically befriend the entire party; they related the usual songs, stories, and jokes… And that same Vaska who kicked the sick prisoner and threatened to finish him off, conversed very congenially with me about many questions interesting him concerning various scientific discoveries and how people in other countries live and think, and was candidly indignant at many of the problems in our system. When I reminded him about the scene with the sick man not long earlier and about his unfairness, he ashamedly mussed his hair and said:

"I'm a passionate fellow!…"

Moreover, the herd forgot about everything, as if what shouldn't be in the order of things is something that never happened. Matskevich-Kozhevnikov talked happily with the commander and, at least outwardly, bore him no malice.

Concluding my reminiscences of the journey, I'll flatly state that if I had a sworn enemy and were to consign him straight to what, in my opinion, was the harshest punishment, I would choose traveling the way-station route for several years. Truly, for me, being sentenced to a long term would not be such a blow to the spirit… Indeed! no worse punishment on earth can be imagined for the intellectual… Writing of the misfortunes and nightmares of this journey, I've forgotten to emphasize perhaps the single most terrible and torturous circumstance: this was the need to abandon a place where you had only just stretched out, warmed yourself, and gotten ready to relax; the need to drag yourself somewhere for some reason through mud and cold, just so you could once again make up your oh so short-lived nest and by your own hands dismantle it again. There's nothing stable, permanent, or comforting in this senseless, turtle's-pace peregrination from place to place… And, like the wandering Jew, every minute you hear a commanding voice against which you cannot protest: "Move! Move!" All this serves to create in the soul of a man with peaceful disposition a fearful and nearly desperate mood…

We finally came to a halt at the last station. Ahead was true, genuine *katorga*, that mysterious world which swallows thousands of people, thousands of souls, rarely returning them to the world of the living…

And when I glanced back at the last station standing alone in an open field, at that long, wet, gloomy, awkward structure that had unfortunately been witness to so many generations of people, people disfigured and insane, to so many wrongful torments, tears, and deaths, I shuddered.

SHELAI MINE[1]

—Greetings, forgotten miner!—
There, where ghosts ran in the evening,
Timid bats lived,
And no bitter, angry cry could be heard—
The laborer's candle now burns anew.
Once again, the mountain's heart is being gnawed at,
The steel augers like maggots,
The hammer sternly resounds, never falling silent,
The heavy chain links clang…
Who languished here in years past?
Was it you, blessed sufferers for freedom,
You dark victims of want and horror?
There is only a cross—and, partner in torture,
I acknowledge you as my only family:
Fraternal greetings equally
To your homeless, tormented ghosts!
Straining with your calloused hands,
You, who are eternal, left your mark in this tomb:
You are not now alive, but your tortures are,
Needfully hovering secretly around me…
—Poor ghosts, mournful shades,
I make you this great vow—
To pour into my cherished poem
All your tears, sighs, and punishments.[2]

P. Ia.

I.   THE ENCOUNTER

Around ten mines are grouped together in the Nerchinsk *katorga* district where prisoners serve terms of punishment. Several prisons are in Kara, where gold is mined. Kara is renowned among prisoners for offering the most difficult work: the "barbarian" Razgildeev's[3] name still resounds throughout Transbaikalia, and though Kara's *katorga* prisons have lately become banal institutions of confinement, where they not only do not mine gold but generally perform no labor at all, the term "Karaian" is still nevertheless imbued with an austere aura. However, ironic notes are beginning to burst forth regarding those who've been in Kara.

"He's seen many sorrows, boys! He was in Kara!" they say about someone, and burst into Homeric laughter.[4]

Silver is mined in the Algacha, Zerentui, Kadaia, Pokrovskii, Maltsevskii, and Akatui mines; the diggings are smelted and the silver extracted in Kutomarsk. The latter works is the most difficult and unhealthy. Several of the mines are close to being exhausted and require very few miners. In the others, by contrast, new mining veins are turning up almost every year; the largest groups of prisoners and huge prisons capable of holding a thousand men are assigned and constructed there. A prisoner's assignment to that or another point depends entirely on chance. I was assigned to Shelai, a new, just barely opened prison that could hold no more than 150 men. The mine to which it was affiliated was long neglected and had only recently reopened. It was impossible to predict the revenue it would generate over many, many years, and so huge preliminary efforts were needed to drain the old shafts and works; in building this prison the administration planned to establish an exemplary *katorga* prison based on foreign models. The accouterments of the regime that were at Shelai—or were said and rumored to be at Shelai Prison—while I was there have reportedly spread in recent years throughout Nerchinsk *katorga*; but when they began, they were something new and never-before-seen and were frightening for prisoners.

"Where you been assigned? To Shelai?" an old, gray-haired locksmith on his way to a settlement asked me in Sretensk.

"Well, pray to God! That'll be your grave!"

"What are you saying? What have you heard?"

A circle of unfortunates who like me were assigned to Shelai, crowded round the locksmith.

"There's a high stone wall," the locksmith said, "'n' a double guard, inside 'n' out, 'n' the wards is always locked, day 'n' night. Prisoners is only let out for work, roll call, 'n' to walk in military formation: 'March in step!'... It's big there, for sure. Eatin', sleepin', workin'—ever'thin's done by signal. Warden's from the military, a Staff Cap'm Luchezarov. Well, in a word, steady on, boys!… There'll be no sign o' cards or mother-vodka!"

"You're full o' lies, ol' fogey! Why, ain't our brother, a prisoner, smart enough to get cards 'n' vodka past Satan hisself into Hell? I'd convince the horned one with a birch rod!" a tall, dashing prisoner with a long, rakish, twisted moustache and arrogant gaze interrupted him. For his part, the locksmith contemptuously sized him up head to toe.

"You'll see!" he said, turning and walking off. "Yet, there's one good thing, boys," he stopped and spoke again, unable to restrain himself, "won't be no slop buckets for you. Yes, indeed. There's a door to a special restroom in each ward."

This consolation, however, little cheered me and my comrades. Everyone's heart sank in anticipation of the unknown future.

On a beautiful September day, at about noon, we arrived at the Shelaia River, on whose banks stood a newly styled prison with snow-white stone walls surrounding it and, nearby, entire rows of clustered houses for the administrators and barracks for the Cossacks. The prison was located three versts from the village in a deep, dark hollow ringed on all sides by little birch- and larch-covered hills. Regardless of the clear sunny day and picturesque (speaking impartially) landscape, the latter made a depressing impression on the party.

"There's Shelai, dammit!" was heard all around. "Geez, boys, whatta hole they're gonna stick us into like mice!"

"'N' there's the tom-cat right now, speak o' the devil,"[5] someone joked, having noticed a stately figure standing with a cane in his hand at the prison gates. I made out the form of an officer and guessed this to be Staff Captain Luchezarov.[6] The long, ginger-colored mustaches on his beardless red face were pointed directly at us and heralded nothing friendly.

"At-ten-tion!! Caps o-o-off!!" shouted a guard who appeared from God knows where. So long unaccustomed to this unforeseen order, the herd lost its head and failed to remove caps immediately and in unison.

"Wha-a-at's this?!" thundered the staff captain, banging his cane on the ground. "Not obeying orders?"

"We're guilty, your honor," a prisoner began saying, "'cause of inexperience, really 'n' truly 'cause of inexperience."

"Mare's worn out, y'see," underscored another.

"Silence!!"

Everything turned quiet. Not a single chain clinked, not a single breath expired. Everyone held onto his cap. Even the convoy guards stood as if frozen.

"Have them put their caps on!" said the commandant in a dark voice.

"Caps on!" the guard ordered. Everyone hurriedly put his back on in a veritable daze.

"Very well!" announced Luchezarov, coming closer and leaning heavily on his copper-knobbed ivory cane. His voice was now quiet, as if fatigued, but it was possible to hear a fly buzzing a hundred yards away, so quiet was everyone. "Very well! Pay attention. You are entering the gates of a prison in which there has not been a single prisoner before you, a prison for which there are special regulations. Yes, *special* regulations! (His voice was getting louder.) For many of you, this is perhaps not your first time in *katorga* or your first time entering a prison. You probably remember the proverb that a new broom always sweeps better but doesn't last long: only the first days here will be difficult, you're saying, but then everything will fall into the same old routine and there'll be cards with vodka and the *maidany*, Ivans, and even husks. Banish these idiocies from your heads, for I will strictly not tolerate them and will not fail to execute my superiors' instructions. I will be strict, but fair. More strict than fair! Do not for a minute forget you are penal laborers deprived of all rights, including the right to be trusted. Understand that I would sooner trust a single guard than seven hundred prisoners. I will punish you for idleness, laziness, rudeness, disobedience, and minor infractions. I tell you straight, I'm not a big admirer of the lash and birch rod, because I well know that they're as if nothing to prisoners like you. No, I will hit you in more sensitive places. In addition to rigorously keeping you on bread and water in the isolator, in fetters and manacles and even shackled to the wall, if necessary, I will make no allowances for the guilty and will haul them before the judiciary. Also, do not think of escaping. You will not escape Shelai Prison! I will be watching you carefully and, at the slightest hint of a planned escape, will punish you without mercy. There, I've told you everything you need to know at this first meeting. Prepare yourselves for induction. Off with all your things, off with your fetters—I know they can be easily removed and I don't need this comedy. Undress yourselves—it's warm and you shan't catch cold."

Shaking from head to toe ("He gave us the shivers," it was later said), the whole party including myself silently began to undress. Guards led stark naked prisoners one-by-one into the duty room beside the prison gate. Watching with suspicion one's body in the corner, they scrupulously went through everything, seized all possessions save tobacco and pipes, and issued new regulation items: two pairs of shirts with thread, footwear, puttees, jacket, trousers, cassock, mittens, and hat; then passed each man into the hands of a pair of barbers who immediately shaved the right half of the scalp. Having endured this entire procedure, prisoners one at a time carried the trousers and jackets they'd worn on the road into the prison yard, where they arranged themselves into two rows. After everyone finally formed ranks the gates solemnly swung open and the staff captain appeared again, with a paper in his hands and an entire retinue of guards at his side. Once more the order sounded: "Attention! Caps off!"

"Very good, old chaps!" Luchezarov condescendingly declared, stepping ceremoniously toward the formation of prisoners.

"W-w-wishing you well, mister com'dant!" the chaps bellowed at the top of their lungs.

"Have them put their caps on," said the commandant.

"Caps on!!" a guard shouted, and then went about counting the prisoners. The number conformed to what should be. After this, Luchezarov delivered us a new speech, this time adopting a light-hearted, paternal manner.

"We've been expecting you and preparing everything for our dear guests for a long time. You'll now take a steam bath and clean yourselves up. I shall not spot a single louse on anyone, and not a single starving man! Yes, under me everyone shall eat his fill. The law recognizes the prisoner's collective, and therefore I recognize it. You yourselves choose a collective headman, four ward attendants, two cooks, and two bakers. With regard to the headmen for the wards and the medical personnel, I myself will assign them. I'll give you the next three days to rest, but afterwards, welcome to work. Yes, indeed. There are nine wards in the prison, and each of you must live in the one to which you are assigned. I'll read from a list."

And he read the list, by which each ward was assigned around twenty men. I was given No. 4, and all my cohabitants became known to me only by surname.

"Guards, you will now order them to pray."

"Attention! Caps off to pray!"

We chanted three common prayers: "Heavenly King," "Our Father," and "Lord, Save Thy People."

"Caps on!"

"Order them to their wards."

Two guards stood on both sides of the formation, a third in the center, and all three shouted nearly simultaneously:

"First, second, and third wards, for-or-ward! Seventh, eighth, and ninth wards, to the left! First, second, and third wards, to the left doors, ma-arch! Fourth, fifth, and sixth wards, to the middle doors, march! Seventh, eighth, and ninth, to the right doors, march!"

Prisoners' heads were in an unimaginable muddle: some turned right, some left, some didn't turn anywhere but stood in place goggling their eyes, and others simply bolted towards the first available door as was usual in the way-stations. Catching sight of the first runners, the entire herd yielded to the infectious example: everyone ran headlong toward whatever door was available…

Pursued by the guards' shouting, the mare bore itself as if possessed, and soon no one remained in the yard save the commandant. The guards disappeared to look for escapees. However, after only five minutes everyone managed to be ejected and gathered once more in the yard.

"I will first of all reprimand the guards," Luchezarov loudly announced, "for it's absurd for prisoners to remember their ward numbers while being ordered to disburse, and their distribution should have been accomplished in accordance with the list while they were still in formation."

The guards were thoroughly shamed.

"Now arrange the prisoners in separate platoons according to ward. Each should remember who's assigned where."

The guards rushed to carry out his instructions, and moreover managed to do so without confusion: barely half the prisoners, especially the Tatars,[7] proved to have remembered their numbers. Without thinking, guards pushed them towards whatever doorway so as only to demonstrate their efficiency to the commandant.

"We're tuckered out, your worship, let us take a bath… Let us catch our breath," one gray-bearded, chubby prisoner, unable to restrain himself, said loudly.

"Who's speaking?!" the staff captain roared. "Take him to the isolator for three days on bread and water!"

Two guards immediately took the ill-starred upstart to the isolator.

"If you do not carry out the order precisely, I'll keep you here till midnight. You won't get a steam bath."

After such a threat, everyone managed to follow the order satisfactorily and punctually.

"Well, he's a six-eyes. A real six-eyes!"[8] muttered the prisoners, dispersing according to ward and sharing their impressions with one another. "He's got the most piercin' gaze. He's gonna send our brother straight to the scrap heap!" Everyone was satisfied, however, with what had happened to the guards.

"He ain't givin' no quarter to no one, brother: that's good!"

From then on prisoners stuck Luchezarov with the sobriquet Six-Eyes.[9]

II. FIRST NIGHT

At day's end I finally lay quietly down on the bare sleeping platform, full of so much activity. Some of my cohabitants were still talking and smoking pipes, others were already snoring—they'd been to the bathhouse, had a good steam, slurped down some regulation tea slops with baked goods, and been satiated. I was trying not to think about tomorrow. Through these behaviors a commoner, especially a prisoner, keeps himself together. He possesses the fortunate inability to see into the future—otherwise life would be unbearable. However, Six-Eyes had clearly put the shivers into most: they were speaking in half-whispers, going for certain necessities in their hard-soled shoes. Indeed, the guards were trying with all their might to perpetuate this fear: they were running down the corridor every minute banging keys and peering through door windows. A song was being attempted in one of the wards ("As should be, young fellas!"); suddenly, we heard several pairs of footsteps and several loud cries ring out—and instantly everyone fell quiet.

"Well, that's Shelai!" my neighbor Chirok, a prisoner still in his thirties with a pale, gaunt face but a powerful, healthy constitution, said in distress. He was sitting on the sleeping platform, cross-legged in the Turkish style, sucking on a cigarette and spitting every minute onto the floor.

"You'll die in this prison under such strictness," underscored the cooper Malakhov, a handsome brown-haired man with splendidly curly beard and small blue eyes. I glanced at Malakhov: he, too, was an athlete, with shoulders seemingly broader than even Chirok's. His gait was level and sure; his movement full of intention.

"Hm!" he groused. "They took away our beddin', so's we gotta sleep on the bare platform."

"Regulation mattresses'll be given out t'morrow."

"Hm!" he continued. "A model prison… But where's the fairness? Why is someone sent to Algacha, Pokrovskii, or Aleksandrovsk Central, where he can easily serve his time in *katorga* eatin' 'n' sleepin', but another gets packed off to a model prison where he's tormented 'n' pushed around all sorts o' ways?"

"This ain't the Shelai, it's the *screwy*, mine!" the metal worker Vodianin, better known by his nickname Iron Cat, sententiously declared. He was a small, unattractive man, not in his first youth, but glib and sharp-tongued. A cheerfully disposed spirit, he always spoke with rhyme and rhythm.

"They took my needle," Chirok complained.

For Malakhov, this was like throwing fat in the fire. He grew still angrier.

"How could it *not* be taken, old chap? You might cut your throat… The command cares about our brother… Oh! But do you know who's to blame for ever'thin'?"

"Who?"

"*Dokhturs*! Them most of all. It's all a pretext, like they want prisoners perfectly healthy 'n' fit. They're tryin' to fill their pockets here, yes indeed, so's to better suck our brother's blood!"[10]

"That's right!" confirmed the metal worker Iron Cat. "Them *dokhturs* is worse'n a swarm o' midges. Them jus' bite ya to death, but *they'll* nail ya to a cross!"

Chirok also found it necessary to take up arms against the doctors and to go further.

"If I were now at large," he enigmatically said, "'n' they shot me in the taiga or anywhere in the steppe, 'n' a doctor was there, I'd choke the life outta him."

Then arose from the sleeping platform a lone figure whose face I couldn't discern in the dimness. It coughed repeatedly and held a hand to its chest.

"No, I know," it hoarsely said, "I know what I'd do with him! I'd strip him naked, set him on an anthill 'n' tied to a tree, 'n' leave him there."

"'N' I would," another character, Iashka Pervanov, exclaimed, "I would strip him of his rank 'n' title!"

This remark elicited universal merriment and approval. At the time, I alone didn't understand the point of this cynical proposal… That evening, I found myself on the whole in very close proximity to the prisoners. Until then, I'd lived in separate rooms in the way-stations, in solitude or the society of intellectuals like me; but now, completely cut off from anyone in the elevated world and made fully level with these outcasts of human society, I had to establish a different relationship toward them and be their brother, their comrade.

I had readied myself for this since my first days of *katorga*; however, comfortable circumstances had till now delayed the decisive moment and, understandably, I'd avoided encountering any grief. That day, having for the first time tasted the bitter chalice of a true penal laborer, having for the first time felt myself humiliated and degraded, I gazed at my comrades-in-misfortune with a curiosity greater than before. I had also gazed earlier, but as more of a tourist, a lord, an outside observer; now, I peered into the soul of these people lying side-by-side me, our bodies almost touching, and saw the humor that they wrung out of those same feelings I found inside myself. A misery shared is so much easier to bear than one endured alone… This was why I avidly attended to their conversation coming from out of the corner and loved, with avidity, every word that found a response in my heart. The notion that I was not alone, that beside me were living and moving creatures similarly thinking, feeling, and striving, similarly taking to heart the insults, the very same insults as I—the hope of meeting such people here warmed and consoled me.

The conversation continued. Malakhov was reminiscing about life in Pokrovskii mine.

"Whatta life! There was no such life in freedom! Weren't so much as a mention of any rules 'n' regulations, 'n' who was the worse for it? When did anyone offend the warden or a guard? The mare kept itself in order, 'cause we understood. 'N' when anyone or any inspection came along, ever'thin' found its place: cards, vodka, knives, money so well hidden e'en the master of the house couldn't find 'em. God's word! We simply got along with the guards like they was our brothers. They'd be with us there drinkin' tea 'n' a little vodka 'n', 'tis rumored, cheatin' at *shtos*. God's word, I ain't lyin'! Warden's name was Sholsein,[11] but we all called him The Finn. Musta been German, though he spoke Russian well; only, he lisped a little—like his tongue weren't fully on. The Finn, as it were, rarely turned up, 'n' e'en then, as it were, jus' rarely peeped in on us in the barracks. 'N' if he came in durin' an inspection, he'd just laugh. Weren't all these orders, 'n' no strictness to mention. He'd drop in on the ward. 'Hey you, kiddo (he called ever'one 'kiddo')!... Lie down, lie down, kiddo, I'm not blind, y'know, I see what's going on. But you there, under the sleeping platform, kiddo, just wiggle your little knife so I can tell if you're alive... What's it matter? Is that all? Anything else? No one's foaled a colt tonight?' The mare goes: 'Ha-ha-ha!' 'n' he's laughin' too, bubblin' over... That's what I remember! This is what a humane attitude means! But, o' course, he was sometimes hot-tempered, 'n' not without reason. Though, for what reason I really dunno! Not o'er a hat that weren't doffed or put on in time. One time, I 'member, he came for an inspection. 'Well, are there knives, kiddies? Just show me them—I won't take them. They just shouldn't be hidden or be too big.' Those of us who had 'em, showed 'em. Mine was just o'er a foot long, 'n' I told him 'bout it. 'Your worship,' I said, 'I'm a master cooper, 'n' I need to use a little one.' 'Kiddo,' he said, 'just don't cut yourself... What, none of you got a bigger one? Headman, isn't there a bigger knife in the ward?' Vaska the Cross-Eyed piped up. 'No, your worship,' he said. 'Will you vouch for this?' 'I will.' 'Vouch with your own hide?' 'In full,' he said. The Finn stood up, reached toward the shelf (as if he knew!), poked around, 'n'—oops! Found a knife jus' bigger'n mine... 'How's this, kiddo?' he said. 'Put him in chains and thrash him, the scoundrel, with fifty hot ones for not coming clean!' We stretched out Cross-Eyed 'n' thrashed him right there... I myself gave him five good licks! For bein' a sonofabitch!"

"Absolutely," put in the listeners, "won't vouchsafe yourself a second time... Couldn't he say: 'Your worship, how can I, I say, speak for the whole ward? I say, find out for yourself...' Then it wouldn't-a meant nuthin' for 'im!"

After this, everyone unanimously agreed that life in the other mines was not life, but Paradise, for which it was unnecessary to die (later, however, I heard a different opinion from these very same people). They resumed their abuse of the Shelai model prison.

"What does *he* want, what does *he* want from us?" the usually meek Chirok suddenly yelled. "I'm lazy 'cause I don't wanna take my cap off again or return it where he commands? I'm to molt 'cause o' this? I'm ready all day to bow to 'im—only, get off my back, Satan!... As I was a prisoner, so I'll remain. But he ain't takin' anythin' from me!"

"Why this noise? What're you bawlin' about?" a guard at the door window suddenly shouted. "You hear the drum beatin' reveille? 'Cordin' to regulations, you're to lie down to sleep at nine o'clock."

Cursing, Chirok slunk into his cassock. The whole ward more or less hurriedly followed his example. Malakhov alone remained sitting on the sleeping platform and indifferently knocked the ashes from his pipe.

"You, big chief, what're you sittin' there for? You were told to lie down!" the guard shouted at him.

"But if I don't wanna sleep, who's gonna make me?" he drawled in a quiet voice in which, however, willfulness sounded.

"No talkin', lie down!"

"Said I ain't sleepy. Were I makin' a racket, it'd be another matter, but since I ain't sleepy, it's up to God 'n' not the regulations."

"Ah! you're the master talkin'? Very well, we'll have a talk tomorrow." And the guard simply went away.

All fell quiet in the ward. Someone attempted to express his sympathy to Malakhov by growling from beneath his cassock, but Malakhov himself maintained a nasty silence. He sat for another five minutes continuing to knock ashes from his pipe, which had long since been emptied, and at last also lay down, breathing heavily. Soon afterward, the guard came again to the door but, seeing that everyone had followed orders and was now lying down, and that the ward, weakly illumined by a kerosene lantern, was plunged into deathly silence, he went away.

I soon heard everyone snoring, including the handsome cooper. But it still took a long time for me to fall asleep. I was thinking... thinking about where I'd ended up and what would happen to me tomorrow; but most of all the idea of my solitude among this mass of people, of the exclusivity of my position, darkened my thinking. Only one evening and the just heard conversations were enough to show me how enormous a difference existed between them and me, an educated man, in our views of life and human value. A question popped into my head: Where would it be better for me to live—in Pokrovskii, under the paternal surveillance of the so famously named "Sholsein the Finn," who would invite me "to wiggle a little knife" and inquire whether I was "going to foal" that night, or here, under the power of Six-Eyes, for whom everything went "according to regulations" in strict formality and machinelike soul-lessness?... Moreover, would I be able to understand and love my cohabitants? Might one of them sympathize with me? In the end, what would our relations be like? It seemed clear as day that, if I didn't become the object of their hatred, then I would in any case live feeling infinitely alone, and that compared to them I would suffer a double, a thousand-fold, *katorga*...

Sleep would not come. My soul was sickened and protesting against something. Against what? I could give myself no answer to this. And for the first time in many years my lips mechanically whispered a prayer: "Lord, merciful Lord! Give me the strength and manliness to face without terror the lot that awaits me; give me strength to endure everything and reach the desired day of freedom!"

III. FIRST DAY'S IMPRESSIONS AND UNDERSTANDINGS

"What's that strange sound? What're those shouts? Is the deluge, the conflagration, already here?" I was thinking in my sleep, but without trying to sit up; my eyes were shut so tight they weren't in any condition to be opened. But then someone violently yanked my cassock off me, and I leapt up: before me was a guard's bearded face.

"Get up for roll call! Stop lazin' 'bout like some nobleman!"

"He really *is* a nobleman," chuckled one of the prisoners.

"Maybe he *was*, but you're all penal laborers now. You devils were so fast asleep you didn't hear the bell or the whistle! The regulations are hanging on the wall and should be read. You noblemen ain't illiterate, are you? At the whistle you gotta quickly get up, wash yourselves, and dress, and as soon as the doors open, go out to the yard and stand at attention. Now, fall out!"

The sleepy herd hurried to wash itself. Everyone hustled over to the latrine where, with the assistance of a single handful of water, each tried to wash his face and hands above the latrine vat. This was accomplished nowise due to the economy of water or because we were late and in a hurry: no, such were the prisoners' ways—they possessed no hygienic habits. Instead of a towel, they wiped off using the shirts on their backs. They then at last pulled on their cassocks, pulled down their caps, and, going out to the yard, formed two rows. At six o'clock in the morning it was still almost completely dark outside. It was almost October, and the morning air was reasonably cool; moreover, everyone's heads were shaved. It occurred to me that morning roll call in the yard was a nasty thing… We'd spent over ten minutes there until, with the aid of shouts and threats, the guards dragged all the convicts out of the wards. Only then did the count begin. But the guard on duty was clearly deficient at arithmetic, because he had to go around the rows twice in order to figure out the count. With the other guards' help, he took a good five minutes to add to the count those prisoners assigned to the kitchen or lying in hospital. Then there was a disagreement. They decided that someone had not been included after all, and counted us once more. This went along like the first time. Then two guards ran like madmen to the wards and, several minutes later, swearing and pushing him by the neck, drove out some sleepy old man who hobbled from foot to foot. Prayers were ordered, and we sang what we were supposed to. We thought we would then be allowed to disperse immediately, but one of the guards boomingly announced the following:

"For arguin' with a guard the com'dant has ordered that Paramon Malakhov sit in the isolator for twenty-four hours, 'n' he instructs prisoners that they are not to address guards as other than 'mister guard.'"

Malakhov was taken straight to the isolator.

"Right, left! Forward, march!"

We returned to the wards and were locked inside again. Only the headmen from certain wards were allowed out for the tea. They brought in a bucket of the same weak, steaming brew as the night before, and we began drinking it. Since we didn't have our own cups and regulation ones hadn't been issued, several men shared one cup while others simply gulped down spoonfuls from the bucket. Bread was brought in. Each received a ration of two and a half pounds (on workdays it was three pounds); we found ourselves with such big appetites that all portions were consumed immediately. I myself was so famished that I ate a good half of my ration with my tea. The cursing of Shelai Prison resumed.

"Well, it *is* a prison! Fortunate is the man with a brief sentence. You could die here."

"Rot in the isolator."

"Even without the 'slator. Was this how you lived in Pokrovskii? There, you always had tobacco 'n' you could buy some milk 'n' meat. But how can you buy what you used to here?"

I decided to inquire as to where the prisoners in Pokrovskii got their money from.

A tall, heroically built old man with red-gray sideburns, Goncharov by name, evidently pleased that I'd breached the silence I'd stubbornly maintained till now, began lively explaining to me:

"Y'see, in this case…"

But I should first make a small note here. Nearly all the prisoners with whom I clashed on the road, excluding the most backward and simple-minded, addressed me with the formal "you." Since arriving in Shelai Prison, I'd intended to start a completely new life, blending fully into the prisoners' environment, sinking into it; but from the very first day these fancies somehow fell apart. Aside from this, almost none of those who came with me to the prison had accompanied me as far as Sretensk during the journey, and although I had benefited in no visible ways from any privileges most recently, I remained as earlier a "lord" in everyone's eyes. I was at first perplexed, trying to explain this strange and unwelcome phenomenon to myself with the expression, "the earth is overflowing with innuendo," but I nevertheless soon realized the principal explanation lay in myself. For one thing, I myself used the formal "you" with each prisoner, as if he were not beneath me but I were a comrade in his eyes. Many prisoners, especially from the city, have a similar manner as well: during the first five minutes or even the whole first day of acquaintance they use the formal "you" with their neighbor; but not one of them can long endure this trial, and after a certain amount of time yesterday's refinedly courteous gentlemen are already zealously invoking each other's parents… This is why it's always rather funny to hear prisoners address each other. With me, it was different. Not noticing it myself, I continually used the formal "you" even among those who used the informal toward me.

No one heard a single abusive word from me; I was always polite and obliging: in a word, in *katorga* I behaved exactly as I would have on a hotel parquet. Everyone finally saw that I was a "scholar," that I had some books with me, that I "knew everything" and could be consulted for advice on the most complicated legal question. Of course, money played no small role in my relations with the herd… A rumor exaggerating the amount of money I received from home even made the rounds; each saw that I always had tobacco and everything that was possible to buy in prison, and that I never refused it to anyone—on the contrary, I myself frequently offered it. In Shelai Prison, where prisoners' material circumstances were especially straitened, one had to spread these favors on a broad canvas. In return for all this I received something unexpected: it so happened that someone learned my patronymic, and so the whole prison was soon calling me by none other than Nikolaich or even Ivan Nikolaich; they would make way for me in a narrow corridor; bow extraordinarily; give me the easiest spot at the work site or help me outright. And if I refused this help, I sometimes incurred a nasty insult. Naturally, the ward headman (until I noticed and forbid it) gave me the best portion of meat… However, I should add that for the majority of the prison (which in general treated me like a special person) the mercenary aspect in this had, so to speak, only nominal significance, since it goes without saying that the direct benefit those living principally in my same ward could derive from me was very slight, whereas I received good turns and help from absolutely everyone. But I'm getting ahead of myself. We return to the beginning of Goncharov's explanation.

"Y'see, in this case," the loquacious old man was saying, "there, in Pokrovskii, they'd do it with incentives."

"What's that mean?"

"Doin' so-called minin' work for pay, that is, in addition to government quotas. On government work, that is, without any pay, if you don't perform all you get is the birch rod or the isolator, 'n' so you ask yourself, 'What am I doin' all this work for? I don't care about their jobs!' I was better off sittin' on the heap[12] or e'en makin' off with what'd already been piled up 'n' given it to the guard. I'd do as little as necessary 'n' then sit down 'n' smoke my pipe. Y'see, we'd collected a *pudovka*. A *pudovka*'s what they call a small tub—holds three poods, fifteen pounds o' slag. You put in the silver ore from the ol' slag heaps, 'n' that was your job. That was good enough in the ol' days. You'd trick 'em. As was the way, the galena would lie on the bottom of the *pudovka*, 'n' only there is where the silver is, but on top 'n' around the sides was the ore you actually mined. You'd dig 'n' haul this with your livin' hand, jus' to give it away. The guard sees there's a pile of ore, 'n' that's good enough. He leads you to the storehouse where the ore is dumped into a pile. Only, it's dumped out carefully. Then, if you ain't thinkin', there's all these plops, y'know, 'n' the guard notices the only galena is at the bottom. 'Stop what you're doing, scoundrel!' Then you gotta wriggle out of it: say 'I couldn't really tell the galena from the ore.' Well, it weren't necessary to give me—an old bastard 'n' a swindler—a demonstration on how to do it. *They* didn't know how to screw them blockheads o'er… I didn't put any galena in the *pudovka*—jus' fill the bottom with *prytes*[13] 'n' put a little o' the real ore on top 'n' along the sides. As such, I'd dump out, I recall, only what sparkled before the eyes! 'N' there the fool'd be with his mouth open… 'N' that was all I did. I was too lazy, y'know, to crawl on my knees around the heap, tear a hole in my trousers peckin' like a chicken for grain. So I'd hustle early, early in the mornin' to the pit face, where the smoke from the explosions hadn't yet cleared. Goes without sayin' that's where the real ore fell. Well, without more fire, you go searchin' 'bout, but as they say, it was close to the bone!… You'd run in there 'n' in jus' five minutes your soul is satisfied, but other times, I'd hide pieces away in old work spaces for later. Once, the guard Izmailka almost caught me doin' this. I hear him runnin' with a lantern, shoutin' in a weird voice: 'What're you doin' there, you bastard?' Only, I didn't slip up, brother! I threw my shirt o'er my head 'n' charged straight at him like one possessed! His lantern went out 'n' I knocked him off his feet… That old man barely 'scaped from out the darkness; hit his forehead square on a rock… He got to the openin', groanin', moanin', 'n' eyein' us. But I'm standin' there with the other prisoners like nuthin' happened, doin' what they was—planin' a board… 'Which one o' you devils knocked my lantern out?' he says. 'You knocked into me 'n' near killed me, you barbarian. Was it you, Petrushka Semënov, or you, you ol' devil?' He's sayin' this to me… Petka 'n' I shake our heads, make our denials, 'n' laugh. That's what we did. That Izmailka was an odd chap. Our brother had nuthin' to fear from him.

"The borin' was also a pure laugh. The government quota was to dig seventeen inches 'n' a full twenty-one if'n it was soft rock. But in fact we dug five or six—at most, twelve inches. No one cared 'cause he weren't 'fraid."

"But weren't you held responsible?"

"What could they do to us? Sure, o' course, if the guard noticed you were a regular loafer he'd send you to the warden with a note. Once, Izmailka sent Senka-No-Finger to The Finn. He reads the note. 'How come you're working poorly, kiddo?' he says. 'The guard's complaining you've dug only three inches, not the seventeen required.' 'It's absolutely impossible, your worship,' answers Senka. 'The mare's hands just can't bust up that pit face, it's such hard rock!' 'Alright, kiddo,' he says. 'I'll take a look. Tomorrow morning I'll send the strongest fellows in all the mines to that spot.' So he sent Grishka-the-Ukrainian 'n' Vanka-the-Zhigan. They chipped out two inches jus' for laughs, o' course. 'Well,' says The Finn, 'if they can't bore any further it means that rock is pure iron. Kiddos, I'm telling you not to work it,' he says. He takes a piece o' paper 'n' writes to mine officials that this pit face ain't gonna yield anymore for folks, 'cause they'd damn well exhausted it… Now, unnerstand this pit face had only jus' opened!… The minin' division sees you can't increase the government quotas, but 'mong Pokrovskii's silver mines there's one that's first-rate: nigh ever'thin' to be found at the time was in this one. So, they created the incentives. We was offered compensation: so many rubles per cubic foot we dug. 'N', oh my God! What happened from there! People had the strength 'n' desire to dig. First, you'd complete the government quota (a full seventeen inches), then, without pausing for breath, you'd dig another thirty-five o' the incentives! Unnerstand that 'cause o' this, each man had tobacco 'n' some milk 'n' vodka… 'N' gambling cards was picked up. For them who didn't work there weren't nuthin'. Malakhov, for example, slept all day 'cause he lived hungry."

"Why was he living hungry? What about his prison ration?"

"He traded his meat ration for tobacco. 'N' as if the prison skilly is food!"

"But why didn't he work? He seems a hearty enough fellow."

"He could knock out a bear… But he jus' didn't wanna… A proverb says that some of us is born lazy."

"Why?! Why talk of trifles?!" Chirok, who until now had been listening silently, suddenly shouted. "I don't like this. Paramon's a fair man. He didn't like them reproaches 'n' self-promotions that was goin' round: the more there was the less he worked… Y'know, 'mong us there's the Ivanchiks 'n' the low-lifes… But Paramon don't like this. He's a fair man. He'll work so long as no one opposes him. He dug almost twenty-three inches in the spot where Grishka-the-Ukrainian 'n' Vanka-the-Zhigan messed around with two outta the government quota. Paramon's a fair man, so he stopped workin'.''

"One dug is like forty: fair's fair! But why're you lookin' at it this way? You really never considered borin'! You've lived your whole *katorga* servin' as a laundress, bathhouse attendant, or nursemaid.''

"Go to hell! Damn your shameless eyes! I've heard worse put-downs: look, I was a servant… But have your hands been overworked like mine? You're sayin' now how much you worked, but I scrubbed all the skin offa my hands washin' your mangy shirts! Only, it means nothin' in your eyes, you Eniseisk whiner!''

"You salty-eared Permian, what're ya barkin' 'bout? Geez, how you flap them gums! What'd you see in your Perm?[14] Whaddya know, whaddya unnerstand?''

"Much you know, I seen many mountains, you green *cheldon*!…''[15]

"Well, I sure ain't no greenhorn: fifty-three years alive in the world, I know a thing or two. But what you know I already forgot!''

I realized that the once interesting topic had now been exhausted and that the interminable wrangling would drag on without end, so I went to my space in the corner of the ward. Later, however, I became aware that such wrangles among prisoners rarely end in a fight; even more rarely than among cultured society, it seems… It cannot be said that this is explained by a lack of pride among prisoners. Oh! I witnessed terrifically inflated self-esteem when the issue concerned relations with men regarded as somehow above themselves… Among them a prickly sensitivity to insult as is never detected among the intelligentsia would manifest itself. Their brotherliness is another matter. My hair sometimes stood on end from the wicked abuse they'd heap on each other: to wound an antagonist there was no curse word, no offensive rebuttal, they wouldn't use—not only against him but his mother, father, and countrymen. I'd conclude that after such serious words nothing could keep the rivals from becoming intransigent, blood-thirsty enemies… But what would happen? After a day, sometimes even an hour, I'd see them talking peacefully and amicably once more. The breaking off of relations, so common in educated society, was for them a completely inconceivable and impossible thing. For them, the most terrible argument was in essence nothing other than frivolous debate, the prisoner's version of a joust. These exist everywhere except among us, of course; but, I repeat, during my several years' sojourn in Shelai mine I witnessed brawls and fisticuffs resulting from verbal insults no more than a few times.[16] Because of the rareness of friendly sorts among prisoners, close and affectionate friendships are rare. Each looks at the other not as at a comrade in misfortune but rather as a wolf at a wolf, an enemy at an enemy… The word "comrade" itself—one of the most frequently used prisoner words in this place—in essence expresses very little: people eating and drinking together, in the same circumstances, are called comrades. Such economical unions are in large part incidental. The word "friend" means even less.

The argument between Chirok and Goncharov was interrupted by the appearance of a guard declaring that the headman for our ward would be old man Gandorin, who'd already been performing this responsibility temporarily. The guard then asked the ward whom it wanted as headman of the work collective and as launderers, cleaners, and bakers. A din arose. I barely knew any of the names nominated. From our ward, Kuzma Chirok was named a launderer and Iashka Pervanov (also called Marmot) a cleaner.

"Iasha, you did this job before, 'n' you got a nose for that spirit… 'N' Chirok, you're used to women's work as well. You know how to wash them pillow cases!"

"How this idiot talks! You should give him a stuffin'."

"Hey-hey!" shouted the guard. "Who do you want as headman?"

Everyone looked at each other quietly. Then Goncharov pointed at me.

"We got lit'rate people of a special type. Won't be no crookedness…"

"Nikolaich, Nikolaich for headman!" boomed the entire ward. But I waved my hands and feet against being nominated.

"Leave off, gentlemen! It's not right for me…"

They tried to persuade me, but I refused point-blank.[17] To my great surprise, a majority of the other wards had unanimously selected me, whereas I'd been naïve enough to believe that most hadn't even known of my existence!

The guard went around explaining I'd just refused, and so after a certain interval of shouting and argumentation agreement was reached concerning one Kolpakov, an easy-going young chap from among the card sharps. Luchezarov, however, didn't approve of Kolpakov, and so the next prisoner chosen headman was a certain Iukhorev.

In the meantime, old man Gandorin brought from the kitchen a container of *kroshonka*—that is, chopped meat—that the twenty men in our ward had been counting on. Each prisoner was allotted five ounces of uncooked meat on a non-work day and seven on a work day. An hour or an hour and a half before the distribution of food the cook, in the presence of the collective headman and an orderly, would take the meat from the cauldron, separate it from the bone, and with big knives cut it into little pieces on a table. Then the headman would divide the *kroshonka* among ten containers according to the number of wards (the kitchen was counted as a ward) and the people living in them. This distribution was done with bare hands which, of course, were not always clean… Ward headmen took these containers to their respective wards, and there commenced a second distribution.

I watched with loathing how the disheveled old-timer Gandorin, not having washed his hands, laid twenty pieces of meat on the filthy table (which he moreover wiped off with his cap). The fat was sticking to his hands; in addition, a suspicious fluid dripped from his nose, which he compulsively wiped with his fat-smeared hand. Because of this his nose and lips had a glossy look. The old man was evidently distinguished by extreme conscientiousness: if one or another piece seemed smaller or larger, then he had to put it with another infinitesimally complementary piece of meat. I could barely tear myself away from viewing this repulsive operation. I lay down on the sleeping platform and faced the wall. But the divvying up was already finished; the prisoners hurried to grab their portions. No starving aunt, as they say, I also went after a certain time to get my share. The modest amount surprised me: I counted exactly five little pieces of meat, each of which could fit into a thimble, and half these were un-chewable gristle. I curiously asked how much meat was allotted in the other mines.

"By law it's the same ever'where," answered the garrulous Goncharov, "only… it's up to our brother that every mouth gets its fill. This is a good portion: one, two, three, four… 'N' look here! I got six pieces. Thanks be to God! It's enough on a non-work day. But in other prisons where our mare's given complete freedom, believe you me, you won't get such a portion e'en on Easter Day!"

"Why not? If you were free there, it means the administration wasn't cheating you."

Everyone laughed at my naïvety. Goncharov chuckled as well and lowered his voice.

"You're judgin' things so simple!" he finally said. "Our brother mare is worse'n the administration. Administration can't rob me, 'cause I'm a swindler. But one's own'll rob ya. But he won't rob mine, I'll rob his! 'Cause we're swindlers…"

"So who's stealing the meat?"

"Who!… Aren't there really some candidates in the kitchen? The headmen, cooks, orderlies, bone-nibblers…"

"Who are the bone-nibblers?"

"Them what's nibble on bones: *zhigany* who've gambled 'n' got nuthin' to eat. They've lost their rations for months to come. So they hang round the kitchen while the meat's bein' cut. Also, the Ivans buy it from the headmen 'n' cooks."

"But I've heard a brother who robs the prisoners is strictly dealt with?"

"That's true. Whoe'er steals e'en sugar or tobacco is seen as the lowest person. 'N' 'member, if a thief gets caught in prison, he's pounded to death! I myself have been a thief my whole life, so why hold back? I was a villain 'n' criminal of the top order; but in prison… Here, I'm an honest man, 'n' I'll knock in the snout o' the sonofabitch who e'en says I stole from a brother prisoner!"

"But isn't it theft all the same: stealing meat from the collective?"

"No, them's dif'rent things! We don't consider this stealin'."

"How can it be stealin'?" seconded Chirok, with a look of profound conviction. "I agree with ever'one on this. It's up to the headman to correct things… But why bother o'er this? He's elected by the collective. Ain't no stealin' whatsoever."

"Course there ain't," the entire ward chorused. Only, it seemed to me Goncharov was chuckling cunningly as he smoked his pipe. This strange prisoner's logic interested me.

"But aren't you complaining," I said, "that food in the other prisons is real slop? You said it's impossible to live for whole years that way: you'll die!"

"You wouldn't die there!" answered my interlocutor. "Ever'one there's got money. I considered it a sin to touch the government skilly there. 'N' in Pokrovskii the guards brought us swinish skilly 'n' kasha by the tub-full."

"Very well, if the over-achievers eat," I heatedly said, "but they're not eating in all of the mines, then only the strongest could work there."

"'N' it really was jus' the o'er-achievers! Like a little kid, you still don't unnerstand our brother: you was born with a silver spoon in your mouth…"

"What he's sayin': it's a lie!" Iron Cat chimed in.

"We got a lotta profiteerin' types, 'n' each can find his exact place. Some win at cards, some stand as the stirrup,[18] warnin' o' the guard (gets his share for this as well); some deal in vodka, some are from families o' pastry cooks, o' dairy farmers, some hold the cards. Oh, my Lord! A sharp wit can get up to dif'rent tricks! The launderer cleans me that towel, 'n' I should pay him somethin' 'cause it ain't government work. Another pretends he's sick 'n' is lyin' in hospital: he's sellin' milk or meat for several days—'n' there's a bit o' tobacco. But he'll gamble it full away—'n' so he may give away his regulation things. Well, o' course, you sometimes pay with your hide: really, for our brother, that's like sweatin' it out in the bathhouse… Ha-ha-ha! Still, it's to the full—the blood's sprayin'… They get by this way. Let's say there's twenty rubles in the prison—they go from hand to hand in a circle, not stayin' long in a single one. They feed ever'one."

At eleven o'clock this curious economic theory[19] was cut short by renewed clanking of the lock that signaled lunch was being served, and Gandorin appeared with a huge container in his hands of the cabbage soup prisoners know as skilly. It simply seemed like slops to me: some buckwheat in filthy water, a little bit of cabbage, several unpeeled potatoes, a multitude of cockroaches, and not a drop of fat. Indeed, some fat would have been possible had prisoners not taken the meat from the cauldron just as it began to boil, so that the meat hadn't come off the bones and there was none in our portions whatsoever. However, my cohabitants unanimously praised the Shelai skilly and emptied the container to the bottom. This circumstance led me to doubt very much their stories about a paradisiacal life in other prisons. Goncharov seemed to divine my thoughts and, lying on the sleeping platform, resumed talking:

"It's really pretty good, if only it don't sit by itself 'n' you don't drag it out too long. But when it sits, clearly, it becomes gruesome. Here in this prison, we'll say, it'd be a great sin to swindle the collective. 'Cause o' the measly crumbs… Won't get no more outta here."

"Not outta here for sure!" Chirok despondently enthused and, approaching me, added: "Gimme some tobacky for a cigarette."

Following him, Marmot and others silently turned towards my tobacco pouch. Having completed this solemn rite, everyone lay back on the sleeping platforms and, it seemed, sank into contemplation of the imminent bitter future. Everyone grew quiet, and soon a friendly snoring resounded through the ward. This inaugurated the post-lunch rest. At five o'clock the dinner alarm rang. A gruel of groats thin as soup and inexpressibly offensive to the taste was brought in; another time, when it hadn't been made as was usual, I caught a whiff of dog in it… Soon after dinner our evening tea was delivered. At six o'clock the wards were unlocked for evening roll call. Along the corridor came a piercing whistle, followed by a guard's anxious shout:

"Fall out for roll call! Line up immediately in the yard, the com'dant himself will be there!"

Frightened by everything that was happening, prisoners quickly put on their cassocks and, jostling each other as if going mad, ran into the yard where they formed two rows, ward separated from ward. An orderly in white gloves ran along the ranks and, gazing anxiously at the gate, made a preliminary count. The alarm finally sounded. The senior orderly standing behind the gate shouted through the grating: "He's coming!" Everyone rippled like the sea, cleared their throats, blew their noses, settled down, and stood as if rooted to the spot. Through a space in the grating the Cossacks who'd been idly standing in the road could be seen dashing to their sentry boxes… And there beneath the gate appeared Six-Eyes's immense figure, greatcoat thrown across his shoulders and walking-stick in hand, circling the retinue of guards. The senior guard quickly ran to him, saluted, and delivered a report that could be heard: "Mister Com'dant, everything's going well in Shelai mine; there are in the prison…" It was impossible to hear anymore. The lock growled, the gates swung open.

"At-ten-tion!! Caps o-o-off!!" the orderly standing in front of the ranks commanded in a voice so shrill it could arrest an unhealthy heart.

Shaven heads were bared in a moment.

"Caps on!"

"O-o-on!!" Caps found themselves on heads. The orderly flew with quick steps to a swaning Luchezarov and, having saluted, quickly reported:

"Mister Com'dant! Everything in Shelai Prison is going well. There are a hundred and seventy men in the ranks, eight in the infirmary, and two under arrest."

"Greetings!" equably replied his commandant, maintaining like he a salute throughout the length of the report.

"We wish you good health, your worship!" barked out one of the prisoners, not having realized this greeting did not concern him.

"I wish you good health, Mister Com'dant!" the guard slavishly answered and quickly jumped to the side.

"Greetings, chaps!" Luchezarov said, having raised his voice, and approached the ranks.

"We wish you goo-ood health, Mister Com'dant!" the chaps burst out, as if having been fortified by a good night's sleep; the echo bounded far off the prison walls and flew out to the hills themselves.

"Order prayers!"

"Begin prayers! Caps o-o-off!"

The prison choir, standing as already ordered between the rows, sang the usual prayers with sufficient voice and harmony.

"Caps o-on!"

Caps found themselves on heads again. Six-Eyes stood for two minutes silently observing the prisoners, who were neither live nor dead. "Here's what!" he began in an imperious tone. "Today, with my permission, you chose a collective headman, cooks, and other collective personnel. Let them know (and all of you as well) that I do not tolerate thievery in my prison. For each case of theft in the kitchen, hospital, or other collective, I will bring the guilty before the court. I won't mention the fact that stealing from your own comrades, even from your prisoner's point-of-view, is a shame and a disgrace. Above all, understand that besides permitting government products for the cauldron, I will allow nothing into the prison. You may apply to purchase with your own money tea, sugar, and tobacco no more than once per week, and in no greater quantity than that assigned for one person. I will not allow any *maidany* whatsoever. I will also not allow servings to be augmented. That one should eat better than others, I shan't permit! I'm not obliged to other prisons. Shelai Prison is a model *katorga* prison, and I want it to be *katorga* not just on paper. It's my deep conviction that a *katorga* regime should also be a food regime. However, if someone wants, he can use his own money to improve food for the entire prison. Guards, escort the prisoners to their wards!"

"First three wards, to the right! Middle three wards, half-turn to the right! Last three wards, to the left!"

"Forward, ma-arch!"

The prisoners ceremoniously and in strict order defiled to their respective locations, quietly misconstruing among themselves "the *prigime* regardin' vittles" that Six-Eyes promised them.

"So, chaps, he's straight to the point: 'Under me,' he's sayin', 'there'll be a real *katorga* prigime.'"

But this ceremony had not ended the day. In the wards we also had to form two rows! Six-Eyes walked around the wards and ordered two final counts. His guard appeared in each ward and shouted: "Attention!" and, having horribly screwed up his eyes, reported: "Twenty men, Mister Com'dant!"

Finally, the door slammed, the lock clicked, and we, dulled and stupefied by all the noise and splendor, were left alone.

"Well-well!" Goncharov summed up the general mood.

"Oh God, a master o' my stomach!" groaned the old-timer Gandorin, and actually clutched his stomach, aching from terror… This set everyone laughing, and the silence was broken by general conversation. But I wasn't listening and, lying down in my corner, tried to relax and gather my thoughts.

IV.   INSIDE THE BARREL-ORGAN

The next two designated rest days were as alike as two peas. The only difference lay in the conversations prisoners had among themselves and in the fact that there was no meat at all in the skilly on the second day, Wednesday, because it was a fast day. However, in instituting two fast days a week for *katorga* the administration had obviously not ordered that this be done out of religious considerations, because on those days it allowed fat for the kasha. Such oddness especially drew attention during Lent, when prisoners were made to fast for three whole weeks (which is why none of us could avoid fasting) and skilly devoid of fat was served the whole time. Save for the Wednesday and Friday fasts, there were only two days a week in Shelai Prison when there was allowed, instead of meat, so-called *oserdie* or, according to the prisoners' pronunciation, "*userdie*," that is, liver, stomach, and lungs. The apportioned amounts were somewhat larger than usual, but only because all this frugal fare was, as prisoners said, "false meat": I could barely choke down the slippery, toad-like lungs and poorly cleaned stomach possessing its own natural aroma. As such, I received real, not-false, meat only three days a week and, having become quickly familiar with Shelai Prison's food regime, now contemplated with horror the several years I was condemned to experience it. "You'll die here!" I repeated the prisoners' admonition to myself...

Luchezarov himself was present during the second day's evening roll call, but did not speak. On the evening of the third day, the senior guard walked around the rows asking prisoners to identify their crafts and skills. Everyone was silent at first, then they pointed out a certain one: "Go, Andriushka... Maybe you can scare up some tobacco... Y'know how this prison is." Vodianin from our ward was assigned to be a smith and, having given his surname, began departing the ranks.

"Don't leave the line! Stand in place! Arms at your sides!" several guards shot at him. Iron Cat quickly scampered into line.

"Who else? Maybe someone's a striker?"

A certain Efimov from our ward identified himself.

Malakhov, now released from the isolator, reported that he was a cooper. Carpenters, joiners, sawyers, metalworkers, and cobblers were identified from the other wards. After this, the orderly read the duty roster. One group was assigned to dig a ditch, another to build a winter encampment, another to construct carts for hauling water or firewood, and, finally, one group to work as miners. I awaited the calling of my name with a sinking heart, but was glad when I heard it among those assigned to the mountain, given that I'd wanted to be assigned straight to the miners because everything else, although much easier, seemed less dignified to me for some reason... Having finished the roster, the guard explained that in view of its considerable distance from the prison and the inconvenience of returning for lunch, there would be a one-hour break and we could bring with us bread and kettles for brewing tea.

That whole evening the herd was excited. Already irritated and hopeless sitting under lock and key, everybody was elated by the prospect of imminent change. They also discussed whether or not an "incentive"—so called by them a "spur"—would be given in the Shelai mine. According to the prisoners, craftsmen who worked in the mine were paid by the mine department[20]; smiths got five rubles a month, crew leaders and timberers four rubles, etc. They were also terribly interested in what the winter encampment was to be built for. The nasally fellow who'd offered to plant doctors on an anthill conspiratorially whispered:

"I know… For the free command."

"For what free command? What're you on about?"

"I ain't jokin', rather, I know… They'll let us out soon… Lots 'ave already left the line. There's Andriushka Povar, Paramon, Marmot, Romashka Pestrov, Letunov, Skoropadov…"

"That's as may be. But here, will they really let us go? It's a model prison, after all…"

"They will… I'm tellin' ya!"

"'N' you know this how, you damned mosquito? With us sittin' here under lock 'n' key all day."

"I know my business… I heard it from a guard!"

"Whatta mosquito we got, chaps! This is no mosquito but an outright double-talker. We don't need any news from him."

I looked at the mosquito. His entire face was beaming with a cunning smile; his long red lips were whispering like those of a Tatar and his consumptive chest kept on convulsing.

Having delivered his sensational news, he laid down on the platform and immediately shut up.

Inconclusive discussions began about who would be released to the free command and when. I curiously inquired as to who from our ward would be going to the mountain. Goncharov and his fellow countryman Petrushka Semёnov, a young Hercules distinguished by his brooding silence, turned out to be the only ones. The smith and striker for the mountain had been assigned from other wards; Iron Cat and Efimov had been held back for the prison smithy. Chirok kindly advised me to get a good night's sleep before the job and, having listened to him, I lay down and slept like the dead. The next morning I slept until the whistle warning that wards would be turned out for roll call in twenty minutes. I dressed, washed, and lay down again, and managed to snatch a bit more sleep before the doors finally thundered open and there was the usual shout:

"Fall out for roll call!" Hence it was five o'clock in the morning. At six o'clock, after morning tea was over, the second alarm at the gates could be heard, and the prison corridors resounded with deafening whistles and guards shouting:

"Get to work! Get to work! Line up in the yard in groups according to where you're assigned."

Everybody poured into the yard trying to locate their partners. I sought out my colossi, Goncharov and Semënov, and stood behind one of them. Every miner had a canvas wrap at his chest containing a round of bread and a tea mug; some had kettles as well. First, those assigned to dig the ditch were called outside the gates, then the carpenters, and, after everyone, the mining group. Outside the gates each man was thoroughly searched from head to toe. We were next led to the drill square in front of the prison, where we halted and a dense convoy of Cossacks encircled us. They counted us several times. The senior convoy officer reported to the orderly room that he had thirty-five prisoners. Then a guard who was to accompany us to the mountain gave the command:

"A-bout face r-r-right! Four men to a row! Forward, march!"

And the mare flew headlong into the further unknown—to anywhere as long as it was far from the prison, as long as it was something new, even were this newness to be ten times harder…

The road led downhill at first. Everywhere around us the stubby taiga greenery—young larch, will, and bushes of wild rosemary and dogrose—had turned yellow, but stretched across the entire horizon were hills stripped completely bare by human ingenuity. We didn't know which of them contained Shelai mine. Rumor had it that all of Shelai's mountains were bored through with pits and shafts. This place was full of vague and even strange legends. We were shown one mound and told that thirty years ago a cave-in killed more than sixty penal laborers there.

"They're denyin' it, o' course," said a not-youthful prisoner with a face as dry as kindling and lively black eyes, "they deny it so's not to worry our brother. But we know!"

"You dunno nuthin'!" a guard who'd come up alongside and heard the conversation barked at him. "A cave-in did happen, only not here, but in Algacha."

"But the duty officer at Algacha said it didn't happen there, but in Shelai."

"Impossible. Algacha's duty officer, Stepan Ivanovich, is my very own uncle. So who knows better'n me?"

"Maybe you *do* know better—I won't argue with this—only that the administration ordered you to hide it from us."

"Hide it for what reason?"

"Well, if the mare knew 'bout it, no one would go off to the mountain!"

"You're lyin', ol' man! If they gots to, they'll go. After all, you're sayin' you know 'bout it, but you was told to go 'n' you're goin'."

The old man stopped arguing, but for a long time continued grumbling to himself. The prisoners were apparently not on their brother's side. Several winked at me and whispered to him:

"What's this hogwash you said? Don't lead us on, brother. We know your crafty ways!"

"There! There!" someone grabbed me by the arm. "Lookie there, Mikolaich." I glanced left, in the direction of the identified mound, and barely discerned several huge heaps of slag dug from the blackened pits.

"Are those pits?" I asked.

"Mine shafts."

"The cave-in was there?"

"Who knows; maybe there."

The road began rising toward the mountain.

Having gone four versts I felt exhausted, and unwittingly shouted in the Siberian dialect: "Ease up!" The guard ordered a halt.

Having rested five minutes, we once more got under way. The climbing became more and more difficult. But we soon came upon the watch-house, a small hut where the mine watchman lived and where prisoners were given labor assignments. A smithy was there as well. Crowding and jumbling up to the watch-house we saw a senile, half-blind old man with a mane of gray, matted hair falling to his shoulders. His sharp nose seemed to be sniffing the wind; and his eyes, regardless of their aged lack of luster, made an impression of craftiness that has lodged in my mind. Such was the mine watchman. Beside him sat the duty officer, a compact, ruddy peasant dressed in black velvet trousers and a threadbare jacket with a red girdle. He was named Pëtr Petrovich. He slowly began questioning us as to who knew which jobs; but I noticed that everyone, even the veterans, tried to convince him that this was the first mine they'd seen. The smith and carpenter (or timberer), who the evening before had identified their skills to the prison commandant, were now lost instead. Of the subsequent conversation I understood even less; I heard only that I'd been assigned to the upper gallery, to some kind of "barrel-organ."

"What's that?" I perplexedly asked Goncharov. It had occurred to me they might be joking with me.

"Don't you worry! Petka Semënov's been assigned with you, 'n' he'll explain 'n' show you ever'thin'."

"But you're going somewhere else?"

"I'm stayin' with the duty officer to man the sledge."

I went over to Semënov and learned from him that we were going to the top-most gallery to pump out water.

"But what's the barrel-organ?"

"The barrel-organ is *that*: pumpin' water," Semënov smiled, revealing two rows of dazzling white teeth.

I confess that from the first moment I looked at his face I found it difficult to tear myself away. Normally sullen and brutal—it was lit up by a smile and captive to a purely childish simplicity; gray eyes in whose depths lurked a menacing strength now glittered with a trusting and prepossessing sensitivity.

"How old are you, Semënov?" I inquired, having become enamored of his smile.

The smile instantly vanished like the sun behind a drifting cloud.

"Twenty-eight," he unwillingly answered, and stalked off.

Watching him go I again saw only the serious cold face and knitted brow. A small, barely noticeable moustache gave to part of his face—in general, very handsome and lively—a sort of unpleasant, animalistic quality. Semënov's forehead was large and completely square; his tall height and iron-muscled arms delineated his physique. Each time I gazed into his large gray eyes I was beside myself: they seemed not to look directly at you but to be penetrating through and seeing something behind your back, and I instinctively sensed a danger that his iron hand might right there instantly grab the back of your head and rip the skin off your skull. I made a mental note to get to better know this man in whose spirit some demon doubtlessly lived.

With the mountain becoming steeper and steeper, reaching the upper gallery became even more difficult, and we had to rest every five feet during the 700-foot climb. However, the five exiles assigned along with me apparently felt no need for a breather, and did so only to satisfy me. They were all heavily burdened: one was carrying an enormous, thick seaweed rope that weighted no less than three or four poods; another, wooden barrows; another two had heavy iron-banded tubs; and the fifth had a half-pood iron sledgehammer, an axe, a hack, and several pickaxes. I carried only an empty cistern for tea and bread. When we finally reached the assigned location my heart was beating like a bird in a cage: breathless, I collapsed on the ground and lay there for several minutes until I recovered. Only then did I look around curiously. We were sitting near a large wooden structure in the shape of a cone or a cap and standing about thirty-five feet, covering the entrance to the gallery. On either sides of it were two locked doors; the senior guard unlocked them. Two Cossacks with rifles slowly stood up along either side of the cap, but the five others began making a fire.

I looked down. The wall around Shelai Prison glittered in the basin; the sharpest eye could have barely made out the black dots of the guards passing along the dazzling white background; appearing in black around the prison, the many other structures gave the impression of a whole small city of chimneys puffing into the morning air. Significantly higher, encircled by a bog, was the mining watch-house from which we'd just come. Still higher, somewhat to the side, stood the beautiful little house of the regulator Monakhov, superintendent of Shelai mine. Directly below our feet towered precisely the same kind of wooden cap as ours, covering the middle gallery. I hadn't noticed it under the influence of my terrible exhaustion during our journey; the galleries were about two hundred paces apart. Only now did I learn from prisoners that another shaft was located near the watch-house; a corridor driven into the mountain horizontal to us; a corridor to which a vertical gallery was later added as an air vent. Satisfied with this preliminary information, I became lost in admiration of the picture unfolding before me. The autumn morning had turned bright; a freshness, a peacefulness, a kind of joyfulness was in the air; not a single cloud floated across the pale azure heavens. The sun had only just begun pouring out an ocean of splendor. Hilltops shone dazzlingly clear, black shadows stretching out from them. The ravine in which the prison lay was dark as well. Across from us, stretching high behind it, the landscape was especially majestic and picturesque. There lay an entire amphitheater of mountains towering one after the other and finally disappearing in the cerulean morning mist. I remembered the poet's words:

Behind far-off mountains
Dark clouds hang,
Blood is drained
By the appearance of misfortune…[21]

Yes! the terrible thought of how much grief, tears, and even living human blood these mercilessly beautiful mountains had witnessed clouded my enjoyment of the landscape and forced away my gaze… I looked toward the other side, up from the mines. There towered the huge mountain, seeming to rule the whole area. Having noticed my curiosity, a Cossack approached and told me that Shelai mine's main worksites were inside this very mountain.

"It's riddled with tunnels, 'n' most o' the mines are there. Only, now, after thirty years, ever'thin's filled with water 'n' you can't get in. My grandfather worked there… He's alive to this very day."

"Was he a penal laborer?"

"Quite likely a penal laborer. All them peasants was penal laborers then… We was the factory's own.[22] As I unnerstand my grandfather, today's penal laborers're livin' in Paradise compared to them. Razgildeev was around then… Go ask the watch-house guard: he was here too, in the same mountain, 'n' he worked at Kara. What kinda *katorga* is this for you now? You ain't bein' asked to own up to your quotas, floggin's is rare 'n' proportionate; but back then, a day didn't pass without a river o' blood!…"

The Cossack went away. Everyone grew thoughtful.

"Alright? Let's see about this tunnel," I suggested to the prisoners, and we went over to the cap.

There was a large quadrangular shaft in the center of it, almost over-flowing with water. I knelt down and almost immediately pinched my nose, so fetid was the stench…

"Thirty years—it's rotten through," a prisoner explained.

"What are we going to do?"

"Duty officer'll come 'n' show us. We're in no hurry. Mother-treasury can wait."

"But aren't we penal laborers? We have to hurry!…"

"Whoe'er's fast makes people laugh."

"I'm not saying why we need to hurry," I tried to justify myself, "I'm just asking: what are we going to do?"

"Crank the barrel-organ."

"Where's this barrel-organ?"

Everyone laughed.

"You're so sad, Mikolaich! Forget 'bout your book collection…"

I became utterly confused and began peering about. Emerging from the well was a hawser with iron handles. I grabbed one of them, and the enormous hawser squeaked and turned ponderously. Only then did I remember the tubs and rope we'd brought.

"Hey-o! This'll go better if we sing a song, chaps!" said the young, very handsome fellow Rakitin, whose prison nickname was "wagger" (so called is the little bell that hangs around a cow's neck so it doesn't get lost in the taiga).

And, needing no encouragement, he began singing in a high, sweet tenor:

"In the silvery waves,
In the yellow sand,
I suffered guarding footprints
For so very long.
I see in the distance
The sea shall rise…"

But he couldn't remember this song, and immediately took up another:

"Bell's ringing, troika's tearing
Along the highway;
On wings of happiness the young fighter
Speeds *along the roof*."[23]

I covered my ears.

"Speeds along *what?*"

"The young fighter speeds along the roof... That means this young chap's jus' like me... A handsome fellow, too... Goin' home to his wife, to his jewel of a spouse..."

"Wait! How can he go *along* the roof? *Along* the road, *along* the field—that's fine, but who goes along a *roof?* It should be sung, *To his own blood's house*, that is, to his relatives' house."[24]

"Very well, then. I'll 'member this without fail, you can be sure. Akh, it was so difficult for me to memorize at first, Ivan Nikolaevich, 'n' it so happens it's extraordinary I remembered anythin'! 'N' I was terribly mad for science. Well, I been right dull since I got married."

"You're married, Rakitin? So where's your wife?"

"Here—she followed me. Didn't you see a woman ridin' in the line o' carts? She's such a nasty, nasty ol' bat that you wanna spit! Fifteen long years she's been with me."

"But how old are you?"

"I been twenty-seven years without a roof. 'N', you'll know, I got a little boy called Keshia who came here with me. Three years old. Akh, thinkin' 'bout 'im makes my little heart ache—it *aches!*"

"But it doesn't ache over your wife?"

"The wife! Mightn't there be twenty wives, specially for such an artist as myself!... A passionate woman loses her mind o'er me, 'cause o' my blessed good looks!"

And suddenly he broke into a dance, narrating like a minstrel:

"Pitchfork, rake, two brooms, and a cock!
Pitchfork, rake, two brooms, and a cock!
Two she-devils and a goblin came,
Dragged away two bags and a sack!"

"Akh, wagger!" the prisoners laughed.

At that moment the foreman Pëtr Petrovich appeared at the doors.

"I'm worn out, boys!" he said, taking off his cap and wiping his forehead with a red checkered handkerchief. "It's gonna be difficult gettin' through here."

Breathing heavily, he settled down beside us on the mine's broad timber framing. I asked him to explain what the mining department had in mind assigning this work.

"Indeed, they'd nuthin' in mind, chaps... It's just, the stupid money turned up... Y'see, they wanna use the ol' works that are in that big hill. Water's there now, 'n' has gotta be flushed outside to the bog near the watch-house."

"When is this plan to be accomplished?"

"There's a lot of it, chaps, 'n' it's a job, but as for when?… If there were free laborers… But with penal laborers, it'll never happen."

"Never?…"

"Well, maybe it'll happen in thirty or forty years. You'd think it'd be better to push for the wealth a bit earlier… Even in the old days Shelai mine weren't 'mong the first-rate: you'd get all o' two 'n' a half ounces o' silver per pood. The veins there in Algacha, for example, produce o'er four ounces. Now, there, without any preparatory work, they take all the silver 'n' jus' feed the men… But with this mine here, you'd hafta dig o'er four hunnerd feet deep into the planet, though now the mine's all o' sixty feet deep."

"In that case, why reopen Shelai mine?"

"For the prison… Without a doubt, so's to instruct your brother!… Boys, howe'er much we waffle, the work still needs doin'. Were it the regulator didn't inspect… He drags his fat belly around, but he can still creep up on us. Put the rope on the hawser!"

We wound the rope onto the hawser and connected its end to a tub or, speaking in mining jargon, a *kibble*. Four of us, including myself, began turning the hawser by the iron handles, and two others took the kibble and poured the fetid water from it into a previously constructed gutter from which it sluiced into a ditch.

"Spinning the barrel-organ" in fours and even threes was quite easy; but it became fairly difficult for a pair, and out of all of us only two could turn it alone: Semënov and another unprepossessing-looking Ukrainian. Pëtr Petrovich also wanted to try his strength, and with great effort turned it one full time.

"Well, I'm off, chaps. Please don't blow off work until I come with a Cossack."

"Hey there, Pëtr Petrovich," Rakitin approached him with a sugary smile, "give us a better assignment. Y'know a prisoner only goes fishin' when he wants to eat, so what's the point of all this? It's as if a young man such as myself was gettin' his lovin' from an ol' lady."

"Maybe you'll do it for me. Pump out three hunnerd kibbles, then come to the watch-house."

"So many!…"

"Any less 'n' the regulator'll get mad."

"Alright, then," said Semënov, "three hunnerd it is!"

"But that little kibble you brought up yourself, you gonna count that as well?"

"Stop chatterin' with me, you buffoon."

"Well, very well then! Hagglin' don't cost nuthin'! Don't forget the beautiful girls kiss *us*, you loser!

"Akh, what you young girls're doin',
Runnin' away from us chaps!…"

Pëtr Petrovich left. I suggested we get down to work, since it was already late and there was much to do. Deep down I was quite surprised my compatriots had haggled so little with the foreman. But as soon as the latter was out of sight Rakitin cried out in joy, jumped around, then neighed like a stallion and finally cuckooed:

"Boil the tea. The assignment's finished!"

The others silently followed his suggestion. Semënov grabbed the kettle and went over to a Cossack to ask where he could get water. I perplexedly looked at Rakitin.

"How can the assignment be finished when we haven't even begun?"

"Oh, don't worry, Ivan Nikolaevich, you'll have plenty o' time. How long's your sentence?" I told him.

"Oo-ee!! You can pump a lotta water in that time! More'n three hunnerd kibbles."

"Does this mean you'll trick the foreman? Tell him you pumped three hundred and not thirty?"

"Tha-a-at's it! You guessed it. Exactly! Always follow my rule, Ivan Nikolaevich: try jus' one turn, so's the gutter gets wet. Is it wet? Well, that's splendid!… Ah, no, no! That edge there is still dry… So it looks real, like we been workin'. Now I'm free, thank God! Maybe you'd like to hear a little song?

"The city noise unheard,
Silence in the pond'rous tower,
And upon the guard's bayonet
The amber moon glowers.[25]

"Or here's an e'en better one:

"A final, dying beam
From behind the dry hill,
Now the dense stream
Barely flows from evening's fill!
Take a rifle long,
Walk outside the gate,
Take a left along
The naked cliff of slate."[26]

During this, Semënov had gotten the water and quickly brewed tea over the soldiers' fire and we made ourselves comfortable.

"We'll drink tea 'n' maybe take a little nap," Rakitin continued chattering. "Lie down, Ivan Nikolaevich, lie down for God's sake, I'll make up a bed for you. I'll break up the twigs Petrushka 'n' me brought in the barrows, 'n' you'll have a splendid rest beside us. I myself can't sleep durin' the day: Got too many ideas, y'know, 'n' my blood pressure's high as well. So I'll sit beside you as a lookout. Soon as I notice an authority comin', I'll give you a little nudge."

But I turned down this curious proposition, saying that I, too, couldn't sleep during the day and so preferred to talk.

"How many years were you given, Rakitin?"

"Eleven. Ivan Nikolaevich, I swear I was sentenced to labor completely innocent. For a hat. I swear it—for a hat!"

"How's that?"

"I was angry with a certain chap… Petka here knows 'im—Alëshka Trofimov. Goncharov, Petka, 'n' me, we're all from the same place, from Eniseisk Province… Well, o' course, it happened 'cause of a girl… I'd decided to do him the honor, that is, stick him one rib away from the heart. I got Senka Ivanov in on it. Me 'n' him saw Alëshka come into the yard from outta somewhere, 'n' we got on his sledge 'n' followed him. We're out on the steppe: 'Stop!…' He turns round 'n' hustles o'er… 'No, brother, don't lay that on me.' I jumped up on the sledge 'n' sprang like a cat, 'n' sunk my teeth straight into his chest… Such is my way, you unnerstand—when I'm angry, out come the teeth… Senka had one arm round his *mashinka* [his throat] 'n' the other tight round his belly. 'We're gonna fix you up, sweety, decorate you, so don't scream mommy!' We grabbed him 'n' threw him in the snow. I powdered him with a bit more snow. Got on the sledge again, 'n' off we was to home. We'd made Alëshka obsolete! All bloody, lyin' there under the snow like a bear… He went straight to the village headman 'n' made a statement sayin' Senka 'n' me stole his hat 'n' seventy-five rubles. There was a search, 'n' right there beside me on the sledge was Alëshka's hat! The stupid idea of takin' his hat had just popped into one of our drunken heads—'n' then we'd forgot 'bout it! What happened next was simply marvelous: 'How'd this happen? Why was it taken?' It turned out to be an important piece of evidence. So, for just a hat, I got sent to *katorga* for eleven years."

"But didn't you steal the money?"

"I swear to God, we didn't steal! I swear on my good looks to you—we didn't steal!"

"And by what honest work did you earn a living?"

"It may indeed be told. Y'see, Ivan Nikolaevich, I'm an adult orphan. My father was an exile-settler 'n' left me when I was tiny. I'd go round with a little sack on my shoulder. Other people would tearfully look at me with bleedin' hearts: 'Akh, you dear little child! Neither a father nor a mother for you!' I grew up in like manner. Got used to work, to the worker's life. Later, the horse dealer Ivan Ivanovich Chashchin hired me as an assistant. 'Cause I was a bold chap, I loved the parents more with every clever turn o' the horse. Then I fell into burnin' love with his only daughter—now my wife—Marfa Ivanovna. As it so happened, there was sin 'tween us… Her father, o' course, was very angry 'cause he saw what'd happened, 'n' made us get legally married. Since then, I've wanted for nuthin', drank 'n' ate well, 'n' lived by the labor of me own hands."

"If it's as you say, then you wouldn't-a stolen, ya wagger!" Semënov, who until now had been silent, interjected sullenly and gravely. "You're sayin' you' ne'er took on risky ventures?"

"Akh, Petia, you're my brother! For sure, how can I know on which side it is completely? I grew up in need, in poverty, had so many friends 'n' comrades, but then I should suddenly turn up on a rich man's threshold? Is that possible at all? No, Petrushka, first of all there was commerce. That's it, my best friend!"

"But, chaps," the old man, coming towards us at the cap, now shouted, "ain't it time to go home? Ain't we goin' to the watch house?"

Everyone roused himself and quickly got underway. Descending wasn't the same as ascending: my feet were slipping and sliding; I had to work to keep from running at full tilt. The Cossacks with their rifles barely kept up with us. I was disturbed by the idea that I'd begun my first day of *katorga* labor as a fraud, not personally, but as a co-conspirator nonetheless, yet, seeing the perfect calm radiating from the prisoners' faces, I completely relaxed as well.

"If the rest of the jobs are like today's," I thought, "I may survive."

Rakitin had such gall that, arriving at the watch-house, he reported to Pëtr Petrovich in the most honest and natural way that not only had we finished the assignment but emptied an extra fifty kibbles…

"But is there any more water?" Pëtr Petrovich asked.

"Mister Foreman, it's hard to know for now. We'll see in several days. If there's a side-flow anywhere, then you prob'ly can't do nuthin' without a hydraulic pump!"

Workers from the other shafts came up behind us. The convoy formed. The guard accompanying us completed roll call and ordered: "Forward, march!…" We turned toward the prison. This first day's work left a confused but, in any case, not especially stupefying impression. It would be my fate to see later the other side of the coin.

V.   IN THE MINE'S DEPTHS

We got back from the mountain at 3:30. Like that morning, we were once again thoroughly searched and counted at the gates, and only then allowed into the prison. We ate a warm supper. The ward cleaner Iashka-the-Marmot quickly told me the prison news. The winter encampment really was being built for a free command to be established soon. Six-Eyes had inspected the prison and toured all the wards. He explained to the headmen and cleaners that they were responsible for washing the wards' floors and latrines every Monday and Friday, and that the janitors were to clean the corridors.

"Our Gandorin nearly died o' fright!"

"What do you mean?"

"He didn't lift his sleepin' platforms. As soon as you all left for work, a guard shouted that headmen were to lift the sleepin' platforms, but our ol' man didn't hear…"

"Indeed," Gandorin plaintively chimed in, "I was cleanin' potatoes in the kitchen. But you yourself didn't do right, Iasha: if you weren't gonna help your headman, you shoulda told me… But, y'see, that's the trouble with you!"

"Ha-ha-ha! That's for you blessed old men. Jus' look at 'im… What's my duty? Com'dant hisself told me: 'this is your job,' he says, '—keep your glasses spiffy, the rest concerns the headmen.'"

"What about Gandorin?"

"Ask him."

But the old man simply sighed and kept quiet.

"Six-Eyes nearly tossed him into a cell under a pine tree! He's sayin' his prayers… It'd be a good match for him," Marmot continued. "How he shouted at him: 'What's this? Disobedience, recalcitrance? Put him in manacles, in irons! Bread 'n' water!' I look: Gandorin's knees're shakin' 'n' his lips've turned white… He fell on his knees!"

"I daresay you'll fall! Wait a little bit, 'n' you yourself'll fall! This is my third year in *katorga*, but not once have I ended up in the 'slator. I'm jus' averse to sufferin' innocently. That's that!"

So as to shift the conversation, I asked what time those not laboring in the mines had to work, and learned they ate at eleven o'clock, rested for two hours, and at the alarm went to a work again; that they weren't given quotas and therefore worked from alarm to alarm, that is, until five o'clock in the evening. After this, following Semënov and Goncharov's salubrious example, I stretched out to relax after jobs well done.

"Thank God! One *katorga* day is ending."

From early October, because the days grew shorter, working hours were lowered in accordance with prison regulations: we would be getting up for work at seven instead of six o'clock. Later, in November, the day would be shortened by still another hour: those not working in the mines finished at four o'clock, and evening roll call began at five. Then again, the post-lunch rest was cut in half. Autumn was clear and bright during all the first half of October; there wasn't any snow, but it was quite freezing in the mornings. The stoves were stoked only beginning with October, but at first rather rarely and sparingly; for this reason, the wards were damp and cold. Although the promised regulation mattresses stuffed with straw had been issued, we still had to cover ourselves with the filthy cassocks worn for work. We were given no sheets whatsoever; personal bedclothes were forbidden for the sake of universal conformity to even the pettiest ward regulations. Better yet, if you did get a newly issued cassock, after two years it was usually so torn, so worn out from the coal mines and galleries, that it could literally be seen through like a sieve and in practice offered hopeless defense against nighttime cold; many prisoners therefore covered themselves with their jackets and even trousers; several slept without undressing at all… Generally, during autumn and spring, but sometimes also during bad weather in summer, when the prison wasn't heated, one occasionally suffered terribly from the cold at night and often caught sick. Winter, when prisoners were distributed sheepskin jackets, was far better.

I was continuously assigned to the "barrel-organ" in the upper gallery for no less than two weeks, but the water was not being emptied from it completely. Pëtr Petrovich finally caught on to what was happening and began threatening to report us to Six-Eyes. Nonetheless, he several times had the patience to sit with us for several hours, personally observe the progress of the work, and note down the number of kibbles. During a span of some four hours of continuous labor we emptied five hundred kibbles, and the water level in the shaft suddenly noticeably dropped. Guilty of impudent fraud, Rakitin, Semënov, and the others were not a little flustered, but they had since begun working zealously; the word "report" had a marvelously terrifying effect… Besides that, Pëtr Petrovich had let slip that the regulator was preparing to specify "laziness." This, too, was an enchantingly effective word. In less than a week the upper gallery was emptied clear of water to a depth of thirty-five feet. Deeper than that was solid ice.

We decided to go to the bottom to look at the mine. Semënov and Rakitin descended one after the other along a rope, clutching it with hands and feet and moving so quickly that I could barely believe it… At least the former had found gloves, but the empty-headed Rakitin didn't even use any. Not having waited until Semënov reached bottom, he grabbed the rope with bare hands and, whistling and bawling out some kind of song, shot down like an arrow so that he landed straight on his comrade's shoulders. Semënov could be heard cursing and calling him a devil… I'd warned Rakitin he'd burn his hands on the rope, but it was as if nothing to him. Now on the bottom, he was singing, dancing, and playing the fool. Followed by Pëtr Petrovich and me, the rest of the prisoners started climbing through the so-called "trap-door," the wooden cover leading to one of the side-galleries; with lanterns in hand we began descending a dark ladder. There was no small danger, since the mine had just recently been filled to the top with water and our feet were slipping on the ladder's wet and icy steps. As Pëtr Petrovich explained to me, behind the thick planks a perpendicular wall separated this portion of the mine, similar to a large room, from the remainder so as to protect the ladder and foreman from dynamite explosions.

"But this protection's hopeless," he added, "ever'thin's really jus' slapped together. Ladder 'n' planks have been blown to hell so many times! I always try to get outta the mine when a fuse is lit."

"Yours is a bad job; but is the pay good?"

"It's *katorga*! Twenty rubles a month… Worst of all are them damned mines where you gotta scale ladders. Gettin' into a gallery's easier: you can go seventy feet harnessed to a ledge or stanchion 'n' stay there without givin' a damn."

The twelve steps of the ladder completed, we found ourselves on a wooden platform. I was surprised the descent was so short, but there turned out to be a further four such ladders and platforms. The fifth, which was called "the stepson" (simply a beam with notches) was sheathed in ice as well. The mines were damp and cold and dark to the unaccustomed eye; only, the stench was less than I'd at first expected: the fetid water had been drained and the ice on top of the first, filthy layer, already punctured by Semënov's and Rakitin's hacks, was white and pure as sugar. I looked up. Owing to its being covered by the outside cap, the wide shaft-opening let in little light; wooden beams were soaked with frozen water, and above our very heads hung in the mine's corners enormous icicles that, had they fallen, would probably have killed us… "So this is what a mine is!" I thought, shivering from the cold and contemplating in secret fear having to be in this cellar for five or six hours a day.

"When did this mine begin operating?" I continued querying the foreman.

"Thirty years ago. In three years they dug down over sixty feet."

"And that's when this framing and the ladders were made?"

"Not at all! This all got made o'er the past two summers, when they was gettin' the mine ready to open. Zerentui's 'n' Algacha's free commands did their utmost."

"That means the water that we emptied…"

"Came in not long ago. Autumn rains was strong."

It fell upon us to chisel the ice. Having chiseled a fair amount, we began putting it, like the water, in kibbles and carried it in the barrows to a gutter. We continued taking out the ice for more than a week. We again encountered flowing water in places without ice, where the rotting remains of rabbits, rats, and chipmunks turned up. One had to plug one's nose against the relentless stench… At last, we got over sixty feet deep into the bottom of the coalmine.

"You're all loafin' about!" Pëtr Petrovich, meeting us in the forward chamber, said one beautiful morning. "Now you can start the borin'."

It was now the last day of October; deep snow had fallen and established true winter; it was already twenty degrees below zero.[27] The old watchman pulled from a trunk around a hundred round iron rods of various lengths (from half to almost two and a half feet) and ordered prisoners to allocate thirty of them to each mine.

"What are these for?" I asked.

"How d'ya think you're gonna bore? These're the augers."

I picked up one of the rods and saw on its tip a cutting edge resembling a chisel with rounded sides. For each mine there were also six hammers and three "cleaners"—long and narrow withies with a trowel on the end: what in fact these were used to clean remained unknown to me. Finally, the old man gave each man a narrow tallow candle seven inches long. An argument erupted over these candles.

"Feelin' remorse o'er state property, you ol' sod?"

"You'll indeed be sorry! I myself will most likely be held to account."

"Each brother gets two candles."

"That's if they're workin' in dif'rent places, but you're all in the same kitchen… Ain't it a beauty of a mine? I know, I worked there meself…"

"Geez, you ol' snake! 'I,' he says, 'was a penal laborer, too'… So why're you 'gainst your brother 'n' givin' him so little?!'"

"'N' you're all such penal laborers? Back in our day, boys, you'd have known how to bore… They gave but a single candle to a pair o' men, 'n' the job 'ad to be done within a day. Dark it was, you're flailin' about, hands a bloody pulp, 'n' you're borin'! Moreover, if you don't finish the job, you're tossed on a slag heap 'n' pay with your back! But nowadays you talk to a foreman like he's your brother 'n' don't doff your caps."

"What nonsense, boys! Akh, you, your shameless eyes, you cursed soul! You're e'en responsible for your own nicknames, ol' man… Indeed, what would the mare have done to you for talkin' like that in the ol' days?"

"What's this? So I'm… I know nuthin' bad comes o' me words, I tell you… But why should I worry 'bout you? E'en though you're livin' better'n we did. You could only get one candle per mine. You shoulda lived under Razgildeev!…"

"Gonna scare us with your Razgildeev? You all was frightened stiff—'n' so you think he's terrifyin'. But today's mare woulda gladly knocked him down a peg. You shouldn't chirp so much. Nowadays our brother ain't quiverin'."

"You'll see how brave you are! Yes, indeed, it shouldn't hafta come to that. You shoulda seen how he'd ride through Kara. More'n a thousand of us was there. I remember 'ow he barked: 'Flog 'em!' So all one thousand of us froze. 'Ow he began pourin' it on, my brothers, 'ow he began pourin' it on… One hunnerd men in a row was flogged half ta death—'n' off he galloped."

"Why'd he do it, little grandfather?"

"Well, y'see, turned out little work was bein' done… So there was two cartloads o' wooden switches always near the work site."

"But couldn't a man who'd stand up for himself be found?"

"One was found, chaps! There was a Tatar, a real strappin' Tatar called Mohammed Baidaulov. 'Well, boys,' he said, 'I'll finish off Razgildeev soon as I see 'im, just finish 'im off.' We're lookin': 'tweren't like he was drunk, but his eyes was bloodshot 'n' his whole face 'ad changed. But the chap 'ad been quite humble earlier. We saw the man 'ad firmly made up his mind. But the mare was still eggin' 'im on: 'Do as you say, clodhopper! Yer hand's froze 'n' you got a screw loose.' 'No, it ain't loose,' he said, 'I'm gonna kill 'im.' Very well. There we was again, workin' through one day as if it were two. We see the colonel ridin' straight o'er to us. Baidaulka's standin' aside me. Guard shouts at the top o' his voice: 'Caps off! Attention!' All the caps come off, ever'one drops their tools to the ground. I look: Baidaulka's wearin' his cap 'n' gots his hack in his 'ands, completely pale… I was neither live nor dead, watchin' 'n' not knowin' what was gonna happen. Razgildeev jumps down from his horse 'n' rushes up in front o' his face: 'Scoundrel!' He cursed him with such vile words… 'What's gotten into your stupid head?' He shouted in one ear! Shouted in t'other! What then 'appened 'tween 'em, I can't 'member to this day.

Jus' seen Baidaulka rollin' on the ground 'n' Razgildeev stompin' on 'im… 'I'll take this scum to the world's end!' Jumped on his horse, 'n' was off. They took Baidaulka away an hour later. No one e'er knew what 'appened to 'im."

"So what was his mistake? Did he turn coward?"

"Didn't turn coward, but… Certainly, Razgildeev didn't find it fatal."

"Find what fatal?"

"The man… the man, to be precise."

"But did they kill him afterward?"

"'Tweren't murdered, 'tis true, though he ended up worse'n death."

"How so?"

"The sovereign hisself heard 'bout his villainies, stripped him entirely of his titles 'n' positions, 'n' ordered him to 'pear 'fore him in Peter.[28] Only, he didn't make it—he kicked the bucket!… He rotted alive—eaten by grubs… But soon after this, us serfs got our freedom."[29]

"Should be time for all you Razgildeev relatives to kick the bucket!" concluded Semënov, having for some reason suddenly glanced at the old man maliciously. "You're just ruinin' another's era! 'Twas indeed bad, but you want another one."

"Absolutely, but you're just stirrin' things up," interrupted Pëtr Petrovich, "better get to work."

Rakitin then approached Pëtr Petrovich and asked with an ingratiatingly sweet smile:

"Which of us are you gonna put in charge o' the augers?"

"That's your business. Whoe'er wants, can be in charge. You can take turns so's you can have some breaks…"

"Here's who you should put in charge, Pëtr Petrovich," the irrepressible Rakitin continued, pointing at me. "These educated people ain't used to work, unlike us simple *tuesy*."[30]

"Let 'im, if ya want. What's it to me?!"

"That's great. Ivan Nikolaevich, assume the responsibilities o' your position."

"How's it my responsibility?" I sternly asked, emphasizing how I'd been appointed without my desire or consent.

"You'll be in charge o' the augers… You carry the augers… We'll be bluntin' 'em, 'n' this means you bring 'em to the smith for sharp'nin'. That's what your job is. Stayin' in this cellar 'n' borin' is a lot tougher, Ivan Nikolaevich! Pëtr Petrovich knows how it goes as well, so let's say he ain't askin' you to do it… Chief, ever'thin's clear!… So, no worries…"

"And how many times will I have to go back and forth?"

"Whene'er you need to. Three, five, seven times… but it's all up to chance—maybe not e'en once, if the augers hold out."

But I felt indescribable horror at the thought of climbing that high mountain three or maybe even seven times.

"No, no, I don't want to!" I shouted. "Better to bore a hundred and fifty feet."

"Ivan Nikolaevich!" Rakitin ran over and whispered. "Agree to it, my friend."

"And what about you? Isn't it easier if you don't have to do this?"

"Not easier, but I'm sorry that you…"

"How you pester, wagger!" Semënov shouted at him. "Man's tellin' you he don't wanna. Well, that's it, it's his business."

Rakitin immediately went quiet and, shrinking up and sighing, began piling a bundle of augers onto his shoulders. We went toward our mine shaft, deciding if we should each choose an auger or go through them one after another. The foreman followed behind us.

We put the augers in a kibble along with the hammers and withies and, having each grabbed a candle, descended the ladder into the shaft's depths.

"Who's gonna bore?" asked Pëtr Petrovich.

Everyone was silent.

"Rakitin, you musta bored before. Where'd you used to be?"

"In Zerentui, Pëtr Petrovich, only, I… bored all o' twice, 'n' it so happened that them two times I bored, with hardship 'n' no rest, three inches. That's 'cause my hand's ne'er closed tight since it got broke when I was a boy."

"Alright, brother, alright! You don't need to hold tight, you need skill. How 'bout you, Semënov, have you bored?"

"No," Semënov gloomily answered, though prisoners had several times described him as having been the best borer at Pokrovskii.

"I see by your eyes you're lyin' 'n' that you know how to do it. Chap, watch the shaft for me, so all the holes go straight. That blast-hole there leads first to the left, then the right… If you see this, shout at the fellow to stop borin' either backwards or forwards. Time 'n' effort'll be lost to no gain. For this first day, it'd be good if you bore up to ninety feet."

"I already said I don't wanna be the leader," Semënov bitterly responded. "Let whoe'er's got a long tongue or wants to wag his tail do it, but I can't."

"For goodness sakes, chap! Why is a tongue or a tail better? Man, I've just seen you puttin' down 'n' makin' fun o' the others as you liked… But you oughta think for yourself: I climb this mountain ever' mornin' just to give you your assignment. 'N' if I want, I can guarantee it'll be more difficult: 'how many feet was finished by evenin', did they complete the assignment?'… I guarantee you this is possible. I oughta rustle up an incentive for you…"

"That'd be good, Pëtr Petrovich, good, for God's sake!" said Rakitin. "Rewards would be even better. As you know, a dry spoon irritates the mouth. Akh! How I've turned out… How my heart speaks inside me!… Before you, I'm cursed by my saintly good looks, but I'll chip away seventeen inches today! I'll be bad to this rock, ooh! So bad! Where do I go, Pëtr Petrovich?"

"You should prob'ly go in this corner, chap." Pëtr Petrovich was rapping at the granite with a small hammer. "You'll find no hard mistake there. You'll find it jus' right on the slope. Move the auger a little to the left, so's this knob is broken off. Now, you, Semënov, go into that corner on the right. Move the auger onto the slope in the same way, jus' so, e'en a bit lower still. It's gonna bounce a bit awkwardly, so steady it somehow. After that, it'll break up fine."

In like manner Pëtr Petrovich arranged boring spots for three more prisoners.

"'N' will you be borin'?" he turned to me, using for the first time with me the formal *you*. Evidently, Rakitin's propaganda about my education and so on had had an effect… I answered unfavorably, having explained that I suffered from shortness of breath and heart palpitations.

"Well, so you'll prob'ly be borin' o'er here," he rapped the right wall of the mine. "It's prob'ly well-formed 'n'll be softer here." And Pëtr Petrovich turned toward the exit.

"So this means," he shouted from the ladder, "I should get fifty inches in six days. One for every auger."

The prisoners smoked pipes before working.

"Akh, he's condemned me to a little rock," Rakitin sadly exclaimed, "now I see I'm condemned! It's harder'n steel!"

"Woman's burstin' out in tears. Now you gonna swear you'll bore seventeen inches with your good hand?"

"But, why indeed, Petia? Why're you depressin' us with these curly-long-haired young girls?! Eh! You're knockin' all four wheels off my telega! Ah well, I'll bless you after we meet with God."

"Better to say the Devil."

Everyone grabbed hammers and augers. I went to watch Semënov to see how he would do it. He grabbed the shortest of the augers, with wide blades.

"This is called a startin' auger," he explained. "The thin augers can't be used for borin' at first, 'cause they're impossible to hold—they'll bang from side to side. For the most part, the blades on the medium 'n' long augers is made narrower. If you make a narrow hole first, the broad augers won't go through it. The auger should fit well. It's most important for the blade to follow: you bore in little bits at first; average-sized augers'll go five or six inches deep, 'n' with the longest ones, you'll only reach ten inches at the very end."

Having said this, Semënov pounded a hammer on the end of the auger. One, two, three… He held the auger with his left hand, trying the whole time to gently turn it from side to side. After some two minutes I saw that in the place where he held the auger a small triangular indentation had formed in the rock.

"You've bored before?" I happily shouted.

Semënov looked at his auger's "feather" and temperamentally tossed it into the center of the gallery. "What a piece of crap!" he said. "It's already blunted. Couldn't take fifty knocks." He grabbed a new auger. I picked up and carefully looked at the discarded auger: the steel blades had been completely flattened…

"Howe'er, it's your turn to bore, Ivan Nikolaevich," Semënov turned to me. "Go ahead, I'll show you."

"No, sit down, Semënov, I want to teach myself."

"No teachin' without a teacher."

And, paying me no attention, he lit a new candle, stuck it into the wall near the place the foreman had assigned me, sat down on a bare rock, and, after no more than five minutes, had bored quite deeply. His hammer cracked against the auger, his left hand turning it every so often—and Semënov cut a strong, masculine, energetic figure.

"Alright, alright!" I shouted. "Don't ignore me."

Semënov grinned, grabbed the iron withy he called a cleaner, and stuck it into the deep hole he'd made. Forcing it back out, he brought it up to my eyes, and I saw in the trowel a whole heap of fine white powder.

"That's a lotta siltstone there," he said, tossing the powder on the ground. "'N' that ain't all. Look how much more can be got out."

Semënov plunged the cleaner several times into the blast-hole and each time extracted a lump of white siltstone. Then he turned it around and stuck the other end into the hole. Pulling it back out, he fixed me a look and explained that more than two inches had already been completed, as shown by the inch markers incised on the cleaner. Semënov stood up and, giving me the auger and hammer, said:

"That soft spot beside you… I can pound o'er twenty inches outta there in an hour. Just hold the auger tighter, push it a little to the right. Take your sheepskin, put it on this rock 'n' sit down."

"I'll probably get cold without a jacket…"

"While workin'? Oh, you! I start sweatin' soon as I take off my jacket 'n' begin. You can't work in a jacket!"

I followed his advice, putting my jacket on the rock beneath me. My hammer was now banging in time with the others in the corners of the gallery. A truly harmonious music was being produced. I hammered… I hammered—and stopped, because I was sitting uncomfortably and had to rearrange the jacket. My work somehow did not go well for a long time. I was working hard, copying Semënov and turning the auger with my left hand while at the same time trying to hit it with the hammer in my right, but was completely unable to coordinate both movements. Whenever my right hand hammered the left didn't move and seemed to be following its friend absent-mindedly; whenever the left began turning the hammer simply admired it in high gesture and did not at all want to descend.

Semënov noticed my difficulty.

"Don't try to be exact," he consoled me, "jus' do it howe'er at first. Hammer twice, then turn the auger… Hammer again, turn again."

Things went well after this. Tick-tock! Tick-tock! went my hammer, resembling a pendulum, and the idea that I was working in a mine afforded me a secret satisfaction… Having hit the auger a hundred times, I picked up the cleaner with sinking heart, plunged it into the blast-hole, and spun and extracted it in the hope that it would be, as was Semënov's, filled with siltstone. But what was my distress when it came out almost empty! In despair, I began measuring. My auger showed it had already gone two and a half inches, but this seemed little compensation for those two and a half…

"Semënov!" I complainingly shouted. "What is this?"

"What?"

"I hit it a hundred times but could only get out a tiny bit of siltstone!… There's nothing more!"

Everyone laughed.

"Ivan Nikolaevich, that's 'cause you're stickin' it in as if you're breakin' up sugar," Rakitin explained. "You need to drive it in so's the earth's all broken up! I told you bein' in charge o' the augers'd be much easier…"

I felt ashamed and, saying nothing in reply, tried to hammer harder. But almost immediately I cried out in pain, jumping up from my spot and running through the gallery grimacing and clutching my left hand: I'd missed the auger and hammered my wrist with all my strength… I counted on hearing a sympathetic word, but everyone had only to laugh at me.

"What, d'you get a Shelai christenin'?" the usually silent fat man Nogaitsev turned to me, himself serving as an object of prisoners' running jokes and known not otherwise as Bruin or Mikhailo Ivanych. This made me explode.

"What's so funny, what's so funny?" I bristled. "It really hurts…"

"Ha-ha-ha! Ho-ho-ho!" Nogaitsev went off and reached such ecstasy that he actually began rolling on the ground and the whole of his plump, dropsical bulk heaved with laughter. Rakitin alone consoled me at that moment.

"You was born an idiot, a vulgar idiot, 'n' you'll die laughin'!" he sententiously told Nogaitsev.

"Yes! you're a smarty… Gonna order me to cry so's you won't punish me?"

"Ivan Nikolaevich, for God's sake, get rid o' that auger, get rid of it," continued Rakitin, approaching me. "It's better you brew some tea for us. A telega's already rumblin' through my stomach… Truly!… My business is goin' pretty nastily as well. These little hands are knockin' all about, but I still ain't done two inches!"

But I decided to continue boring. I didn't hit my hand just once that day (all the better that my glove protected it), but I was nevertheless able to bore almost four inches on top of the two Semënov bored. Semënov himself bored the most of all, followed by Nogaitsev. The latter came up to me afterward and for a long time stared at my work in silence. He saw that my hand was growing numb and the blows were becoming lazier and more inaccurate.

"Lemme bore," he at last rudely said, pushing me aside, but said this so simply and straightforwardly that refusal was made impossible. I quickly noticed the vast difference between his and my blows, mine being four times weaker… I watched how Nogaitsev worked without respite and stopped not a moment, how he swung the hammer three hundred times and then stopped only because he'd knocked down so much siltstone that the auger *had* to be pulled out. In half an hour he bore seven inches for me.

"Well, your area's soft, Mikolaich," he said, standing up, "'n' if you weren't here I could do more'n twenty inches with a watery arm."

"What do you mean 'watery'? Is it really easier with water?"

"No comparison! You're draggin' out cartloads of earth then! Quite another matter if it's hot water. Won't work with jus' any kind: with hard rock, borin's the same with or without water."

"But where would I get water? Can it really be brought from above?"

"We could try it here, we could try… warmin' it!"

"Well, get some, and I'll see."

"Ho-ho-ho! Shouldn't in front o' you…"

"It's our prisoners' secret," underscored Rakitin, smiling cleverly. "Go ahead, Ivan Nikolaevich, but you might get wet."

Suddenly, from the side where the unfriendly red-headed prisoner Koshkin was boring, I heard the gurgling of water in a bore-hole and, turning around, felt my face get covered in earth. I instantly understood where the water shot from…

"That's vile! This is an outrage!" I shouted, wiping my face and hurrying towards the mine's exit.

"Ho-ho-ho! Ha-ha-ha!" Nogaitsev and Koshkin burst out after me.

I was thus made familiar with the secrets of the art of boring.

Later, my whole night was interrupted by a burning pain in my right arm. Awakening the next morning, I was able neither to open nor tighten my fist. In their comfort the prisoners however told me this was always the case with lack of habit, and that my hand would loosen up later. Nevertheless, having bored over five inches the second day, I felt I'd be utterly incapable of working the following day.

"Y'know what, Ivan Nikolaevich," Rakitin whispered to me, "let's you 'n' me wag a tail at the medic today. Everyone wags a stretch: 'such 'n' such,' I'll tell the medic, 'let us rest a day or two.'"

"Aha!" said Semënov. "You got a screw loose? You bored two days 'n' you're all ready to wag your tail?"

"That's what you'd do, Petia! You can see for yourself I'm delicately built… I was written a song to sing for a family as a bargain for a loan… But all of a sudden a parable happened… 'N' *katorga* did away with all of it! Am I such a fool I should give my life to it?"

"You're not a fool but a wagger! You shake ever'thin' up, you shake ever'thin' empty!" Rakitin fell silent, and after a minute began singing in a high, sweet tenor:

"'Tell me, my beauty,
How can you go with another?'
'I go gladly with him':
He cried—I laughed…
And the poor thing came to me
Put his little head on my breast:
Laid his little head
On my right side,
The right and the left,
On my white breast…
And for a long time lay silent,
Warm tears dampened my shawl…
But I, his faithless one,
Could not believe why he bawled!"[31]

Infected by Rakitin's example, everybody roused themselves into a chorus and began singing another mining song:

At dawn it was, at daybreak,
Earliest morn at dawn—
I, maiden butter-churner, milked
And strained milk through a skein,
And after straining fed dear Vania,
And after feeding, I told him:
"Dear Vaniushka, don't marry!
If you marry, you will dim,

Lose your youth
'Midst orphaned girls,
'Midst widows young and slim..."
—Hail, green mother-forest!
As a youth, I walked through you;
But not for long did I walk …

It was awful to listen to these melancholy tunes in the depths of the stone vault. With every day my soul was gripped with greater and greater hatred for the mine… Extremely freezing weather set in. You'd try several times to strike with the hammer, but you'd feel your fingers completely numbed by cold. You'd look around to make sure the prisoners wouldn't notice and laugh, and warm them over the candle. My legs also suffered from the cold, since I couldn't muffle them with my jacket. The sooner I became familiar with the mine and its secrets the more animate this granite cell became. It seemed to look upon us all with callous derision, bearing an icy breath and saying: "Aha! have you caught it, dearies? I've buried many here like you."

As if hearing this sepulchral voice, I'd spin around to look tremblingly. The tallow candles burned dimly in the murk; here and there, casting black shadows, contorted prisoners sat pounding their hammers with all their might. Some produced sounds similar to groans or heavy breathing, others the vicious growls of a beast.

"Akh! Akh!" the fat man Nogaitsev burst out with every hammer-blow.

"Hoo! Hoo!" Seménov angrily said.

I barely discerned their faces and physiques in the dim illumination, and at that point, it seemed, not human beings but some kind of subterranean gnomes were working beside me there. I looked skywards in the hope of detecting at least one sunny ray that would communicate a consolatory word to me, would verify I was not yet an utterly dead man and that the time would come when I would live again and be happy and free. But the pitiless cap covered the shining sun, and only a dull, niggardly reflection of the winter day came through the shaft's aperture. I saw there only the ends of two dangling ropes hanging from the hawser shaft, and two kibbles blackened in the heights like a pair of hanged men suspended above our heads. It was unsightly, dark, cold… My heart was painful and lonely, and I so pitied myself…

"Whatta ya think, boys?!" suddenly shouted the savagely cheerful Rakitin, emerging from his melancholy and dancing through the gallery.

"Pitchfork, rake, two brooms, and a cock!
Pitchfork, rake, two brooms, and a cock!"

And in a bass he sang:

"That's you! That's you! That's you! That's you!"

Bitter thoughts took flight, and I laughed along with the others.

VI.   WE BEGIN

It took a week's work to prepare the blast-holes in the gallery. Pëtr Petrovich appeared before us bearing an armful of dynamite charges with long black and white fuses, and a vat of watery, broken-up clay. I asked Pëtr Petrovich to explain the construction of these gadgets.

"Strictly speakin', this ain't dynamite," he said, handin' me one, "but det'natin' jelly."

I unwrapped the paper from around one charge and saw a small tube consisting of a yellow, jelly-like substance that resembled regular beeswax.

"It's a simple construction," continued Pëtr Petrovich. "A powder fuse is connected with a capsule to the blastin' charge. You jiggle it into the very bottom o' the blast-hole 'n' well coat the outside with the clay, so's the explosion's stronger. Then you light the fuse 'n' take to your heels… So, who's gonna climb down with me today? I prob'ly can't manage down there alone. What about you, Rakitin?"

"Pëtr Petrovich, I dunno how… I…"

"Aha! Lost your nerve?"

"No, Pëtr Petrovich, it ain't that I lost my nerve, but I broke my arm as a boy 'n', moreo'er, 'twas badly… Once, a horse… 'appened in summer…"

"Alright, alright… Now don't start a fairy tale. How 'bout you, Semënov?"

"Let's go."

They went down, and the rest of us lay down on the shaft's framing and hung our heads over in curiosity. Nothing could be seen for a long time save fleeting glimpses of a candle moving to and fro. Finally, we heard the foreman's voice:

"Go, Semënov, now!"

The prisoners—especially Rakitin—jumped to their feet and ran away from the mine. Yet, noticing that I was still lying down, and reckoning that Pëtr Petrovich and Semënov were still below, everyone laughed and lay down.

"Are you afraid?" I asked Rakitin.

"Ech, Ivan Nikolaevich! Y'know I got a wife 'n' little one!… You save yourself mostly for them…"

Suddenly, something hissed and exploded below… In one, then another, then a third spot… Everyone started and rushed off with a shout of "It's fired!" This time, I ran, too… Semënov soon climbed out of the trap. While still in front of the shaft's opening, Pëtr Petrovich had ordered us to stand no closer than twenty steps from the cap during "the burn." A minute and a half of tedious waiting passed, but Pëtr Petrovich still didn't show, and we thought he'd decided to wait out the explosions on one of the ladders. But suddenly his solid physique with its red, puffing face appeared at the doors of the cap, and at almost the same time two blasts followed one after the other. The first of these occurred comparatively deeply, with a kind of seriousness, as if it were an angry, sharp knock; then the second came as a deafening boom. It seemed the entire cap trembled and shook… As if insane, two small pigeons that were perching on it and stupidly stretching their necks toward the roof didn't know what to do at first, but then they flapped their wings noisily and, soaring higher, began circling in the air. A bit later, Pëtr Petrovich ignited four more charges, two of them simultaneously, moreover, so that I couldn't be sure there were two separate explosions. The final one, the seventh in number, took so long that Pëtr Petrovich grew quite uneasy.

"It shoulda gone off, the damn dud!" he muttered. On the heels of this came such a deafening boom that it made the previous explosions seem weak.

"Ever'thin' should be blown to pieces!" Rakitin remarked.

"On the contrary," responded Pëtr Petrovich, "it's worse if the explosion's in the air. Those explodin' deep are better."

Fifteen more blast-holes remained to be exploded, but this was completely impossible at the time because the whole gallery was full of sulphurous, suffocating smoke that only evaporated slowly. So as to make it clear faster, we began lowering and raising the kibbles attached to the hawser, but still had to wait a long time until the foreman, grumbling and spitting by the minute, could at last set out once again for the bottom of the shaft. This second time he managed to explode eight blast holes: he had to go back a third time for the last five. Upon finishing the burn, he was fatigued, pale, coughing terribly, and spitting saliva black as soot. Fortunately, none of the twenty charges were "duds," and next day we were able to break up and remove the rock without difficulty.[32] The morning of the following day I entered the mine, curious to survey the results of the explosions. I was first of all astonished that, regardless of the seventeen intervening hours, the unpleasant smell of smoke still remained in the bottom of the mine. But I was most of all struck by the destruction's insignificant dimensions. I'd expected such enormous blasts to produce rubble at least seven feet deep, but fissures and heaps of fallen rock were to be seen only in places. Needless to say, I was most interested to view the spot where I'd bored my two holes. One of them—hurrah!—remained in the same exact spot as before the firing…

"Weren't blown out, blown to smithereens" Semënov explained to me, "it was a better one! That means your hole was jus' right."

On the other hand, the only thing left of my other hole was a long abrasion in the rock; all that was left of most of the others were "beakers"—remains several inches deep.

"Blew up real well!" Semënov decided.

"You call this good?!"

"But what're ya thinkin'? Don't you know how the rock-breakin'll be? Won't take longer'n two days. Look: here's the rubble, 'n' here, fissures ever'where."

And he began lightly knocking a sledgehammer against different spots in the gallery: the last blow echoed dully ("it's rubbled up"). I little understood all these technical terms and therefore decided to refrain from comment.

"Hey, you devils, what're you doin' up there?" Semënov shouted at his comrades who were hesitating above. "Get ever'thin' in, let's get started!"

Several fellows came down immediately. The nimble Rakitin and the clodhopper Nogaitsev, dragging his corpulent body down the ladder with difficulty, came down via the rope. I was told to hold and light a candle. Semënov tossed small rocks into a corner, noticed a fissure, and, leaning a pick-axe against it, ordered Rakitin to use the sledgehammer.

"I'm puttin' you here! Stop talkin' so much!"

Rakitin submissively took the half-pood sledgehammer, raised it high over his head, screwed up his eyes, and... slammed it with all his might into the pick-axe's wooden handle: the pick-axe flew to one end of the gallery, the broken handle to the other, while Semënov was barely able to move his hand in time.

"Akh, you mangy bastard!" he shouted. "Is that how it's hit? Was you aimin' for my mug? Where're your eyes?"

Rakitin looked away dejectedly with a guilty face.

"How'm I the worker for this job, Ivan Nikolaevich?" he complainingly whispered to me. "I grew up an orphan... I knew commerce once... I'm naturally inclined to unnerstand anythin'... Had I been taught grammar, I think I coulda gone far! 'Cause my eye's sharp that way!"

"Yes! You woulda been made a priest right off!" Semënov cruelly said. "You better go up now 'n' make a new handle for the pick-axe. There's a hatchet up there."

Rakitin went up top as he was told. In two minutes we heard him singing a song and joking about something to the Cossacks. Instead of Rakitin, Semënov ended up hammering the pick-axe, held by Nogaitsev. Semënov's entire face and figure were instantly transformed. Whereas he typically looked healthy and strong, he now seemed nothing less than a mythological Titan materializing out of a mysterious world. Regardless of the considerable frost, he took off his jacket and worked only in a shirt, without a hat. His hero's chest and steel muscles were outstandingly defined and startlingly elastic. He raised and swung the half-pood sledgehammer without apparent effort, as if he were playing, and from this every movement flowed beautifully, almost gracefully. Yet, the entire mountain shook beneath our feet amid these beautiful blows... He easily grabbed and tossed aside many pieces of granite I probably could not have budged... Only, his face during this labor was terrible to view: something brutal and unpleasant had fallen over it. Yes, this man did not stop to decide ahead of time if he could find what he needed—so I unwillingly thought about Semënov... I asked him to let me try. He silently passed me the sledgehammer.

"Well, I sure ain't gonna hold!" declared Nogaitsev. "Hit it on the rock like this."

I struck it four times; but my blows were so childishly weak and clumsy that I felt quite ashamed of my efforts and, hearing the general laughter, let the sledgehammer fall to the ground. All the same, I was gasping for air and unsteady on my feet after these four blows. Nogaitsev began pounding it after me. I expected something clumsy and ridiculous from his awkward, ursine physique, but to my surprise, I had to admire him as well. His labor, too, displayed an agile, poetic strength, and also summoned up a hero of fabled times... I could barely avert my eyes from admiring these "children of nature"! A piece of rock suddenly chipped off and hit me in the eyebrow, cutting it and drawing blood... The prisoners then told me that such things often happened during rock-breaking and one had to be careful. Frightened by these incidents, I subsequently protected my eyes with my fingers during rock-breaking (which, of course, hardly improved my productivity)…

Rock-breaking at last completed, everyone went again to the surface to lie around and drink tea. After tea, we began talking frankly with each other. Rakitin, as usual, was gabbing most of all, but my attention was no longer drawn to him. Meanwhile, prisoners began "egging on" the friendly, yet also extremely touchy, "Mikhailo Ivanovich," and we managed through our combined energies to squeeze out of him his curious and horrible past prior to arriving in *katorga*.

"That belly got itself into *katorga*," one prisoner put in. "So, how was this so?"

Nogaitsev was quiet, just sipping tea and breathing heavily into his filthy Chinese mug.

"He's a *telushechnik*," said Rakitin, "really 'n' truly, a *telushechnik*, as anyone can see. I'd recognize one of 'em from three versts."[33]

"A *telushechnik* indeed!" snapped Nogaitsev. "You caught me?"

"But if not, what got you sent away?"

"You must be told. Quickly. So's you don't get mad."

"You didn't come here 'cause of a woman, 'cause what kinda woman would fall in love with you?"

"She sure loved me."

"Some cousin- or sister-wife? Don't count, brother."

"Weren't family… But there was *a* wife…"

"You're believin' in a fantasy, brother…"

"Like you'll believe me."

"Well, tell me, then I'll believe. Another's woman loved you? 'N' she had curves? Or was she missin' a nose?"[34]

"Quite a gal indeed! A gal 'n' her mother both."

"What're you sayin'?!"

"Well. I lived 'mongst those workin' for a rich merchant in Tomsk. Matrëna, this same merchant's wife, 'n' I were connected… 'N', after her, her daughter, Paraskovia… What'd you s'pose? That I was this way on the outside? It's 'cause o' prison I'm fat 'n' outta breath, brother, but, before, I was as fine a young man as you."

"Well, I'll grant that. But for how long did the husband, the merchant, not know anythin'?"

"Knows nuthin' to this very day. What happened is in the dark, brother. You're wond'rin', how'd I get sent away? I was no fool, y'know. But I went to *katorga* all 'cause o' them damned women!"

"He's talkin' truth, boys! So many of our brethren's destroyed by them wolves in sheep's clothin'!"

"'N' don't they destroy! Were it up to me, boys, all the world's women'd be in chains, 'n' if one weren't submissive enough, she'd get tossed in the water with a stone tied to her neck! Why'd you put up with 'em, you fool? You're a softy!"

"Indeed. The master was off tradin' in Barnaul 'n' ordered his lady 'n' son 'n' daughter home to Tomsk. I planned to steal away to Tara with his wife. He'd paid me what he owed 'n', without waitin' around to see his family off, high-tailed it to go trade in Biisk.[35] Soon's he left, Matrëna 'n' Paraskovia stuck to me like glue: we went trav'lin' on 'n' on together."

"But how'd you get by with both of 'em? Weren't they hidin' it from each other?"

"But o' course! For sure, they was keepin' secrets… Naturally, they may have had suspicions… I led 'em to sin 'n' they agreed. We was ready to go off together. There was still her brother with us, Matrëna's son, I mean, a twelve year-old chap, 'n' there was a boy worker. So we go. We're goin' along well. Summer at the time. Once, we spent the night on the edge of a swamp. Such a terrible bog, surrounded by a fir grove… We made a fire, ate, drank. Paraskovia's brother Antip 'n' I knocked back a few. I can't remember how the night went, but when the sun rose next mornin', Antip found me with his sister… O' course, she hadn't needed to be drinkin': there we was in each other's arms, sleepin' in the covered wagon. Antip pulls the blanket off 'n' sees us in that way… Then he grabs a switch 'n' lays into me! I wake up right away, 'n' now Paraskovia's stirrin' awake… I jump outta the wagon 'n' try to run. But he's behind, whippin' me all over. I'm burnin' inside: 'What,' I'm thinkin', 'are ya doin' to me, fer Chrissake?' I look: there's a good, strong branch lyin' there… I grab it. 'Stop,' I says, 'don't commit a sin!' He ain't hearin'. It's like the chap's gone mad—'n' he keeps lashin'. Well, as I'm spinnin' round I hit him in the head… So's half his skull flies off! Then a red fog filled my eyes… That means the blood was a-flowin'… 'Now,' I'm thinkin', 'I'll kill ever'one the same way!' I run over to the telega where the old woman's sleepin'—'n' bash her on the head. Her head fell to pieces. The boy worker's lookin' at me with eyes neither live nor dead. Boy was fifteen years old. Such a humble chap, a weaklin', 'n' I lived with him soul to soul. I didn't lift a hand against the boy, but raised him a banner. Then I remembered that Paraskovia was still left. I fly to the wagon—she's sittin' there bare-headed, white as a sheet, tongue 'n' mind lost to terror… I grab her foot like it's a wood block, swing, 'n' smash her head on the wheel! Brains flyin' ever'where. Then I went over to Vaska again: 'Lissen to me, Vasia. We've lived together like natural-born brothers 'n' I don't wanna hurt you. Remember this: you ain't seen nuthin', all this was a dream. I myself never had this in mind yesserday, 'n' it ne'er woulda happened if they hadn't driven me to it.' Then I went over to Antip 'n' found two thousand paper rubles on him, 'n' another two thousand hidden in Matrëna's skirt; 'n' there was one 'n' a half thousand lyin' under Paraskovia's left tit… I collected the money 'n' dragged 'em all at once to the swamp: one on my back, the two bitches under my arms… Tossed 'em into such a bog they shoulda stayed there till kingdom come… I e'en piled rocks on top of 'em… Evidence was all wiped out, not a speck o' blood left… I burned all the surroundin' grass… Sold the horse 'n' telega to Gypsies… Gave Vaska five hundred rubles 'n' said g'bye. Went to Tomsk 'n' began partyin'. I'm thinkin', 'Can't be no evidence at all 'gainst me, 'cause the master left thinkin' I was goin' to Tara.'"

"Certainly, Vaska squealed on you? I guess it musta been him."

"That's it, exactly. A little kindness destroyed me. I'd decided to forget about Vaska. But, like me, he started partyin'. People was marvelin' over where he got that money. 'N' when the merchant learned his whole family was missin', Vaska got nabbed. Young fellow was arrested, 'n' he named me."

"Some natural-born brother!"

"Indeed. Only, I learned 'forehand they was gonna arrest me, so they didn't find a kopek on me."

"What'd you do?"

"I already managed to blow two thousand, 'n' I gave a thousand to my grandfather—I really loved my grandfather; I gave five hundred to my godchild; I'm thinkin', he'll grow up, 'n' my sins'll be God's secret. But the last thousand 'n' a half I hid."

"Where'd you hide it?"

"'N' what's it to you?"

"Well, if I was to escape, I'd go 'n' get..."

"No, you wouldn't get it. Them notes is outta circulation 'n' completely worthless now."

"Then why'd you hide 'em, you devil? Woulda been better to give 'em to someone to use."

"A fool's been found. 'Twas better to lose 'em, let 'em rot. Always worry 'bout yourself."

"But, tell me, Nogaitsev," I asked him, "why did you murder Paraskovia?"

Nogaitsev laughed:

"'N' what's it to you? Is it shameful?"

"Well, it's all the same... The matter's now past: but did you love her?"

"I loved her. What's this 'bout?"

"You loved her—but you killed her? How did that happen? What for?"

"Here's what for—they're all the same snakey breed! Why should she live in the world?"

"But why should *you* live?!"

"I'm a man... So, 'cordin' to you, I shoulda let her live? So she could inform on me 'n' destroy me?"

"Very good, Mikhailo Ivanych!" his listeners approved. "Well dealt with! You've piled on more stones."

"How he smashed her to smithereens on that wheel, boys! Ha-ha-ha! Such is our Siberians!"

"You also splendidly entertained Antipka, so's he'll be remembered in the next world!"

"Nogaitsev, when they arrested you, did you confess?" I asked.

"No, denied ever'thin'. Got twenty years without a confession, 'n' for what?"

"How 'for what'!... Is this really much for three souls?"

"Sure, it's a lot... They suf'rin' now? They're fine... But I'm sufferin' here 'cause of 'em! I didn't kill 'em for profit but for insultin' me. What was he whippin' me for?"

"How not for profit? Didn't you take their money?"

"That's *another* matter! What, I shoulda thrown their money in the bog? Anybody woulda done the same in my place..."

I wasn't about to argue, seeing as we were speaking completely different languages and would never understand each other. His story and callous attitude toward listeners made a heavy and depressing impression on me. I was enveloped by a feeling of horror and revulsion at this apparently mild and simple-hearted chap in whose soul there seemed a kind of hostile, dark, sick (and possibly unknown to him) power... Not a little time passed before I was able to steel myself and begin appraising him as would an elder. This was possible only after the terrible story I heard that day paled before others rendered ten times worse by their heartless cynicism and self-conscious depravity, when, having gotten to know Nogaitsev better, I realized that he laughed at the Virgin as well as the Holy Trinity, at Christ as well as St. Nicholas and the rest, and I appreciated that his soul was essentially the same as grass shaded in a meadow or a cloud floating through the sky and obeying the first breeze that comes along. In actual fact, he was more guilty of having been victimized by life's temptations, by urban culture and his own libidinous desires, and of having never and from no one received that blessed Promethean spark of which we are proud and is a formative part of humanity and which, however, may somehow include our wild animal impulses. Who could resolve to permanently anathematize him?...

"Howe'er, boys, time we got goin'," Semënov, who'd participated almost not at all in the discussion, suddenly said, "we can't lissen to ourselves chatter fore'er. Nogaitsev, go down into the gallery 'n' load the rocks."

"You're used to pilin' rocks, Mishenka," Rakitin added, "you'll cook up a sweat down there: m-m! m-m! m-m!"

Three prisoners—Semënov, Rakitin, and me—began to crank the hawser to raise the kibbles and bring the rocks in barrows to the slag heap. Two of us could barely tip a kibble now: the rocks were heavier than the water and ice. At one point, when we were tipping a kibble, Rakitin, grabbing awkwardly, dropped a chunk of granite weighing no less than two poods, and it fell with a terrible clamor and whistling to the bottom of the shaft.

"Look out!" Semënov managed to shout, and his warning happened to save Nogaitsev from instantaneous death: he was just able to jump beneath the ladder as the rock crashed onto the very spot where he'd been standing.

"Ooh, you hay-stuffed beast, you soft-belly!" Semënov and Rakitin blasted him. "You should stand under the *varshaft*[36] ever' time the kibbles get raised... But that won't keep you from gettin' soaked!"

"Here's some monsters possessed!" Nogaitsev shouted in turn from the shaft's depths, obviously scared half to death. "You'll likely sooner send the leadership to Hell... Why're you tryin' to pester my life? Devils!"

"Well! Well!" they shouted to him. "You're most guilty for stackin' poorly, but still you're complainin'... Fat-bellied hog!"

The work went along as before, though for a long time I was unable to shake my earlier anxiety. But the irrepressible Rakitin was soon cracking jokes:

"But would it be a calamity if a demon like you was killed? They'd just rustle up a new one, e'en fatter. Lotta our brothers get executed in Mother Russia!"

"But are there cases where men are crushed to death?" I asked.

"So many get crushed," the prisoners answered. "Take this place—it's almost sixty feet deep, but the shaft's a hunnerd 'n' seventy-four. Grab that little rock there 'n' it's part of a bigger one, 'n' your head'll likely get crushed to a pulp. Last summer in Zerentui a barrow snapped off a rope 'n' fell on a Tatar. So's his head's completely in pieces 'n' his arm gets torn off at the shoulder 'n' thrown two feet away... But another time it turns out so lucky that you just marvel. Once, in Algacha, a kibble broke 'n' fell thirty feet straight onto Vaska Mikitin's back... Let's say he was a hearty fellow, a real hero... So he spent all of a week lyin' in hospital, 'n' moreo'er, that was jus' 'cause he wanted to… There was also the time a calf fell down a shaft at Pokrovskii—but it didn't get hurt! Angry fella was down there mooin', 'n' it took all our might to pull 'im back up."

"Also had me a fright once, boys. I'm sittin' in the shaft, borin' away, thinkin' absolutely nothin'. Andriushka squeezed hisself into the kibble to bore next to me. I ain't noticed the end o' the cable from the other kibble got left hangin' on the hawser. Well, I'm fidgetin' 'bout, sittin' there in the kibble. Suddenly, there's a crackin' sound!… As the hawser's spinnin' the cable's comin' off… I'm borin' 'n' payin' no 'tention, but Andriushka's eyes go wide with terror 'n' he's lookin' up 'n' waitin' like an idiot. Hawser's spinnin' faster 'n' faster… Then he runs into the *varshaft* 'n' yells: 'Run!' I jus' managed to hug the wall, 'n' the whole cable come crashin' down! Fell four inches from me on the very spot I was standin'. If'n I hadn't jumped, prob'ly woulda been the death o' me."

"Also often happens someone'll drop an auger from a buncha augers. You'll suffer hor'bly from that as well. Be some inj'ries then, some inj'ries!"

"No one cain't reconcile that damage."

That day we raised eighty kibbles of stone and, upon leaving for the watch house, I felt worn out and beaten up.

VII.   PRISON WORKDAYS

Life in the prison followed its usual sequence of events. Roll call at its time, dinner at its, work would finish, sleep. Everything, positively everything, was arranged so that people were reduced to machine-like beings, living not otherwise than by command and "in accordance with regulations." By appearances the latter were, however, not thought-out, such that in the depths of a regimented prisoner's life a nook was possible into which an instruction had not been forcefully inserted, so that in the soul of even the most incorrigible people there existed a holy of holies to which no one was admitted. With such a holy of holies a prisoner was able to summon up a memory of the past, a yearning for freedom, and an instinctive hatred for any type of "spook," that is, soldiers, guards, authorities in general. True, a clean, unspoiled soul would likely have shuddered gazing into this terrible sanctuary; but what of it? It didn't matter for the outcast from human society; his soul felt satisfied and happy in this world only, and not in any other one, better and more elevated in our eyes. In Shelai Prison, where life was a mixed entanglement of all possible statutes and formalities, no possible regime could take away a prisoner's freedom to think and feel according to his knowledge and understanding; and since, as such, those regulations only slightly impinged upon a man's surface and his behavior in the wards and corridors such that clothes were regulation-issue, tasks fully completed, and caps doffed in time, the result, of course, was that not a single human soul was rehabilitated. Understanding the goals and notions of life, all eyes remained absolutely unfazed by these things, and a prisoner, transferred to the free command or a settlement, began a new life with the same template as in his earlier life, albeit with this difference, that he'd now try to carry out his business "better," more precisely, without leaving any possible clues or evidence. In a word, I got the impression that *katorga*'s terrorizing regime was legally advisable for only a small group of people, hearty by nature and uncorrupted by upbringing, who landed in prison owing to a sudden temper tantrum, a moment's temptation, or a fatal mistake; but there was actually no reason to terrorize this type: they would either way not end up in *katorga* a second time, and if they did, would do so no sooner than any other average fellow living in freedom. On the other hand, external terror ultimately simply corrodes a man to the core by making him cunning and hypocritical. It does not eliminate the evil bacilli that produce the illness of criminality within his soul, but, so to speak, pushes them deep into ventricular caches where their presence is however no less dangerous to the social organism… For gallant Staff Captain Luchezarov, who based himself purely upon external indicators, such as his being told "all is well" in the prison, that there were no card games, no squandering of regulation items, no drunkenness, and no assaults, it seemed completely natural that, in his hands, the prison's business was going along smoothly and flourishing and that he was forging ahead of the times, or at the very least not one step behind the latest conclusions of criminal science; but, for me, before whom the secret depths of the criminal soul were sometimes revealed, there was nothing essential, nothing good, that could be accomplished by this terrible regime… I saw how all these strict regulations, orders, marches, all these shouts to attention and timely doffing of caps, became for the prisoner after several days a habit he followed mechanically, just as he mechanically raised a fork to his mouth but not his nose when he wanted to eat, and so these things caused him not the slightest fear or suffering. For their own preservation, prisoners were ready all day to take off and put back on their caps, if only so as not to wear out their other, more vital, capabilities… And could you expect anything else from these people, whose comprehension of human dignity, of probity, of debasement, had completely atrophied? Moreso this: that among these people, among whom you were at that time, there were representatives and defenders of culture (in the person of the authorities and administrators) who tried as possible to stifle, not develop, this comprehension? Only the intellectual man can suffer in this way, and, in actuality, I can state positively that during the years of my vegetation in Shelai Prison, out of the hundreds of prisoners who arrived there, no more than two or three intellectuals who had, like me, the misfortune to end up in *katorga* experienced in depressing fashion *that side* of prison life. In actual fact, it gave me personally, truly, the most inexpressible torture, and the knowledge that none of my involuntary partners was sharing these tortures with me made me especially wretched and depressed. Even though I tried to lull myself with the idea that this was no more than an unavoidable arrangement that would not humble my human dignity, something in my soul's depths ached and rebelled. Every time one of Six-Eyes's guards ordered caps doffed while the gallant staff captain was in no hurry to permit them to be put back on, so that we sometimes had to stand before him for several minutes humbly holding cap in hand, I wished the earth would swallow me. This feeling forced me to resort to what was, at first glance, a funny ruse. I'd voluntarily doff my cap long before the commandant's appearance and, as such, would not obey the order while at the same time would not be opposing it. I well recognized this was no more than a pathetic compromise, a bargain with my own conscience, though it felt no less soothing or satisfying… As for the mass of prisoners, there actually seemed a kind of enjoyment in every superfluous time they doffed caps before the commandant.

During bad weather the evening roll call was normally conducted in the corridor, where standing without a cap was possible. Upon my request, the collective headman Iukhorev had proposed to the mare to do this.

"Really, lads," he shouted, "what the hell? It's just havin' to obey this order one more time. 'N' Six-Eyes himself can go to hell with it."

He informed the guard that prisoners would be standing in the corridor without caps because the "caps off" order was unnecessary. The guard agreed and when Luchezarov appeared simply shouted "attention." But when roll call took place in the corridor two weeks later, the prisoners were everyone of them wearing their caps, and to my reminding them of the situation they laughingly responded:

"What, are we too lazy to doff our caps? They shout 'take 'em off'—we take 'em off."

And the same headman who last time so passionately took to heart my request had now forgotten it and was also standing in his rakishly cocked cap. I dropped the matter.

Thinking about corporal punishment was, needless to say, immeasurably more terrifying. It seemed that should I myself ever be subjected to the horrible outrage the whole of my spiritual being would be forever broken and destroyed, and I would no longer be able to live and appreciate God's world. Worse than any of the mid-century's leftovers, use of the lash and birch rod on the eve of the twentieth century seemed something ineffaceably disgraceful and barbaric… Among my cohabitants this opinion was completely alien and incomprehensible. They feared only one element in corporal punishment—the physical pain. When I first time saw the long, thick lash wound out of string like a woman's braid; when they brought it to the little courtyard near the prison isolators to punish those sentenced by the court, and in addition to the executioner there arrived Luchezarov himself, a doctor, a medic, and several guards, I was shaking all over as if in a fever, and for a long time after the punished had returned to the ward and laughingly told how this one was "pro forma" I still couldn't relax.

"Only glanced at Mikitka… Barely, barely ironed me trousers… Six-Eyes made it clear: 'I don't worship the court's punishments! Don't influence me. But if you get into trouble *here*, I won't spare you.'"

All the prisoners unanimously approved of Six-Eyes for this and were generally satisfied with his conduct. Following this incident, his reputation rose in the mare's eyes. I was incarcerated during the times even women were cut;[37] but, from the point-of-view of it being a disgrace, it troubled no one…

Of course, the loss of free will was for all inmates similarly difficult. But, to tell the truth, I think an educated person bears this loss more easily. He has a fuller interior world and is a man enriched by treasures no one and nothing can take away. The interior "I" of the ignorant man is poorer because it depends upon purely external stimuli to fill his spiritual void and distract from bitter meditations. For those same reasons, he's more powerfully drawn to free will and purely physical instincts and needs. I was frequently surprised and unable to comprehend why prisoners so yearned for the free command, from which, for some theft or drunken assault, they often returned with their term reductions nullified or even with an additional *katorga* term. I realized it would have been better for many to complete their sentences in prison and not enter the free command, where it was easier to earn a new *katorga* sentence; each of those acknowledging this nevertheless strode pathetically through the yard inside the prison walls gazing enviously at the hills rising beyond them, sighing and counting his months and days until the free command… Let sigh those who dreamed of escaping to freedom, who had twenty or thirty years' *katorga* on their shoulders: them I could understand… But those with all of two or three months left before entering a settlement yearned for the command… Subordination, it's true, was weaker in the free command: "the spook with the bayonet" was not felt from behind; yet the work was no less difficult. Life in its barracks was simply much worse, darker, filthier, and noisier (thanks to the greater freedom); the food was worse than the prison's because the administration didn't look after the free-commandees so sharply and strictly. Given this, what there attracted these people? The freedom, of course, as expressed principally in open games of cards, the drinking of vodka, and the tubular nursing of penal laborers…[38]

In purely physical terms, Shelai Prison imposed upon prisoners a truly enormous mass of difficulties. Principal among these was the prohibition against emoluments of food and the requirement, even for those with money, to eat the regulation skilly. Folks among the prisoners found themselves sufficiently well-off, but not a single one could achieve such—primordial, in essence—altruism as to consent to increase his contribution to the cooking pot (as determined by the commandant).

"Why should I give my own money to feed the whole prison? I'd be called a fool!" each reasoned, and preferred to die of starvation.

True, however strict Six-Eyes was, however threatening his speeches and promises about their punishment, various little gaps and flaws immediately formed in the Shelai model prison. The hospital's cook sold "superfluous" milk on the sly, and the sick themselves their own meat rations, etc. For a long time, I couldn't understand how this conspiratorial commerce earned any money, since prisoners held not a kopek in their hands, and if they brought a ruble into prison it was confiscated during the search to which all were subjected. One time in the barracks old Goncharov laughed while I was expressing perplexity about this.

"Like them searches always find a prisoner's money! What're you thinkin'? Don't they play cards here?" he whispered at me.

"Cards? Where do they get them? Cards are even more difficult to bring in."

Saying not a word, Goncharov entered the latrine and, returning a few moments later and smiling conspiratorially, revealed two packs of old, greasy cards.

"So! Do you really gamble?"

"No, ne'er gambled in my life, 'n' 'ave ne'er e'en wanted to watch a game. Petka 'n' me jus'… hold onto 'em. Let's say he's a gambler, a first-class card-sharp. 'Member, he marched the whole way (we walked together six months) 'n' didn't lose once. He knows all the gamblin' ins 'n' outs to a tee."

"But does Semënov gamble here?"

"What game can there be here?! Is he gonna get his hands dirty? At the very most, there's all o' twenty rubles floatin' round in this prison."

"So why are you keeping the cards?"

"Whaddya mean 'why'? If someone wants to play he comes to us. We'll make a percentage."

"Ah, that's it…"

After this, I several times happened to witness card games. One would typically take place in a corner of the ward on the sleeping platform or behind the oven in the kitchen. A stirrup would obligingly stand at the door-window and, upon a guard's approach, typically exclaim: "Twenty-six!"—the prison cheats' conventional signal. For the most part, the stirrup was Iashka the Marmot, a great lover and expert of his business. Fortunately for the card players the orderly was always given away by little bells, the ringing of keys that jangled with his every move and forewarned the guilty. I remember one time how excited the whole prison was when gamblers were "nabbed" in the kitchen: the stirrup had been yawning and a guard took the cards and money straight out of their hands. We expected Six-Eyes to deal strictly with the guilty, but to everyone's surprise he limited himself to confining them in the isolator for several days and didn't even call for a search of the prison. Another time, a guard spotted a card game going on in the ward. He silently unlocked and quickly pushed open the door and went to grab the cards, but they had vanished.

"Where's the cards? Where's the cards?" the nonplussed keeper of order shouted.

"What cards? God bless ya, Prokopii Filippych. We're just sittin' here talkin'.'"

"You're lyin', lyin', you sons-o'-bitches! I was just watchin' Petin dealin' with my own eyes. You got 'em, Petin? Confess!"

"I sure don't."

"Take off your shoes, I'm gonna search you. I'll stake your life on 'em. I'll stick you in the isolator!"

"Search as you wish."

The guard picked through every last thread on Petin, a strapping fellow of enormous height who submissively positioned his arms and legs per his demands and took off his shoes, trousers, and jacket. The cards seemed to have been swallowed by the earth.

"Very well, it won't be good for you, dear fellow! You won't be able to do a thing… I'll be keepin' a close eye on you."

The guard left and prisoners began laughing.

"Petin, where did you manage to hide them?" I asked.

He cheerfully flashed his white teeth.

"On my head the whole time. Soon as he ran in, I made like I was adjustin' my cap 'n' slipped 'em under it… His eyes was rovin'—but he didn't notice. He searched ever'thin', only, he didn't have sense enough to look under my cap."

This clever prisoner's trick truly amused me. Another time Iashka the Marmot performed something similar. A different guard, suspecting a game in the bathhouse dressing-room, similarly rushed headlong at it and began searching everyone. Primary suspicion fell on Marmot, but no cards could be found on him all the same. It later transpired that during the entire search Iashka was holding the pack of cards in the palm of his left hand, having skillfully grabbed it with his pinky and huge fingers… However, regardless of similar instances, I can't say that prisoners were in general exceptionally skillful at conspiring to hide contraband. All that their illustrious ingenuity and cunning consisted of was audacity and brazenness. The Russian nature's usual qualities of light-mindedness and carelessness they possessed in high degree.

However, the very fact of cards' and money's appearance in prison showed that Six-Eyes's will and terrorizing rants alone were insufficient to make the model Shelai Prison always stand on one and the same level of strictness and formality. Many instances convinced me the prisoners had constant interactions with the outside, with those few free-commandees who even before our arrival served the commandant and guards. From time to time appeared extra mittens and shirts that had been brought to the mountain and given to the old watchman or left beforehand in agreed upon places. The gaps were widening a bit. Step by step, victories were being won on the most essential points. Hence the guards themselves didn't want to conduct morning roll call in the yard, to freeze in the forty-below-zero frost standing with head bared during prayers, and thus soon began conducting it in the corridor. Luchezarov would wake up later and there was no danger he'd appear any moment. The prisoners went further and, after long arguments with the guards, introduced the custom of not singing but instead just reciting morning prayers. Prayer in the morning was a generally more blasphemous than blessed affair. Hungry, cold, sleepy, even witless prisoners spread out in the corridor and stood in the draft for a certain ten to fifteen minutes until guards managed to enumerate them. Shelai's guards generally knew arithmetic very poorly, and at the time, instead of counting everyone in succession, they for some reason counted each of the nine wards separately, adding one to the other.

"Sixteen 'n' eighteen is thirty-three."

"Thirty-four, Prokopii Filippych," one of the prisoners, running out of patience, corrected him.

"Oh, leave me alone, chap! Now I gotta recount again."

And everyone had to be counted all over for a third time. Finally, the order was given:

"To prayer! Caps o-off!"

Everyone was silent.

"Why're you bein' quiet? Start."

"No one sings, Prokopii Filippych."

"Whaddya mean, 'no one'? Don't you sing in the evenin'?"

"Evenin's another matter… But now, just woken up, each of our throats is hoarse 'n' dry."

"Well, you can recite, anyhow."

Everyone was silent.

"Well, you, Penkin, recite the words!"

"I dunno words, Prokopii Filippych."

"Why don't you know? You're a chorister. You want the isolator? This is jus' scandalous! I'll inform the com'dant."

"Swear to God, I dunno words, Prokopii Filippych. I can sing by ear, but can't read."

"Bulanov, you read the words."

"No voice, Prokopii Filippych."

"What nonsense! Says he gots no voice. Read."

"I'm a Mordvin,[39] Prokopii Filippych," squeaked Bulanov, "what kinda reader can a Mordvin be? But I'll read if you want:

"Our Father, who art in Heaven. Hallowed be thy name, thy kingdom come, thy will be done, on earth as it is in Heaven. Give us this day our daily bread. Forgive us our trespasses, as we forgive them who trespass against us. Lead us not into temptation, but deliver us from evil. Amen."

"March into the ward!…"

With noise and laughter the mare dispersed throughout the ward.

"Aye, a Mordvin indeed! Says he dunno how, but he performs like he was a priest—jus' exactly!"

After that we heard every morning "Our Father, who art in heaven…"

The indulgences went still further. At first, guards were strictly given only an hour a day to completely turn out the wards for fresh air and for those "weaklings" permitted by the medic not to work to take a stroll. Headmen were let into the kitchen for the lunch, and the wards immediately locked and closed behind them; they'd return with lunch and in turn the guard would let them back in. But there were nine wards. As such, during the space of the day, from morning to evening roll call, he opened wards fifty times and locked them as many times. It absolutely goes without saying that even the most diligent guards felt themselves the most wretched in the human world on the day of this duty; and since just one internal orderly was assigned for all prisoners (another was at the gates), it was natural that he had almost no time to watch the kitchen, the infirmary, the isolators, and the workshops where linen and footwear were mended. In light of this, Luchezarov soon decided to keep wards unlocked all day on holidays, and on working days from the morning work-bell until the miners' return. After this toleration on the part of the supreme commander the guards became bolder. For their part, prisoners didn't stop egging things on.

"Ech, Prokopii Filippych, you're scared of ever'thin', 'fraid of ever'thin'."

"I, brother, follow orders… Do as I'm told."

"An order's an order, I won't disagree. Only, a man's also gifted with unnerstandin'. How come neither Ivan Pavlovich nor Vasilii Andreevich ever bolts the wards? Though, o' course, if they suspected the com'dant was to suddenly appear, they'd lock 'em. That's what the alarm's really for: senior orderly's s'posed to give a warnin'."

"That's impossible. I don't believe that Ivan Pavlovich or Vasilii Andreevich don't lock the wards. What crap are you bubblin' up, you sonofabitch?"

"God's word, I'm tellin' the truth, they don't lock up. O' course, they jus' forbid speakin' 'bout it. 'Cause they're people o' refined unnerstandin'."

"Doubt that," said Prokofii Filippovich, walking past and shaking his head, though lapsing into a certain pensiveness all the same.

Prisoners tried at the same time to influence Vasilii Andreevich and Ivan Pavlovich with Prokofii Filippovich's purported disdain for them. Exaggerated praise of rivals often reveals one's self-interest, and any of the guards could quickly become the audience's true darling.

"It ain't Ivan Pavlovich, but simply a feast!" they said among themselves, not knowing how to compliment him.

Yet, despite all the unimportant and insignificant indulgences and concessions prisoners won over time, *for me* life in Shelai mine remained as inexpressibly difficult as before. The nauseating and poorly nourishing food; the laboring in damp and cold shafts; the degrading structure of barracks life, trampling to filth all my most cherished feelings and aspirations; the deprivation of liberty and intercourse with the wider world; the crowded cohabitation with a people with whom I had so little in common and familiarity; the bitter days and black nights of gloomy sleeplessness or nightmares—akh! even now, after many years' passage, I shudder every time I remember all this… My heart is thumping once more, filled with wounds and sorrow once more… Peace, peace, unruly heart! Leave off this fit! We will turn again into impartial chroniclers despite our own horrible past. We will accordingly discuss what was most significant and interesting in it: perhaps this will do someone good!

VIII.   MY SCHOOL BEGINS

As winter set in and nights grew longer we got locked in earlier and earlier. I confess that even I was gladdened by this. Only then, when evening roll call had at last concluded with all its fears, shouts, thundering, and splendor, when the lock had clicked to make way for the blessed Luchezarov, only then did I breathe freely and feel that no one would impinge upon my freedom until morning, that no one would burst in on my soul, that I was insured against any new injury or insult for a whole twelve hours. There were many disgusting features of this long time under lock and key, but, for me, there were far worse things than the stuffy, asphyxiating air and proximate interaction with the offal of humanity. However, I'll try to give the reader a clear idea of the atmosphere I happened to breathe. The ward, at first reckoning, had been built for sixteen men (this number appeared on a plaque nailed to the door); but, as I've already said, the group became large, and in each ward there were twenty or even twenty-two men. Five of our number didn't have places on the sleeping platform and had to sleep on the floor (the Tatars and Sarts[40] were usually bunched together on the floor). The ward contained a double-paned window, but since a Russian fellow is knowledgeable in the science of opening, that pair of bones wasn't cracked and it got opened only rarely and reluctantly. It would probably have never been opened but for my insistence; however, I was too shy to abuse my influence, meeting at times the sidelong and frankly hostile gazes of old men like Gandorin. This venerable and honorable elder was, for his part, a bit severe; after exactly two minutes he resolutely crept like a cat toward my opened vent and, with a pious, wizened expression on his face as to a headman's rights, slowly closed it; but at the same time, so as not to offend, he gave me a kind of satisfaction and, on the sly, opened it part-way for a little while and, holding his pipe in his teeth, whispered to me:

"This works, too… Jus' better."

This Gandorin was my veritable tormentor. With a haggard, saint-like face and gray-tufted goatee, he was a glutton the whole prison marveled at. Scrupulously devouring until the last drop his portion of skilly, however vile it was, he even scooped up, without fail and in his capacity as headman, what was left of all the other portions and ate them, too. He ate all the bread—his and others' leftovers. He drank all the leftover tea… The mind boggled at where all this went in this frail old man! But, at the same time, he gave back a hundredfold what he took in: forever suffering from an upset stomach, he had to run off somewhere every minute, and when he returned, his neighbors were not grateful for his misfortune… Unfortunately, he slept all of two persons away from me: Chirok, Marmot, then him… My spot was right next to the wall. However, not just Gandorin suffered from catarrh of the stomach, made unhappy by the terrible menu the gallant staff captain introduced to Shelai Prison; hence the atmosphere of the small ward where twenty-odd grown men were crowded together almost touching each other was, in the evening, utterly asphyxiating and repulsive. The puttees prisoners unwrapped and laid on the stove to dry emitted a particular stench as well. Certain prisoners wouldn't wash these puttees for a whole year, and so loathsome was their rotten smell that they might have caused the unaccustomed man to vomit… Many prisoners' feet themselves reeked horribly from constantly sweating (the illness is very widespread among working people).

Nonetheless, I repeat again, I always felt glad when roll call ended and we were locked in.

As for the selection of my cohabitants, I was with few exceptions completely satisfied. These people weren't able to give me much, but it would've been ridiculous to complain to them about this. From the very beginning, the relations established between us were amicable. In the early days, an acquaintance of mine expressed a desire to be taught to read and write. I'd mentioned the idea just once, half-jokingly, half-seriously, when the expansive Nikifor Burenkov bounded off the sleeping platform and, running over to me, shouted:

"That'd be great! Y'know, Mikolaich, I wanted to ask you for a long time, but didn't dare… But you yourself thought of it… Oh-ho! I'm gonna learn to read 'n' write soon, the Devil take it! I'll go home 'n' everyone'll marvel: 'Is it really Mikishka?' You can teach me *rikmatik*, too… I wanna know how to count… I'll be one o' the clerks here—I'll wrap ever'one here round my finger!"

I answered Burenkov that one studies not for wrapping people round one's finger, but, on the contrary, for unwrapping them from the web of darkness and various untruths. Nikifor got embarrassed and hastened to assure me he was "only jokin'."

This man was a real "child of nature"; I'd never encountered in another man such an inability to conceal feelings or thoughts that changed by the minute. His face was the truest mirror of his soul. Tall, bony, he was all ardor and fire; jerky movements, an always cheerful demeanor, wittiness, a forgiving nature, and flippancy rendered him a universal favorite. True, a certain craftiness glowed in his large gray eyes and thin lips stretched by a long, soft mouth and yellow goatee. He did not refer to himself as other than "we rascals"… But one had only to observe Nikifor a little while to be certain that he was not only a good comrade in any kind of "lucky" undertaking, but also a straight-shooter. He came from the priest-less Old Believer Seedlings of Verkhneudinsk District;[41] but an early familiarity with mining, a natural penchant for trading, and dash transformed him into one of those heroes of the main roads whose specialty is stealing tea from the caravans.[42] For this, he and his cousin Mikhailo were sent to *katorga* for four years.

The notion of establishing a school keenly interested the entire ward. Old men were urging on the younger, prompting them to study. The literate are an insignificant percentage in prison. There were all of three literates in our ward: Semënov, Paramon Malakhov, and a certain Vladimirov. But there were wards where universal illiteracy reigned. I asked who was ready to learn. A terrible desire could be read on several faces, but everyone was quiet.

"What about you, Pestrov?" they shouted at a certain very young chap—flaccid, silent, and shy.

"Got a bad mem'ry, boys."

"How he talks! Does us ol' men got better? Who's gonna learn if not you? Chap's nineteen years old, very prime o' life."

"So, you'll study, Pestrov?"

"I'd like to… But, for God's sake, ain't nuthin' worth 'memb'rin'."

"We'll see about that."

"But how we gonna study?" Nikifor suddenly shouted. "We got no pencils, no ink, no *paker*! Akh, you hateful prison! Ever'thin's forbidden, 'n' there's nuthin'!…"

And from raucous joy he suddenly passed into gloomy despair. I myself grew thoughtful. A little book, let's say, would be the Gospels; there was also paper: the steward gave prisoners gray writing paper for rolling cheap tobacco, though, following the restrictions against writing implements in prison, he cut it into irregularly shaped pieces. It was more difficult to think where to get pencils. Paramon Malakhov, who with his pipe normally sat importantly on the sleeping platform ruminating at length over something, suddenly hit his forehead and shouted:

"I ain't Paramon Malakhov if'n I can't git 'em!…"

"What?"

"A pencil 'n'… an alphabet. Let Six-Eyes have his way, let 'im have his way e'en more, I'll git 'em. Nikishka, have faith in Paramon!"

However, for a long time he didn't try to live up to his boast. He'd go to work in the joiner's shop located outside the prison wall, and every time, as he was returning from work, Burenkov and Pestrov would pepper him with questions. The handsome cooper would just wave his arms and shrug his shoulders:

"Well, I'll git 'em jus' the same. Come the right moment. If I don't, they can call Paramon a bottle-fly!"

In the meantime, I'd gotten the idea of using a piece of coal. Nikifor found a long, beautiful piece of coal; I sharpened it and drew several letters on the tobacco-paper. As it turned out, my students were not a delight. In the evening, just after roll call and the locking of the ward, everyone crowded up to the table… and Nikifor and Pestrov hunched over me. The former's face beamed at me like a well-buffed copper basin; sweat instantly began pouring down his and Pestrov's face, even though the lesson had not even begun: both were terribly nervous…

"Well, Mikishka, help us out 'n' don't throw dirt in our faces!" Chirok and Goncharov admonished Burenkov.

To my great surprise and chagrin all my students in the ward proved to be terribly slow-witted and manifestly untalented. For a long time, I consoled myself with the idea that they were simply timid and confused, but after a week I was able to discern that Pestrov was an absolutely blunt chap who could not memorize. Seeing he'd reached a similar conclusion, I didn't let on, of course, and didn't tire of drumming the same thing into his head every evening; but the ward soon reached the same conclusion on its own, and got terribly angry at Pestrov: it seemed to everyone that he aimed to offend…

"Well, you really been cramming, Romashka!" Chirok said. "Are you really this way? Ever'one calls me a Permian, a chop off the block… I grew up in the woods 'n' I'll grow old in prison… But, considerin' you, sev'ral goats coulda mem'rized the lesson by now. 'N' you're a youngster, *and* a *Raseyan*!"[43]

"Jus' stop it!" Romashka would flare up like gunpowder, and every time I'd have a hard job convincing him to continue the educational experiment.

On the other hand, the ward praised and reassured Nikifor:

"You'll be a priest for the Seedlings!"

These praises were, of course, highly exaggerated. Nikifor was not, it's true, a hopeless blockhead, but his natural impetuosity harmed him in his studies as much as in life. Without having looked carefully at a letter he'd instantly shout its name, inopportunely, for the most part. Moreover, he didn't like to confess right away to the most obvious errors and, possessed of a rich fantasy, would try to vindicate its resemblance among letters with which it obviously had nothing in common: thus, according to his words, *м*, since it was like two drops of water, resembled *ф*, and *a* resembled *з*... It goes without saying that he constantly confused assonant letters: *ж–ш*, *с–з*, *д–m* (I taught using the phonetic method).

"Well, Ivan Nikolaevich's patience is a virtue," they'd say about me in the ward.

Apropos all this only Malakhov held a high opinion of himself.

"This ain't teachin', it's jus' pamp'rin'," he groused. "Why ain't you teachin' us like in the ol' days? First: there's the ABCs, letters, 'n' you go on to words, very well... Each letter had its name, like it was alive... But nowadays? They peck 'n' peep... Unnerstand nuthin'! Zh-zh-zh-zh! S-s-s! Makes you jus' plug your ears."

I tried explaining to Malakhov the beneficial sides of the phonetic method, but for naught: he was a blind worshiper of tradition, and therefore resisted like a bull anything more persuasive.[44]

"Secondly," he said in a guard-like tone, "a teacher can't manage without givin' a slap."

"That's true, Mikolaich," shouted Nikifor, "punch me, for God's sake! 'N' pull my hair as you like... Won't say a word if you do."

"No, brother, that won't stir things up," Paramon corrected him, "that's jus' for science, for causin' a fright. Know how we was beaten? Our village sexton taught me. As it was, us kids ne'er visited him 'cause he was always soused. First thing after prayers he grabbed all us by the hair without interrogation... Pulled 'n' pulled it till he got tired... 'Well, kids, now you're ready to learn!' he'd say. But when he beat us we hadda fight back or he'd 'ave beat us to death! Once, when he was pullin' my hair 'n' thrashin' me with branches, I bit his arm."

"You had some spine then, Paramon," prisoners laughed.

"Well, but what was good about that kind of teaching?" I asked Paramon.

"Whaddya mean? There was less spoilin' 'n' we began learnin' grammar."

"I don't know about spoiling, but wouldn't you have learned grammar just as well if the sexton hadn't beaten you? As it is now, you can barely read a syllable."

"I've forgotten now," the proud cooper answered, evidently getting annoyed, and passionately knocking his pipe on the sleeping platform. "But I can still read alright for my own use. Why do us fools need to be well-learned?"

Nonetheless, except for the students themselves, the propaganda for beating failed to rouse anyone in the ward and Malakhov remained alone in this regard.

"'N' if I should beat my own child?" he said with genuine indignation, walking up and down the ward. "That's nuthin'! Once, I'm ridin' home like so on a gelding.

Hear a scared cry 'n' see beside a fence a teacher pullin' the tanner's boy by the ears. Child's seven years old, but he's gettin' his ears turned inside-out. I ride o'er, tie the gelding to the fence, 'n' go straight up the teacher. 'What're ya doin' this for?' I ask. 'What's it to you? I'm a teacher.' 'Ah! You're a teacher? So you can learn from me first!' Then I knocked him down 'n' laid into him such that his flanks prob'ly ache to this day…"

I gazed at Goncharov's huge, ursine physiognomy with its broad, pock-marked face, thick nose, reddish-gray sideburns, and large blue eyes, over which sullenly glowered red eyebrows, and thought it a real shame that he had to encounter that teacher…

"'N', later, it'd so 'appen," Goncharov continued, "you'd catch his eye from afar 'n' call out: 'Hey, Trofim Evstigneich, come on o'er, let's talk hand-in-hand…' 'N' he'd jus' take to his heels! I'm laughin', threat'nin' to come after 'im with a knout!"

IX. MALAKHOV AND GONCHAROV

Goncharov and Malakhov were certainly not overly fond of each other, though they didn't show this openly, one sensing in the other a practically similar physicality and moral fortitude. Theirs were natures contrary to all ideas, and Siberia and its metropoli seemed to heighten this very contrariness: Malakhov was from Pskov,[45] and had lived in Peter itself as a coachman and obtained while there a certain superficial gloss. People for whom he felt respect or sympathy he could treat with refined courtesy, without giving off, however, that loathsome refinement so distinctive of lackeys copying lordly mannerisms and phrases. Goncharov was in this regard more vulgar and uncouth. On the other hand, the traces of civilization that had been left on Paramon were limited to a superficial gloss. In spirit, he remained a real Vendée provincial[46] wedded to traditional views and prejudices. To his expense, he was distinguished by enormous egoism, regarded himself a very intelligent man, and believed he had firm, fixed views on things, though in fact he was always off the mark and perhaps even slow-witted. This was why, when talk moved to something burning hot and he was caught out by persuasive questions, he became bilious and forgot every delicacy and refinement. He responded to every "smart thing" with scorn and therefore, against my will and desire, we rarely entered into stormy altercations. He nevertheless had nothing against the experimental sciences and any discovery or invention that caught the eye; yet, from the starting gates the issue turned into general conclusions and positions encroaching upon—it seemed to him— humanity's eternal blessings, and he would be up against a wall, beside himself and eyes defensive. We grappled especially often over questions of astronomy, such as, Because it is true the Earth moves in a spherical pattern, why does the Sun comparatively stay in the same place?, and so on. Paramon usually listened long and silently to my stories to a prisoner about the miracle of nature as revealed by modern science. Finally unable to contain himself, he'd say:

"But which gentleman scientist has climbed to Heaven so's he can know all this so well?"

I'd begin my explanation anew, trying as possible to express it more intelligibly and still more simply than before. He would listen patiently once more and then decide in a powerful and imposing tone:

"All this is nonsense, rubbish! I can see, see with my own eyes, how the Sun moves. Well, but how the Earth moves—this no one has e'er seen 'n' ne'er will! I'll stand the whole day in one spot 'n' look over at that hill there, 'n' it won't move a step to the side."

I'd vainly try to show that the entire Earth moves simultaneously, with all its mass evenly on any point; I'd vainly produce the typical example, that when you're moving in a machine it appears you're staying in one place but the Earth is moving away from you. The more clearly (it seemed to me) I explained my view, the more agitated and angry Paramon would become… One time, thinking I'd win him over by using his own views, I showed him the place in the Book of Job where it says that God, having suspended the Earth in the air, did *nothing more* to fix it; in response to this, he tracked down other places in the Bible talking about the Earth's immobility and the Sun and stars' subordination to it. He didn't want to undertake any kind of allegorical exegesis whatsoever, and in the end pronounced a harsh philippic against science.

"All this high falutin' learnin' ain't worth a copper penny! Today's science has gone so far as to say God don't exist!"

"You're talking nonsense, Paramon," I answered, "there's no such science can show God doesn't exist; science doesn't concern itself with such questions."

"Ha! I myself 'ave met scientists who said this!"

"But aren't there completely unscientific people, among prisoners, for example, who don't believe in God?"

"Well, I depend more on my own ears. Believe me, boys," my opponent suddenly appealed to the entire ward for sympathy, "one scientist in Peter showed me that man comes from the ape… A fool indeed! He should at least known you hafta shave an ape once a month for it to be a man!"

Everyone joined in a burst of laughter, and Malakhov appeared the winner. True, two or three of the young men were on my side, but they were too afraid to fully announce their support for science; and to a man the old-timers shared Paramon's view and indignation at my free-thinking. Only Goncharov was chuckling, and evasively said:

"Well, but I'll believe anythin'… I'm ready to believe *any*thin'… 'cause I well know what we are. Blocks o' wood, tree-stumps—nuthin' more! 'N' all we got in our heads is trash!"

Goncharov's mind was quite practical and little interested in abstract speculation, though by the same token he'd grant others freedom in this regard. Paramon, by contrast, was an idealist. Regardless of the solidity of his mannerisms and entire physique (he was less than forty), he was to a large extent a passionate and enthusiastic man, and rather immoderate. He typically spoke with pathos, accenting several syllables, and was inspired and openly excited and sometimes capable of electrifying not just listeners but especially himself with his ardent talk. Then again, he happened to talk about completely absurd things. Hence, he once told us the following story.

He was returning home from Peter with a comrade. He entered some village and saw in one hut a sick woman who had been bedridden for several years. The patient's relatives asked the travellers if they knew the cure for her illness. Paramon and his comrade were young lads, light-minded and always ready to make a joke.

"This was my answer: 'Sure, I know! Jus' do ever'thin' I tell ya. Bake me a doll made out o' dough.' Course, that very day they made me a huge statue with great pleasure. Then I sent ever'one out o' the bedroom, laid this doll on the sick woman, 'n' prayed 'fore the icons… Had to been seen to be doin' *some*thin'! Then I called back all her kin 'n' told 'em I'd take this doll with me, but that the patient would be healthy right soon. Then they sent me on my way with all kinds o' supplies, 'n' even gave me some money, 'n' my comrade 'n' me went on our way. We're laughin' to ourselves. We stop on the way to have a bite. We decided to taste the doll. So, I break off an arm… 'n' whaddya know, boys? I see—blood!… Break off the other arm—it's livin' human-bein' blood!… I swear to God this is true!… Then we got scared, threw away the doll 'n' all the supplies, 'n' ran. But what'd happened in the meantime? At the very same moment we was breakin' the doll that woman, the sick one, got up from bed completely healthy—Swear to God I ain't lyin'!… How can scientists explain that, huh? Let 'em try!"

This story made a strong impression on those listening; but I was personally interested by it in a different way. I sensed that not all in it was right, that being concealed was one of those secrets by which tales and popular superstitions usually arise. Later I often pestered Paramon concerning this, asking him to tell me the story about the doll yet again; and each time he'd tell it he'd conspiratorially laugh at my curiosity. But once, after a space of six months, in a moment of good will and expansiveness towards me, he straightforwardly confessed he'd exaggerated about the blood.

"Ever'thin' was correct as I described it. Only, I was jokin' when I added the bit about the blood," he explained, a bit ashamed, although I recalled in particular that *at that time* he'd not been joking.

A particular circumstance caused Malakhov to ask me all this stuff and nonsense: it was his unselfconscious innocence compared to the rest of the prison masses. I knew he'd come to *katorga* for murder; but it was a singular fact that the Siberian court had sentenced him (he had formerly been an exile-settler) to all of six years' *katorga* and mentioned several words in his favor. General opinion among prisoners was that Malakhov was an honest and self-sufficient man. Paramon himself loved to boast that he had never engaged in usury and that in future he would earn his own way. In general, his disposition was far from gloomy; much humor and occasionally purely childlike carelessness hid beneath his exterior seriousness. To get a rise, "to stroke the bagpipes," as prisoners say, to play with Chirok, to pick on him, to provoke an argument and even push it to a fight, was Paramon's favorite occupation.

"Why don't you put your puttees in your spot?" he asked, as if threatening Chirok.

"'N' you're such a lord you can't move?" came the answer.

"Take 'em, I'm tellin' you, take 'em now, if you don't want 'em rubbed on your snotty mug. D'you know who I am?"

"Who?"

"I'm Paramon Malakhov! I'm pedigreed! But what're you? A vag-a-bond?"

"How'm I a vagabond? Come 'ere 'n' you'll get knocked out."

"You was exiled to live in Ishim, 'n' from there you 'scaped underground into Ialutorovsk Prison[47] so's you could run the *maidan!*"

Laughter filled the ward.

"D'you know he ate a dog, Paramon?" Iashka-the-Marmot interjected.

"Shut up, vermin!" Chirok shouted at him. "A creature's mangy mouth is gapin' o'er there."

It must be said that among his comrades, Chirok was a constant object of ridicule because of his escape from Algacha's free command. Prisoners told with humor the story of this notable escape. Just out of prison, tight for money, and in league with his comrade the Tatar Malaika, he had set off down the road. The fugitives lay in the bushes by day and travelled along the telegraph line by night.

"We're goin' by *egraph*, by *egraph*, Malaisha!"

By the second night both were very hungry, and they approached a certain village and saw before them something white.

"Malaisha, Malaisha," whispered Chriok, "it's a little sheep… This is what God's sent us!"

They snuck up, intending to seize the proffered sheep—and suddenly found themselves being attacked by a huge white dog… Chirok and Malaika took to their heels as fast as they could. On the third day they were arrested, returned to Algacha, "given a fifty,"[48] and put in prison until the end of their terms. Since then, prisoners had given Chirok no peace: they barked at him like a dog, bleated like a sheep, cuckooed like a cuckoo, and jokingly called him a vagabond (for a long time among penal laborers there had been hostility toward the vocation of vagabond). Jokers even said he'd eaten the dog but that his guilt had been established by the tail-feathers he'd left at the crime scene; that a priest excommunicated him from confession for his meal of a dog and that his prison records were imprinted with a dog's tail… With sufficient composure Chirok endured all such stories and laughter and only sometimes met a joke with a cross face; Malakhov alone could get a rise out of him and push him to a so-called white heat.

"Hm!" He wasn't letting up. "Others are at worst tempted to become husks or run the *maidan* or become vagabonds, but he wanted a taste o' dog. He was goin' hungry on Algacha's skilly!"

Chirok was silent.

"Here this devil's caught 'n' brought to prison. 'Where're you from?' 'Boys,' he says, 'I seen many mountains…' He says, 'I 'scaped Sokolin Island,[49] swam in prisoner's irons through the sea, 'n' traveled forty versts underground… Boys,' he says, 'gimme the *maidan* to run… For I am—General Cuckoo!…'[50] Ooh, he's a damned vagabond!"

Lying in his spot, Chirok once more remained stubbornly silent, sucking on his cigar and spitting on the floor by the minute. Paramon was sitting in a row of us and continued recounting vagabonds' tricks, turning to everyone in the ward and only now and then to Chirok himself.

"So, he's livin' in prison: like them devils he dons a red shirt 'n' walks around with his arms crossed… 'Your spot—*not* your spot!…' Ooh, those damned devils! Them salt-ears from Perm!"[51]

Again, the response was silence; only those listening broke out laughing.

"On the road it's e'en worse: he grabs three feet o' the sleepin' platform jus' for hisself. 'Brother,' they tell him, 'push over.' He answers, 'Don't y'know who you're talkin' to? Who're you? Are you pedigreed? As for me, I'm an Ivan, o' the *Nepomniashchii* pedigree![52] Reckon that! There's my leg, 'n' there it's gonna lie. Git down under the sleepin' platform!' 'Cause o' them, 'cause o' such devils, our brother, *our* pedigree, ends up suf'rin'… All 'cause o' those… like that there… right there, what's lyin' there!"

Paramon pointed his finger at Chirok and, maintaining for a long time a comically gloomy and serious face, repeated:

"All 'cause o' those very… such as that… 'cause o' them Tobolsk leaves, cow-tails, unconscionable dirty-bones, creatures!…"

"You're the creature!" Chirok suddenly screamed, defending himself against neither Paramon's denunciations nor even his insults but, as such, his finger, which for so long had been in the air pointing everything out to him. For some reason, Chirok could never accept this pointing finger, and in those rare instances when nothing was happening Paramon always resorted to it.

"Mangy louse! Black-striped demon!" the completely aggravated Chirok would shout in his sing-song Perm dialect, and sometimes, having jumped up, he even took to pounding his tormentor. But, for the black-striped demon, this was merely what had to happen: smug in his own success, he peacefully endured the strongest blows by lying on his back and breaking into cheerful laughter.

Offering an utterly different type was the native of Eniseisk Province—old man Goncharov!

Prisoners often loved to crack jokes and laugh about the "*cheldony*," the "yellow-beaked *cheldony*," that is, the Siberians.[53] There is something callous, coldly calculating, and egotistical emanating from this Siberian type figuring in prisoners' stories (moreover, when imitating Siberian speech, they always talk through the nose for some reason). I can't forget a particularly characteristic story by the vagabond Dorozhkin,[54] about how *cheldony* once arrested him in some Western Siberia village. They brought him to a bathhouse and, having firmly tied his hands together, left him there to go off and drink vodka in the changing room.

"Ol' chaps, my hands was swellin' up 'n' gittin' bigger... I e'en overheard they was gonna hang me. I hoped to be able to loosen 'em a little. I look round, 'n' there's a window. So I run me head into the frame! The *cheldony* run into the bathhouse... So's they start pourin' water on me!... They toss me outside: I'm sittin' there neither live nor dead, head hangin' down. Unnerstand, they're layin' into my back. Thrashed me a good half hour, 'n' the twilight was up to me eyes. Two stayed there, the other two left. 'Ol' men, have pity not for me, but for me hands,' I says. 'Wouldn't you rather they plow the soil?' 'But that's it indeed, chap... Our hands is worth more'n... his head.' They beat me again 'n' left once more to drink vodka in the changin' room. I'm sittin' on the floor. Up comes an ol' man, white-haired, all hunched over. Looks at me. 'Grandfather,' I says to him (so pitifully), 'grandfather!' 'What, dearie?' he asks. 'Gimme some water to drink... Me throat's all parched... Y'see how they've beaten me?' 'Akh,' he says, 'they're barbarians! Why'd they do this to you, child? Even if you'd killed your own birth-mother, what's it to them? You'll answer 'fore the Lord in heaven. Everyone'll answer.' Ol' man gave me some water with the bath ladle. This water was like pure honey to me, 'n' I drank it to the bottom. 'Drink,' the ol' man's sayin', 'drink up, dearie!' Then, just as I was finishin' the water, he hits me on the head with the ladle as hard as he can—so's the ladle flew into pieces!... Later, the whole gang of *cheldony*, 'long with the canton headman, came again for me. I pleaded with him: 'Your highness,' I says, 'order 'em to grease me hands with somethin'. Y'see, blood's flowin' from 'neath the rope.' He looks: 'Oh!' he says, 'chap, they've really gone too far. Loosen his hands a little 'n' lubricate with some clean tar.' A *cheldon* grabs a dauber of tar (there was a box of tar sittin' there) 'n' shoves it in me mug... Smear, smear! Smeared it all over, in a stripe. Then they tied me to a telega 'n' dragged me to Achinsk. Gnats swarmin' round me the whole way. I ran behind the telega like a demon, hot as can be… Kids in the villages saw I was hurryin' to me maternal home…"

Such were the stories about Siberians' callous, nearly voluptuous, cruelty. A smidgen of truth can be acknowledged. The Siberian's practicality and sobriety, the complete absence of poetry in his soul, his cunning and capability for self-restraint, immediately strike a Russian person's eye.

Yet, at the same time, he possesses traits and qualities infinitely superior to those of the latter and that position him nearer to the Western European type. His mind is less obstructed by obsolete traditions and prejudices, more capable of being open to and absorbing new ideas and concepts, and he's distinguished by great independence and a love of freedom. This must be understood: the Siberian has not known serfdom,[55] and does not recognize a connection between himself and landless, impoverished, disfranchised peasants;[56] servility before authority has clearly not been beaten into him, and so native Rus[57] does not strike him so unpleasantly.

I changed my opinion many times about this or that prisoner, including old man Goncharov, but it never entered my head to deny in him a clear—purely Siberian's—mind, always able to quickly orient itself toward each of life's problems and situations and to grasp, so to speak, the bull by the horns. Owing to this quality and a sharp, razor-like tongue that never pocketed a word, he played the role of father-commander in the ward: he taught the young men to use their heads and happily intimated his former journeys and adventures to them, and listened with the indulgence of an older brother to the more mature or similarly knowledgeable, without, however, ever allowing anything to be interpolated into his didactic observations. For this conceit, prisoners did not love him. Goncharov was a very tactful man and permitted himself bluntness towards only utterly unthreatening people, and therefore rarely got into face-offs and only abused everyone with something hot from his eyes. He was friends with Semënov only, his countryman: everything they had they split in half, and they ate and drank together. Having obviously been exhausted by the garrulous old man, the sullen and silent Semënov for some reason found it necessary to spare him and to patiently suffer his indefatigable loquaciousness and ratiocinating.

"A most highly advanced hypocrite!" Malakhov, so praising his best friend that he was cutting him down with a mother-oath before his eyes said of him. "A Siberian fox! He's so thrifty you'd think he's a real monk, livin' by his own hands; but—shameful to say!—many here knew him on the outside: to a man ever'one says our brother didn't go hungry as an exile-settler… God grant me as many years to live in this world as all those he killed! He was a first-rate evil-doer… But now he's pretendin' to be such a chemist!"[58]

"Not in those days. In another prison he woulda been shown how prisoners treat their brother for this," Iashka-the-Marmot declared.

"No, fella," said Chirok, "what don't I like Goncharov for? 'Cause he censures ever'one 'n' ever'thin', 'n' he knows ever'thin'… 'I, yes, I!' is all you hear. But no one else dares open his trap to him."

During one of these quarrels, Chirok got up in Goncharov's face to reproach him over the exile-settlers; he got up in his face, and bit his tongue. Goncharov had knocked him off his feet.

"What're you stirrin' up?" he shouted in irritation. "Stirrin' up trouble. Y'know, there's a lot who know me here in prison. Petka o'er there knows me well, Rakitin in the sixth ward knows me, so does Vasilev, Grigorev… Ask them who don't got their mouths painted on. Ech, you fool, you fool! Kill exile-settlers… 'N' what does one such as you take from him? I'm ready to get my hands dirty. Better to wait till you're gray 'fore figurin' out how to get a kopek? Petka o'er there knows how I lived. A lord don't live like that! When I was runnin' a tavern ever'one around knew 'n' respected ever'thin' 'bout me. 'N' they always came to me 'cause I knew who to take in 'n' how to treat 'em. The lucky folks always stuck by me. If someone needed hidin', again, they came to me. Ask Petka there, he won't lie: he escaped from Kansk Prison three times, 'n' I hid him ev'ry time!"

"Yes, I'm sure!" Chirok vindicated himself. "I'm sure that people… It's said you killed a lotta folks…"

"A lotta folks? What is this? Is it bein' added up who's killed more? 'N' who's gonna trade the medal they give for bravery for a quick trip to Paradise? Well then—an education in Shelai Prison. Bravery's gotta be earned… No, you already got this bravery, 'n' as 'tis, it's needed, though us without bravery is gonna live to be a hunnerd. We came to *katorga* as scoundrels 'n' bastards; this means we ain't gonna eat our only cabbage soup with you! Y'see many folks I killed? They envy me. Am I really wastin' away here? I killed a certain Pole 'n' buried him under a tussock in a swamp. Twenty years went by—'n' no one knew a thing. God alone saw it. That's why I don't suffer insults 'n' always avenge an offense, whether or not I'll survive. But I'll 'member my days happily!"

And, continuing to argue for a long time, Goncharov strode through the ward, heavily turning his vast bulk that weighed close to seven poods and reminded one of an angry bear standing on its hind paws… He had in a moment become terribly angry. He was talking about how, ten years ago during a comedic struggle with one such as himself, with a bear from Eniseisk—his own brother-in-law—he knocked him so hard to the ground that the unfortunate man's skull split in two, for which Goncharov was sentenced to all of seven months' internment and to religious confession… If in a sober context such things were a joke, then what might a spark of fury or drunken oblivion produce?

Malakhov didn't utter a word during the clash with Chirok, though his opinion of Goncharov hadn't changed. I later heard more than once from many others ill-disposed towards Goncharov that his infamy had resounded throughout Eniseisk Province, until the government was finally able to capture and convict the experienced taiga wolf. I asked Goncharov's countrymen about his past, but even the talkative and simple-minded Rakitin responded evasively:

"T'ain't much to say 'bout that, Ivan Nikolaich… 'N' it's hard to talk 'bout now."

Once, when we were talking, I asked Goncharov himself about what brought him to *katorga*, and he began swearing and cursing that this time he'd done nothing.

"Here's what I'll tell you, Ivan Mikolaich. I've swindled my whole life, it could be said, I've robbed 'n' e'en murdered—but I ain't languishin'. Well, but at that time I happened to suffer another's sin. I'm speakin' to you as honestly as to God! I was a tavern keeper. One evenin', no one's in the tavern 'n' in comes my comrade, Birukov. 'I'm goin' to the city with Pakhomov,' he says. 'He's drunk as a sock 'n' lyin' in my telega along with his money, but we'll be back.' We laughed. He drank a bit 'n' left the tavern 'n' kept goin'.

Go off to go sleep. But next day I hear they've found the telega 'n' horse without its master 'n' Pakhomov's lyin' murdered in the telega. Birukov 'ad disappeared like the vodka. They start investigatin'. One o' the neighbor women turned up… That she be five times cursed, the stinker! She tells 'em she saw how Pakhomov was lyin' in that telega at my tavern, that it was there a long time, 'n' that we both left together in the telega."

"Why did she testify to what didn't happen?"

"Go ask that slut. I think that when Birukov left again to get into the telega Pakhomov, even though he was very drunk, raised himself up a little: she took him for me. He's almost the same height, 'n' just as wide in the shoulders, 'n' his face was similar."

"So they never found Birukov?"

"Ne'er found him at all. I should think he escaped."

"If he got tossed in the Enisei, you'd-a found him there!"

"Who'd-a tossed 'im?"

"*You.*"

Goncharov said nothing, only puffed his pipe and spat scornfully onto the floor.

"Here's what spites me, Ivan Mikolaich," he continued after a brief silence, "what's annoyin'. Thirty years I swindled 'n' took ever'thin' 'n' ne'er got caught, but then, 'cause o' some wolf, some bitch—God forgive me—I got fifteen years!"

Another time, when we were alone in the ward, both of us having been released from work because of illness, the old man talked to me again about this affair; once more using almost the very same words as the other times he'd spoken of it and similarly passionately bemoaning his unfair lot. There was only one small feature that was new in this retelling—a feature that made me suspicious.

"My comrade Birukov drops in. 'I'm goin' to the city with Pakhomov,' he says. 'He's drunk as a sock 'n' lyin' in my telega along with his money. *There's prob'ly two thousand there. What,' he says, 'is to be done?'* I laughed. He drank a bit 'n' left the tavern 'n' kept goin'."

"But did you answer his question, 'What is to be done?'"

"Absolutely not… I jus' laughed, like so: 'Play a joke on 'im,' I says, ''n' drop him in a gully.' I said it as a joke, o' course. But what a joke it turned out to be."

But enough about Goncharov. He killed maybe many, maybe few, people in his day; in the case that sent him to *katorga* he was either guilty, or innocent as a dove—but, in any case, he had sufficient blood on his hands and he himself didn't try to hide it. He was a beast, of course; but now and then a beast remembers well about himself! Hence there remains in my heart a pleasant imprint of this beast-man. If we're fated to meet again in this life, I believe we'll encounter each other as friends… A trait purely humane and rare in prisoners particularly attracted me to Goncharov—the paternal tenderness with which he adored young children. This love came out in all his stories about them. Once, I was writing per his request a letter to his wife and a granddaughter he'd left in freedom as a three-year-old girl, and when he came to expressing a phrase typical of the common man—"My dearest granddaughter Dasha, I send you a grandfather's kind wishes, never to fade"—a hail of tears was falling from this fierce man's eyelashes… He also loved to feed pigeons and other small birds beneath the prison windows… Of Goncharov's subsequent fate I will speak in its place.[59]

X.   MY STUDENTS THE BURENKOVS

The students continued their studies. In the ward, Burenkov and Pestrov were called nothing other than "students"; at the same time, many confused the words "student" and "teacher" and often called me "student" as well.[60] Pestrov would freeze up over syllables and be unable to continue; but he devoted every spare minute to studying: he'd sit on his sleeping platform holding the alphabet I'd written and whisper to himself, exactly like a wizard doing the same with his incantations. He could make out individual syllables sufficiently well, but while connecting them to a word he changed them or they went the Devil knows where.

"H… a… ha! a… y… ay!"

Pestrov would turn thoughtful.

"What would that be together, Pestrov?"

"Pen!" he would answer after long rumination, pushing me to the limit.

One fine day Malakhov, beaming and triumphant, had concealed inside a mitten a pencil and some old worn-out alphabet. Nikifor could hardly have rejoiced more over these. Even the sluggish Romashka, discouraged by his own lack of success, roused himself considerably. But at that moment I detected a malevolent shadow falling between the students. Nikifor greedily snatched the pencil and alphabet, regarding them as inalienably his.

"Didn't you promise 'em to me, Paramon?… I'll pay you."

Pestrov fell silent and looked at Nikifor in obvious hatred. I then remarked that he should share the pencil with his comrade.

"What's it to you, Mikolaich? Don't he already know syllables? He… But I wanna learn by writin'."

"God knows you should both be writing."

"But didn't you yourself say that to learn, one can read 'n' write a *yetter* at the same time? Though it's a pity there's no *baper*."

"In the first place, there're no such things as *yetters* and *bapers*, as I've already told you. In the second place, it's not good to be greedy. You can certainly give the alphabet to Roman: you don't need it anymore."

"But how'll I repeat? Without the alphabet, I'll forget… How can I study without the alphabet? We'll look at it together."

However, after a several minutes fit of avarice he laughed in a burst of magnanimity, and I listened as Nikifor himself told Pestrov to share the pencil and alphabet with him. But the latter felt very offended and behaved capriciously for a long time:

"I don't need 'em… I quit studyin'… Can't mem'rize…"

As such, the entire ward finally started cursing him.

"Geez, you're really a vile fellow, Pestrov! So much bile in you. Mikishka's a simple chap, ever'thin's from his heart—but not you."

During all this everyone was surprised by the appearance of a third student, such that no one knew what to make of him. Nikifor's cousin Mikhaila, whose surname was also Burenkov, had been standing for a long time beside the table with arms folded during one of our evening lessons, and suddenly leaned forward:

"I see you're a birch-bucket, Mikishka! You can't get such little things into your head. Quit studying, and stop embarrassing yourself and torturing the teacher for nothing!"

Nikifor blew up.

"So you take yourself for a student? You'd get it into your head better?"

"I certainly would do it better. I know the syllable better than you."

This boast interested me, since I knew that Mikhaila was illiterate, and so I joked to him:

"Well then, read this word."

And, to my great astonishment, Mikhaila, having thought a bit, correctly read the denoted word, confusing only the ending (the word was long). Nikifor was similarly astonished. Having been up himself somewhat, he'd wanted to prove his cousin wrong but had enraged himself even more definitively. Amid this, I began testing Mikhaila and realized that he, having listened from his corner to our lessons and gazing askance at the letters, had managed to learn far more than the "students" themselves. After this, I began advising Mikhaila to enunciate the proper conjugations. The ward buried him with laughter. Everyone found it extremely surprising and hilarious that a forty year-old man wanted to study grammar! It need be said that Mikhaila had for a long time not needed the prisoners' sympathy, and I had long ago observed that he did not get along with his cousin. Mikhaila was fifteen years older than Nikifor and possessed a character opposite his in every way. As the latter was talkative and expansive, the former was quiet and always serious and closed. Nikifor loved to parade his camaraderie and beliefs about prisoners' ways and traditions; Mikhaila despised the popular opinions with which he did not agree, and was not afraid to openly express views on things directly countering the opinions of the ward or even the entire prison. There was in him an ocean of pride, of "spite," as prisoners put it... He remembered every little offense and never asked forgiveness. He was an individualist to the core. I've already spoken about how there is in contemporary prisons a quick and completely insupportable smugness among older prisoners regarding tradition and how things are, and of the difficulty of living under new regimes and the conditions of life in the Dead House; nonetheless, if not in action then in words, prisoners' sense of honor and camaraderie is to this day alive and strong. Thus, for example, it is a sacred honor and duty for everyone to assist by whatever means those comrades sent to the isolators, regardless of the reasons for their arrests. Prisoners give them their last pinch of tobacco, their final lump of sugar, cut for them the best portion of the dinner meat, and so on. It goes without saying that the transferring of all this is done in secret from the administration, though in prison there always exist several knights without fear or reproach who, risking their hides and freedom, care for those who've been "secreted" and stand guard, go to them, or find another way to transfer everything. With regard to assisting those in the isolators, Mikhaila more than once expressed a contrary view.

One time, when he thought his portion of dinner meat too small, he once again didn't hesitate to take up arms against the philanthropists. Then the entire ward fell upon him as one man, cursing him as an Asmodei,[61] a snake, and reminding him of instances of his previous behavior that he himself had forgotten. But Mikhaila did not cower, and calmly and methodically continued to defend his view warmly.

"I've been in the isolator and, well, you sit there. It's your affair. If I find myself there, you can't help me. Why do men go to the isolator? For gambling, being rude, laziness— and what else? So our martyrs have been found! They come to *katorga* and aren't scared, but fall apart in the isolator? They're in *katorga*, but want to live as though they're free, barking at guards and playing cards."

"Look, chaps: a man of honor's 'peared 'mong us!... A priest's arrived. Why, don't you yourself cheat?"

"Sure, I cheat; but do I hide it? I just don't cry, like you, that I'm in prison."

"Yes, you carry yourself honestly. But you say you don't loaf around on the job? Indeed, you're the top loafer! You try to dodge 'n' blame someone else where'er possible. It's a pain to do bargain work[62] with you, 'cause all you do is pull strings."

"And why should I pull myself to death? I don't keep you from loafing; you just need to do it sensibly, understand when it's possible and when it's not."

"Akh, you Seedling fox! Chaps, I really don't like chemists like this here, prigs who're so full o' spite!" shouted Malakhov. "Y'see, he got fed too much in the isolators... I starved!"

"Starved, indeed. Why have the portions gotten so small lately? I'm not blind. Something's being sent to the isolator painfully often... Now, it's better not to give them anything. Why are we feeding our free command? It's fat and drunk, but I should feed it? It gets vodka, but I should give it my last crumbs? A fool's been found!"

"Brother, you're no fool, 'n' no one's sayin' that."

Mikhaila reasoned logically and, it seemed, absolutely correctly, but for some reason his ruthlessly logical reasoning proved unappealing and he was incapable of inspiring sympathy. But his undeniable giftedness for the unexpected, his independence of character, and all the energy, passion, and originality of his spiritual temperament attracted me to him. I've said already that the ward burst out laughing at his wish at the age of forty-two to study grammar, but he scorned popular opinion and, joking or saying nothing to the painful jibes, he began, over some three months amid the most insalubrious conditions for studying, to read and write tolerably well and learn the four rules of mathematics. Toward the end of this period he even began studying Church Slavonic;[63] he was, like Nikifor, a Seedling, only simply more devout than he. Nikifor smoked tobacco, but Mikhaila considered him cursed by seven churches.

An old, unspoken enmity evidently existed between these two cousins. This enmity had for a time ceased upon their arriving at Shelai Prison; under the impact of external oppression their hearts softened and Nikifor even asked Six-Eyes about putting him in the same ward as his cousin: Mikhaila was then transferred to our ward. But the business of learning brought everything into daylight and, as much as I went to pains to keep the peace and harmony between the two rivals, I could not permit my authority as teacher to be lost, and their enmity reemerged and reached most critical heights. This enmity was bitter to the last, poisoning the joy that students can in time experience through successful persistence, as well as me and the entire ward. Jealousy and hatred constantly burned between Nikifor and Mikhaila. Now and then their unfriendliness towards each other was redirected at me. The principal reason for this was the conditions of prison life amid which it was necessary to study. Between evening roll call and the drum-roll signaling bedtime, only two or three hours were available for teaching. During this time I had to be able to administer to the students, deal with each separately (since their levels of ability and accomplishment weren't the same), and hope for a moment to somehow remember a little something of the previous lessons. Therefore, those students with whom I didn't deal for several evenings in a row unfailingly grumbled at me: it seemed I was taking more time with someone else than with him… Mikhaila was more intelligent and tactful than the others, but Nikifor and Pestrov often took offense. It was impossible to evade their suspicion, since I really did enjoy dealing with Mikhaila more than with them and gave him more approving comments. Of the latter I was, without a doubt, guilty: my admiring the occasionally instantaneous achievements of my favorite student and not refraining from loudly praising him pierced others to the heart like a poisoned arrow! These were, in truth, adult children, utter children, in whose minds and souls, like in virgin soil, could easily grow a good or a bad seed… Unfortunately, the conditions for our undertaking were so insalubrious that it was difficult to grow the better seed. There were so many pointless struggles over the alphabet, the Gospels, and the pencil, the resolution of which was so difficult! During every prison search the pencils were ruthlessly seized and it became necessary to painstakingly hide them. There was also a struggle over seating. A small tin lamp, mercilessly blackened and throwing off a sufficiently lackluster reddish light, served as the ward's only illumination. The table was huge, but there were no benches specially for it: during the day the benches that supported the sleeping platforms were moved to the table, but in the evening, when most prisoners were flopping down on their sides, these couldn't be moved, and students had to use only those places in the corner where the benches themselves served as sleeping platforms: this sufficed for only a pair of readers or a single writer. In this spot next to the wall slept Mikhaila Burenkov, and when he was not studying grammar Nikifor freely used it; but when Mikhaila took up his work he, per a master's rights, commandeered the spot at the table. Oh, then how many arguments and all sorts of dramas there were because of this spot, how much hatred sometimes agitated the entire ward, having been brought to life through participation in the matters of my school! Pestrov soon dropped his studies altogether, and I no longer spoke to him. For a long time Nikifor quietly grumbled at me and his cousin. He'd get up at night, after everyone had gone to bed and the spot was free, and begin writing or reading by himself, listening keenly for the guard's footsteps and, at each approach, diving into bed. Thus he sometimes sat up until daylight, without the slightest advantage in succeeding at his studies. For a long time I didn't know what Nikifor was grumbling over, because he wouldn't deal with me, but one day he and Mikhaila generated a stormy explanation, during which they brought up all their past grievances, beginning with their domestic trash and ending with the affair for which they were sent to *katorga* and shared a life at Pokrovskii mine.

"It's 'cause o' you I ended up in *katorga*," Nikifor heatedly said, pacing about the ward with huge steps. His large blue eyes burned with fire, but melancholy and a deep conviction resounded in his voice. "'Cause o' you… You was older, you knew better… You shoulda warned me, but instead, you pushed me into that stealin' business."

The ward, normally on Nikifor's side, began laughing at him this time.

"What, Nikishka, sorry you didn't take monastic vows?"

"He was an honest man, boys," Mikhaila poisonously responded, "that's why the devil combed his hair and the comb broke. What's he done up to now that I could shame him for? He pinched eighty rubles from his father and ran around with the girls; he climbed into a store and stole a thousand in goods for a Chinaman; it so happened he wasn't squeamish about snatching tea from a caravan… Well, but if you don't count all that, he was an honest man…"

"Ever'thin' what's happened, all o' that, don't cut me down, don't cut me down at all," continued Nikifor, with the same melancholy and seriousness in his voice. "Only, if my mind hadn't been bewitched, I'd still be on the right path. In a sober state, I was actually 'fraid to steal… D'you really forget why I made friends with you? Ain't you noticed no one in our family liked you? Absolutely no one liked you, 'cause you're an arrogant man. Didn't you know I considered you a scoundrel? You think you can come at me like some chemist? 'N' you say you're devout, saintly. Why'd I wanna break from my other comrades 'n' stick to you? 'N' why're you here stickin' to me?"

"So, so, seems I'm guilty. It's a shame your memory's so short. It wasn't me—for sure—who idly talked like you did, it wasn't me proclaiming my thefts from the rooftops; nope, and you're just lying, lying, Mikishka, about me being saintly. You knew about my life, knew everything for certain. And if you dropped other comrades for me, this was for a different reason."

"What reason?"

"It was that you thought I was smarter than the others, and you hoped that with me you wouldn't land in a trap so soon."

"Indeed, with you I landed in a trap e'en sooner! I was robbin' with you all o' ten months, but I was already up against it, 'n' drunk or sober I weren't bein' honest."

"I'm guilty, but you, brother, aren't guilty of anything!"

"Precisely, you're guiltier. Didn't you run when they was shootin' at us, 'n' left me to get outta the kasha myself?"

"Dare I say you fenced me off, and took all the wine for yourself? You snared me in a trap, and your kinfolk arrested me."

"Stop, you devils! Tell straight out how ever'thin' happened," someone interrupted the disputants, one of whom began to narrate, interrupted every minute by the other with corrections and venomous barbs. I recognized in the brief sentences the following. One night, having on a main road snatched two crates of tea from a caravan and loaded them in a nearby telega, the Burenkovs tore along in the direction of Troitskosavsk.[64] The caravan drivers chased but didn't catch them. By dawn, the thieves had arrived at the coach house of a known "lucky man." In the meantime, the pursuers had notified the police and the latter were already quickly descending upon this coach house long enjoying a shady reputation. Noticing the police, the Burenkovs hurried to their telega, flung open the courtyard gate, and took off. Policemen tried to prevent this but were simply shoved aside; the several shots fired point-blank at these Kiakhta daredevils failed to scare them; escaping the courtyard, they were able to run the horses out of the city… A mounted pursuit began following them, but they were already far away and would soon have been hiding in the woods—had the mountain road not turned to loose sand. The horses became exhausted. The police drew close and began shooting again. The cautious Mikhaila reasoned that the stolen tea couldn't be saved and left the telega to its fate and hid in the bushes; but the hot-headed Nikifor did not want to drive the horses into the woods. To stop the pursuit, he even fired a blast from the shotgun he carried… The police did actually stop, but some of them, having dismounted, took a short-cut through the forest. Just barely noticing this maneuver (albeit too late), Nikifor was thinking how to save himself. Just as he managed to reach the edge of the forest and throw the shotgun into some tall grass, he was surrounded from all sides and captured. Fortunately for him, in all the confusion the police forgot about the shotgun and, after they remembered, the investigator didn't include it in their belated hearsay report. Had Nikifor not thrown away his gun he would, of course, have received twenty instead of four years' *katorga*… Mikhaila, meanwhile, escaped and hid for a whole eight months: Nikifor had named him in all his depositions. He couldn't disown himself of this.

"I thought they'd ne'er catch you," he naïvely tried to vindicate himself. But he then vehemently disavowed himself of Mikhaila's other accusation, that he'd told his kinfolk to track down and arrest him. According to Nikifor, his relatives had their own reasons for luring Mikhaila as a guest to their house and turning him over to police. This betrayal had terribly embittered Mikhaila and, for his part, he himself acknowledged that, in revenge, he'd blamed everything on Nikifor and furthermore linked some of his relatives to the case…

"I'm thinking, 'Let the devils go to prison and get a bread ration!'"

In the end, both Burenkovs were sentenced to four years' *katorga* and sent, first, to Pokrovskii, and then Shelai, mine. En route they were peaceful toward each other, and in Pokrovskii lived without any special arguments; but now I had the misfortune to be the unwilling cause of new disputes between them. All the bitterness of their past encounters and deeds had come to light and elicited general discussion and laughter. The ward, as I've said, was for the most part on Nikifor's side, but it was apparent that both men wanted to know my opinion and to win my sympathy. My situation was extremely ticklish, and I tried as possible to forestall discussion of the past.

"I'm a simple chap," said Nikifor about himself, "ever'thin's from my heart, not my head… But you're cunnin', a double-dealer!"

"I'm not cunning, but I do have a brain," objected Mikhaila, trying to appear calm, though he was just as red as Nikifor. "You love to praise yourself, Mikishka: you're simple, as you say, and certainly without cunning… But what about when your comrade gets sicker of your simplicity than he would if you were cunning?"

"Is that so?"

"Just so. I'm cunning, but I never threw away your portion, and because of your celebrated simplicity I ended up getting hungry on the way. 'Ever'thing'll be ours, Mikhaila!' he says. 'We're gonna live like brothers, share ever'thin' 'tween each other.'

I answer: 'Very well, let's try it…' I toss the money and everything into one pile. But he goes and plays cards? If he's got a brain in his head, then now I'm telling myself he's lost his mind… But he's got to go and stake the money on *shtos*! Well, he gambles away mine and his full and finally—and we both go hungry for several days."

"'N' how often did it happen? Your shameless eyes. Once or twice we lost ever'thin' on the way."

"But it *was* everything."

"Well, so you've jus' lost ever'thin', Mikhaila," Paramon Malakhov suddenly intervened, "but you're alright. What was you doin' in Pokrovskii?"

"What?"

"Indeed, I already know what… I saw. Maybe you think no one saw, but people was watchin'. As it was, away from Mikishka he'd secretly buy meat pies, stick one in his mouth, 'n' go round the prison howlin' like a wolf!"

"But what's this? You're saying there was no sharing between us? He was playing cards, but I was feeding him!"

"Well, you shoulda told 'im to his face! But that was hidin'… Oh, you saintly Pharisees, you righteous men! You high-minded men!"

Paramon spat vehemently, lay down on the sleeping platform, and grew silent. The disputants also finally grew silent, though for a long time, still agitated, they stalked like beasts back and forth through the ward, one-by-one and from side-to-side.

Having grown fond of one student for his buddy-buddy disposition, but having been stuck with another who could be a hard character, I should have stopped trying to keep the peace between them. Mikhaila was actually inclined to be peaceful, and making use of his superior intelligence, he agreed to give Nikifor his place at the table during evening lessons, but Nikifor acted capriciously, like a young child, and didn't want to resume the lessons. Once, I even happened to hear a bunch of the most vile things from him.

"Why are you mad at me, Nikifor?" I asked. "What wrong have I done you?"

"Whate'er wrong someone does to me," he answered, not looking me in the eye, "is done to all of us. All the scoundrels, the penal laborers, is in the same boat…"

"How 'in the same boat'? They've come to *katorga* for different reasons…"

"How do I know you weren't a scoundrel like me, 'n' didn't rob or kill someone? Did anyone help you?"

In the meantime, Nikifor was looking at me with such insolent and hateful eyes that I unwillingly fell silent and walked away. But the other prisoners grew indignant and contradicted Nikifor on my behalf.

"These devils here is reckonin' to study, to torture themselves," shouted Chirok, truly indignant, "they'll be thankin' you, jus' wait!"

"Ah, you're a fool, a fool, Mikishka!" Goncharov shamingly shook his head. "Tomorrow, you're really gonna be embarrassed you wagged your stupid tongue."

"What kinda schoolin's this?" Paramon became indignant in turn. "So the teacher's gotta beg the student to study? Where's this e'er been seen? In our day, you'd get a good canin' on the back—then there'd be some learnin'!"

Mikhaila also felt ashamed for his cousin and, pacing through the ward, said:

"You're a Kolyvansk birch-bucket… trying to jump into science with your crap-for-brains!"

Nikifor sat quietly behind the Gospels. I lay down and, though I couldn't fall asleep for a long time, pretended that I quickly had. After the entire ward had been snoring awhile, I saw Nikifor approach my spot several times and look at me for a long time, though I didn't open my eyes wide. The next day in the mine he asked my forgiveness, and with extraordinary naïvety several times implored me to strike him on the cheek. This offer I, of course, refused, but I did readily agree to make peace since, in essence, I was no longer angry. That same evening our lessons resumed. Nikifor was cheerful, lively, and distinguished by atypical comprehension. He also tried to butter up Mikhaila like some naughty boy buttering up his father. Mikhaila held himself in stolid reserve. The ward had also not forgotten the day before.

Nikifor did his utmost to try to overtake his cousin in writing but was not at all successful. His clumsy, rough hands broke the pencils, crunched up the paper, and punctuated and scrawled such anonymous characters that a teacher would have recoiled in horror at the calligraphy. But, in the meantime, all Shelai students cherished the dream of learning to write: a commoner believes writing to be the quintessence of all knowledge, the epitome of learning. Lord, with what suffering and diligence they scribbled on paper for entire days and nights; only, you could hardly distinguish one letter from another! Occasionally perceiving a poisonous—it seemed to him—laughter on Mikhaila's lips, Nikifor would stop, throw away his pencil and paper, and begin complaining.

"How can you learn in prison? Where there can be laughin'? Sittin' there on that bench, you like bangin' the anvil 'n' pumpin' the bellows, but if you worked like I do you'd 'ave bored seventeen inches a day! 'N' I daresay your hand would shake, too!"

"And I don't bore?" Mikhaila shot back. "Did I stop boring a long time ago? No, you're only better inside your bucket, so complain to your empty head."

"I'm droppin' the writin'!" Nikifor then decided. "As should be, 'n' in fact, I don't like writin'. I'm better off wearin' myself out by readin' well."

And, suddenly lapsing into complete despair, he shouted:

"'N' what's all this lit'racy to us scoundrels? What?"

"Shoulda quit a long time ago!" Chirok mockingly assented, having set his cigar down in its spot.

"Mikolaich! What's lit'racy to us? What?"

I tried, in answering this question, to explain literacy's usefulness, saying that it makes a person intelligent and therefore honest; but, while asserting this, I now and then doubted myself: what did it, all this literacy, mean for them, the prisoners? In subsequent instances I several times became convinced that many of my best students, who had studied and read and written conscientiously, very quickly forgot this and that upon release to the free command, and a bitter vexation sometimes whispered in my soul, a conviction that so much of my gift of labor and time had been squandered. More than once I also happened to hear from prisoners themselves that literacy is actually harmful for them, that a swindler can become a bigger swindler with it, whereas an honest man, having dreamt of the easy work of a clerk and acquired an aversion to physical labor, can be corrupted thanks to it. I well understood, of course, the utter superficiality and perniciousness of such generalizations on the basis of salient, exclusionary facts, but I do confess I was often seized by all sorts of doubt, and would then abandon my school for a long time. Struggling with the obstacles raised at each step by administrators also got on my nerves: they would close their eyes to the existence in the prison of pencils and writing tablets, then suddenly confiscate everything and reinstate the ban. However, a certain time passed, and I returned to it with love. My "pedagogical" activity was strewn with bitterness and poison from all sorts of brambles and thorns that bled my soul, nevertheless, there was something kind, blessed, and warm in it that illuminated and comforted not only me but, it seemed, the entire ward. Prisoners somehow unwittingly became accustomed to regard paper and book with respect, and the ideas attuned them to a higher tone and harmony. In the other wards, listening to exaggerated stories about the Burenkovs' accomplishments and my teaching abilities, they gazed at them with envy, and most of the men dreamed of transferring to our ward and also becoming "students."[65]

I can't forget the day when the Burenkovs decided for the first time to send their wives their own handwritten letters, and began readying themselves for this triumph. Few scribbles were completed and sent without my final approval. Because only a few of Nikifor's disconnected scribbles, with hundreds of improbable mistakes and misconstructions, could be understood, his letter, in truth, was completed by me in whole, and for his part, his belief that he had produced this letter was merely a pleasing self-delusion. By contrast, Mikhaila's letter was truly his own child, and written so intelligently and coherently that I couldn't refrain from expressing the most sincere admiration. I found only one problem in it: the appeal to his wife seemed too dry and cold… It should be said that in August of that year (the letters were written in January), both Burenkovs were to complete their *katorga* terms and go to settlement, though where was unknown: natives of Transbaikal District are removed to Sakhalin or Iakutsk District, or are even left there, in Transbaikalia. The latter, of course, was the Burenkovs' dream; both were terribly afraid of Sakhalin… Needless to say, and as made clear earlier, the worst had to be prepared for, and in the meantime, preparations were made for their respective wives to follow them. Ardor and emotion emanated from Nikifor's letter to his wife, completed with my help; but Mikhaila's letter, as I've already said, exuded coldness: it was a simple notification to his wife about the impending change in his fate, without even a question as to how she, for her part, was hoping to arrange things.

"You ought to write a bit more warmly," I advised Mikhaila, and proposed among other things adding to the word "wife" a modifier such as "dear" or "sweet." Mikhaila laughed:

"That won't do."

"Why?"

"The wife doesn't merit such an honorific: 'Dear'—what's that for? A horse may be dear, a house… 'Sweet'—this, too, isn't our custom; 'loving'—that's neither here nor there."

"Well, so add that you miss her, that you're looking forward to seeing her and living with each other again."

"No, that's not necessary," Mikhaila sternly responded and, the next day, I noticed but one brief addition in his scribbling: "Now, wife, pray to God."

I considered asking Mikhaila about his relations with his wife to be awkward (according to my understanding); but Nikifor soon parsed the matter for me. During his removal to *katorga*, Mikhaila had wanted his wife and family to follow him; but she expressed no particular desire to do so, and observed that his term wasn't long and was not enough to make her leave with small children for a new, possibly very difficult, life, only to change to yet another one soon again. Nikifor's wife, by contrast, had yearned to follow her husband, but he'd told her to delay her arrival until he entered settlement.

That following Sunday, with fear and trepidation, all three of us entered the orderly's room, where letters had to be written. To write with ink was completely different than with pencil, and I greatly feared for my students. Not for nothing did Paramon predict, staking his head on it, that having never in their lives held a quill, they would embarrass themselves, and so he advised stealing the guard's ink and undertaking several preliminary experiments. The latter idea terribly pleased the rash, always enthusiastic Nikifor, and I had great difficulty persuading him not to do it. With the very first strokes, Nikifor put down such blots and scrawled such Egyptian hieroglyphs that he was brought to despair, and I had to draft the letter for him; he simply signed it. It took him a good ten minutes to produce his surname (moreover, he adorned it as well with a pair of blots, smeared with his tongue), and all the same, it was quite difficult to make out. Having finished and laid down his quill, he was literally bathed in sweat.

"It's easier borin' seventeen inches," he declared, breathing heavily. Regardless of his lack of success, he nevertheless sat tall and looked like a victor. By contrast, Mikhaila, having sat almost the entire day in the orderly's room, wrote his entire letter himself. I followed every motion of his hand and gave advice. At first, his letters wobbled across the paper as if they were drunk, but then grew more stable and strong. After returning to the ward, he victoriously demanded Paramon's head.

"Just so I can give it back," he eased off, "because it's big, and stupid!"

After that, Mikhaila wrote several more letters home; Nikifor immediately abandoned writing entirely, having despaired of ever learning so difficult an art.

XI. SEMËNOV

My teaching served among other things as an occasion for a particularly difficult scene that has since remained among my gloomiest memories, though at the same time intimately familiarized me with the inner world of a man whose personality had excited my greatest curiosity much earlier. I'm speaking of Semënov, one of our ward's most incommunicative and sullen residents. He almost never participated in general discussion, only occasionally interjecting some caustic remark, whereby was revealed his hostile attitude and disdain toward everything commonplace and vapid, toward all of sorts of cowardice, hypocrisy, and "tail-wagging," toward every form of mediocrity. He established friendly relations with me, but neither intimate nor such as would have allowed on my part the possibility of asking him about his earlier life. I simply knew that Semënov had a violent temper and, in a drunken state, became positively dangerous, grabbing a knife and sticking it into the first person whose face he didn't like. In Pokrovskii, where prisoners could procure vodka without difficulty, Semënov immediately endeavored to establish a contact, and his friend Goncharov, having by that time lost any power over him, was the first to ready the noose or the hammer.

One day, having awoken just before morning roll call, I heard a squabble between Nikifor and Gandorin.

"Where'd you put my notebook, you ol' devil?" Nikifor angrily demanded.

"I didn't put your *botenook* nowhere," mocked Gandorin, "you students stick 'em ever'where. That's it, over there! It's with Semënov, next to the Gospels."

"Well, brother Petka, the students have been takin' notes on you!" joked Goncharov.

Semënov nervously approached the shelf, tore the Gospels from Nikifor's hands, threw his notebook on the table, and shouted:

"Don't dare write in my book! Ain't gonna happen no more! Stu-dents!… You been wavin' the flag 'bout your studyin'… Aimin' to be priests!"

"'N' what're you bullyin' us for, brother? What're ya barkin' 'bout?" bristled Nikifor, recovering from his surprise. "Didn't you study yourself?"

"When did I study? Did I study in prison?" said Semënov, voice still rising, and his nostrils flared and quivered menacingly.

"You're studyin' now," Nikifor boldly continued, "jus' like a student."

"I'm a student?!" Semënov didn't ask, but growled, as if having received a deadly insult.

"Precisely. You're always readin' the Gospels, too, 'n' you also wanna be a priest…"

(I should point out here that this Gospels, which I never actually once saw Semënov reading, was, in Goncharov's words, a maternal benediction.)

Nikifor had hardly gotten his last word out when there was the sound of paper being torn and the pages of the relevant book were flying through the ward like goose down. Marmot, Chirok, and Iron Cat, seeing such rich spoils for rolling cigars, fell down to gather and capture them. Meanwhile, Semënov, shaking from head to toe, pale and clenching his fists spasmodically, roared at the entire ward:

"Here's how I read!... How I wanna be a priest!... I'm better'n all them priests o' yours (a subsequent, cynical word sounded in Semënov's mouth like a knife-thrust)... I believe in your Holy Scripture, in the law!"

The abuse hurled at *katorga*'s residents was made all the more horrible by terrible blasphemies; the whole ward had long ago awoken, but it was quiet as a grave.

"Petia, Petia!" Goncharov's voice quietly whispered. "The guard's listenin'."

"What's a guard to me?" Semënov continued roaring. "When 'ave I hid from the guards? Didn't I sit in solitary with manacles for two years? Am I afraid of Six-Eyes? I'm better'n all of 'em..."

And once again, a terrible vulgarism caused me to wince.

Fortunately for Semënov, there was no guard in the corridor, and all turned out well. Semënov at last managed to calm down. The Gospels was never afterward mentioned, and I never knew whether he ever repented of his blaspheming over the maternal benediction. Without a doubt, he had a strong connection to his old mother. He'd send her completely proper letters, and moreover never asked for money like the majority of prisoners, but, on the contrary, once gave her a dressing-down for having sent two rubles. It's also notable that after each of his three escapes from prison he had first of all visited his mother, dangerously risking, because of this, falling into the hands of the authorities or those fellow villagers who deeply hated him.

The same day as the event with the Gospels, I had a talk in the mine with Goncharov about his friend, and learned about my curiosity. The old man was reverential toward Semënov, and failed to notice, even while passing them on, the most uncomplimentary— in my view—facts and qualifications. He completely, absolutely completely, found in his "Petka" a beautiful and astonishing wonder.

"I actually knew him as a testy little thing, 'n' held him on my knees... 'N' I knew his father, mother, 'n' brother. They was Raseyans. For murder, the father'd been sent for settlement to our province. He was a bitter drunk. 'N' such a barbarian: I recall he was so miserly, so miserly towards his wife 'n' children that e'en an Indian woulda called it a shame. Their only salvation was to be found in my home. But when the father claimed 'em again, I chose to keep the children. Only, they went bad. Started drinkin', brawlin', 'n' got to know prison from the age o' seventeen. But prison certainly didn't make 'em good; prison is above the saint, 'n' beats the righteous from his path. Stepash, the oldest, was eighteen, 'n' got slapped with four years' *katorga*. He 'scaped the march 'n' went straight to Petka. There, in the canton, they boiled the same kasha they'd been boilin' all o'er the district. A posse was formed 'n' captured 'em sleepin' in the woods. Their hands was chained together 'n' they got run along on foot! They was so worn out that Petka was close to death for three weeks after. His case, howe'er, got buggered up for lack of evidence. Stepash got slapped with ten more years for 'scapin'. He 'scaped from the march yet again 'n' killed a guard. They captured him again 'n' have him cooped up for eternity in Tobolsk Central.[66] He's there now. But Petka finagled another two years in freedom. He formed a gang… He picked all o' the baddest to work for him, 'n' in those days they wouldn't-a gotten caught but for the vodka… It destroyed him. Petka has such a foolish temper: he can drink four bottles 'n' still stand straight; well, but he can also suddenly become a mess 'n' lose all reason. He broke into a shop in broad daylight. They caught him, o' course. He sat in Kansk Prison for six years 'n' couldn't tell what to do: only, while they was decidin' what to do—presto!—he broke out! They'd stuck him in the isolator, arm 'n' leg irons, 'n' he finagled an escape from there: sawed through the grille, smashed the wall, 'n' dug a tunnel. Came out in front o' the watchman: 'I'm Semënov, 'n' you're nuthin'!' With that word he grabbed his rifle 'n' ran. Then Petka came to me. I'd already decided where to hide him. Only, the vodka would wreck him ever' time. He'd drink for two or three days, lose all sense, 'n' go stealin'. But the circle was closin' in… They caught him again, beat him half to death, 'n' tossed him in jail. Ever'one in the jail was scared of 'im. Warden approached him on tip-toe 'n' gave him little books to read. As with the Gospels today, he'd curse all the officials to their faces. If you saw his rap sheets, Ivan Mikolaich, you'd simply marvel at how many crimes is written in 'em, at the twelve years of *katorga* he's drawn, the 'scapes, attempted robberies, acts 'gainst authority, all kinds o' scandals… For these they beat 'im last time they got 'im… Beat the life outta every part of 'im, dislocated all his joints! You can't see, 'cause he looks so healthy 'n' hearty, 'n' he's quiet 'bout it all 'n' never complains 'bout it. I'm an ol' man, but I'm prob'ly still healthier'n him 'cause I weren't beaten… But I know 'im, know that when there's just a tiny change in the weather he's racked all o'er. 'N' I 'member how in his day the peasants of Ura[67] (Petka's from Ura, y'know) was so scared of 'im… Each summer they'd fear his return! 'N' he had one idea in his head. He'd show 'em, those blessed ol' men, he'd give 'em his blessin'!"

And Goncharov added in a whisper:

"Pity the prison here ain't like that, it's hard stayin' here… Let's say it don't frighten Petka; 'n' Shelai's walls won't hold him 'n' I talk him outta ever'thin': 'Wait, Petka,' I says, 'soon you'll be in the free command. You can hold on one more year.' I'm scared o' one thing, Ivan Mikolaich: I'm scared of his character. Were it not for this mornin', you'd prob'ly think him the meekest prisoner, but if you knew what this humility costs him! He lissens to the guards' barkin' 'n' resigns himself to ever'thin', ever'thin' he sees—'n' stays silent! But, back then, with his cousin, he'd-a sooner puked. He shoulda been in a dif'rent spot long ago 'n' not arrived as part of a pair. But now he's gotta suffer, though the free command'll give 'im a break soon…"

Actually, having for some time watched Semënov, I noticed that he exerted a terrific strength of will to keep his vicious nature in check. One time, our ward attendant Marmot had fallen ill, and the most hated guard shouted without thinking at Semënov:

"Tomorrow, you'll be the ward attendant!"

In prison, this responsibility is usually borne by volunteers who have a penchant for similar types of employment or derive some benefits from them; the Ivans, of whom Semënov was undoubtedly one, consider it shameful to be an attendant. I watched Semënov turn suddenly pale and clench his fists spasmodically. But he got ahold of himself and stayed quiet. The ward attendants' business somehow managed without him.

Soon after this, I ended up working with Semënov in the gallery for about two weeks running. The gallery offered a narrow corridor in which no more than two men could fit for boring. This physical proximity and quotidian residence by both of us underground in the dark for many hours naturally evoked a certain spiritual affection between us. Semënov became—unbeknownst to him—more garrulous and open, and he repeated much of what I'd learned from Goncharov. To my great surprise, it turned out he was familiar with many classic works by Russian and even foreign authors: he'd read Gogol, Pushkin, Nekrasov, and Victor Hugo's *Ninety-Three*,[68] and was in possession of an outstanding literary memory; but, of course, he'd read still more the various boulevard rubbish and French hacks' sundry products in Russian translation, and his baggage of literary knowledge consisted of improbable romantic adventures and stories of romance and gore, in which he blindly believed and that without a doubt made a certain impression on his mentality and temperament. This temperament was savage and terrifying and I was struck by its callous egoism and somehow persuasive—if it can be so expressed— depravity. It was impossible to argue a point with Semënov, since he acknowledged nothing save a crude materialistic logic. A single red stripe ran through all his feelings, thoughts, and desires: uncompromising hatred toward all existing tradition and order, beginning with economics and ending with religious morals, toward everything that put however small a restraint upon his refractory will and unquenchable thirst for pleasure… "Spit on the law, on faith, on society's opinion, 'n' kill, rob, 'n' live to the fullest"—such was the motto of this present-day Stenka Razin…

At first this worldview amazed me, and for a long time I tried to track down its source in one of the books he'd read and pretended to understand; but, in the end, I was forced to the conclusion that life itself creates Semënovs, filling their souls with a certain boundless evil and depriving them of any guiding principles or ideals.

"If everyone became as depraved as you," I told Semënov, "then what would happen? Life would become constantly murderous and violent, and people would become even more wretched than they are now."

"What dif'rence is it to me," he answered, "if I frighten others, when no one frightens me 'n' no one e'er pities me? They follow the law, punish the starvin' man who steals a piece o' bread, but are known to steal thousands from the blessed! The long-hairs[69] tell us 'bout God, but God Himself… No, let them honorable men do as they will, but I spit on that honor!"

"But do you murder only the guilty and scurrilous? You're only after money. Yet… say someone finds money in the sweat of his brow, through working with his hands? Is he guiltier?"

"No, if he's a rich man it means he's become a snake like the rest of 'em. But if he ain't, then God'll reward him in that world of the priests burnin' frankincense 'n' actin' holy!"

"But, your conscience, Semënov?" I timidly asked, deciding not to speak of God, in whom he obviously did not believe. "Can you explain why, in the deepest soul of every man, even the cruelest and most dissolute, there is nevertheless shame? If there's nothing sacred in the world, if man is also an animal and his soul doesn't exist, then can you say where this shame comes from? Can you remember a time when someone you were simply kind towards offended you unfairly? Weren't you unhappy after this? Isn't this the same? How do you explain it?"

Semënov wasn't able to answer, since at that moment we were relocated; but it seemed that it wasn't just because of this he couldn't answer, but that he had in general been caught unawares by my unforeseen questions. For the first time Semënov turned reflective—sufficiently enough, I decided; and conversations with me would occur at other times. However, my victory did not last long and proved premature. No more than three days later he approached me in the prison yard and said:

"D'you know what I wanna to talk 'bout with you, Ivan Nikolaevich? This accountin' for a conscience that you told me 'bout. I 'member that a dog had it, too."

"What do you mean a dog had it?"

"Jus' so." And he told about an incident in which a dog supposedly became ashamed of its own foolish action.

"At first I taught it to fear me, but then it started gettin' ashamed. It's the same, I think, with a person. Boys also really have no shame at all, but then they fear the birch rod, well, 'n' as they grow up…"

I shrugged my shoulders and simply walked away. Another time I posed him the following question:

"But what do you expect lies ahead for you, Semënov? Your life is really awful, just awful! You're not even thirty years old, but you've already—with just a little interruption—spent eight years in prison! And even earlier, at the age of twelve, you got to know it… Also, your brother's a permanent resident of prison… And did those few years of freedom you had give you joy? Are such horrible torments worth a drunken revelry? You'll probably escape again—not from the prison but from the free command… Well, you'll be captured again, of course, and be slapped with another ten years' *katorga*… No, Semënov, truly, this is awful… Wouldn't it be better… to live honorably? You hate honor, but by a simple calculation it's better."

"Is there land to plow? A little grain to sow to earn a few kopeks? No, thank you very much. Let honorable me occupy us-selves with this!"

"Does this mean prison is better?"

"Yup, better. But I'll escape—well, then… I'll do whate'er I want!…"

Whatever I want—such was the quintessence of all the worldly ideals of persons like Semënov. But, besides this, he had still another "notion," in Goncharov's expression: the notion of avenging himself against one of the villagers who'd beaten him during his last arrest. Every time he spoke on this topic his eyes burned with a gloomy fire, his fists clenched angrily, he ground his teeth and growled like an animal that's seized a tasty morsel but not lost hope of seizing it again in his claws. Goncharov knew of his student's and friend's notion, sensed it with all his soul and, like a cat whose ears are being scratched, voluptuously screwed up his eyes at these moments of blood lust. Like his offspring, he cherished the hope that Semënov would escape from *katorga*. It's possible he had his own accounts with Ura's peasants and that his sympathy was not simply platonic… Semënov's dream was not just a dream or a captive's fevered thoughts: I do not doubt that it was in his blood and was one of the principal demons guiding his soul… Then there were the other prisoners. If their words are to be believed, vengeance was for almost each one a primary stimulus inspiring their continued existence and forcing them to dream of escape and freedom. "I'll get revenge 'n' then I'll snuff it—so what!" a dozen dreamers similarly told me. Goncharov dreamed of vengeance, and Rakitin, Chirok, Nogaitsev, Malakhov, and all the multifarious, multi-characteristic majority of prison residents I was able to get to know dreamed of vengeance. Even Iashka the Marmot, this prison "weed" without a name, the lowliest man in the labor collective, sometimes said with comical gravity after having listened to Semënov's or some other leader's vengeful talk:

"If God grants it, I'll also finish my term 'n' visit home, 'n' find someone to pay back good."

Taken at face value, all this nightmarishly bloody atmosphere of cruelty and vengeance to which nearly the entire prison mass down to a man contributed would horrify the Russian people, so glorified by their Christian humility and forgiveness and, however, generating from their very depths similarly cruel and hateful monsters! Fortunately—I think—not every one of the prisoners' words was to be taken as serious or meaningful.

Nonetheless, I've often posed myself the question as to what society should do with such undoubtedly harmful members as Semënov. Of course, it shouldn't produce or create such members in the first place… But, once they exist, what's to be done with them? Were I the government, what would I do with them? I confess to still being categorically vexed in answering this terrible question… I would of course not execute or flail them with those heartless scorpions the modern prison and *katorga*; but should I decide, on the other hand, to free them? Prisoners themselves sometimes posed me the same questions… It must be said that they, almost without exception, regarded themselves as innocent victims… Aren't martyrs—in their words—tortured? Does this not impoverish the rich men they've lightly fleeced? Why must they languish for so long because of them? Ten, twenty years, life… Why, upon conclusion of even *katorga*, are they not allowed to return home, thus branding them with the eternal mark of the outcast and, as such, pushing a man toward new murders and crimes? And the majority has decided that were they in authority, they would immediately free all inmates…

"But I," Semënov, having listened to my opinion, once jumped up and shouted, "I'd gather all of us from the whole world, put us all in the same prison, 'n' burn it down 'n' finish us off! There's no honor in an evil man, 'n' the wolf can't live with the sheep in brotherhood!"

These words evinced a profound, somewhat even shameless, sincerity, and at that moment I sensed in them many bitter truths. I sensed—and was most horrified… I was horrified because, of course, I would not have lifted a hand to do as Semënov would have, because I was striving to understand and love these terrible people, in whom I was trying to find some of those same human characteristics as were in me, the same ability to suffer and to feel suffering. During these given instances and circumstances they seemed victims, but not executioners, to me … And I frequently caught myself sympathizing with Semënov's dream of escape and wishing him complete success, preparing to assist even superficially his return there, to that verdant wood, those wide-open hills, a wild freedom far from the soul-encasing Shelai Prison, where so much strength and young life was extinguished without a trace… In the presence of this kind of suffering, this living suffering, you relate and become close to even a sworn enemy, you even sympathize with the beast languishing in an iron cage only to exit it impotent!…

XII.   READING THE BIBLE; IASHKA-THE-MARMOT; THE POET; THE PENAL LABORER

"All the students, yes, the students, for us, the ward, they don't mean nuthin'. Boys, let's have a riot!" said Paramon one day, puffing his pipe on the sleeping platform in an especially good mood. "We gotta give Nikolaich somethin' to read us."

"That's right: read!" the others emphatically chorused.

"But what can I read," I asked, "when there are no books? I have just the Bible and the Gospels."

"But what could be better?" replied Paramon. "Start the Bible. I'm already sick o' Gandorin's stories. 'There lived a Tsarevich Ivan 'n' a gray wolf, 'n' a Tsarevna Paraskovia 'n' a firebird...' He's lyin' just o'er there, see—'n' he's mumblin' to Iashka—'n' so you got no choice but to lissen. Though, in Pokrovskii, he could tell a story well, such as 'The Charmers,'[70] for instance: that blockhead there could make a connection!"

"I'm an ol' man, what can you take from me?" Gandorin sang in his own justification. "In the ol' days I listened, 'n' so now I'm *tellin'* the stories."

"You, an ol' man? Oh, you're lyin', you pious old-timer! No this or that ol' days... Brother, your eyes weren't seein' then. I lissen! I can tell from your own stories what landed you in *katorga*."

Everyone burst out laughing, since they well knew that Gandorin had gotten twelve years for raping a little girl.

Gandorin's stories, which he accurately related every evening at bedtime to Marmot and Chirok, often deeply angered me. They were evidently all his own inventions; he'd lump into one all the stories he'd ever heard, and the tall tales and even the lives of the saints were completely covered over with the crepe of some toothless old man's cynicism and libertinism. Even the most typical story adapted for young readers he managed to saturate with his own Gandorinesque miasma. Prisoners were generally great lovers of his cynical conversation and stories; but Gandorin's tales were distinguished by such a complete lack of tact and even simple ability that no one, save the non-exacting Chirok and Marmot, ever heard them out to the end.

"Very well," Gandorin would begin in his usual manner of continuing yesterday's endless tale, and from the very beginning everyone would start lying down to sleep, and soon the ward would actually suspiciously drift off under the rhythmic babbling of these oft-repeated and melodious "very wells."

The idea of reading the Bible had long intrigued me, and I thought: how would my neighbors regard this or another veritable artistic creation affording so grand an enjoyment to educated humanity? What impression would Shakespeare, Dickens, Gogol make on them? Well knowing that prison regulations forbade prisoners reading any kind of literature except the morally religious and the strictly scientific, but knowing at the same time that in most prisons this rule was in practice not strictly enforced, I had mailed home while still on the march route a brief list of belletrist books I asked to have sent me. I now awaited this parcel with impatience, nourishing the secret hope that the brave staff captain would, as sometimes happened, show less formality regarding his charges' spiritual food than the somatic. At present we were limited to the Bible. Everyone seemed to hold his breath when I first began reading. However, after not more than an hour I noticed that many were no longer sustaining this tension and were already snoring in good order. Goncharov and Marmot had fallen asleep sooner than the others; and they were followed by the "students." Subsequently even Nikifor, during the most gripping readings when the rest of the audience became excited, laughed themselves silly, or ground their teeth in rage, was unable to listen for long and distracted himself with something. By the same token, the most zealous listener after Paramon turned out to be—to my surprise—Gandorin. He was somehow surprisingly able to combine in one the most disgusting libertinism with the most sincere and emotional sanctimoniousness. Tears were in his eyes and he was clenching his fists by the minute while I read the story of the handsome Joseph, sold by his brothers into slavery. Yet, this story made an equally strong impression on everyone. And my listeners couldn't have just this: what I gave them in one dose was less than they wanted. It wasn't enough. Malakhov, Chirok, and Gandorin were prepared to listen all night, and each, as I closed the book saying that was enough for the day, would raise a hue and cry and begin haggling with me. Unfortunately, I soon had to acknowledge that my listeners were more passionately captivated by the story's superficial plot than its internal content and ideas: at the very least, I did not once hear at the end of a reading any kind of pious conversation apropos what had been read. They listened—and that was it. Each resumed his own affairs afterwards: one immediately fell asleep; another began yesterday's interrupted story. And if the reading occasionally provoked conversation, then it was some trifle related to this or another prisoner's specialty or a point whose discussion was hardly informative or desirable. Thus Iashka-the-Marmot very often laughed about Sodom's residents and the abused angels and, evidently, deeply regretted he hadn't been there… The better portion of the ward would already be asleep, but he'd still be nudging his neighbor and, choking with laughter, saying:

"How 'bout them *andels*, brother, them *andels!*…"

But Goncharov, who for the most part had been dozing senilely during the reading, would nod and say as I was closing the book:

"As you're lissenin' 'n' mullin' it o'er, so it's been one 'n' the same always 'n' ever'where in the world. Fights, murders, violence… 'N' so it'll fore'er be, unnerstand, fore'er 'til the end o' time!"

I finally became completely convinced that my listeners had still not come to an understanding of the Bible, this book filled with such high poetry and great simplicity;

I then came to understand why precisely the reading of the Bible so often elicits various mental confusions in simple and devout people. They approach it with a profound, essentially childlike, belief, insofar as each of this "holy" book's lines must be pure, pious, and edifying, and so when they instead find a truthful, unbeautiful chronicle of primitive morality and vital clashes of all sorts in all their dark and occasionally dirty details, they're absolutely nonplussed and, being unable to grasp the generally inspired idea, don't know what to think. A commoner relates to the spiritual exactly as he does to the beautiful. He perceives and comprehends the beauty of—for example—a woman only when she strikingly, protuberantly, and banally confronts his gaze, with her beauty as form and color and when everything about her is dazzling and clear, without a single blemish to indicate you're dealing with a living creature possessing a soul and not a marionette or an icon painter's cheaply depicted angel. The sacred must therefore be simply irreproachably sacred. But what becomes of these sacred people when certain of their actions in real life fall under the penal code and get them sentenced to *katorga*?

I also tried reading the Gospels. The peasants' suffering made a huge impression, and with regard to the discussions of those in the ward, I was reminded of the words of the barbarian Frankish king Claudwig: "Oh, why was I not there with my Franks!"[71] This touches on the rest of the Gospels, insofar as they generated little interest. The most powerful and beautiful (in our view) section—the "Sermon on the Mount"—produced absolutely nothing. Even Paramon himself, our ward's principal supporter of the faith, declared:

"No, I approve o' the Bible more… This weren't written for today's people… An eye for an eye, a tooth for a tooth—that's what's for us!"

"I believe in two eyes for one 'n' all teeth for one!" added Chirok, laughing.

The impenetrable darkness reigning in the majority of these primitive minds horrified and despaired me, and I often asked myself: Is there really, "in Russia's depths," still greater darkness and every sort of cerebral nonsense? Are these people, only slightly glossed by urban culture, wizened and corrupted by it, also the Russian people?

To the point, I'll familiarize the reader with several of my ward's residents, so that that mental and moral atmosphere in which I happened to live and participate will become absolutely clear to him.

Meet "the prison weed without a name," Iashka Pervanov, "Marmot" by nickname, the ward attendant I've mentioned more than once.

In his own way, he was an extremely interesting exemplar. As it turned out, he was borne into the world only to live in prison, namely performing a ward attendant's duties. Small, a bit plump, with a flaccid red face and sagging belly and stubby legs on which he stood somehow heavily and awkwardly, taking mincing little steps, he vividly brought to mind the figure of that Siberian animal whose name he bore.[72] To cap off the resemblance, his small beard and hair were yellow in color. Nothing in the world concerned and agitated him to such a degree as purely prison problems and interests, cards, striving for and squandering things, paying for them with his own hide, etc., and it was difficult even to imagine that Iashka-the-Marmot had ever lived on the outside and worked at any job other than carrying chamber pots. But, among other things, he'd at one time thrived, at one time been a man and had a wife and children… He was a native of the Kuban.[73] When he was fourteen he spent an entire year in the local prison on suspicion of horse-stealing and it was there, in his own words, that he was corrupted for the first time. Forced to be a soldier, he was assigned to serve in Riga, where he soon ended up in a penal battalion and received corporal punishment. But, having even as a baby come to learn about prison and the prisoner's life, he feared no punishment whatsoever and quickly slid down the decline of drunkenness and thievery. Only a single circumstance barely sobered him up. He was caught stealing a horse, got tied up and, after being beaten with meat hooks seven ways from Tuesday, was left to the four winds. Iashka's legs hurt for a long time after, and he even showed me the marks on his calves from the meat hooks… But he soon ended up in the affair for which he was sent straight to Siberia. Several soldiers beat him half to death in their unlovely sergeant-major's filthy den and were brought to trial for this; Pervanov was sentenced along with them to deprivation of all rights and to settlement in Eniseisk Province.[74] He lasted no more than a year in the settlement, doing nothing and existing on "*mantuli*" and "*savateiki*," that is, by begging beneath windows.[75] Finally, he along with another knight-errant murdered a peasant for a sack of millet flour and, as such, he earned himself ten years' *katorga*. I don't doubt that the whole of his future life will proceed in exactly the same way. He cannot and does not want to work, and if living "on the window-ledge" becomes difficult he'll leave the settlement for vagabondage, will be caught again for some "exchange,"[76] and wind up back in *katorga*. Ultimately, he'll go to Sakhalin. Extremely characteristic of Marmot's moral equivocation was his relationship to his homeland. In his words, for seven years he heard nothing whatsoever from home and himself decided never to write, so as not to grieve his mother over his *katorga*.

"Better to let her think I'm dead."

Then, one day, he turned to me with an unexpected request to write a letter home for him. Surprised, I asked why he'd suddenly changed his mind. Marmot grinned somewhat sheepishly and said:

"Who knows! There's a chance I'll get some money sent to me."

Having written the letter, I noticed that Marmot had in the meantime been losing his shirt gambling… He'd been told he'd be going to the free command. Encountering me outside the prison one time, he began happily waving and doffing his cap and shouted:

"I got a letter!"

"What did they write?" I asked out of courtesy.

"I got sent a ruble… Wife's been missin' six years now… Mother's alive 'n' well."

For a single ruble, which he immediately lost at cards, this man had not troubled himself to give his mother peace!

It was strange, however, that inside this eternally sleepy, fattened-as-if-it-were-made-for-prison head, a dream of freedom constantly wandered. Often, after I'd returned from the mine, he would approach and, smiling broadly, dancingly whisper:

"They say I, too, will be goin' to the free command soon… A present's already come."[77]

I nodded my head sympathetically and smiled at him. But what does freedom seem to mean to such a character? What is freedom to a mole, a marmot, a weasel, whose whole world consists of a burrow and for whom all in life is his food and safety?

But Marmot's appearance would be far from complete were I not to say several words more about him. Without a doubt, he embodied not only the stupidest but the best side of the prisoners' world. True, he was corrupt to the marrow; the most loathsome prison habits and perverse tastes he mastered to the full. Shelai Prison's regime did not allow prisoners to let loose completely; the population was comparatively small, everything was in view, and, when anything reached Six-Eyes's ears, he would quickly make short work of the guilty in his own way. As it was, people were therefore constrained to verbalized lusts, but it was in this regard that Marmot could outdo the rest. Although he said little, his words were always borne by his desired object. He actually gazed at women themselves from a peculiar, purely marmot point-of-view; their natural charms attracted him little... Yet, as I've already said, Marmot also had his good sides. Like the ever-present prison rat, he considered it his duty to defend prisoners' traditions and ordinances, holding high the flag of prison honor and comradeship. True, during meetings his voice was never heard and prisoners themselves called him "the grass without a name," but without such grass the prison's internal life would have immediately lost its form, and without these nameless heroes the prisoners' world would have fallen apart completely. Thus, for example, Marmot was the exclusive seller of tobacco, meat, etc., to the ward's inmates, and no one questioned his responsibilities and rights in this matter. However, I generally noticed that prison leaders, the Ivans and "throats," were in most cases limited by the goods that could be carried by a stirrup—those "watching" the guards, playing the most insignificant role in the prison, even serving as an object of ridicule, and always most dangerously near the fire. No one "snarled" at guards more ferociously than Marmot. His marmot-yapping was, in truth, very funny, and often those at whom it was directed simply laughed; but beneath the banner of this comedy he sometimes confronted one with a sharp truth that no Ivan could have divined... Such was Iashka-the-Marmot.

Apropos, I report one amusing general observation I had regarding the ward attendants of Shelai Prison. They were all precisely well-matched, all most precisely naturally suited to their craft: slumberous, clumsy, unwashed, slovenly, ragged... Hence, following Marmot, another worthy representative of this esteemed corporation was a Moldovan by the name of Ababii and by the nickname of "The Angry Cockroach." Never in my life have I seen an angry cockroach; I confess that I don't even know whether a cockroach can be angry or, if so, what form this takes; but it was only necessary to look at this small, toothless, constantly mumbling figure with long flowing mustaches to immediately appreciate in it an astoundingly precise resemblance to an angry cockroach... Only later, when Shelai Prison's administration abolished the practice of electing, and began assigning, prisoners to all prison jobs, did this corporeal being lose its universally shocking appearance.

There was another curious specimen in our ward whom I would also have probably named an herb had I discussed him earlier, though all that remains for me of his moral composition are the borders of a certain secret aureole. This was one Vladimirov. An incoherently complex chap, twenty-three years old, without a hair on his face, downcast and with a crestfallen head always hanging and seeming to dangle (wags said that it hung by a thread), he forever had a kind of sleepy look and walked like a clumsy old man. The expression on his face was at the same time strange and changeable: it could be that of a calculatingly senile seventy year-old man or, by contrast, an entirely young boy. Chirok successfully christened him Bear's Ears. Always silent and speaking in a quiet, worn voice, Vladimirov sometimes abruptly broke out of his chains and suddenly intervened in an argument and, declaiming something clearly absurd and nonsensical, shouted so loudly and with such animal-like basso that everyone plugged his ears and looked in alarm at the window panes. Vladimirov at first impressed me as a true cretin. But, among other things, he had completed two courses at the district school, wrote completely grammatically, and, when my books eventually appeared, himself undertook a course in arithmetic and algebra. In general, he had a great inclination towards mathematics: solving puzzles was his favorite occupation. At the same time, he had practically no interest in the other sciences and, as such, confirmed my low opinion of his intellectual capabilities. But then, one day, he brought me on a scrap of paper (hitherto owned by me) the following poem composed entirely by him:

O, Nature! Nature! Nature!
You have no end or beginning.
Stars simply twinkle
In your limitless unfoldings.
They shine, and burn, and float…
They float there, where is eternal gloom and cold,
Where no creatures live.
—O, I am mistaken, and I do lie!
There is another, blessèd, world
Where living creatures thrive!

This poem, I confess, moved me… I hastened to explain to Vladimirov the technique of poetry and recommended he read more. He did not take to reading in the first place, and expressed the strangest and occasionally wild views regarding extensive reading, yet continued to write poetry. He soon presented me two further productions of his muse, where the metrical demands were much more satisfactory.

I hear a voice, a voice going:
"God's free world is now, now!"
Freedom's come, my chest heaves,
And then, as tears flash
In my eyes… instead of this fate,
Sweet freedom, freedom, freedom!
Physical weakness,
Cerebral sloth,
The sermons at roll call
Really torture a man.
Days and years continue—
Will I achieve freedom?!
When my sick wife and mother

Are sheltering beneath a roof?
When will my country, my homeland,
Return my consolations to me?

Another poem, of which I remember only the first couplet:

The forest stirs and greens
        And rustles the feather-grass;
In the field the wind blows, whirls,
        Raises the dust—

did not represent anything original but bespoke an imitation of Koltsóv, Shevchenko,[78] and other populist poets. Of course, I did not see in Vladimirov's lines anything of the proffered great hopes, and I soon even completely stopped encouraging him toward further experiments, though I repeat—this discovery took me by surprise. It turned out that within this clumsy, perpetually drowsy bumpkin living side-by-side me for so long and seemingly ridiculous and dull-witted, there coursed a sufficiently complex process of ideas and feelings essentially very close and related to what I myself experienced and felt.

Physical weakness,
Cerebral sloth,
The sermons at roll call…

Akh! had this not tortured and tormented me as well?

I hear a voice, a voice going:
"God's free world is now, now!"

Was this not my secret wailing soul being overheard in so poetic an expression—and by whom? Bear's Ears!…

Vladimirov soon gave up poetry and resumed his usual physical and intellectual lethargy. His inner world closed me out and became impenetrable once more. I've never met another person so reserved. No laughter or jibes by his comrades could draw him out of himself and make him say who he was, where he'd been born, or why he'd come to *katorga*. They knew only that he'd been arrested as a vagabond in Irkutsk and, as a vagabond, been sentenced for six years to temporary mine labor without right to the free command. I even heard from Goncharov that Vladimirov was a Tobolian,[79] had been a merchant's son, and was concealing his identity, not wishing to distress his parents and hoping upon completion of *katorga* to return home a "clean" man; this may or may not have been true, but to this day I don't know what exactly brought him to Irkutsk or why he was arrested. In a moment of candor, Vladimirov himself merely told me that he had no reason to return home after finishing *katorga*, since he expected to find nothing good there, and he would try to establish himself in a settlement. But it's possible he was deceiving me and only appeared to open up, and for some reason really wanted to turn my eyes away from his true future trail—only God knows.

Vladimirov possessed a certain indubitable quality that sharply distinguished him from the rest of the herd; the latter all believed (and only about him alone) that Bear's Ears wouldn't steal a crumb from his brother prisoner or the collective; once, he was even elected to join the prison headmen. But—inhabiting his own internal world, unknowable to anyone, sitting there deciding algebraic formulae or composing verses and so little attuned to reality—he demonstrated such indifference to this desideratum that the meat in his pot turned out to be less than that of that inveterate thief the headman: cooks robbed him, he was cheated by the accountant, and soon Bear's Ears fell sick and had to be rushed to the hospital in order to forestall a general reprimand. In general, being a headman gave him a sour stomach; his incorruptible honesty was extraordinarily prized by the public opinion and he worried over every trifle in which he saw or suspected prisoners' dissatisfaction, and in this concern was extremely droll. Religious and profoundly devout, he actually reached such a bitter—but, for the outside observer, comical—moment in his life that he loudly proclaimed doubt in a living God!…

XIII. CHIROK

I vividly recall a certain evening. In the ward there was the usual talk about "our stupid gov'ment, not lettin' prisoners free, 'n' holdin' 'em their full sentences in prison 'n' controllin' ever'thin'." Someone asked me: What did I think of this? I confess, I struggled to answer such a direct question.

"Well, would you let one of us out?" Goncharov laughingly asked. "Right now, which of us would you let out?"

I glanced around and named my neighbor Kuzma Chirok, an object of universal ridicule and laughter and a completely harmless man, it seemed to me, who'd ended up in *katorga* through some judicial error. Everyone erupted into deafening laughter at my answer.

"You've found the devil! Don't y'know how many folks he's killed? Didn't he tell you? You can't tell, 'cause he's quiet 'n' gentle as a calf. There's a lotta cleverness in that Permian's head!"

"Don't believe it, Mikolaich, don't!" shouted Chirok, smirking archly and, turning to Goncharov, saying, "You spoke the complete truth, the holy truth. I woulda let an old-timer like me out a long time ago!"

"Yes! So you could lay another five down to eternal rest?"

"But did you really dispatch five, Chirok?" I asked.

"Mikolaich, they'll tell you anythin' if'n you lissen to 'em. I'm suf'rin' completely innocently."

"For what?"

"For a brother. He killed his sweetheart, 'n' I helped him box her up in her husband's cellar."

"Indeed, you buried her alive," someone said.

"Oh, you black demon! Why're you lyin'? Alive… She weren't breathin', she'd been strangled! Why'd I get sentenced to eleven years 'n' Egorsha to eighteen? I came to *katorga* jus' for hidin' a body."

"Well, brother, tell how you finished off that Cheremis."[80]

"*What* Cheremis?"

"What happened behind the hay wagon…"

"Shut up, demon, shut up! Y'know Mikolaich'll write this down…"

"No, Chirok, I won't mention what you're saying."

"You ain't lyin'?"

"I'm not lying. How did you finish him off?"

"Around the neck, o' course… How else do you finish off a scoundrel? Egorsha 'n' me 'n' another little brother, Vaska, was pilin' up hay… that is, someone else's. We piled two huge cartloads 'n' was on the way home. But we meet this Cheremis. Why was he there? What was he doin' there? So, y'know, we had to stop the scoundrel from reportin' us 'n' sendin' us to prison. So we tied his neck up with a timber-hitch."

"'N' can you tell how you bumped off that peasant for a loaf o' sugar?"

"That's what you remember. We still scared o' what happened like it's a crime?"

"Tell us anyway," I said.

"A peasant I know, three sheets to the wind, went visitin' his daddy. There he was, sittin' 'n' drinkin' vodka with daddy, 'n' us boys found a bag o' various candies in his sleigh. Whole loaf o' sugar there, some spice cakes… We only wanted to make off with the bag, but look—the lord o' the manor's comin' 'round. Could hardly walk, 'n' his daddy's leadin' him. He somehow got into the sleigh. 'Give us a ride, uncle,' we says. We get in with him 'n' go. The little horse knows the way itself 'n' was takin' us where we needed. Then I took the reins 'n' wrapped 'em round the sleepin' fellow's neck. He let out a wheeze. Then we left the horse, grabbed the bag, 'n' ran. But the horse goes home. So, it delivers his body. Well, daddy, as he shoulda, figured it out 'n' comes callin' 'n' threat'nin' us with the knout: 'You killed him, you sons-o'-bitches!' But no one knew. The drunk ran o'er his own reins, that was all."

"But how old were you then, Chirok?"

"I was eleven, 'n' Egorsha was eight."

"'N', for sure, you strangled more? Well done, Kuzma!"

"'N' he knows 'ow to use a hatchet, boys," approved Marmot. "Kuzma, tell 'ow you split that other peasant's noggin with an axe."

"Oh, you foul scoundrel! You lousy creature!"

"No, tell it, brother, tell it, since you've started," the whole ward was shouting, "'n' if you don't, it'll be for the worse. Hey, Iron Cat! You'll hafta give 'im a grindin'!"

"To grind"—this meant tickling the heels, which Chirok mortally feared. He instantly sprang to his feet and began running along the plank beds, threatening everyone with his powerful fists.

"Jus' you bring it on!" he rhythmically shouted. "I'll show you! The old-fashioned way…"

But enemies came from all sides. Nikifor, Semënov, and Iron Cat went for his sides; Paramon advanced directly, terribly, decisively… Chirok, back to a corner, readied himself for a hot fight, but Marmot suddenly somehow knocked him off his feet, everyone flew at him and piled on, and after long and dogged resistance on the sleeping platform they "nailed the horseshoes." Chirok was meanwhile yelling so mercilessly that his mouth had to be stopped up to keep the guard from hearing. Chirok finally begged for mercy and, coughing and swearing, sat down in his spot to tell how he split the peasant with an axe.

"What's to tell? It was 'cause of a bound'ry dispute. He came at me with banners wavin'… I'm wonderin', what's all the bawlin' about? I grabbed the axe from him 'n' clopped him straight on the noggin. Bastard gave up the ghost right there. I got sent straight to court 'cause there was witnesses."

"Note this, Mikolaich: what kind of a soul is this?"

"Still has one. Last night he told me… First…," interrupted Paramon, but Chirok began pummeling him so fiercely and such a row erupted between them again that the guard came to the peep hole and shouted at the combatants. Row quieted, the conversation came to an end, and little-by-little the majority fell asleep. Only Chirok, Paramon, and Iron Cat, having gathered on the blacksmith's spot on the opposite sleeping platform, still sat for a long time with legs folded Turkish-style, puffing cigars and pipes until sometime late into the night and speaking to each other in half-whispers. Chirok was now talking about his youth… Fragments of these stories reached me and I often shuddered at the enveloping horror, though, by contrast, sometimes I was prepared to laugh most deeply and heartily.

Chirok's personality was in general a rather odd mix of the serious and the joking, the comic and the tragic, the purely childishly naïve and open-hearted with the most clever cunning and slyness. His gray eyes, always gazing curiously from the wrinkles of a knitted brow and the corners of a large, awkward mouth set off by hard, ruddy lips, gleamed with innate intelligence and craftiness; yet, at the same time, something so simple and good emanated from this pale, lean face with its long, horse-like cranium, from the whole of this simply cut figure, frumpy from head-to-toe, that one rarely disliked Chirok. As an object of perpetual and universal ridicule, and now and then returning the abuse like the coarsest drayman, Kuzma was, even in a moment of rage, essentially harmless, and the most terrible of his curses merely elicited laughter. He was a great sage and master of swear words; they were almost always on his tongue, but, on his lips they were not as terrible as those on, for example, Semënov's, nor had they the cynicism of Marmot's. During the several years of life together in Shelai Prison I grew strongly attached to Chirok, and among the many upsets and events of all sorts that caused me more than once to change my opinion of other prisoners, Chirok forever remained in my eyes the very same harmless and kind-hearted Chirok, the same faithful and loyal friend, never discomfiting himself with prisoner's squabbles. Yet, among other things, this same buffoon Chirok had, while at large, dispatched a dozen souls to the other world, and now felt not the slightest regret about this…

For a long time, I couldn't understand why they teased him about (among other things) Sakhalin, saying he'd soon be delivered there to his sister. I thought this no more than a joke; but, listening one time to secret nighttime whispers, I learned from the mouth of Chirok himself the following explanations for this ridicule:

"I was really done in 'cause o' Lukeika. Even as a thrifty hay-girl she was a pure thief. Her eyes was big, as they say, 'n' terrible… When she was seventeen she hooked up with the vagabond Senka Pelevin 'n' started fixin' deals! I didn't bother with that crew 'cause I was tryin' to be more relaxed: they'd crawl into someone's shed or barn, grab some sheep or geese… Where'er there was hay, where'er there was firewood… Well, I weren't too squeamish 'bout wheat 'n' carp, neither…" His listeners laughed quietly.

"So, y'know, murder was bound to happen. So, I drummed up a little hitch-knot or some mercury chloride."

The others laughed again.

"I was a suspect, o' course, a suspect in many cases, only, they couldn't investigate me that time. Once, they turned up with a search warrant. I'd stolen three sheep from my neighbor, had cured the meat 'n' sold the skins… 'N' I was startin' to chop up one o' my own sheep. 'Ah,' they say, 'here's the meat!' I say: 'This here's my sheep, 'n' Timoshkin's little skin is hangin' up o'er there.' My sheep had been named Timoshka. They say, 'Sure, 'n' there's eight kidneys in one sheep?' 'Good Lord,' I say, 'it was *such* a big, fat sheep…' With that they left, 'n' didn't take away nuthin'.'"

"Well, but did your God-given brother-in-law 'n' little sister wind up doin' such things?"

"No. Those decided to kill 'n' rob a certain ol' lady. Seventy versts from us was a rich ol' lady livin' jus' like a nun with an adopted daughter. They went there, killed 'em both, cleaned the place out 'n' left, 'n' was walkin' away, as is customary. They got arrested 'n' convicted on suspicion. Lukeika got twenty years 'n' Pelevin life. Both got assigned to Sakhalin. Their case had jus' finished when Egorkino's came up. If Lukeikina hadn't committed murder I prob'ly wouldn't-a been convicted. But that *procuror* was a hardliner: 'you so-'n'-so,' says he, 'if your sister's such a criminal then her brother must be an e'en worse criminal.' It was 'cause o' her, that rascal, 'cause o' that snake in the grass, I copped eleven years!"

"But what's the scar on your head for? We're to think it was all outta your hands, as you say?"

"That's it precisely, fellas: I was stumblin' about so many times I 'appened to taste glory. One night, me 'n' Egorsha was gettin' some flour. I'd set him to watch with the horses, 'n' nose-by-nose, unnerstand, I'm gettin' the sacks from the barn. Only, Egorka notices ever'thin's quiet, no one's there, 'n' he opens his trap: standin' there with his finger in his nose… 'cause he was still young 'n' stupid! There I am, haulin' a sack on my back… Suddenly, it was like someone knocked me on the head with a flag pole!… I'm on my back, seein' red 'n' green stars. Like when someone fires a rifle—pheasant all 'round… I drop the sack 'n' grab a log (thankfully, a log's lyin' nearby), 'n' stand up 'n' look. But, *he's* standin' 'n' lookin' at me, too. As should be, he was scared stiff, too."

"I daresay, you shoulda been scared o' that demon, what with his flag pole!"

"I 'member then how fast I ran! I yelled to Egorsha, we got in the telega—'n' off to home! My head was cracked badly… The blood was gushin'! When they came to investigate, I jus' told 'em: 'the horse,' I says, 'kicked me.'"

Broken now and then by suppressed laughter and individual listeners' observations, such whisperings continued on Iron Cat's sleeping platform for a long time. Terrible shapes and bestial, bloody scenes played out before me, weaving into a single gruesome phantasmagoria. Lukeika with her fiery orbs instead of eyes, killing the old lady and little girl and travelling to Sakhalin with her vagabond-lover; ten-year-old children being strangled in a drunken peasant's looped rope; Chirok stealing hay and then murdering the Cheremis witness… A timber-hitch, reins, axe, mercury chloride… Blows to the head similar to shots from a rifle… Wheat flour, carp, logs, Timoshkino's skin and eight kidneys… Blood, jail, *katorga*… The storyteller's cunning face, the listeners' sympathetic laughter… I finally fell asleep; but in my dreams the same visions continued, the same bloody nightmares poured out. I tried to save myself from them, I was running and gasping for air… Luckily, I was passing by a guard with a bayonet, I was running past a foyer with an old night-watchman suspiciously looking out of it at me, I was running through a bog, along a hill… Suddenly, having stumbled, I was falling into the depths of a dark, cold mine shaft! The air was whistling past my shivering body, and there came another person's strange, hateful whispering: "Aha! You're fallin', dearie!…" Just then, I hit one of the granite ledges and my skull smashed to pieces…

"Ah!…"

I awoke, entirely bathed in sweat and mortally terrified. I heard in the corridor the guard's whistles and shouts: "Fall out for roll call!" The windows were still dark but the grueling *katorga* day had already commenced and my neighbors, yawning and stretching, lazily began getting up.

XIV. LUCHEZAROV

One Sunday morning in December, a breathless Marmot burst into the ward with news that I'd been called to the gates. Beneath the gates I learned from the orderly that the commander had summoned me to his quarters.

"Perhaps to his office?" I asked.

"No, ordered to quarters."

A Cossack was discharged to me and I went with him to the brave staff captain.

"You're entering through the back steps?" asked the Cossack, revealing a certain perplexity.

But I decided to go up the front steps and to ring the bell. This, however, turned out to take a long time. Eventually, a woman appeared and, upon seeing a prisoner, vigorously slammed the door and cried:

"Why're you loafin' round the front porch? Master'll be angry."

Confused, I was properly directed to the rear steps and entered through the kitchen. Several female characters were squabbling there. Upon my entrance they fell silent.

"Whaddya want?" rudely asked one with an elderly face and sleeves rolled high, evidently the cook. I told her. They left to announce us.

"The master's ordered you to his cabinet," the housemaid who'd chased me from the front porch informed me in surprise. The Cossack and I followed her down a long and dark corridor, along the sides of which open doors revealed rooms with basins and flower vases in windows and vivid oil paintings—the subjects of which I could not discern—hanging in every corner on the walls. "Here," pointed the housemaid, and I timidly entered a small room floored with carpets and occupied by glass cases of books and various papers. In a large armchair behind a writing desk sat Luchezarov himself. Having heard the noise, he rose from his place and quickly walked straight up to me.

"Ah!" he drawled, his round eyes inquisitively fixing upon me and a contented smile covering his face, ruddy and radiating healthiness.

"Only in recent days have I," he had to confess, "recognized that… completely by chance… a prisoner with higher education is here in my prison."

I confess to having been surprised by this casual lie on the part of the brave staff captain: from my communications with relatives alone, not to mention my prison records, he must have known from the very beginning my social status prior to conviction.

"I value education," he continued familiarly, "though I suppose it's not the most important thing for a Russian. It highly disciplines the mind and character. Honestly, I fail to understand how a person with higher education can end up in *katorga*?"

Such a turn of conversation was difficult for me, and I evasively responded that my sentence was of course detailed in my records.

"Oh, yes, needless to say," said Luchezarov, "I know, I read it… But all the same, there could have been a judicial mistake, perhaps mitigating circumstances, something that escaped attention…"

"No," I dryly interrupted, "as I understand Russian laws, I was convicted completely fairly."

"Indeed?…" Luchezarov gave me a searching look for several moments, smiling, as before, ironically. Then his face suddenly became stern and official. He quickly turned on his heel towards the table and said:

"A parcel's been received… It's strictly for this I called you."[81]

Until that moment he had in addressing me used no personal pronoun, neither the informal nor the formal "you," evidently hesitating between them as if to reconnoiter the ground; but he had now suddenly banished hesitation and spoken thoroughly courteously.

"Books have arrived in your name… From your mother.[82] Judging by her letters, she would seem to be a wonderful person. You may know I dislike nervous ladies, always whining and sentimental. But she's not like that at all. Such cheerfulness, even joy, emanates from her letters. A completely masculine temperament. Yes, these are the books she mailed you. I myself once loved to read, but now, of course, I've fallen out of habit. I'm up to my neck in business and am never idle. The choice of books, I might say, is not bad; these are generally known names. Your mother herself writes that she tried to choose classics."

"Does this mean I can receive them?" I rushed forward.

"W-well, let's say this still doesn't mean so," Luchezarov answered, and quickly frowned.

"How so?"

"May you know: I unfortunately do not have completely clear and concise instructions regarding prisoners' reading of books. I like precision in all things. I'm a soldier; I want that each of my steps be proper and correct. If I've stepped with my left foot, then it's understood I'll follow by raising my right, and not hopping on that same left foot. Thus, for example, I have the most detailed and indubitable instructions regarding how to conduct roll call, labor, and what should be the prisoners' relations towards the administration, their rations, and so on."

"However," I couldn't restrain myself, "in the instructions posted in the prison it doesn't say, for example, that purchasing food with one's own money is prohibited, yet you prohibit this?"

"Yes, perhaps… If you like, you're right: the point is insufficiently clearly stated in the instructions. That will be done! Do you know the level of intelligence of most of those who copy out these instructions? You're right: there are many omissions. But the prohibition on private rations flows logically from the entire *katorga* regime. In the instructions it says precisely and down to the letter exactly what the prisoner gets from the treasury: how much meat, how much bread. Evidently, the law recognizes this quantity of food as completely sufficient."

"Perhaps it does not recognize it as sufficient at all, but the treasury is not wealthy enough to provide more."

"W-well, I don't think this is… In the end, this accords with my personal beliefs: the *katorga* regime should be just like the food regime. A soldier—mark this: a soldier!—receives little more from the treasury. It's abnormal. Yes, yes! I will petition, I will insist before the governor that this point of the instruction be outlined precisely and exactly according to my orders. Prisoners come to *katorga* not to sleep but to suffer and endure retribution. No, no, you still don't know these artists; double their bread and rations and they'll pour like a wave into prison! A bridle is necessary and strict limits are needed on everything and, among them, rations. I repeat, this is my profound belief…"

I looked at Luchezarov's flushed face radiating healthiness, at his round belly and sufficiently prominent chest, and understood that such was actually his honest and profound belief… But something inside me was boiling, and this something pushed me to make one or two more objections.

"But it is really… inhuman," I said, "to exist on the same food for many, many years, performing difficult work without having freedom—it is unthinkable! People will inevitably weaken and become sick. Can prisoners and soldiers really be equated? Soldiers are the best pick of people, the healthiest portion of the youth, whereas prisoners are people of all ages and all possible degrees of healthiness. Soldiers are not exhausted like them by long preliminary detentions in prison, and they anyway receive large rations. Finally, they're not forbidden to spend their own money. It seems to me your 'food regime' amounts to a slow death penalty for us, which is hardly what the law intends!"

Having apparently listened very attentively, Luchezarov frowned and even nodded his head sympathetically.

"All this may be so," he answered, shrugging his shoulders, "but… there's one way out of here: don't end up in *katorga*."

He had substantially lowered his voice and was smiling pleasantly. I stopped arguing.

"What was it you wanted to say about the books?"

"Yes, the books!" Luchezarov joyfully ejaculated. "I want to say that I find myself in great difficulty. I am, you may see, a man who is, in essence, not cruel, and I hope this will become evident as you become more familiar with me. I would even be pleased to give you a certain surprise: I can see you want these books very much. But… as before, I must say that my arms and legs are tied by the regulations. But the authors of Shelai's regulations certainly did not foresee prisoners such as you finding themselves here. As a matter of fact, where and when does a prisoner interest himself with reading? Mercy, don't these artists really need a little book! Hence, in the regulations, I read only: 'They are permitted books of religious and moral content.' Even that's not right: there's no conjunction 'and'! It says: 'religious-moral content,' but since books of religious-*im*moral content are impossible I regard this as a simple slip of the pen, and have voluntarily inserted the conjunction 'and.'"

Not believing in the brave staff captain's proffered comparison, I went against my conscience and hastened to affirm that this proposal was completely appropriate and well-founded.

"Oh, yes! I've thought much about this… I've thought about it day and night… I do believe I'm right. Thus, except for purely religious books, the law also permits books of moral content. But there's the rub! I'll frankly admit to you that I will refuse to be the judge of the moral or immoral books sent to you. Of course, at some point I, too, read and memorized all these Gogols and Shakespeares, though it was very long ago… I've already forgotten so much. Yes, in my opinion, it's not worth memorizing every piece of rubbish. Reading all these now would be like new—thank you very much! I don't have time for this. This is the first thing. But second and most important: what on the outside may be called moral reading could for those sitting in prison have an entirely different impression! You know what they'd say—what's this about Gogol? Take, for example, *Dead Souls*… It's true, I don't remember. Won't they find something of an allegory there? It can't be said that the censorship would allow it…"

I warmly defended Gogol, arguing that it came from one of the most moral Russian writers, was a classic universally allowed in middle and lower schools; I also explained the existence in Russia of the 1865 law, by which the majority of books are published without preliminary censorship.

"All this may be so, and so on," Luchezarov nodded his head, "but please tell me why you need these books. Apparently, you know almost all of them by heart. Honestly, do you intend to read them to the prisoners?"

I answered that I actually had this goal in mind, and began broadly developing my view on artistic literature's educational role, saying that the reading of good books and the development of higher intellectual interests in prisoners may reform them sooner and better than all regulations, restrictions, etc.

This idea astonished Luchezarov, and we fell into a lively argument.

"Of course," he said, "reforming prisoners is a good thing. I've set this goal for myself; but this is the first time I've heard there may be a way other than terror to deal with these people. Strictly speaking, for a long time I've not been an admirer of, for example, corporal punishment; I've said this more than once to prisoners themselves. If you like, I'm actually opposed on principle to the lash and the birch rod: what use are they? What do they matter for such prisoners? The arsenal of punitive measures in my hands is sufficient without these… I repeat, I am by nature not at all a cruel man. I strictly adhere to legality, to the letter of the law, in all things. Therefore, I don't envisage other means of reform save those instructions issued me. Contemporary prison planners recognize only one method—terror, and I fully agree with them. All these other things you're telling me are still mere guesswork… No! you cannot get through to such a commoner using these books. I've been living in Siberia for ten years now and know him better than you do. They are rotten canaille down to the marrow! However, you may try. Towards elucidation of this problem for the higher administration, I'll probably give you some of these books. They won't fully avail themselves of them, of course, but I think there'll be no special harm…"

"Nevertheless, which of these books will you give me?"

"Certain ones. Well, take these, perhaps. Gogol in two volumes, Pushkin, Lermontov… Though poetry, in my opinion, is completely unsuitable for prison… Well, let it be so, for the time being… *Othello, King Lear*—I don't remember these, but I suppose they're alright. Kostomarov, Mordovtsev…[83] historical… Well, I suppose. But these foreign writers here I can't give you: Hugo, Dickens… I confess I don't know them at all. No, no, I can't! And don't ask!"

"But why forbid Flammarion?"[84]

"Isn't this about heaven, the stars?… No, this can in no possible way be given out. Heaven, you may know, is a ticklish thing… I don't want to assume the role of spiritual censor at all… And understand that you will write your mother that she will send no more books. What for? These are enough."

I bowed and hurried toward the exit with the pile of books in my hands. Luchezarov courteously ushered me to the front porch himself. I flew toward the prison, not feeling my feet beneath me for joy, frightened every second that the brave staff captain would suddenly repent and order me back. But he'd already become interested in something else, I could hear, as he was loudly shouting at someone:

"Why this mess? Why's there litter in the courtyard? You well know I don't like this. It should be noticed and cleaned up. Do you want to go to the isolator?"

In the prison yard, I was surrounded by a crowd of prisoners.

"Books, Nikolaich? Books, m'boys!"

"Mikolaich, come, come o'er to us in the second barracks… We want one, the tiniest one!"

"Ohh, whatta heckuva book… Boys, there should be a lotta smarts in that one! Who wouldn't git tired writin' *that*?"

"To us! To us!"

"You're gonna get torn to pieces, Mikolaich. In all our wards Grishka alone knows how to read jus' a little."

"Spare me a little book now, Ivan Nikolaich, one now, for Chrissakes!"

"'N' you're more saintly than the rest?"

"Stop, stop, gentlemen, I'll satisfy you all. We'll distribute fairly. Come to my barracks."

With uproar, din, and tramping nearly the entire prison burst into my ward and surrounded me and the books.

"Now don't go for the books, boys! Give Ivan Nikolaevich a chance, see, he's sweatin' buckets… You'll still be satisfied!" said collective headman Iukhorev, an athletic man with an imposing and energetic physiognomy sitting next to me and pushing aside the impertinent, clambering herd. "Read somethin' to us now, Nikolaich," he ordered.

"Now! Now!" everyone simultaneously droned. I took one of the Pushkin volumes and opened to "The Bandit Brothers."[85] Everyone slowly quieted down. I began:

This is no flock of crows that's flown
To a breast of smoldering bones—
Past the Volga, at night, a gang
Collected round the fires of the courageous.
What a mix of clothes and faces,
Tribes, dialects, and fortunes!

"It's 'bout us!" several voices suddenly shouted. All faces had become animated and taken on a daring expression.

In winter, deep at night,
We'd harness a daring troika,

We'd drink and whistle like an arrow
Flying over the snowy depths.

During these words some of the prisoners tried to break into a dance. Iukhorev barked
at them; but when I began reading further:

Who hasn't feared our encounter?
We've spotted candles in a tavern—
Over there! towards the gate, we knock,
Loudly summoning the keeper,
And enter—everything's for free: we drink, eat
And fondle the beautiful girls!—

he himself suddenly jumped from his spot, crossed his arms, stamped his feet, and in a fit
of delight uttered such words that I had to stop in embarrassment.

"Goodness, that's how I was with Marva in Olëkma!"[86] he shouted. "Goodness,
that's us!"

I confess I absolutely did not expect such a surprise. I became ashamed for both
myself and for Pushkin… Most of all for myself, of course, since I'd chosen for a debut
such an unfortunate thing, not having imagined I'd be dealing with such an audience. I
wanted to stop and read something else, but there was such uproar that I was forced to
finish "The Bandit Brothers." However, the guard appeared amid the din.

"What's this mob for?" he shouted. "To the wards! D'you wanna get locked in again?"

Iukhorev and other prisoners ran to talk to him and smooth things over.

"You yourself can hear how we're havin' a lecture. Nikolaich is readin', 'n', y'know, it's
so enjoyable! Don't worry: the com'dant hisself sent these books, y'know."

The guard fell silent and approached the table out of curiosity as well. I resumed "The
Bandit Brothers." Upon the poem's conclusion there was, of course, little happiness: in a
moment a cloud of grief and reverie crossed over the faces of even my reckless listeners.

But this lasted only a moment. Everyone quickly brightened up again and became
enraptured by the tale's beginning. The guard then ordered prisoners to the wards. Arms
reached out at me from everywhere, begging for the books. Very many demanded "The
Bandit Brothers."

"I'll mem'rize it by heart, Ivan Nikolaevich!" enthusiastically shouted Rakitin, having
only just begun the alphabet.

I distributed all the books, keeping the Pushkin for my ward.

XV. GREAT POETS FACE THE *KATORGA* TRIBUNAL

On that first evening nearly all the wards continued reading until midnight, so that the guard came to the doors several times and ordered the audience to go to sleep. I was seriously alarmed that this circumstance would reach Luchezarov and he would take away the books. Fortunately, it was a liberal period; the guards had not for a long time been adhering to the originally strict punctuality, and no report ensued. I read Pushkin to my neighbors all evening until I became hoarse. Of the entire ward only Goncharov, whose practical mind struggled in vain to maintain attention, quickly fell asleep. Nikifor and Marmot fell asleep considerably later. Everyone else listened with absorbed interest and was prepared to the very end to give me no trouble. Chirok was nervous and unusually funny in his curiosity. He sat beside me all evening, raptly attentive, with an extremely sly expression in his gray eyes and a deeply furrowed brow. From an abundance of sensations he continually fidgeted on the sleeping platform and scratched his belly… Malakhov listened importantly and stolidly but, also unable to contain his delight, clapped his hand on his thigh and emitted child-hearted laughs and, more frequently, other expressions. Gandorin, Semënov, Vladimirov, and Mikhaila Burenkov listened attentively, albeit silently. The somnolent Marmot gazed wide-eyed and constantly uttered his usual rejoinder: "All the better!"—typically completely inappropriately. This first time the students listened attentively, but friction subsequently arose between them and the ward: the students selfishly preferred to read, the wards to listen to me reading. There was a lot of absurdity because of this, though some difficult episodes at time.

Pushkin entertained and was understood by almost all without exception. The greatest success, however, was enjoyed by "Boris Godunov," *The Captain's Daughter*, and "Dubrovskii." Among other things, the famous scene in the tavern elicited such irrepressible joy and laughter that many were rolling along the sleeping platform in convulsions. Meanwhile, Iashka-the-Marmot was nearly dying, and Malakhov had to jam a fist into his throat every minute so that the reading could go on. Godunov's personality was so well comprehended by everyone that they later began calling a certain prisoner by his name, and in Shelai Prison it came to be generally used as a synonym for any hypocrisy or intrigue. Yet, alongside good impressions from recital of these Pushkin works there remain gloomy, difficult memories for me. The horrible scene of Fëdor and Ksenia's murder in "Boris Godunov" brought forth recognition and happiness in some listeners.

"Ah, the vermin, they was howlin'!…" Chirok said, and was supported by Marmot, who began laughing more ignorantly. I recall many such instances, when some tragic, soul-arresting moment elicited from prisoners a sudden burst of joy and cynicism… This circumstance at first drove me to despair, and I remembered Luchezarov's mocking smile as he handed me the books:

"You won't reach them with these little books!"

During recitation of *The Captain's Daughter*, "Dubrovskii," and even "Boris Godunov" some of them said with sincere conviction:

"That was quite a time!… What if we'd had such kasha… Chirok, we coulda warmed our hands."

"The long-hairs, the long-hairs woulda had to comb their manes!" Chirok argued in a tone of deep conviction.

Prisoners in similar conversations generally evinced hatred toward clergymen. The latter were unpopular among everyone, all *katorga* residents to a man, and I was never able to successfully fathom the reasons for this visceral hatred. Once, I was reciting by heart to my neighbors what I remembered of that section of "Who Lives Well in Rus?"[87] dedicated to defending clergymen. Most of the ward, it seemed, agreed with the poet's idea; but after a certain time the earlier conversation and earlier put-downs of the clergy reemerged… One world-weary prisoner (the same who'd acquired the sobriquet "Godunov") expressed particular hatred and bitterness toward priests, yet during his detailed retailing of his personal past I discovered, among other things, not a single instance of any conflict between him and this class. This is a sort of tradition of hostility that gets passed from one generation of prisoners to another, in parallel to which may be posed the enmity towards medics and physicians.

But no reader can imagine that Pushkin's best works have a demoralizing influence on all prisoners. I mean only certain personalities; and of these it can be said that the individual and cynical comments they made during readings were more a matter of habit and thoughtlessness: it was not because of this, but rather for another reason, that these comments would have been made all the same, during readings or absent readings, as a result of their tongues' habitual lack of restraint. In essence, they revealed absolutely nothing. On different evenings the very same Chirok spoke completely contrarily, expressing indignation at the murder of Fëdor and Ksenia, and in general he seemed even more than others the defender of strict morality and humaneness. What would he not have supported, since, as for a child, everything was for him sincere in the extreme. This touches on the inappropriate laughter and jokes during the most tragic spots in the reading, jokes that naturally exasperated and jarred me insofar as they demonstrated only one thing—the backwardness of their aesthetic taste; but to make on the basis of these some sort of universal conclusions about the fruitlessness of the readings would be unfair. True, various hopelessly depraved individuals, having encountered each other, conspired to eke out still more overflowing bitterness, filth, and cynicism here, there, and everywhere: and such listeners often spoiled the impact of the most irreproachable works and, through their example, infected the unspoiled portion of the audience; but the majority—I assert this unequivocally—always gave themselves straight over to that mood which the author had pursued, and received the same impression as normal readers and listeners receive.

I remember not a few instances when hopeless cynics and scoundrels were, in turn, infected by the majority's good-humored attitude, and in a completely healthy and civil fashion joined in the argument. I cannot forget the heartfelt nervousness with which I began reading *King Lear* and *Othello*, the only Shakespeare works I had with me. I thought the great poet would suffer complete defeat in this environment, and that if he didn't appear deathly boring, then it would only be thanks to a certain melodramatic plot and by no means the depth of psychological analysis and everything more that Shakespeare captures for educated humanity. But what was my surprise when both tragedies generated unprecedented (and, for me, unforeseen) furor, as roughly understood as they were! True, the audience's attitude was reserved, even cold, during the reading of *Othello*'s first two acts; despair soon began creeping into my soul: extraneous conversations could be heard here and there and, contrary to usual, the majority wasn't trying to stop them. Semënov alone struck me with a surprisingly piercing observation regarding Iago, whom he saw through after the first scene:

"Well, he's foolin' 'em all!"

But the attitude suddenly changed with the beginning of the third act; a real electrical current ran through the ward.

"It's startin' to make sense," said Chirok, jumping to his feet.

Soon, many were jumping up one after the other from the sleeping platforms and surrounding me with burning eyes. The drama was making a staggering impression. Upon the reading's conclusion everyone started talking and making a fuss… They pitied Desdemona (whose name, unfortunately, no one could pronounce correctly), they pitied Othello; they cursed "Iaga" with one voice and surmised about the torture Cassio devised for him. In a word, the power and strength of profoundly great works of art was revealed with the utmost brilliance during the reading of Shakespeare. *King Lear* made nearly the same powerful impression, and after these two dramas there was a greater demand for readings.

Each time circumstances alone seared me to the depths of my soul. In most cases the impression that was made simply evaporated some half hour (and even this is too long) after the reading, and conversation returned to something superfluous and quotidian, so that what had been read served at times as simply an extraneous, purposeless exercise. After a half hour they would be speaking completely contrarily to what had come out in the first gush of impression. Hence, almost everyone pitied (I remember this well) Desdemona, saying that Othello had strangled her wrongly, but after only an hour they were cursing women in general and wives in particular, asserting that even when innocent they should be strangled like dogs. After priests and doctors prisoners cursed women most of all, and if every word was to be believed it could have been imagined the world had created no more terrible women-haters! Paramon Malakhov, whose entire life, in his own words, he destroyed for a woman, was especially indignant over them. Pursuant to Othello, I remember I came to learn his story of the double murder for which he came to *katorga*.[88]

He lived for three years without rights in Irkutsk Province, working, as he was now, as a cooper. There he fell in love with a certain girl, a local peasant's adopted daughter. There were dark rumors about how the peasant lived with his adopted daughter, but Paramon dismissed these rumors and simply took the girl's word that whatever had happened between her and her father in the past, there would be nothing of this in the future and she would be his faithful wife. The wedding cost Paramon, in his words, seventy-five rubles, and he placed enormous significance on this fact. The young newlyweds lived joyfully and lovingly for the first three months, but then rumors about Katerina and her father began circulating once more. Paramon beat her once, and beat her again, telling her not to be naughty. Then one unbeautiful day, she ran away to her father for good… Neighbors began laughing at Paramon. Added to his sense of insult was the sorrow of money spent in vain.

"The very next Sunday," Paramon told me, "I dressed in my Sunday clothes 'n' went to talk sharply 'bout the matter with my father-in-law. There was only one thing I wanted to know: would Katerina change her mind 'n' stop with her debauchery, or break with me completely, 'n' then would they gimme back my money. As for murder, I was o' two minds 'bout this, 'n' so it was only for a possibility that I was packin' a knife on my shin. I ran into both of 'em on the street, in front o' their house: they was comin' back from mass at church. I go up to 'em. 'Stepan, you so-'n'-so,' I says, 'I wanna have a word with you,' 'n' he came o'er. 'I know why you wanna to talk with me,' he says. 'For my part, that there's my business only. If she don't wanna live with you—what can I do?' 'Katerina,' I says, 'come 'ere 'n' tell me yourself.' I call her a little to the side, 'n' say this calm 'n' quiet like. But, for God's sake, 'n' I ain't lyin', she didn't have a single dumb idea in her head! She, the piece o' filth… she grabs her lover's hand 'n' dances off to home. 'No,' he says, 'I don't wanna, 'n' *we* ain't gonna talk 'bout it.' That fired my heart with boilin' blood. I grab her by the hand as well 'n' pull her towards me. So we're standin' there in the middle o' the street—right there, 'pon my honor, it's the truth!—I'm holdin' onto one hand, he's got the other. Then she turns to me 'n' says: 'Get outta here, you scoundrel, or I'll scream or spit in your face.'

"'Ah! so *I'm* a scoundrel?!' I bend down, grab the knife offa my shin, 'n'—one! two!—jam that little devil of a knife into her chest twice. He, her lover, comes after me… I grabbed him 'n' he got the knife in his belly. He fell on the ground 'n' gave up the ghost right there. But Katerina… That wolf had such life she managed to run to the door of her hut. Then I caught up to her 'n' stuck her once more in the back: die, you snake in the grass!…"

His listeners were without exception in absolute rapture over Paramon's action and urged him on with warm approval: she deserved it, the bitch. You couldn't live honestly—so you're eatin' dirt. Lie down with your lover 'n' kiss each other!

Questions as to what internal drama may have occurred in Katerina's soul, what reasons pushed her to break with her legal husband, popped into no one's head. No one had a shadow of doubt that her marriage with Paramon had a single goal—to serve as a cover—and that she was deceiving him all during those six months he was her suitor and those five months he was her husband.

"She died the next mornin'," Malakhov was continuing his story. "The whole village, ever'one to a man, stood behind me 'n' didn't e'en want me arrested. 'Such a man as you,' they said, 'shouldn't run.' I myself insisted I be arrested. Katerina, it turned out, was carryin', though I still don't know from who, him or me, 'n' I was tried for triple murder: for her, her lover, 'n' the little one. In court I told ever'thin' truthfully, ever'thin' as it happened, didn't hide nuthin', 'n' e'en the judges sympathized with me… Although they sentenced me to six years, I consider that an acquittal. Six years for three souls—*that's* an acquittal! I acted righteously—killed 'em for the insult, for the shame, for my money! I acted honor'bly!"

I tried to interject several words condemning murder in general, but these only completely incensed Paramon, and he, not wishing to listen to me, pathetically exclaimed:

"I acted correctly! Anyone would say: '*Good man* Paramon! *Artist* Paramon! *Hero* Paramon!'"

"It's possible that's so," I answered. "I really do not hate you. I'm only saying it would nevertheless have been better not to murder."

"No, killin' was necessary!" Paramon, turning beet red, shouted, energetically tugging at his huge black beard and beating his chest with his fist. "Murder was necessary, 'n' the whole world would say: '*Well done* Paramon! *Eagle* Paramon! *Othello* Paramon!'"

I stopped arguing, and Malakhov beamed in a glow of triumph and victory. All the prisoners were definitively on his side, and Goncharov, having also witnessed the unusual stupidity and baseness of women, did not fail to tell something of his own life apropos this. Someone else, provoking universal laughter and merriment in the ward, then told how he'd one day finished off his lover like an animal...

"I got her in the side, under the rib, in the pussy, in the belly, again in the side..."

I plugged my ears so I couldn't hear. However, after some time I posed Semënov the question how, in his opinion, should a husband behave towards his wife, and what should he do in case of her infidelity?

Semënov was surprised.

"But should she really be forgiven? So that she, the dog, should laugh at me? Indeed, better I chop off her head, the wolf, jus' for suspectin' her of it."

"And you, Vladimirov, what do you think?" I turned to our poet, who'd been silent the whole time and, it seemed, was dreamily lying on the sleeping platform thinking and musing over God knows what. Bear's Ears, as usual, stayed quiet for a long time and refused to answer, saying he knew and thought nothing, but then jumped suddenly from his spot, twisted his head, and spoke so loudly it seemed to threaten my eardrums:

"But, o' course she should be killed!... A wife should obey... A husband shouldn't fear his wife!"

The conversation ended on an absolutely comical note when we heard Marmot suddenly say that he, when he returned home, would also "instantly" murder his wife if he learned she'd been unfaithful.

Upon a single glance at this filthy, grease-swollen and fat figure of a creature who also dreamed of performing his own Othello, everyone burst out laughing and began cutting him down to size.

"'N' you got a wife? Ain't conjured her up in a dream?"

"Ain't you married to that pack o' cards that's in our pigsty?"

"No, boys, he's married to that eye-catchin' little bitch what's runnin' round behind our prison. She came to *katorga* for him."

Marmot grew angry and, as he did, gnawed at himself. He couldn't parry jokes with jokes.

I've since failed to understand the fact that in Shelai Prison Lermontov was undoubtedly more popular than Pushkin. If I'd been previously asked my own opinion as to which of the two poets the prisoners would value and like better, I would not of course have hesitated to name Pushkin. To my surprise, Lermontov not only didn't bore anyone, but even snippets of his lyrical poetry pleased them more than anything that could be said of Pushkin. It goes without saying that it's another question as to how accurately they understood them, but the fact is that we read Lermontov more often than Pushkin and they more willingly talked about him. True, they listened to "The Demon" the first time very coldly, evidently understanding absolutely nothing; but several days later, something I absolutely could not understand happened: for some reason they were suddenly mad for "The Demon," such that they were prepared to listen to it every evening… A certain half-Russian Tatar named Ravilov especially admired this poem; he and many others memorized separate parts of it by heart. Whether it was the charming music of Lermontov's verse or the titanic form of the poem's hero that made such an impression, I can't say. For some reason, "The Boyar Orsha" and "Mtsyri"[89] produced less enthusiasm; on the other hand, "Song of the Merchant Kalashnikov" was able to strongly compete with "The Demon." Upon release to settlement certain prisoners planned to subscribe to the books, and when, asking me about prices, they learned that Lermontov and Pushkin cost nearly the same, they gleefully shouted they would purchase Lermontov first… These words were possibly never carried out (for either Lermontov or Pushkin!), but most important is their regard for both poets. They loved Pushkin as well, and undoubtedly understood him even better, but preferred Lermontov nevertheless. Among other things, his youthful melodrama "The Spaniards" enjoyed great success, perhaps because it responded to the prisoners' general hostility towards the clergy, about which I've already spoken. As is known, this drama lacks an ending, since its proprietor lost the final pages of Lermontov's manuscript. My listeners were in no way able to grasp the idea of this "loss," and appealed to me more than once "to look hard" for the end of "The Spaniards"… I was most of all surprised that Lermontov's popularity in Shelai Prison depended primarily upon his poetry and not his prose. *A Hero for Our Time* elicited a kind of indifference compared to the more admired "Dubrovskii" and *The Captain's Daughter*. With regard to the poet Vladimirov, he valued it significantly lower than those Pushkin works.

"What's there to him?" he boomed, laughing idiotically. "Nuthin' to him, nuthin' special…"

So I read Lermontov day and night.

But the undoubted idol among Shelai's penal laborers, the writer who commanded greatest love and respect, was Gogol. Unfortunately, we didn't have his complete works. There were the following: *Dead Souls*, *Taras Bulba*, *Evenings on a Farm*, "Nevskii Prospect," "Notes of a Madman," "Old-Fashioned Landowners," and "The Overcoat." Of these only "The Overcoat" was received completely indifferently and never given a repeat reading; all the rest were learned almost by heart. In our prison, Gogol's heroes became common names—the best measure of success. *Evenings on the Farm near Dikanka* was always heard with intense interest and, for that matter, summoned up the most intense laughter. One day, someone called Kuzma Chirok "Cherevik" (from "The Sorochinsk

Fair"), and for a long time afterward this sobriquet stuck to him. The devil, the witch, the blacksmith Vakula, and Chub, spluttering with pain whenever the voices in the sack encircled him, became general favorites; even the drunkard Kalenik who fleetingly appears in "A Night in May" was recalled fondly. But the greatest furor was of course produced by *Dead Souls* and *Taras Bulba*. The impression made by these two works was different, but nearly just as huge. Vladimirov alone expressed, as usual, a unique opinion regarding *Taras Bulba*.

"What's this? Nonsense, pure nonsense. Nuthin' special there… Jus' empty prattlin'."

Collective headman Iukhorev admired the character Nozdrev from the moment of his appearance on the scene, to the point that he couldn't constrain himself from declaiming:

"That's me!… Good Lord, it's me, boys!…"

However, later, when Nozdrev's character was more fully explained, he wanted to back away from this identification, but it was already too late. From that moment on, prison jokesters didn't give him a break and constantly teased him with Nozdrev, and also with "the Kherson landowner." Shelai's Nozdrev-Hercules, forgetting all responsibility and the title of headman, chased his offenders furiously through the yard, and those he caught in his iron claws fared poorly. He mercilessly crushed noses, tore lips and beards, and mangled arms and legs. But even after this lesson he could not quell Rakitin, Nikifor, Marmot, and the like. Rumor finally reached Six-Eyes himself, and he, laughing generously, asked Iukhorev why he was being called Nozdrev…

Korobochka, Pliushkin, Manilov, Sobakevich, Petukh, General Betrishchev, and Chichikov himself were for everyone living beings, general acquaintances, and favorites. It is significant that even Gogol's humorous digressions did not escape attention. There is a spot where Gogol talks about the bureaucrat Prometei, who appears cocky before the division head but tries very much to please his subordinates. Even the misunderstood word Prometei[90] was for some reason recalled, and for a long time afterward Luchezarov himself was called by this name.

"A Prometei, a real Prometei!" they'd say of him when he appeared at evening roll calls with an entire retinue of guards.

On the other hand, it's curious that Sobakevich was perceived not as a negative but as a positive character, and Malakhov raved terribly about this.

"I 'member that fellow! He's a real gentleman, 'n' that's no grist to mill. He is… Paramon Malakhov! Yes! I myself am Sobakevich."

Unfortunately, a number of listeners, often pretending to be the most gifted and clever element of *katorga* and usually influencing the rest, were always rotten to the core. Sometimes these people cast a thoroughly undesirable glow on the reading. Thus, the vagabond Dorozhkin tried to make a pearl out of the behavior of *Dead Soul's* principal character—Chichikov; he went into rapture over his clever enterprise, praised to the heavens his scurrilous talents, and shouted:

"That's what you do to 'em, the stupid simpletons! So's they don't fatten yer lips… Ech, if they freed me right now I wouldn't fire the same bullet again, I'd make like Chichikov hisself, 'cept, not the governor but the *governor-general hisself* would gimme his daughter!"

Of course, this was simple bragging, and Gogol so poorly taught Dorozhkin the art of fraud that, having been released to the free command, he was immediately returned to prison almost the very next day for stealing a shawl from one of the guard's wives; nonetheless, I happened to compare his self-promotion to a similar passage in *Dead Souls* and made the usual explanations. On the other hand, I think that in the end this epic, even without my help, would have been properly understood and that most, despite agreeing with Dorozhkin's words, did not in the depths of their souls consider Chichikov a praiseworthy character worthy of emulation but well recognized that this was satire. I always terribly regretted that we had neither *The Inspector*, nor *The Marriage*, nor "Ivan Ivanovich's and Ivan Nikiforovich's Argument," nor "The Nose," nor "Vyi,"[91] nor "The Portrait," for what then might have been Gogol's popularity? In any case, it is without a doubt that this is an essentially populist poet, unique among all Russian writers, who is now neither understood nor valued by the masses and, consequently, it is soulfully desired that there will be a time when Gogol's works appear in affordable popular editions.[92]

I was unable to familiarize my listeners with the works of other classical writers—Turgenev, Tolstoy, Dostoevskii, Ostrovskii, Nekrasov—and I can only conjecture as to the impression these or other writers' works might have produced.

Among other things, the question as to what they would have said about Dostoevskii's *Notes from a Dead House* especially aroused my curiosity, and I was terribly happy when several chapters of this work covering the prison theatrical were found in Filonov's old reader.[93] I calculated that so close and familiar a subject would summon an explosion of enthusiasm from my audience and arouse lively interest, and was mightily surprised when the fragment I recited was received quite indifferently, almost coldly. This failure impassioned and, I confess, almost annoyed me; I began to explain to Chirok, Malakhov, and others that this wouldn't be so were I to read them *Notes from a Dead House* in full.

"But what's that scribblin' there?" old man Goncharov asked.

"It's scribbling about how prisoners lived forty years ago in a fort," I answered, "and how they worked, suffered, and were oppressed by the administration—in a word, it's all about prison life."

"As if we dunno 'bout that, Ivan Mikolaevich! What else is there to read?… Now, if they'd scribbled there 'bout various battles 'n' adventures—for instance, 'bout Ataman Roshchin 'n' his Lieutenant Bura, now that'd be another thing."

"He should be given what for 'n' not read!" Semënov suddenly said, rising from the sleeping platform and lighting his pipe. His nostrils flared angrily and his eyes cast an unfriendly and at the same time disdainful look.

"Who do you mean?" I asked in surprise.

"Well, who wrote them notes—Dostoevskii, if'n that's his… I read this little book."

"You read it? And you say you should give him what for?! You must have read something else."

"Not somethin' else, but that. He should be given what for, 'cause he gave away all the prisoners' secrets to the leadership, 'n' thanks to this our brother's livin' e'en worse!"

I became excited, showing, on the contrary, that with his work Dostoevskii rendered *katorga*'s inhabitants a great service by explaining to the leadership that prisoners are just the same as all people and should be treated humanely; but it was no use arguing with

Semënov. Having expressed his opinion exactly as if dropping an axe, he laid down in his spot once more and fell silent with the same look of hatred and scorn on his face. Other prisoners in the prison put down what was read of *Notes from a Dead House*, and all blamed the author for revealing prisoners' secrets and the various intimate aspects of their life, asserting that had he been caught by the mare in his time, it would have been the worse for him… It's to the point that in their naïvety, the majority of prisoners had thought till then that the administration was completely ignorant of their ability to conceal money in so-called "gophers,"[94] their various arrangements and forms of deal-making, breaking of shackles, etc.

Among the foreign works we had besides Shakespeare was Victor Hugo's *The Last Day of a Condemned Man*. I anticipated that this little book would also make a staggering impression on my listeners; however, as with Dostoevskii, I was mistaken… The reading soon wearied the bulk of the audience, and before the end they were completely asleep: in the absence of extrovert actions the in-depth psychological analysis and fascinating plot held no sway over them. This touches on those among the more terrible lovers of the readings, insofar as they truly listened to the story to its end with great—apparently— attentiveness, albeit in absolute silence, as if something were melting through them, and I felt that the impression they were getting was difficult to the point of incomprehension and that they were regarding me in the same way. The topic's realism was obviously close to their own life, fed their soul, but rendered it less susceptible to the work's artistic side, as in other cases. Perhaps my listeners felt that with each of them there was or might in the future be a similar story, and of such things as gallows prisoners naturally do not want to speak or think. In a home where a corpse is soon expected any conversations about death, moreover verbose and illustrative, are inappropriate…

My library was not extensive, yet the prisoners could not become familiar with all of it even during the time it was kept in the prison. I therefore skipped some definitive and decisive selections on the basis of the above observations. I will simply say that these evenings devoted to recitation comprise the best and most gratifying part of my memories of Shelai Prison, and, regardless of all the personal disappointments accompanying my dreams about the humanitarian impact of artistic literati on *katorga*'s residents, I personally stick to my opinion to this day. Sown into the soil readings can, I think, just like lessons, play a large role in prisoners' rehabilitation, gradually and imperceptibly broadening their intellectual horizons and rebuilding their moral understanding. Even were it shown that, in practice, this is a chimera, a poetical fantasy and nothing more, I would staunchly appeal not only for permission, but for construction by the authorities of *katorga* prisons themselves for small libraries of classic writers of foreign and Russian literature and the best works of secondary writers. The library would be small, but just right. Novels of a bloody/criminal nature or of a risqué/romantic content should, of course, be unconditionally excluded from it. I've always personally felt that of all the world's writers, Dickens (none of whose works I was fortunate enough to have) would be best suited for this kind of library, given his utterly tender warmth and charming images and portraits, his profound love for suffering humanity, for children, the poor, and toward all the unfortunate, degraded, and aggrieved. Dickens's novels alone would take up great space. I generally noticed that big things especially enjoyed the most success and had the greatest impact among prisoners, readings of which continued night after night, drawing listeners' attention to the most secret and complicated depths of daily life and psychology, inspiring not only ideas but, as such, allowing time for harmony and tone to be firmly established. Shorter stories and tales often only annoyed my listeners: the undeveloped intellect is barely able to concentrate attention and enter the proper mood by the time the story's already ending. Very short tales and stories are, in my opinion, completely unsuitable in most instances for a prisoners' library, since prisoners require solid and profound, and not fleeting, impressions. But they also meet these goals when read over a very long period by poorly lettered prisoners themselves; then each such reader is somehow his own storyteller with whom he carries on like a chicken with an egg, and apart from which does not for a long time wish for any other book whatsoever. Among my books the following enjoyed the greatest success: *Socrates, Teacher of Life*, *Christopher Columbus*, and *The So-Called Alexander the Great of Macedon*. Besides Dickens's novels, I would also recommend for reading aloud to prisoners the historical novels of Walter Scott and Cooper, as well as the best works of Mayne Reid (such as, for example, *The Plant Hunters*).[95] I won't even mention such notable children's novels as *Robinson Crusoe* and *Uncle Tom's Cabin*. Cervantes's *Don Quixote*, I know, should also be among the top books in this select library. By the same token, I vociferously oppose for children and young people all abridged and bowdlerized editions.

XVI.   SHAH LAMAS

Month followed month, and all of no one was released to the free command. It was said that construction of the winter camp had not been completed, and for some reason the administration was holding up the "offering" Six-Eyes had made. Rumors about the offering had fallen nearly silent, and as soon as the prison became animated and started gossiping again, candidates for release to the free command raised their ears. The prison "heralds"—Buzzy, Marmot, the cobbler Zvonarenko, and others—time and again ran from ward to ward verifying the news: the offering would accommodate thirty-five men; the most hopeful persons had communicated this in secret: one of the favored guards, a clerk from the office, and, finally, Six-Eyes's favorite housemaid, Mariushka… Excitement was written on everyone's face. Even those who could not at all reckon on freedom from prison—the lifers and those with thirty-year terms—were excited. Under these conditions, the unbearable oppression of the prison walls and Shelai's regime told more starkly. The sole idea that all thirty-five men living the same life here, suffering for the same reasons and from the same conditions, would, in however many days, become practically free men and not see behind their backs a "spook" with a bayonet and hear every minute the guard's terrible calls—of all joys, this sole idea fired the heart, vicariously compelling one to gaze rapturously ahead toward freedom…

But the yoke really was considerable, regardless of the trifling indulgences mentioned above. Most penal laborers are not devoid of a sense of their human dignity, and they were undoubtedly sickened when their personhood was flouted at every step, when every second they were made to feel that they, in essence, were not people but some kind of unique animal species that had been named penal laborers. Not without a bitter taste did a rumor emerge from somewhere in the prison that Luchezarov would, in cursing for some offence a free-commandee, shout:

"You're a penal laborer! You're a slave and nothing more! You have neither God-given nor human rights, you're like those oxen over there who bring me water! And, like them, you shall unquestioningly obey!"

The majority skeptically regarded the construction taking place before their eyes as a structure for corporal punishment.

"Mark my words, boys," said a fire-haired, practically comic, and diminutive old man nicknamed Prickly Weed, pacing the ward and forever embittered towards everything in the world and especially himself—lovable, according to the prisoners' expression, only once a year—"Mark my words, boys, he'll tear someone up first thing, 'n' they'll be brought to death's door! He's already drunk on our blood, he loves human blood. 'N' the reason he ain't had our shirts ironed up to now is 'cause he's a six-headed 'n' six-eyed serpent. Look at his paunch: he's come 'fore us to do nuthin' other'n gobble up a livin' man—he'll do it 'n' be happy… I feels, my little heart feels, that it'll come to no good at his hands… Either me from him, or him from me, it'll come to no good. Won't be otherwise!…"

And having thoughtfully fixed his gaze somewhere in the distance and spread his legs ridiculously wide, the half-mad Prickly Weed grandiosely stood in the middle of the ward. Great was his malicious glee when a rumor once went through prison that the brave staff captain had with his own hands beaten two female penal laborers living in his service, giving one a bloody nose and mussing up the other's pigtails. Of course, living under lock and key, it was difficult to verify the accuracy of prisoner gossip, but Prickly Weed didn't think to question it.

"Now he'll get us soon, soon!" he prophesized, raising an index finger and sadly shaking his head, exactly as if he was prepared for some epic deed.

Fortunately, that prophecy was not fulfilled. Not only did the brave staff captain never lay a finger on prisoners, he never abused them with bad words. Nonetheless, everyone feared him like fire. Luchezarov's personality unintentionally weighed upon and pushed one toward the ground; in his presence, each felt like a dog before a raised knout… A complete disdain for the human being was evident in his every look, word, and action. To him, everything was somehow soullessly legal and inhumanly impartial. Luchezarov was proud of his incorruptible honesty, and, actually, prisoners unanimously acknowledged that nowhere had everything come to them so timely and completely, as prescribed by law, as in Shelai Prison; nor was such trouble taken over cleanliness and hygiene in another prison. But for all the positives there were, on the other hand, motives behind this incomparable fairness and solicitude; they did not flow from a fervid love for living people but from a craving for glory and distinction before the senior administration, and mostly from a love of the very principle of legality and justice, of artistry for artistry's sake. Luchezarov slighted prisoners themselves, seen and unseen, like animals, not suspecting, of course, that these animals caught his every word and were sometimes able to be clever and unmerciful critics. Hence, they were never able to forget his comment, made the first day he met them, that he would sooner believe a single guard than seven hundred prisoners. Another time he somewhere declared (and this, too, passed from mouth to mouth) that the distance between penal laborers and guards was the same as that between them and Staff Captain Luchezarov, and… he was God himself! He apparently put the utmost effort into ordering his executors in general to gird his grandiosity and authority with the greatest possible pomp. His was a wise rule, undoubtedly toward this very end: never to countermand too quickly a single one of his orders, even if it was immediately proven to be clearly absurd and unfair. Obviously, he was a great politician, dreaming of going far… By the same token, one time, Luchezarov himself was embarrassed when, amid the festive ceremoniousness of evening roll call, collective headman Iukhorev unexpectedly shouted from the ranks a loudly voiced complaint on behalf of all persons in the collective, against one of the guards standing right there who allowed himself to push prisoners in the chest and use the most foulmouthed words against them. Luchezarov seemed to be taken aback by surprise at this; he stood in silence for a certain time, clearing his throat and staring as if not knowing what to do. But then, having briefly mumbled: "I'll flog you!"—he more majestically than ever ordered the guards to take the prisoners to their wards. It absolutely goes without saying that thereafter no one heard of a general investigation having been conducted… The unloved guard remained, as before, a guard, and although he stopped pushing prisoners in the chest he became still ruder and more brazen. This guard, Bezymënnykh by name,[96] was Luchezarov's right hand and was hated not only by prisoners but also his comrades in the service. Being an informer by profession, he did not reach any agreement with the mare and was, like his patron, formal and soullessly legalistic; but he brought passion and fire to his business, and Luchezarov was quite captivated by him, saying that of all the guards Bezymënnykh alone took to his duties with a "religious" devotion… He'd dart about the prison all day, now prowling like a cat pricking up its ears, now swooping down like the wind and catching the guilty; all day he shouted, cursed, nagged, and threatened arrests and denunciations. Several men were always sent to the isolator while he was on duty. Bezymënnykh's puny little physique with a red face suffused with gloom inspired disgust even in me, with whom he was courteous in private. He demanded that in the merest instances prisoners should turn to him with nothing other than the words "Mister Guard," and that when meeting him—although this might be a hundred times a day—should unfailingly doff their caps, and one time, while dressing down an insubordinate person, he shouted to everyone in the corridor:

"The com'dant orders you to yank off your caps 'fore our wives!"

This especially angered the mare.

"What! So we gotta meekly doff our caps 'fore a woman, 'fore ev'ry wolf?" everyone freely said, glancing, however, at the door. "Better put us in the isolator, freeze us inside!"

Bezymënnykh armed himself against the prison not so much with strictness and formality as with contempt for the man who'd become a penal laborer, a contempt evident in his every word and gesture, even his voice's intonation.

This guard thought himself, among other things, an educated and well-read man and, actually, none of his comrades read more willingly than he. The days he was on duty he could be found with some translation of a French novel with a harrowingly sanguine title. Moreover, he carried a notebook in which he wrote Tatar words and their Russian translations, and, having once curiously glanced in it, I noticed this dictionary had all possible curses and vile words.

"What's this for?" I asked.

"For the next time you go past those animals," he answered, grinning smugly, "'n' dunno what they're mumblin' behind your back… Maybe they're cursin' you! But you can't send 'em to the isolator!"

Of this, however, there was little. Bezymënnykh was also a poet, composed hateful satires of prisoners and fellow guards, and wrote denunciations in verse, which he sometimes presented to Luchezarov to curry favor. Once, he had an entire battle over this with the guard Petushkov. Bezymënnykh wrote a satire about him that became widely popular in the world of Shelai and included the following couplets:

Like a skeleton, dry 'n' brittle,
He's a poet, a poet o' words none,

'N' so has been suitably laconically
Named: Petushkov![97]

These murderous couplets and especially the misunderstood word "briefly" struck Petushkov as a lethal insult impossible to endure. He dressed in parade uniform and gave the brave staff captain an ultimatum: either he, Petushkov, or Bezymёnnykh would have to go… But Luchezarov managed to put a comical spin on the affair and to avoid the proffered ultimatum. He had an exceedingly high opinion of Bezymёnnykh.

"He's vulgar, that's true," he normally answered all charges against his favorite, "but this, in essence, he cannot change. Such a gentle-natured commander as I clearly needs an executive-executioner!"

This is why all the dirty tricks and intrigues of the prisoners and the guards themselves against Bezymёnnykh were for a long time in vain. He carried himself well and was later ruined only when God deprived him of reason and, seduced by his gift for versification, he composed a satire about his protector. His enemies hastened to deliver this to the appropriate address, and in less than twenty-four hours the bilious poet was dismissed from his duties…

Another of the guards hated by prisoners was Voronkov,[98] an absolute boy with a smidgen of down growing on his lips, pretty like a beautiful young woman but as impudent and depraved as the absolute worst penal laborer. Power obviously intoxicated him. During searches at the prison gates when we returned from work every day, he was particularly impudent and cynical. Wary of "chirping"—as prisoners would say—too much at me, yet at the same time wishing to make me uncomfortable, he limited his search to an especially impudent clap on the top of my cap when I passed by; this he never forgot to do. By the same token, Voronkov was a terrible coward, and if he met with any serious repulse on the part of a prisoner, then, like a hare, he'd instantly pull his tail in and fire off cutting responses and even direct insults such as could be lost on no member of the herd.

Unfairness and penal injustice could be felt at every step, in all the minutiae of life. Luchezarov was not pleased, for example, that there were too many sick in his prison and that the drunken medic came to the prison only to drink or grab a bottle of spirits for himself from the pharmacy, and so he expressly ordered the following: no more than half of the infirmary's beds should ever be occupied, and if it became impossible to admit newly sickened prisoners, then one of the previously admitted prisoners should be discharged without fail, even if he was weak. Furthermore, the brave staff captain wasn't pleased there were *bogoduly* in Shelai Prison, that is, weak prisoners incapable of hard physical labor.

"My prison is a working prison," he declared, "and not an almshouse. It's not my fault I've been sent old men, the sick, and cripples. I therefore wish not to acknowledge any sort of *bogoduly*. Without exception, all shall be put to work, and not a single one should be in the infirmary!"

And, in actuality, he did manage to find some occupation for those old men distinguished by their senility and to devise work responsibilities for them. During this, he expressed the prejudicial and often completely false opinion that the jobs of ward headmen, attendants, and the other "cleaners" were the easiest of jobs and most suitable for *bogoduly*, and so he assigned them to the old and the weak. Among other things, these responsibilities were some of the most difficult and time-consuming. Twice a week, attendants and headmen had to wash tables, benches, sleeping platforms, and floors using a rag and on their hands and knees, since for some reason mops were strictly forbidden. Wards had to sparkle like glass. Headmen had to clean potatoes in the kitchen every day, and when there were few prisoners in the prison, also to haul water and firewood. In summer, they had the function of planting and watering cabbage in the gardens. In assigning ward headmen the medic never thought to question the health of these job candidates, and it therefore often happened that notorious syphilitics and consumptives were washing our dishes and preparing our meat and bread. Free laborers were at first assigned as ward attendants, but later Luchezarov began telling prisoners to assume this position with or without their consent and sent those who refused to the isolators. For some reason, he eventually arrived at the belief that this job had been purposefully created for a Tatar whom he, like the mare, indifferently counted among the true Tatars as well as the Caucasians and Sarts. This situation incidentally pertains to a certain episode that ended tragically for a prisoner and marked for the whole prison the beginning of a new, still gloomier era.

There was in Shelai a certain elderly Lezgin[99] with a head already quite gray, who'd more than once run away from *katorga* and thus more than once been pierced or wounded by bullet or bayonet—a man obviously sick and feeble. Only Shah Lamas's eyes, large and black and gazing proudly from beside a long, handsome, aquiline nose, spoke of a still unquenched inner energy and burning hatred for his massed enemies. He was poorly suited for physical labor and Luchezarov, passing through the ward one day during evening roll call upon having learned the attendant had fallen sick and been sent to the infirmary, stopped before him.

"Assign this old man to do it, then," he decided, pointing out Shah Lamas to the guard, "it's Tatar labor, after all."

With these words he majestically sailed out of the ward. Shah Lamas, having learned from his comrade what just happened, first went dumb with astonishment and rage, then began shouting loudly:

"Me—ward attendant? This work for Tatar? Me show you Caucasian work! Me now cut your head off!"

He could barely be calmed and told to say, next morning, without going into a story, that he was sick. In this way he was indeed able to avoid this unpleasant work for a while; but the day came, and guards, remembering their commander's orders, again assigned the ill-fated Lezgin to be an attendant. Then Shah Lamas flatly refused to obey. For this he spent a whole week in a dark isolator and, having been released, was once more ordered to haul the waste vats.

Departing that day for the mine, I was convinced that Shah Lamas would again refuse and, I confess, I looked forward with some curiosity to the outcome of this struggle between the authorities and the stubborn Caucasian. Having returned from work and reached the gates, I guessed that something unusual had happened in the prison. We were searched with distracted thoroughness and rudeness for a long time; everyone's kettles and knapsacks were peremptorily confiscated.

"What're we gonna drink tea from?"

"There's a government kettle for government tea," the orderly answered, "but your tea is forbidden."

"Why's it forbidden? When? What for?"

"Y'know why."

The prisoners spilled like peas into the prison yard and briskly hurried to the wards to find out what had happened. Running into the corridor, we were surprised that all the doors were again padlocked, as when we'd first arrived at Shelai Prison. Marmot's chubby face gazed out of my ward's door-window, obviously burning with impatience to communicate anew the epic news of what had happened; Buzzy's red lips were flapping behind him. They both let out a stream of words as soon as the guard let the miners into the ward.

"Stop, you devils, 'n' tell us straight out what happened!"

"Six-Eyes was almost killed!" Iashka blurted out.

"He weren't almost killed, but he got showed a good time," corrected Buzzy.

"But that's what I'm drivin' at!"

"Talk sensibly, don't torture us. It's like draggin' 'n' draggin' a dead man by the nose. Marmot, you tell us!"

"Shah Lamas refused to be an attendant again. They reported it to Six-Eyes… He himself shows up in the prison: 'What *is* this?' he says. 'Disobeying the will of the authorities? Don't you know what will happen for refusing to work?' At that moment, that Circassian was slicin' bread on the sleepin' platform, gittin' it ready to eat. 'Me,' he says, 'know what!' 'N' then he yawns!… Well, the mare weren't gittin' into this mess, 'cause at that point no one else was in the ward… Some say he got Six-Eyes with the knife, but others, that he got 'im with the loaf o' bread. With the knife, more likely."

"With the loaf!!" hissed Buzzy, interrupting Marmot and losing his voice with completely atypical forcefulness. "He couldn't use the knife 'cause the guards grabbed his hand."

"Here he still wants to argue, the rotten scoundrel!" Marmot suddenly flared. "Zvonarenko knows better. He was in the shop when Six-Eyes came back 'n' saw with his own eyes a flap of his greatcoat was cut out…"

"You're sayin' it weren't his head that was flappin'? You 'n' Zvonarenko was both gone. Prokopii Filippych hisself told me—so who knows better? He grabbed the Circassian first. Says they used all their might to hold the brute; he was cursin' terribly 'n' spittin' in their eyes. Well, for that the guards smashed 'n' bashed him in the side—'Don't cry, little mother!'[100] But they say Six-Eyes hisself, m'boys, grabbed a *levolver* from his pocket 'n' shouts: 'I'll kill you and won't answer for it.'"

The offended Marmot receded to the side for the time being, and Buzzy exclusively commanded the arena's universal attention.

"He jailed all four blacksmiths, m'boys," he hissed.

"The blacksmiths? What for?"

"But, the knife? Who'd he get the knife from? The guards right off said he got it from someone at work. There'll prob'ly be some good trouble for them, too."

"Indeed, for ever'one now," Nikifor Burenkov gloomily observed, "they already took our kettles…"

"What a woman!" Semënov shouted at him. "He won't cry 'cause Six-Eye's belly weren't sliced open, but will o'er kettles. What are you? A prisoner? D'you come to *katorga* to drink tea? Don't you know he was almost cut in half? Would that the Devil scratch them honorable men… Took away his kettle—'n' he's scared!…"

Semënov's sharply expressed opinion suddenly set the tone for our ward and determined how the rest should view the offender Shah Lamas. Everyone for the first time expressed sympathy for him and complained about his unfortunate experience. In the meantime, Marmot once again commanded universal attention and began telling what he himself had witnessed.

"Jus' as they was takin' the Circassian to the isolator they locked all the wards. I was in the kitchen, 'n' the ord'ly dragged me out by the neck. They locked 'n' searched it for an hour. Ever'thin' to the last was sorted through 'n' raked over. They took ev'ry single one o' the kettles 'n' mugs on the stovetops. Any rags found unnecessary, needles, any little thing—swept up like with a broom. They also found several little knives 'n' took 'em. All of Ivan Nikolaevich's, Chichikov's, 'n' Sobakevich's books got hauled away!…"

"What! The books, too?" I shouted, deeply saddened that our blissful evenings full of poetry and gusto could no longer continue.

"Ev'ry last one. Only, they didn't take the Bible. There's a rumor they're plannin' to put the whole prison in shackles."

"Wha-at?!"

"Nah, I'm pullin' your leg."

Everyone shook his head.

"Akh, you rotten Shelai!" Nikifor said again. "I had a tetchy little pencil 'tween my teeth, 'n' they took that. That's how upset they was!"

"They was 'fraid you'd poke Six-Eyes's eye out," someone shot in.

"No, that you'd write a note to your parents in the other world."

We got up to look over and divide up our bedding and things that had been tossed into a single, disorderly pile, and hastened to determine what had been lost or broken. Alas! the destruction was total… Malakhov, returning in the evening from the workshop, brought more bad news: they were planning to divide the wards anew!… It was truly unpleasant, having over several months accustomed yourself not only to people but even the sleeping platforms, to suddenly find yourself in a new place beside new, often completely unfamiliar, neighbors whom you'd have to get along with and get used to.

"Well, now the free command's fallen through," Paramon said, adding fuel to the fire and thoughtfully knocking his pipe on a sleeping platform.

He especially had anticipated imminent departure to the free command, and a definite disappointment could be heard in his voice. Undoubtedly, many other prisoners were experiencing this disappointment (Gandorin, Marmot, and Pestrov had also been anticipating the free command), and it probably would have extended further had it not been for fear of Semënov; everyone could well see his glowering, scornful, and wrathful gaze directed at them from the sleeping platform, and stayed silent. Only Gandorin sighed heavily and whispered some kind of oath.

That day we went to evening roll call shuddering and shivering throughout our entire bodies. We believed there'd be new difficulties. We were waiting for Luchezarov himself… And then he literally appeared, surrounded by the usual pomp and circumstance. His greatcoat flapped on his shoulders and his white fur hat towered high on his head more ceremoniously than ever. His face was crimson and his long red mustaches hung menacingly. He did not allow us to put our caps back on, and when everyone was holding his breath and had resumed a deathly quiet after prayers, he stood silent for a long time, slowly looking over the clean-shaven ranks of prisoners' heads.

"Very well!" his speech began with the usual introductory words, and our hearts jumped. "Today there was an audacious assault against me by one of those artists such as you. Evidently, this artist didn't know that I'm not a coward, that I go about well-armed and ready to shoot anyone who tries to accost me. He will suffer, of course, the deserved punishment, but all of you… yes, all!… are in my eyes answerable for his deed. The headman of the ward he lived in is first of all answerable. He was unable to learn there was a knife forbidden by law in the ward, but also that this artist possessed the courage to… that he had the courage. For this itself all of ward number seven is answerable. Therefore, I declare this ward under arrest for a month, that is, deprived for this period of tobacco, tea, and walks, and also chained at night in manacles; furthermore, I am subjecting the headman to incarceration in a dark isolator for a week. That's ward number seven. But the entire prison is guilty. After today, per my instructions, searches will be conducted in all the wards for the knives I've forbidden. Whoever's not prepared will suffer special punishment. But for tomorrow, I'm ordering all of you put in leg fetters, and the wards will henceforth be bolted tightly. You were unable to take advantage of my kindness—now you'll rattle your bracelets. I'm also taking away the books which… which I gave you, acceding to the request… of an educated man, who dreams to his wits' end of teaching you with these books. I was told they gladdened and amused many of you, but artists such as you do not care at all about yourselves and are not worth any indulgences. In conclusion, there is one thing more! Many of you are now ready to begin terms in the free command, but know this: no one will be released until I see sincere repentance and full improvement. The circumstances of the ward headmen are especially great and significant: their job is not only to keep wards clean and orderly but also to see to their comrades' moral conduct. For any incident similar to today's, I will make them answer foremost. Orderly, read out the work order to the exclusion of arrested ward seven."

During the distribution of prisoners to the wards there was an innovation: the wards were immediately locked and, during Luchezarov's tour of them, each was unlocked again. During this the guards first rushed into the ward, timidly surrounding the herd in a tight cordon. The brave staff captain entered the center of the room, threateningly cast his merciless gaze, and with the same overpowering menace, departed.

We all spent this fateful evening gloomily and silently. The students, depressed and grief-stricken, soon laid down to sleep; Gandorin didn't tell Marmot his stories and stayed silent for a very long time, kneeling and loudly banging his forehead on the floor; as for Marmot himself, he would have no stories. Malakhov honestly tried to show that everything in the world was just the same for him, and began singing in a cloyingly drunken voice, leaning toward Chirok and provoking him:

> Now I'm sittin' 'neath a little window,
> Gazin' at the red sun—

but Chirok, evidently not well disposed towards the joke, limited himself only to giving "the black-striped demon" a good slap on the back, cursing his drunken mug, and going to lie down to sleep. Even Goncharov was not sounding off that evening, and soon fell asleep…

XVII.   THE USUAL OUTCOME

A gloomy, difficult time began. It seemed that the prison divided into two groups hostile to one another. One of them, smaller in numbers, it's true, but nonetheless more influential, consisted of people who absolutely approved of Shah Lamas's act and only expressed the wish that he'd dispatched Six-Eyes to the other world. Among others belonging to this group were all the Mohammedans, though as always they kept themselves isolated from the Russians, did not bespeak their sympathy for their fellow believer aloud, and walked around pensive, sad, and enigmatic. Then there were the "Ivans," the prison hot-shots and worldly people who, having come to stand atop the mountain on the force of old prisoners' values and ways, looked with hatred as the "new breed" of cowards, the "tail-boxers" (lickspittles) and "tongues" (spies), were ascending the throne, rearranging and heaping in ruined piles the honored customs of the glorious past. Some of these leaders, like Semënov and Goncharov, were undoubtedly stalwart and sincere; but many others did not at all vindicate Shah Lamas because they believed in his rightness or because a fire of irreconcilable hatred and enmity truly burned within them, but only because they sought popularity and primacy among the mob. The majority of the prison consisted of a faceless mass, pushed and pulled here and there by its supposed leaders; the terror before it revealed for the first time its real (cowardly) views and feelings, concealed in the depths of its soul and imprecisely expressed according to whoever's voice was loudest and most persuasive. Yet there had now appeared amid its existence an extreme truthfulness, consisting for the most part of pious old men and others aching to be released to the free command; and it could not conceal for long its hatred and indignation toward the culprit for the new repressions. However, the constrained old men—left out, ignored, dependent upon the faceless, cowardly herd before them—had won a first, decisive victory and were biting their tongues and holding tight. In one ward prisoners even wanted to beat up their headman, so affected were they by Luchezarov's dictates… Regardless of locked doors, the shepherds quickly managed to communicate with each other in a sustained campaign, and soon the opinion that it was by no means at all necessary "to reproach" a comrade to Six-Eyes held sway throughout the prison.

"What can he do to us?" shouted the ringleaders. "He took our kettles 'n' tea? Well, he 'n' the tea can both go to hell! He put us in shackles? Since we're prisoners, this is how it goes in *katorga*. Abolished the free command? But to hell with his free command! Them blessed ol' men who serve with tail 'n' tongue need it, but we can do what we want in prison!"

"But, I suggest, boys," orated someone in another corner, "that Six-Eyes himself'll still answer for this, 'cause he got no right at all to punish ever'one for one man.

The authorities'll investigate 'n' discover this can't be; that we're all treated as one man; your worship, they'll say, you so-'n'-so, this full-scale 'pression ain't possible. Unnerstand: he'll be in hot water! All this villainy may uncover 'n' expose 'im. Our case is correct 'cordin' to the law, boys, so how can we be reproached? Nuthin' may e'en happen to the Circassian, 'cause there ain't no law tyin' a man to a waste tub."

But on the army's flanks there was a breach, a weak point, that no one could at first point out: this was that Shah Lamas was not a Russian but a "Tatar." Russian prisoners generally regard Tatars, that is, Mohammedans, with extreme hostility. This hostility is mutual, and the reasons for it manifold (among them, historical memories that have passed into instinct possibly play a role). It cannot be completely denied, for instance, that Caucasians, Sarts, and other foreigners are unaccustomed to hard physical labor, try with all their might to shirk it, and, where possible, "ride on the back" of Russians; but the latter exaggerate this inadequacy of theirs and frequently accuse even the most hardworking Mohammedans, on whose backs they themselves ride, of laziness and wanting to loaf about. Mohammedans' ignorance of the Russian language and obvious disinterest in learning to speak it also perpetuates mutual animosity. Mohammedans keep to themselves in small, isolated groups in the prisons, irritating Russians with their guttural dialect, monotone singing, repetitive nasal recitations of the Koran, and ritual ablutions, which, I remember, nauseated me. For their part, "Tatars" have few reasons to love the Russians, meeting at every turn their high-handed attitude toward them and hearing shouts of "Ooh, you animal! You mumblin' Tatar," and so on. An Oriental hot-temperedness sometimes lets loose, and out come the knives. On the road, bloody confrontations between Russians and Circassians are frequent.

As regards Shah Lamas, regardless of the overall dislike for his co-religionists, he personally enjoyed popularity and respect in the prison. Everyone well knew that he was a man who had more than once fled *katorga* and was generally able to look after himself, that he was in fact sick and wasn't just shamming an incapacity for work. The old man was moreover distinguished by a cheerful character, ably spoke Russian, and, being the only Caucasian in Shelai Prison, he socialized more with Russians than Tatars. In this sense he was rivaled only by the Uzbek Marazgali, whom I will introduce in a later chapter. Upon first hearing of Shah Lamas's situation, it didn't enter anyone's head to think of him as a "Tatar" rather than a Russian. But under the influence of the reprisals and petty fear, this was soon remembered.

Light whispering could be heard in the corners; and the oblique comments begun against Tatars, Kirgiz, and Sarts soon became utterly unstoppable.

"Ooh, the animal! The mumblin' Tatar!" could be heard everywhere with and without cause.

A clash occurred in the kitchen between the cooks, candidates for the free command, and Sarts who had come to fetch some boiling water. One Sart responded with boiling water to a cook's spitting at him and was beaten up for this by the cooks and other prisoners in the kitchen. They somehow put a stop to the Russian's spitting, but regarding the Sart's scalding him with boiling water the whole prison insisted "they all gotta be taught a lesson." Leading up to this, it was significant that even Semënov, who was fairly intelligent and seemed essentially capable of understanding all this agitation against the Tatars, got swept up in the general fervor and even gritted his teeth at the sight of a pair of funny Kirgiz who lived beneath his sleeping platform in our ward and were irritating him with their incessant "grr-grr-grr," as he characterized their speech with one another.

In actuality, prisoners similar to Semënov were unable to appreciate how the increasingly pointed enmity against "the Tatars" had already carried over to Shah Lamas and his deed, and conversations in this regard became open and careless.

"I say, whatta lord!" bellowed Iashka the Marmot. "He didn't wanna drag a waste tub!"

"Over there in the Caucasus, they're really all boyars 'n' princes," Gandorin chimed in.

"So these non-Christians always are," added Malakhov. "You say but one word 'bout this 'n' he grabs a dagger or a knife. Off goes your head!"

"Ooh, those forest creatures!"

"This Shah Lamas is an unhealthy old-timer. I said this 'bout him a long time ago… His eyes dart about like they're shootin' bullets. Anyone's eyes dart about is a no-good fellow, boys!"

"But now there's sufferin' 'cause o' him… They e'en took our kettles!" complained Nikifor, who had been especially struck to the heart by the removal of his kettle.

Burenkov was terribly fond of tea and could drink almost an entire *vedro* by himself.[101] Before evening roll call he would take his kettle filled with steaming tea from the kitchen and wrap his cassock tightly round it. As soon as roll call began, he'd take the kettle to the table and commence a solemn act of tea-drinking that neither calls to work nor roll call nor guards' shouts could disturb. I don't know how, but even during this thankless time Nikifor had conspired to get himself a somehow available kettle, and one day an hilarious event happened concerning this. He had just pulled the kettle from its hiding place and begun performing his ritual over it, when the guard Bezymënnykh came to the door-window and shouted:

"Burenkov! You drinkin' tea?"

"Tea! There's no boilin' water!"

"But don't I see steam risin'?"

"Good Lord, that's from the cold water… from the frost…"

And as evidence Nikifor scooped up a cup of cold water from the cistern beneath the table and drank it in one gulp. The guard wouldn't go away and was watching. Nikifor scooped up another cup and drank it all again… And so he drank at least five cups in a row, for some reason believing it possible in this way to convince the guard of his innocence! The guard, however, was not convinced and, unlocking the ward (at that time keys were not brought at night to the commander), took the kettle and tea away amid the mare's universal laughter, leaving a dismayed Burenkov foolishly "transfixed" by the hot water…

"Know what, boys," a thoroughly aroused Nikifor suddenly shouted, "I suggest it's jus' better we resign ourselves to ever'thin'… We gotta forego a feast 'cause o' someone else's hangover? We're really in a corner… What about how we was livin' in the first place? Mikolaich was readin' to us, we was studyin'… The wards was open… 'N' there was kettles…"

"Damn your soul 'n' kettle both!" Semënov shouted at him, unable to contain himself. "Scorn me if you want. But go round with our kettles 'n' bang 'em on your head!"

"Well, I *will* scorn you. Who're you? What're you to me? I ain't goin' to the free command. Am I only out for myself? I'm for the truth…"

"A noble, honorable man has appeared!…," wickedly snickered Goncharov, rising menacingly from his spot and supporting Semënov.

"You won't be ennobled, it certainly won't be offered you," Nikifor snapped at him. "As for me, I'd convert to Mohammedanism, but you'd marry Shah Lamas hisself!"

An enormous squabble ensued, during which Goncharov and Semënov shouted:

"You all scorn, scorn who supports you! Damn all your souls! You 'n' the Tatars can both go to hell. There's someone else stabbin' us in the back. We ain't for the Tatars but for prisoners' rules. Scorn us, you noble souls, 'n' wag your tails!"

But events forestalled the noble souls' intentions. A rumor soon spread through prison that a special commissioner, very important, almost a titled personage, would arrive to interrogate Shah Lamas. After a day or two the "personage" actually showed up in the prison. He was a still quite young and very courteous man, who smiled pleasantly and inquired whether the prisoners in each ward had any charges or complaints. The mare responded, as usual, that everything was absolutely fine. Out of 150 men only one daring fellow, whose surname itself was generally unknown to that point, piped up, but then, having suddenly broken the universal silence, he lodged a complaint about the food. In that instant the courteous young official knitted his brows and his voice became dry and serious.

"The food's bad?" he coldly asked through his teeth. "They're not giving you all your rations, is that it? Old chap, think well before making such a charge."

"You often can't stomach the food you git," the oblivious prisoner bravely continued, "once we was given completely rotten 'taters…"

"This matter will be investigated," snapped the official, and he immediately left the ward.

Luchezarov felt deeply offended. What?! He, the brave staff captain, wasn't issuing full rations? He was feeding prisoners spoiled provisions?… He and the official immediately descended to the kitchen cellar and examined the potatoes stored there (before them went flying the panting quartermaster, who ordered the cook to pile all suspicious food supplies to the side). The potatoes turned out to be of outstanding quality. The prisoner's meal that was served for the authorities to taste (greasy fat skimmed from the kettle) was also found to be tasty and uncommonly nourishing.

"Such glorious cabbage soup isn't cooked at my house!" the young official exulted, and gave the cook fifty kopeks for tea and sugar.

During evening roll call that same day it was loudly announced that the prisoner who'd lodged a false charge against his superiors had been incarcerated in a dark isolation cell for one month, chained in manacles. Next morning, the exalted personage summoned Iukhorev and all the ward headmen to the chancery and strictly reprimanded them regarding their responsibilities. It was later said that many of the old men, including our Gandorin, fell to their knees and immediately gave the names of various "unreliable" comrades. After this the personage left, having first ordered Shah Lamas transferred to

Zerentui mine pending trial. The sick old man was carried almost motionless from the isolator, thrown into a cart, and, regardless of the extreme frost, barely covered with a cassock. I later heard that he died soon after arriving at Zerentui, prior to a judicial sentence that would undoubtedly have been severe.

After all these events the mare was certainly frightened, and each man thought only of saving his own hide. Every time Luchezarov appeared in the prison he was appealed to in this or another ward with entreaties about release to the free command and assurances of reliability. There were also many secret discussions and whisperings going on with the guards. You firmly bit your tongue…

XVIII.   IN THE MINING GALLERY

During those difficult times the mine turned out for me to be the only place of relaxation and comparative peace for the soul. To go as possible further from the prison's hateful walls, from that kingdom of oppression and every evil, to depart as possible for a long time and lose with all strength of body and soul one's entire existence in physical labor, to pound without interruption the hammer against the auger, to measure and calculate inches so far completed and then to again swing and swing the hammer—once more became for me a delight in which there was something sick, almost agonizing... Pëtr Petrovich had already long ago given me another assignment, moving me from the mine and to the so-called gallery, where it was warmer and the rock much softer. Here even I could bore fourteen to seventeen inches a day without becoming especially fatigued. Only the piling of the slag was difficult, which is why on those days one of my stronger comrades like Semënov was assigned me, though Rakitin normally bored with me.

It is perhaps not mistaken to explain what this gallery was. It was a so-called horizontal subterranean corridor, leading from the watch house to the mine. Prior to our arrival in Shelai Prison, almost 500 feet had been dug through it thirty years ago. But work in this narrow corridor didn't require many hands: only two borers and one haulage-man, dragging the blown-up rock to the slag heap in a specially built cart, were necessary. As far as deepening the gallery into the mountain, there were also occasionally needed carpenters who built new braces (frames) and extension bridges over which the haulage-man pulled his cart. As such, for the most part I happened to work completely alone, since my comrades finished their boring assignments much earlier and, having completed work, left for the watch house; not pushing myself and requiring long rests, I sometimes swung my hammer right up until the last prisoner left for the prison.

In one regard this gallery was, without any comparison, better than a mine; in winter it was much warmer than outside, and in summer there did not flow from all sides, as in the mines, the cold water that dribbled down the neck and into boots.

For me, those long, long hours I passed all by myself in my subterranean world are drawn vividly and clearly. The tallow candle affixed to a rock glimmered weakly, flickering and waning by the minute; left and right, at a distance of seven feet from one another, rose the corridor's granite walls; a rock ceiling, which seemed just about to collapse, hung overhead... But it held firm; small rocks shot away during hammering, but it remained a single, flowing rock with many buttresses. Before me stood the same dark granite into which I pounded; yet, behind me, my candle's light wrestled with the darkness, soon gave way to fugitive shadows, and finally completely drowned among the eternally reigning gloom there. Only in the distance, at the far end of the gallery, was a small window visible—the exit to the blessed light; with it came the means by which to always deepen the gallery in a straight line. Sometimes, having accidently extinguished the candle in the pit-face, I noticed how this distant shaft of light was reflected on the rock-wall ahead in the form of a small, bright patch, producing in full an illusion of moonlight… In the gallery, despite the comparative warmth, it felt continually damp, and I could even see evaporation along the walls. Just then, gazing at this mist, you could gradually imagine vague, strange outlines betokening all the world's forgotten sufferers, obsolete and passed into oblivion, but who now, however, seemed real and alive. Initially inchoate shapes gradually assumed sharply defined forms, and there seemed to appear the pale faces and bony frames of people who had at some time actually suffered inhuman torments there—torments before which present-day *katorga* was an idle game—who spilled not only sweat but their own life-giving blood… In the name of what? Who were these people? Unwitting victims of society's discontents, of destitution, ignorance, and feral desires, or bearers of all sorts of high ideals? I didn't know; but all, all without distinction, presented themselves to me in their moments of equal suffering and therefore seemed equally to be brothers and comrades in misfortune. I saw eyes filled with tears and horror perplexedly asking me: "What for?" I saw fists raised and clenched in impotent rage, exactingly seeking out the enemy who should be ripped to pieces; I clearly heard in the air the despair emanating from a sunken, exhausted breast, and the wheezy laughter of a fury thirsting to get drunk on the place…

Pale shadows, terrible shadows!
Malice, madness, love…

Even the sound of my chains seemed to come from out of the past… And, shuddering, I hurriedly turned away from the horrible hallucination. It was truly gone, and would exist no more. There now remains only a pale shadow of what was, and it is possible to hope that this last shadow will disappear with the sun's first rays… But at the time, I shuddered once more, albeit for an entirely different—and actual—reason: a weak, distant boom, nonetheless clearly distinguishable to the ear thanks to the crypt-like silence reigning all around, rolled from out of the mountain's depths. These voices of the mountain spirits frightened me at first, because they seemed forerunners of an earthquake; but they returned so often that I soon neglected even to pay them attention. There was not one real earthquake during my time in Shelai mine, but they were frequent in the old days and gave birth to entire legends. One such legend was told me by the watch house's old watchman. Similar to the mare, he asserted that one time in Shelai there was a collapse that trapped several dozen penal laborers; only, the old man ascribed this event to a more distant past that he himself could not recall.

"One time the boys was workin' in the mountain," he told me, "they're workin' 'n' ain't thinkin' nuthin'. Suddenly, the orderly flies in 'n' shouts: 'Get out quick, the mountain's goin'!' Ever'body threw down their tools 'n' run out. They get out, 'n' the orderly meets 'em: 'Where're you goin', you scoundrels? Why'd you quit workin'?' 'You so-'n'-so,' they say, 'you yourself jus' called us out: you said the mountain's goin'.' 'Have you all lost your minds?' he says. 'Or are you drunk? The mountain's not plannin' on movin'.

Someone from *katorga*'s playin' a joke on you. I been in the watch house the whole time. No more chatterin', now off to work.' What could they do? They hemmed 'n' hawed, 'n' went back into the mountain. Then, they was really wrong… They'd jus' gone into the mountain, jus' picked up their tools again, 'n' it went… it *went*!… So, all was lost. Sixty men, they say, was lost."

"Who had warned them, grandfather?"

"God knows him. Accordin'ly, 'twas the master o' the mountain."

"But you yourself saw him, this master?"

"I ain't seen him, but peoples have… That's the reason, to this day, it's strictly, strictly forbidden for workers to whistle 'n' sing where there's a lotta work goin' on."

"But, why?"

"Well, accordin'ly, is why. Accordin'ly, *he* don't like it!"

I gradually grew close to the old man, who had at first seemed unfriendly and cunning and whom prisoners called "the ghost of the mine," and I found in him a pitiful, downtrodden, and completely desolate creature, enamored of his own self-pity. His intellectual world was very narrow and simple: in his past there was Razgildeev, but at present and in the future there was constant worry over those wretched ten rubles a month the regulator Monakhov paid for his watchman's duties. Fortunately, having been tempered in the fire of the *Razgildeevshchina*,[102] the seventy-year-old man was still hale and hearty, but irregardless of this he consumed only black bread and steaming tea. I'd chat with him for a long time on those days I finished work early. The old man talked about the terrible things during the Razgildeevshchina, about how difficult and excessive the work had been at Kara, how convicts got sick and died just like flies in autumn, and how cholera dragged hundreds of those still alive into the grave during that time… *Katorga* stood upon disgraceful unfairness and insult. During work, even resting or smoking was forbidden; a bite of bread, hidden in one's blouse, was taken stealthily. Beatings and intimidation were normal…

"Was Razgildeev really never kind?" I asked one day, and the old man livened up. A pleasing smile covered his wrinkled face, and his lifeless, faded eyes sparkled.

"Not so! 'Twas said he was a beast. First off… As I now recall… 'Twas rainin' cats 'n' dogs. A comrade 'n' me was both up to our knees in water in the mine shaft; we was soaked, chilled, 'n' laborin' at our task with all our might into the evenin'. As we're leavin', my comrade says: 'Brother, let's drag a song outta the mountain.' We struck up a song:

> Behind the quiet ford o' the stream
> No feather-grass sways in a field:
> I began swayin', a kind young man…
> Service for the tsar tired me,
> The tsar's, the sovereign's, service,
> The tsar's service hardened me,
> That service from mornin' to evenin',
> From evenin' to midnight!
> From midnight, with stars fallin' from heaven…
> Our strong army, strong army,

Razgildeev's party, deployed.
And it descended, descended broadly,
Through the shaft, the deep shaft!

'Twas a long song, 'n' I don't 'member more. There we was singin' it, 'n' suddenly… we hear: 'Who's singin' there? Come 'ere!' We look, 'n' there's a man standin' on a house roof. We go o'er, doffin' our caps, 'n' see it's the colonel hisself. 'Drunk, are you?' he asks. 'Not at all, your worship,' we answer, 'we're leavin' work for the barracks.' 'Why're you singin' with such joy?' 'What do you mean,' we say, 'with joy? Here we are, drenched, chilled to the bone, starvin', but we've finished our task. We're goin' to the barracks, 'n' we'll warm ourselves up 'n' dry off.' 'Get behind me!' he says, 'n' he leads us both to his quarters. 'Well,' we're thinkin', 'this is awful!' He leads us into a large room, shows us to a table: 'Sit down,' he says, 'be my guests.' Then he calls the cook 'n' orders him to give us ever'thin' there is to eat in the house. But he himself gives us a huge goblet of wine. 'Drink,' he says. He can't be misunderstood. We drank. We dunno what we're doin' from fright. But we see he's givin' us another goblet still: 'Drink more.' 'No,' we say, 'that's enough, your worship, we don't wanna get tight, or tomorrow we won't make it to the trench.' 'Don't worry,' he says, 'I'll answer for it. You'll remember how Razgildeev has hosted his powerful army.' Then he grabbed a piece of paper, wrote down some message, 'n' stuffed it in my blouse: 'In the mornin',' he says, 'show this to the orderly.' As we was reachin' home, I was already gone. We was both well 'n' truly drunk, 'n' weren't it all the more so for an already weakened man? They woke us for work early, early in the mornin'. They really had to nudge me, but I couldn't unnerstand a thing. My tongue wouldn't come back, 'n' all I did was stick my hand into my blouse: 'Here,' I says. The orderly looked at the note 'n' his mouth fell open: 'Yes,' he says, 'you been freed from work today by Razgildeev hisself.'"

Around this time I got to know the regulator Monakhov. Pot-bellied, with a swollen red face and placid laugh emerging more from a well-fed belly than from his throat, he little recalled by outward appearance that word from which his surname was derived.[103] He seemed unconcerned by any daily cares or any intellectual interests, and of all the emotions capable of directing his mortal soul, he was open to one only—a feeling of stupefying boredom, salvation from which he sought during the day in the watch house through bantering with prisoners and Cossacks, and during evening and night through cards and drinking. With regard to the latter, he became renowned throughout the entire Shelai region: absolutely no one, not excluding the brave staff captain, little surpassed his portliness, nor could anyone out-drink him. If higher interests and aspirations had ever existed in Monakhov, he'd forgotten them long ago; he read snatches of the newspapers, journals, and articles that happened to turn up and in which he'd heard there was a reference to persons or local affairs known to him. But beyond this he did not go. His political views at any given moment were formed according to the views of the nearest mining authority, before whom he presented himself from time to time to report on the progress of work in Shelai mine. Monakhov, of course, understood perfectly well that the mining department anticipated neither any results nor fruits from all these labors, and so he didn't worry much about them, having left the foreman to direct and answer for everything; he himself followed only the success and productivity of work by the joiners, coopers, carpenters, and smiths who provided him furniture, cabinets, tables, and samovars and who banded with government iron his chests, wagons, and so on. Excluding those instances when he'd been recklessly drunk the day before, Monakhov didn't let a single day go by without rolling into the watch house early in the morning to banter with convoy guards and prisoners about anything that popped into his head, to tell anecdotes, play tricks, crack jokes—in a word (to use the prisoners' expression), to squeeze the bagpipes. He soon recognized, of course, what I was like, and was exquisitely courteous toward me and even tried to discuss other matters, but I sensed that these discussions taxed him, that his atrophied brain tissue was trying with difficulty to surmount long forgotten summits, and I quickly left for the gallery even if there was absolutely nothing there for me to do. After receiving its assignments, the mare would exit the watch house and form ranks—following behind it came pot-bellied Monakhov. For a long, long time he'd stand in one place looking after us, as if wondering whether he should go home to eat or go off visiting somewhere. But Shelai's *beau monde* was small and, having hesitated and thought it over, Monakhov would begin clambering up the mountain to his bleak bachelor's den. Yet, on the way to the prison, we would encounter the pealing bells of a troika in which he was flying to visit some guest from the plant or a mining or other official.

"Well, now that our Monakhov's gone," the mare said among itself, "he won't show up for a week."

On those days when there was rock-smashing in the gallery I felt uncomfortable. It was then I witnessed to the fullest my helplessness and uselessness, witnessed that I was riding on someone else's shoulders. The most I could do was to hold a candle or hand over a pickaxe; Semënov or someone else stronger than I worked the sledgehammer. Not one of them, it's true, grumbled at me; but to me, my weakness, my nobleman's litheness, was pitiful and disgusting. Listening to how the mountain groaned beneath Semënov's powerful blows and how he himself growled with each hammer-blow like a hungry tiger, seeing how the heavy blocks of granite—which seemed indestructibly hard to me—shuddered and fell beneath his hammer, I, squatting somewhere off to the side with a candle in my hands, shrank, contorted, and regressed spiritually and physically to being an actual baby in fear of this elemental, all-embracing power… It seemed that this strength could crush me at will, like a worm, and that any resistance on my part would be ridiculous and useless. It occurred to me in a moment of despair: here's the truth of the common people and the intelligentsia! How powerful and also how benighted and blind is this unfortunate toiler the common people, and how pitiful are you, idle intelligentsia, burning with ardent love for them, dreaming of universal brotherhood and happiness, but possessing such weak hands so useless for realizing the supreme ideal! Shout, cry, call out—your wailings are fruitlessly rooted in the deep labyrinth of reality and cannot be strengthened even by titanium, and are being drowned out by the savage music of daily toil, by these sounds from which mother earth excretes from herself our weak, timorous heart. Covered completely in his own sweat and blood, Titan hears nothing. He simply growls like a lion with every stroke of his gigantic arm, and woe, woe to you, should you manage to tear him from this work, for then you will have to tangle with *him*! The lion will tear you to pieces—and what will remain of your bright dreams, your passionate, loving impulse?… Parasites alone will be left to continue your vile affair…

"We'll keep on with our work, Ivan Nikolaevich!" shouts at the top of his voice Rakitin, whose appearance Semënov and I, wrapped up in our work, hadn't noticed. He'd finished his assignment in the mine and now ran over to see what I was doing.

"Petrushka, lemme have the sledgehammer. I'll bust that wide open, I'll smash it my old-fashioned way, so's sparks'll fly…"

"Show me," says Semënov, handing him the hammer.

Rakitin does really slam it five or six times, but soon tires of this activity and, sitting himself down, starts blabbing some nonsense.

Not without pleasure do I recall those days I worked in the gallery paired with "the wagger." That was when work went slowest, but was on the other hand most enjoyable. Even when Rakitin found himself in a melancholy mood and was inclined toward philosophical and lyrical outpourings, just a single one of his words suddenly drove all melancholy out of me. Once, he was in a profoundly tragic situation. Having already bored twelve inches, he suddenly made a sad discovery:

"Ivan Nikolaevich! Ah, Ivan Nikolaevich," he beseeched me. "I got a real disaster."

"What sort of disaster?"

"That rock there, look, it ain't sound!… See, it's gonna completely collapse."

"So what? All the better. Pëtr Petrovich is keeping it as his patron saint. Bore in another spot."

"In a-*nother*?! 'N' these twelve inches should jus' be for nuthin'? All my work, jus' gone? Who're you, Ivan Nikolaevich! As if they'll really unnerstand? As if they're capable? They'll gimme a harsh reprimand that I was borin' incorrectly; they'll e'en send a nice chap to the prison with a report."

"Well, that hasn't happened up to now. I don't think Pëtr Petrovich is that kind of man."

"For the time bein' they all been good up to now! But, in my opinion, Ivan Nikolaevich, that white sheep is really black—he's jus' a spook. I wouldn't cry if they all kicked the bucket tonight 'n' was gone tomorrow mornin'! No, my most estimable gentleman, 'tis always better to watch them people carefully. You gotta see for yourself that ever'thin's in good shape for certain."

"But is all this rock really going to fall at once? Look how long that crack's been there."

"Shh! Don't move. Oh! If we laugh is it gonna fall on us, Ivan Nikolaevich? On Egor Rakitin? It should fall on Egor Rakitin? Twelve o' my inches should disappear, my bloody difficult twelve! Indeed, this shouldn't be at all… Oi-oi-oi! It's fallin', Ivan Nikolaevich, good God, it's fallin'… it's gonna fall right now… It's gonna knock us to our knees. Might's well do thirteen inches as do one. We won't have to do more, a full thirteen'll be enough."

And with grim seriousness and tragic visage he slowly began boring, the whole time supporting a two-pood rock with his knees. I laughed myself silly looking at this picture, but Rakitin didn't stop boring, and all the while wagged his tongue, complaining about his fate and cursing the ill-starred day he entered the world, and then he suddenly switched to a cheerful and happy mien by which nothing in the world mattered! At last he was, in this manner, able to bore the thirteenth inch, and the rock did not collapse. Rakitin was as happy as a baby about this, and danced, yelped, and even did a somersault. He then sat down, propped himself up, and, turning sad, began singing a favorite, leaning his cheek on his hand:

> In the silver breakers,
> In the yellow sand,
> For a long, long time I tried
> To guard my little footprints.

However, disaster still threatened: the crack in the rock was so large that the orderly, having arrived to give orders, noticed it without fail. Because Rakitin had gone to the watch house, conspiratorially prepared some clay there, and returned to the gallery to carefully fill in all the cracks around his bore-hole, Pëtr Petrovich was summoned.

"But what more could we do?" said Rakitin, smiling craftily. "So's the gutter stayed wet 'n' the hole was ready: as it is, this a matter for God 'n' the orderly."

Rakitin numbered among the forty men destined for the free command and who had the patience to wait to be released to freedom. But it was a strange thing: I never noticed in him the least animosity toward Shah Lamas, the culprit who'd been given his own liberation. "Certainly weren't lucky"—this was his sole explanation for his misfortune, and he preferred not to grieve over the past but to dream of the future. Yet, time and again, he returned to talking about the free command.

"It woulda been good, Ivan Nikolaevich! For three years I been thinkin' o' the open world I don't see; that I hadda be taken in such an inhuman way to a meetin' with my wife 'n' little boy: in leg fetters 'n' ornamented with half me head shaved! What I'd give for freedom, Ivan Nikolaevich, yes, to dress in a free man's clothes so's you, havin' met me, would exclaim: 'Say, where in the world is such a handsome fellow to be born?' I got, y'know, *my wife's* got a downy little hat in a little box that's so well made it'll last as long as a pot…"

"It's just a pity you don't love your wife… She's old, you say?"

"Ech, Ivan Nikolaevich, what our brother says! The tongue also don't really like gettin' bored. How *can't* you love your own wife? It's true, o' course, that she's ten years older'n me 'n' is like an ol' woman now. Well, but I gotta observe all the laws… specially when sober. Drunk—well, that's another matter. If that dev'lish spark hits us in the throat, then no fella's gotta answer…"

"How will you earn your bread in the free command?"

"We're complicatin' things, Ivan Nikolaevich, complicatin' things! First off, I got a great inclination for tradin'. Second, me wife's greatly handy at ever'thin': she sews, cooks, 'n' trades, too. But, primarily, Ivan Nikolaevich, you only gotta know one secret to trade."

"What's that?"

"The Devil's water itself."

"Vodka, that is?"

"Well, indeed, ya hit the nail on the head."

"But if you're really going to sell it, won't you end up in prison again?"

"That's down to luck. Anythin' can happen. Then you're sittin' in prison. It's really very simple. Only, my mind, Ivan Nikolaevich, can control it. Lord God 'as put so much in this noggin, won't you know! There's all kinds o' worlds 'n' ideas floatin' round in there! Ech! I'm sorry 'bout one thing: that I lived in the same ward with you a short time 'n' didn't stick to grammar in the modern way. Well, but all the same, a big thanks to you, Ivan Nikolaevich, for showin' me the light. Without you, my head wouldn't-a busied at all with the books put there, 'cause I'm a complete dunderhead, a simpleton. But now I begun little-by-little to knock out all the syllables. I read through a teeny-weeny bit o' 'The Robber Brothers'—though them monsters took it! A miraculous book; I'll buy it soon's I enter freedom. Come summertime I'll send you little berries, Ivan Nikolaevich. I swear, every blessed day bears fruit! If I don't got time to gather 'em I'll send that scamp Keshka. He's already three years old 'n' it's time he helped his father."

"But, Rakitin, doesn't it ever occur to you to go… over there, beyond the hill?"

"You mean, *go home?*"

Rakitin's carefree face suddenly darkened and wrinkled over.

"How can it not occur to me, Ivan Nikolaevich," he mysteriously said, "only now, my hands 'n' feet are bound by me wife 'n' son. Well, all the same, mark my word, Ivan Nikolaevich"—and Rakitin pounded his knee with his fist—"I ain't Egor Rakitin if you don't hear 'bout me! I'm already reachin' my limit! 'Cause I gotta get home immediately!"

"Whatever for? Tell me, if it's not a secret."

"I already gotta little deal goin' on o'er there. When I'm eatin' there's one such man, whene'er I think of 'im, who stops my heart's blood! If I don't chew out his heart I won't live… I'll rip it out with my teeth soon as I see him!"

"Stop talking nonsense, Rakitin. There's probably no such person, and you're not at all ready to escape."

"Who? *Me-e?*! I'll take to my heels, Ivan Nikolaevich! Only, when I reach a certain point, o' course."

Once, after one such conversation, we returned to the prison and the long desired event proved to have occurred: around forty men had been released to the free command, including Marmot, Malakhov, Pestrov, and Gandorin. Rakitin soon passed through the gates as well, and upon leaving waved his cap and enthusiastically shouted to me for a long time:

"We're grateful, grateful for ever'thin', Ivan Nikolaevich! Don't forget the dashin' Egor Rakitin. I'll get the berries for you quick. I'll flatten myself 'fore mister com'dant 'n' ask 'im to allow it."

By contrast, there was in the prison a most unpleasant surprise with regard to the new ward arrangements; having arrived at my previous ward, I learned that it was now No. 1. Besides those released to freedom, I lost Goncharov and Semënov, who had been put in another ward, Buzzy, and several other of my old cohabitants. Still with me were the Burenkov cousins, Chirok, the poet Vladimirov, and Iron Cat and his blacksmith striker Efimov. Joining us five were twelve new prisoners—by which number the ward's atmosphere was barely tolerable. From time to time the prison administration made similar transfers, having in view the same goal it pursued in all things—consistency.

In the given instance, it had in view an ecclesiastical consistency, since it was supposed that with the passage of time each ward developed its own special physiognomy and character, and could produce a shared spirit and outlook that made possible dreams of undermining and opposing the leadership's will. I've already said that Luchezarov was a great politician and had every chance of going far...

Upon entering the ward and recognizing there had been a "pivot" to another location, I each time somehow felt personally offended (strange, it would seem, in *katorga*!): you were dealt with exactly like cattle, capriciously moved from one stall to another! It's said that a prisoner will forsake with regret those stocks to which he's been chained a long time, and I think there's a measure of truth in this assertion. I remember extremely well that gloomy displeasure I felt after each forced separation from old walls and cohabitants and relocation amid new, practically unknown people. It felt exactly like the first time. I inexpressibly missed Goncharov and Semënov, and Marmot, Malakhov, and even the pair of wild Kirgiz who slept beneath my sleeping platform and often made the whole ward laugh with their pranks. Only the presence of Chirok softened my dejection; but he was evidently bored without "the black-striped devil," Marmot. Since my books' confiscation my students occupied me little, and they themselves grew somehow lazier and more vulgar: a rumor was constantly going round that in spring a "sample" would be sent to Sakhalin Island... Vladimirov (Bear's Ears) was more sluggish and uncommunicative than before and inspired no affection. Finally, I hardly knew the blacksmiths: they'd been in the background in the first ward for some reason. For the most part, the new prisoners seemed always unfriendly, morose, and hostile.

"No, these are far from what the others were!" I thought to myself...

THE LITTLE EAGLE OF FERGANA[1]

There may be noticed in every prison a group of prisoners keeping off to the side from general prison life, exclusive and estranged from the majority of comrades. These are the non-Russian Mohammedans—Kirgiz, Sarts, Uzbeks, and Tatars (without distinction, Russian prisoners call all "Tatars," just as they call all inhabitants of the Caucasus "Circassians").

When free from work they either sit somewhere in the corner listening with grim attention to their mullah's sing-song monotony and rather nasal recitation of the Koran, or pace through the prison yard with slow, silent, almost ceremonious strides and conduct among themselves an enigmatic and also, as it were, grim conversation.

But it always seemed to me that the most serious impediment to affinity between Muslim prisoners and the Christian majority was their ignorance of the Russian language, and by no means their religious fanaticism. As soon as a Mohammedan begins to learn to understand Russian speech and to employ it, mutual estrangement quickly vanishes and he practically blends in with the general mass of prisoners. Unfortunately, most non-Russians have neither the stimulus nor the desire to study Russian, since each of them constantly dreams of returning home. They soon flee the free commands and settlements by entire dozens, which is why the greater part perishes along the way or ends up in prison again, and only rare individuals manage to make their way to Khiva, Bukhara, or even Afghanistan.

For some reason, a special hatred of Russian prisoners is enjoyed by the Sarts, among whom may be discerned two types: one serious, silent, and frankly lazy; the other, by contrast, garrulous and cheerful, but crafty and able to skillfully shirk labor, heaping it on comrades. I remember one such Sart, a young, healthy fat boy with a big, bushy black beard who amused the whole prison with his talk. He loved to tell about his adventures in freedom and, winking slyly, said of himself that Aidar Iakubaika was "a swindler, a *hy-uge* swindler," and that if the "Urus"[2] captured and put him in prison he'd only become "betterer," that is, smarter, and the Urus wouldn't fare well next time he escaped. Iakubaika was humorous, risible, inquisitive, attentive to any talk, and, regardless of his poor understanding of the language, somehow always managed to understand everything. These qualities would have won him the prisoners' general approval had he not been terribly lazy and crafty during work-time, when he simply *appeared* to be working but was piling anything difficult onto others; added to this was a loathsome greediness, touchiness, and peevishness. He got into a fight every minute, and for all his strength and burliness was often beaten, since he was clumsy and comically slow; they'd crack him in the head, then rip a tuft of hair from his beard… You should have seen Iakubaika during these fights: that was when he'd turn into a real animal, bare his teeth, terrifyingly show the whites of his eyes, and snarl and growl just like a tiger. On the other hand, I should say to his credit that his rancor was not excessive: after two hours he wouldn't remember those offenses for which Russians, even for just words, will spend many years dreaming of revenge. Having been released to the free command, Aidarka soon escaped and, they say, was killed by steppe-Tungus. He'd probably wanted "to borrow" (steal) something, but Shelai's "bestest" didn't get his way: the Tungus turned out to be better "scoundrels" than he.

The Kirgiz, or, as they called themselves, the *Kyrgyz*, were far more attractive.

I loved to watch these children of nature, practically untouched by European urban culture. Among them were individuals with slender, delicate features, pleasantly drawn lips, tenderly expressive, deeply set velvety eyes, and graceful, un-worked hands. At the sight of these striking figures hailing from the depths of our Orenburg and Turkestan steppes, I often recalled Cooper's novels about Indians and his moving story of the last of the Mohicans. Thus were the brothers Stambeki—Telenchi and Eskambai—engraved into my memory. They were sent to *katorga* for robbing caravans and repeatedly stealing others' cattle. Telenchi was the elder, and possessed one of those attractive appearances about which I've just spoken: a slender and narrow build, a long, dark-complexioned face of European type with small, Spanish, profoundly thoughtful eyes. He was frail and weak and, exercising his rights as older brother (*ará*), barely worked. Eskambai normally performed double assignments, for him and for himself. This display of fraternal regard infuriated the mare, and curses and reproaches were hurled at Telenchi from every quarter.

"Ooh, you lazy Tatar spade! Are you jus' gonna ride your brother? He's glad he's found a fool!"

Telenchi was silent and always sad. It seemed that if he could have, he would have lain on the sleeping platform from dawn to dawn without getting up. But he slept little, and often at night I'd see he'd opened his long eyelashes from behind which he gazed with his large, dark eyes. Eskambai slept undisturbed, but Telenchi was always thinking...

Eskambai had a completely different character and even different facial features— coarser, more distinctively Mongol: protruding cheekbones, sallow skin, somewhat slanted eyes. Owing to two missing front teeth he had an utterly savage appearance. But all this was made up for by his surprisingly friendly, childlike, happy disposition. Eskambai was kind and helpful not only towards his brother but everyone who regarded him without rancor. Hence, he shared a great friendship with Chirok, who for his part was favorably disposed toward him. Having been stuck beneath the sleeping platform, Eskambai barked like a real dog, bleated like a thoroughbred sheep, and cuckooed like the most indubitable cuckoo. Chirok couldn't restrain himself and would jump up and began beating the offender out from under the platform with a belt, shouting:

"Akh, you Tatar spade! Vermin! Creature!"

But for his part, Eskambai would snarl:

"Ooh, *id palás! Kuchuk palas* (sonofabitch)!"

And the whole ward would smooth things over with laughter.

Chirok also taught Eskambai to beg for alms in Russian villages.

"I'm quite familiar with your wild sort, 'n' you'll surely take to vaggin' immediately. Go to a milit'ry unit 'n' soon there'll be a cauldron on your shoulder—'n' you're on your way home!"

And Eskambai, slyly smiling at this prophecy, would study his "shootin' 'neath the windows" and "pickin' up the *savateiki*,"[3] bowing from the waist and hilariously saying:

"Little mother, little father, gimme some alms, for God's sake!..."

Later, the Stambekis really did escape from the free command, and of their subsequent fate I know nothing.

During the transfer to No. 1, I joyfully noticed my neighbor on the sleeping platform, the young Uzbek Usanbai Marazgali, who had much earlier attracted my sympathy and pity. Something special that cannot be put into words was in this lithe, graceful creature, in his easy gait, his face now young and lively, now as if suddenly faded and aged with discernible, small wrinkles on the cheeks and a bitter expression on his angular lips and in his beautiful black eyes. I painstakingly questioned the prisoners and, to my surprise, it turned out nearly the entire prison was favorably disposed towards this strange youth.

"Usanka?" old man Goncharov said. "Yes, he's the only one of all them beasts I e'er seen act close to a human bein'. We call 'em all the same, Tatars 'n' Sarts, but Usanka's no Sart, really. He e'en gets mad when he's called a Sart: 'Me,' he says, 'Uzbek, 'n' we, too, no like Sarts.' This Usanka's a strange chap, so jolly, an en'ertainer. Whole party fell in love with him durin' the march... Unnerstand, there's no trace o' Iakubaika's laziness in 'im: he tries hard to do his 'n' others' work. I often says to 'im: 'Usan, why're you o'erstrainin' yourself? Y'know there's a buncha loafers here... You ain't gotta wear yourself out in *katorga*...' He just laughs 'n' waves his hand: 'It's alright! Me not scared!' But how alright: he ain't at all well, unnerstand! He's really all worn out... Durin' our march there was an escape, they got far away; but the soldiers kilt his father 'n' brother, 'n' he was close to death... Another time the poor man looked like he'd cough hisself to death... He's grabbin' his chest: 'It hurts here,' he's sayin'. He's a weak chap, ain't clever, 'n' there's nuthin' more to say!"

Marazgali wasn't assigned to the mine, which is why for a long time I couldn't get closer to him, encountering him for the most part only during roll calls; but in prison the prisoners spoke about no one as they did about Usan, about how he was not clever at work, how he poured out his strength, not understanding that "there really are scoundrels 'mong us brothers." Everyone unanimously complimented his cheerfulness as well, and lovingly mimicked his poor pronunciation of Russian words. Among other things, a rumor ran through prison that Marazgali was a remarkably skillful boxer and, in a fight in the kitchen with the cooks, he knocked out in succession three Russian brutes whose humiliation no one foresaw. The prison was excited. Most were delighted with Usanbai and egged him on to further triumphs; the minority who aspired to glorify their good fighters was indignant, confirming that they would not only soil but immediately "disembowel the Tatar vermin"... But Usanbai laid out a quintet of braggarts on the floor one after another, many of whom were twice as strong and bigger than he; he won with the mobility and dexterity of his flexible young body. His opponents finally brought into the kitchen Andriushka-the-Boxer himself, a hefty fellow terrifyingly tall and enormously strong. Nonetheless, he had a problem—he was said to be a coward... Having no faith in his own strength, as he should have, Andriushka resorted to a scurrilous trick: not letting on beforehand how he was going to fight, he suddenly lobbed a rubber ball over Marazgali's head… This is done with tremendous risk and near barbarity: after several practice throws one of the fighters suddenly drops straight onto a knee, yet at the same time throws again with all his might over the head of his stupefied and surprised opponent. It's said that mortal outcomes often conclude such a battle… The unfortunate Marazgali smashed his shoulder against a log lying on the floor and was in pain for a long time afterward. The whole prison was up in arms against Andriushka, but the injured man himself would simply smile and, contorted by pain, say:

"It's nothing, nothing, I'm alright."

However, after this incident his pugilistic exploits ended.

I tried my best to get close to Marazgali, but it was a strange thing: cheerful and easygoing with other prisoners, always joking and carrying on with someone, he was for some reason embarrassed by and avoided me, delivering typically nonsensical phrases and hastening to get away. Imitating the prisoners, he for a long time referred to me with the formal "you," though this was completely alien to his native language, and he addressed me as nothing other than "ma*h*ster." When I, as it happened, approached him in the ward, then, having no possibility of hiding anywhere, embarrassed and flustered, he was willy-nilly compelled to engage me in conversation. A volunteer who appeared as a translator in difficult moments would come and sit down next to us. Marazgali spoke Russian hilariously poorly, and I often understood literally nothing he was saying. But in coming to the story of his escape, he usually livened up, stopped being embarrassed, and, with glittering eyes and rapid gestures, told how he'd fled and how they shot at him… He fell… A soldier swooped down on him with a bayonet… He jumped up, grabbed the rifle, began fighting back… Struggling, he bit the soldier's hand and ran off with a shout… Then an entire horde of new soldiers came tearing along, knocked him down, and stabbed him with their bayonets. Poorly understanding his words, I nonetheless imagined this young tiger who, surrounded by enemies and seeing no salvation anywhere, screamed, scratched, and bit, dearly sacrificing his life and freedom…

Marazgali would then come to the most important part of his story. From the road he wrote his mother that his father and brother had been killed, and that his *katorga* term had been doubled to ten years. But his mother, in his words, returned this letter, wishing to believe that not Usanbai but some "fraud" had written it.

"She not believe… Well, let not her believe!" Usan passionately exclaimed, angrily waving his hand, though with tears in his eyes.

Because of his own inconsistent stories and self-assigned translators' poor translations, I managed to learn only a little bit about Marazgali's past. One day, I heard a rumor that he had demonstrated an unusual understanding of grammar and had by himself already mastered half the Russian alphabet. I joyfully seized upon this circumstance and immediately suggested to Marazgali that he study with me. Having heard this, he for some reason became embarrassed and began entreating me to leave him in peace.

"Ma*h*ster! Pr*w*ease, no need, pr*w*ease!"

I pressed and prodded him to study, believing that he himself would be glad to be a literate man upon release to settlement. Having turned away, Marazgali listened in silence, but then whispered again:

"No need, ma*h*-ster!, be*s*ter, no need!"

I actually noticed tears in his eyes, and stopped pressing him.

"It's all a scheme by their mullah Safarbaev," a Russian who'd overheard our conversation told me, "he's forbidden 'em to learn Russian."

I instantly started out for Safarbaev, a quite young Sart who read Arabic and knew the Koran better than Shelai's other Mohammedans and so was regarded as their mullah, and frankly asked him: did he tell Marazgali he didn't want him studying Russian grammar? The mullah, smiling and explaining that Mohammedan law does not at all forbid sciences and languages, promised for his part to discuss the matter with Marazgali. But soon there was a new reallocation of prisoners among the wards and Marazgali unexpectedly found himself my cohabitant and neighbor. After this, we quickly grew close and became friends.

As a cohabitant, Usan was indispensable, cheerful, always courteous, and serviceable. All the prisoners liked him and strictly distinguished him from the rest of the Mohammedans, most of whom they disliked; Marazgali himself stood apart from them, rarely going near their group and listening inattentively to the mullah's nasal recitation of their holy book. He was generally unable to concentrate his attention on any point for long. When I again suggested he take up studying Russian grammar, he joyfully agreed, having explained his earlier unwillingness as his being very frightened of me and, considering himself for some reason incapable, thinking I'd be angry over this... Able to read Arabic, he quickly acquired the Russian alphabet and phonemes, and even began learning tolerably well how to write those words I dictated. But, alas! His poor knowledge of Russian vocabulary did not let him understand what was read, and this greatly cooled his ardor for learning. To quickly learn to speak Russian he would have needed to have not been living in the same ward with any Tatars at all, but this almost never happened. Therefore, he eventually did not begin learning Russian correctly, though he read and wrote tolerably well.

I soon learned the circumstances of his sad history.

He was a native of Fergana District, from near the city of Margelan,[4] where his parents worked as farmers and fruit growers. From time to time they travelled to the city itself to trade. The family, consisting of a father, mother, and two sons, lived together very amicably. But the older son Marasíl, who'd begun drinking vodka and playing dice, grieved his parents. Norbiutá Marazgali, Usanbai's father, often severely beat Marasil for this, but was unable to restrain him. He soon piled up debts his father did not want to pay, and one night a Kirgiz to whom Marasil had lost a significant amount at dice broke into their lodgings, stole their best horse, and galloped into the steppe. Norbiuta, however, noticed the theft, woke his sons, and all three tore along on horseback after the thief. They caught up to him next to his own village, and Marasil immediately brought the enemy down with a kick to the head. Marazgali senior cut his head off with a saber. Usanbai promised and swore that he himself hadn't touched the Kirgiz and had limited himself to handing his father the saber; but he fully approved of the murder and, when I began arguing with him, said half-jokingly, half-seriously:

"Why such man live, Nikoliaichik?" (Thus he called me, unable to pronounce "Nikolaevich"; a prisoner named Kanarevich living in our ward he called Kanareichikom.) "Thief, gambler... Why he live?"

"But didn't Marasil gamble?"

"Marasil die… God punish him."

"But you yourself, Usanbai, did you ever try gambling?"

"I try, Nikoliaichik," he said, embarrassed and in a guilty voice, "once I lose five rubles at dice… served me right… Also lost ruble at card in Algacha…"

"Not good, Usan!"

"I am indeed, Nikoliaichik… I can't… The Devil knows! I can't do nothing at cards!"

When the killing took place it was already morning, and a passing Kirgiz saw the murderers. Norbiuta and his sons were soon arrested and sentenced: he got fifteen years' *katorga*, Marasil got ten, but as a minor, Usanbai got two years. He could not without tears recall his farewell to his mother, who evidently loved him terribly. Indeed, he was her favorite son. One time, a prisoner praised Marazgali's hair, which was rather curly and black as a raven with bluish tints. He became animated and told how at his home, according to their religious custom, his entire head was shaved except for a long top-knot on the crown.

"Mama stuck in clay, in clay, like so…," he said about this top-knot. "Akh, how mama cry—said good-bye, scratch face, scratch till blood, screamed… Akh, how scream mama!…"

And each time, reaching this point of the story, he fell silent and hurried to bury his nose in his pillow and sigh deeply… Deep, powerful emotion, joyful or mournful, he expressed in the same comically clipped language.

Marazgali's party consisted of thirty-two Uzbeks, Sarts, and Kirgiz and was guarded by a convoy of all of eighteen soldiers. At the third or fourth station from the city of Vernyi,[5] where they had a day of rest, an escape was planned. The convoy, suspecting nothing, had stacked their rifles together in the same ward as the prisoners were and settled down for a game of cards; just one watchman was standing outside the doors. By prearrangement Norbiuta was supposed to shout "Allah!," attack this watchman and disarm him, and the others were to grab the rifles and dispatch the convoy. Norbiuta did like so—with a cry of "Allah!" he overpowered and killed the watchman; but the other nineteen men who were in on the plot evidently froze at the decisive moment and, without grabbing the rifles, scattered helter-skelter wherever their eyes led them. Among them fled Usanbai and Marasil. The convoy, having regained their wits, flew out of the station and began shooting at the escapees. Right there on the station's threshold Norbiuta was hoisted onto bayonets. The heavy irons fixed to everyone's legs caused them trouble; and there were no bushes nearby. Only three managed to hide themselves; the other sixteen were either shot or stabbed. Usanbai was wounded in the leg and fell; but when the soldier who'd shot him rushed over and was about to stab him he got to his feet and grabbed his rifle. There ensued between them a desperate hand-to-hand struggle in which Marazgali so badly bit the soldier's arm that he ran off screaming. But then the other guards arrived and finished him off with rifle-butts and bayonets. So they thought, at least. According to Marazgali, he lay unconscious for over twenty-four hours, but when on the second night he awoke, he realized there was a watchman standing over the murdered bodies and that the slightest groan could ruin him. The sixteen year-old boy, seriously wounded and dying from unbearable thirst and pain, had the strength of will not to emit a sound, and did not make a move until after another twenty-four hours when a doctor from Verny arrived and began certifying the dead. Only then did Marazgali groan and stir. Even then the brutal soldiers attacked and probably would have killed him had it not been for the doctor. Even those twelve men who hadn't tried to escape and had spent the entire time in the station were beaten. Marazgali was taken together with them to Verny and put in an infirmary; while he was recovering a military judicial commission tried him and, taking into account his age and the aggravating example of his father and older brother, gave him only eight more years' *katorga*…

Having recovered, Marazgali was again assigned to a party and dispatched along the regular route. At the third station, where the escape had taken place and his father and brother killed, he cried so bitterly that even the convoy's sympathy was aroused. The senior officer (who was the same as the first time) went up to him and said:

"Thank the Lord, Marazgali, that none of the guards here now were here then! They'd finish you off right now… Why'd you try to escape?"

"I cried and not able say nothing. Officer pitied me and say: 'We go, Marazgali, and see grave where Norbiuta and Marasil lying.' I go. Akh, I cried so! I pour earth in little rag… that earth where father lies… and always carry it here."

And Marazgali showed me the little bag hanging round his neck safeguarding the precious granules.

Often, lying on the sleeping platform with his arms folded behind his head, he sadly hummed—in the same way as Mohammedans generally read the Koran—some kind of prayer/plaint developed by a certain Sart mullah who'd marched beside him into *katorga*. Unfortunately, I don't remember it verbatim, though Marazgali more than once translated for me this beautiful, truly poetic song; but every time I heard this monotonous, sad melody, melancholy and pain gripped my heart:

"We forsook our homeland, wives, mothers, children, and brothers," went the mullah's song, "we forsook our beautiful fields where grow sorghum, rice, and madder, and where ripens juicily the sweet apricot… Lord! Forsake us not, forget us not in a foreign land!

"The terrible foreign land where we are going, where the pitiless enemy binds us in chains, imprisons us in the dark underground, makes us do hard labor… No one will come to comfort us… Great Lord! Do not forsake us in the others' land, do not forget us!

"On the terrible anniversary of separation, when our wives and mothers will mourn us as dead, tear their hair, scratch their faces bloody, and call upon You to witness their grief—Great Father! think of their and our tears, remember us in a foreign land!"

I've already recalled above that Marazgali wrote his mother from the road, and that she returned this letter with the words that some "fraud" had falsified it and that Norbiuta and Marasil were alive… Upon arriving to *katorga*, Usanbai sent her a second letter in which he repeated the sad news and asked her to believe him, and exactly eight months later, in my presence, he received it back with the Margelan post office's stamp: "Returned due to addressee's non-appearance." These two circumstances: his mother's "non-belief" and her "non-appearance" terribly confused and worried Marazgali, and he often asked me:

"Why mother not believe? Why not come for letter? 'Due to non-appearance'—how non-appearance? What for?"

I myself was as if in a dark forest, trying vainly—based on Marazgali's unclear and inconsistent story—to make any sense out of Fergana District's postal affairs. The poor man absolutely did not know (though I knew for a fact) that not one of the countrymen to whom I'd written letters home for him ever sent an answer.[6] The idea finally popped into Usan's head that his mother might have died… I then urged him to make one more attempt and have a letter delivered to an uncle, Pirmat, who lived in the same village but often traveled to Margelan to trade and had good connections there. So as to definitively guarantee success I called upon Luchezarov himself at his office and, having outlined the whole tragedy of Marazgali's situation for him, asked in view of this unique situation that a letter written in Tatar be permitted. To my surprise Luchezarov granted permission almost without hesitation: evidently, my appeal to his humanitarianism flattered him… Marazgali and I had triumphed.

The next Sunday mullah Safarbaev wrote under our dictation a letter in the Tatar language; I, for my part, wrote the address on the envelope with precision and placed an envelope with Marazgali's exact address inside the letter itself. It seemed everything was accounted and assured for down to the letter. The letter was mailed by registered post and its receipt most painstakingly guaranteed. It remained to patiently await an answer. Almost every evening after that we mused about how Uncle Pirmat would get the letter, how he would immediately inform Usanbai's mother about it, and how the latter would be glad and hurry to answer. But, alas! day after day, month after month, for some reason no answer came… And Marazgali fell into gloomy despair…

"All dead, all!" he said, wringing his hands. "Mama dead, uncle dead… No one left!"

He was even seized by a kind of bitterness from time to time.

"Why, Nikoliaichik, mama not believe, not go to post office? Why mama bare me? Should kill mama, should kill!"

"God save you for what you're saying, Usanbai!"

"God save you, God save you… What a God! Where is God? Why God made *katorga*?"

I didn't know how to answer this question, but Marazgali sadly muttered something in his normal language and, lying down on his bed, abandoned himself to his "*khapá*." So he called his gloomy depression, in which he sometimes found himself for several days and when nothing could distract him or cheer him up, when during all his time off from work he lay on the sleeping platform like a sheet, hiding beneath his cassock, breathing heavily, and constantly thinking, thinking… Old man Goncharov translated this "*khapa*" well with the Russian word "brooding."[7] One evening he was especially sad and, when I pestered him with questions, explained:

"Akh, Nikoliaichik! The day mama cried… The day I go *katorga*… Father, brother… Mama screamed, cried… Akh!…"

Suddenly, clasping his hands, he himself bombarded me with questions:

"Tell me, Nikoliaichik, why man come in world? Why *katorga* in world? Why *Urus* law bad? Our side's law betterer: man murder, earth take him! Chop off head! Stick on pole! But this *katorga*… Torture, tears… Akh! Our law betterer… Have to die, Nikoliaichik!"

He looked at me with eyes full of tears, and I had the terrible notion that a bad end lay in store for Marazgali… But I consoled him as I could, trying to dispel his black ideas of death and turn them in a different direction.

But his *khapa* continued, becoming gloomier and more relentless than the fast approach of summer, more vivid than the greenery on the hills behind the prison walls, and reaching us more strongly than the aroma of the blossoming dogrose and purpling rosemary. Marazgali's health was utterly shattered; the entire summer he coughed, sometimes even bloodily, and grabbed his side, cursing in pain.

"Marazgali," even the guards said to him, "did the medic kick your ass? You're such an idiot, you're really gettin' a taste of it."

"I don't want to be a canvas," he answered, smiling sadly. "They say, 'Beat Marazgali the canvas, beat the canvas!' I won't be that!"

Frequently, against his wishes, I asked the medic to release him from work for several days. Then he'd lie in the yard all day in the sun, wrapped up in both his cassock and gloomy brooding. By summer's end, however, he'd righted himself and once again become the spirit of the ward and was cheering up the whole prison. He was hobnobbing, fighting, and joking with the prisoners once more, and working hard. A hope that he'd get a letter from home had returned…

"Sing us somethin', Usanka," the prisoners playfully said to him, and he began one of his favorite songs:

Got me spoilt by a little bit o' gin,
Got me spoilt by a little bit o' love…
I'm a-goin' sixes and sevens,
Ooh, my nutty little dove.

He didn't know the rest of this song, and didn't understand what this couplet meant; but the greater the laughter these mangled words produced, the sweeter they sounded to his ears.

"No, sing 'Ol' Lady,' sing it in real style 'n' dance!"

Blushing, Marazgali refused. Then one of the wrestlers entered the middle of the crowd encircling him and began to dance and sing:

'N' the ol' lady's got forty years,
But the young girl's got none!

Hearing this familiar and favorite motif, Marazgali couldn't hold back and hauled himself up and started swaying just slightly, stamping his feet in place, just like young women do in circle-dances, and to top off the resemblance he started waving a kerchief.

Oi, the ol' lady's gotten old,
So, young girl—cheer up!…

A third person was clapping time.

But, suddenly noticing either myself or one of the guards nearby enjoying his singing and dancing, Marazgali became terribly embarrassed, broke off the song mid-word, and, accompanied by universal laughter, fled into the ward…

He was forever moving. You might encounter him in the corridor fighting a prisoner or cheerfully singing his "Got me spoilt by a bit o' gin, got me spoilt by a bit o' love," and next minute see him sitting behind a little book or fitting himself out with a Tatar fez made from my worn-out wool socks; but next minute he'd be strolling through the yard curiously searching for swallows circling round their nests. Once at that time, his attention was drawn to a young dove settling itself undetectable to any approaching human on the prison roof behind a wooden column. Usan was instantly transformed: coiled like a cat, he stretched his head forward along one arm while strangely keeping the other behind him, and decisively and silently stepped through the yard in tandem to the peeps so as to steal upon his motionless victim. His face assumed a cunning expression, his eyes burned like those of an animal in whom the hunter's instinct has been aroused, and he was entirely transformed from the delicate and soft-hearted Marazgali I knew and loved into a primordial savage, a blood-thirsty son of the steppe… A single instant—and the gawking dove was quivering in his powerful hand, knocking against the roof, and dropping helplessly into the yard. Hearing the noise, the prisoners hanging about in the corners ran to the spot of action and laughingly and exclamatorily saluted Usankin's dexterity. I also approached, readied by my pupil's brutally devised game to morally admonish him… But this was already unnecessary—Marazgali had once again entirely transformed himself: he was so tenderly pressing the fallen bird to his face, and so softly and lovingly passing his hand carefully across its feathers and head, that my lesson froze on my lips. And before I could even get beside him Marazgali, raising the dove skyward, released his grip. The dumbstruck prisoner seemed to think for several seconds, but then shot straight into the sky and began joyfully circling there to the mare's delighted laughter and Marazgali's beaming gaze.

However, I followed this shining Sunday with suppressed alarm, fearing that it was only temporary and would go no further. And, actually, in October, when a damp, windy autumn along with snow, rain, and sudden frosts begins in the north, Marazgali caught a bad cold and fell ill with pneumonia thanks to his carelessness at work, from which I wasn't powerful enough to protect him. The drunk medic didn't want to intern him in the infirmary and kept interrogating me: "Why should I worry 'bout that 'little wild animal'?" But I threatened to complain to the prison leadership and so, believing my exaggerated stories of influence upon the latter, he immediately fulfilled my request. On the other hand, if Marazgali fortunately endured this illness it was thanks only to his naturally healthy organism, and by no means to this dark physician's solicitude or artistry. For my part, I did all I could for Marazgali, did more for him than he himself could do, and spent all my free time sitting next to his bed. I refused to talk to him too much, but he looked at me with warm, grateful eyes and smiled affectionately. One day, he asked in a whisper:

"Am I going to die, Nikoliaichik?"

Needless to say, I hurriedly responded negatively and even forced myself to laugh, though deep in my soul I believed there was a danger—Marazgali gripped my hand warmly. He was enduring this difficult illness, but then again, he often confessed that he greatly feared death and wanted terribly to remain alive…

Among other things, a plan ripened in my head to free Marazgali from *katorga* and return him home. This plan consisted of presenting to His Highness a petition in Usanbai's name that detailed his entire sad history, unvarnished and without excuses. To me, it seemed clear as God's day that if only the petition reached Petersburg and was read there, Marazgali's freedom would be assured. Having arrived at this conviction, I once again decided to rely upon the brave staff captain's "human" emotions. This time, Luchezarov was astonished at my request and immediately expressed doubt that my effort would succeed.

"You can write a thousand petitions," he said, "but only one will get noticed."

I answered that this very petition could be the one out of a thousand, since I deeply believed in its correctness and lawfulness. Luchezarov shrugged his shoulders.

"But how will it help him?" he went on asking me. "Really, isn't it… all the same if he dies? Doesn't he practically have consumption?"

To this I responded that all people die but each is nevertheless hoping for a better future.

"Very well, then," Luchezarov at last decided, "write it, and perhaps… Then I'll order my clerk to make a copy immediately."

I immediately wrote the petition after returning to the prison, pouring onto paper the better part—it seemed to me—of my heart's blood… Having read it, Luchezarov gave his full approval:

"You have a powerful pen, powerful."

He again repeated his promise to give the petition to his clerk for copying and to then direct him where to send it.

Afterward, Marazgali and I lapsed into reveries even more optimistic than the time we wrote his Uncle Pirmat. We concluded that within exactly one year, in the following autumn, an answer should come from Petersburg… Insofar as I tried to believe the answer would be positive I did not for a minute imagine a different response. But one day we quarreled almost severely. One more time (it seemed like the tenth time already), I'd made Usan tell the story of the Kirgiz's murder, and I immediately seized on the fact that he gave his father a wooden block, but that it seemed he'd earlier concealed this important detail from me.

"Why were you silent about this earlier?" I angrily pressed. "The tsar's there now, saying that he's received a petition and that you're lying because your file shows you gave a different story."

Marazgali became terribly upset.

"I said, Nikoliaichik, I said," he whispered, justifying himself and looking at me imploringly. "You forgot…"

"No, you were covering up, Usan, you were covering this up, and maybe you've been lying to yourself."

But then other prisoners who, like me, had many times heard his stories about his past, intervened on Marazgali's behalf and confirmed he always remembered about the block and that I was wrongly accusing him of lying.

Marazgali looked at me reproachfully.

"You see, you see," he shouted joyfully. "Marazgali said… He covered up nothing!"

I was ashamed… And although Usan immediately forgave me and forgot my injustice, he'd already been disturbed as to whether the petition had been correctly written. I calmed him with great difficulty, having myself recognized my error in assuming because of a simple unintended elocution that he'd been trying to alter his case's negative outcome.

Unforgettable evenings, full of faith and hope! We both vividly pictured to ourselves that Marazgali had already received a full amnesty and would be going home to his warm and sunny Margelan… He would find there his mother alive and healthy and all his relatives and, with his own hand, write me detailed letters about everything… Sometimes our reveries strayed so far that I was already entering a settlement and journeying to visit Marazgali in his Margelan; he was hosting me to dried apricots, rice, and braised mutton, and at that point Fergana District would so appeal to me that I would decide to settle there forever… In the end, Marazgali would get me married to an Uzbek girl and dance at my wedding… Naïve, golden reveries! What happened to you?

Among other things, the brave staff captain, for his part, wanted to show kindness to Marazgali, and on New Year's Day itself declared his release to the free command, for which he could've waited for almost another year by law. For both of us, his release was so unexpected that Marazgali at first completely lost his head, though he was nonetheless evidently overjoyed… I, too, was overjoyed…

However, having realized that we would be parting, Marazgali suddenly turned gloomy and made me understand he did not welcome the free command and that prison would be better. I consoled him, shaking his hand and constantly repeating:

"Remember, Usan, what I told you: don't play cards, don't drink vodka, and don't escape! If you flee, everything will fall apart, and you won't see your home or mother because you'll be captured anyway. Better to wait for an answer to your petition."

"Alaright, alaright, Nikolaichik… Farewell!"

And we parted…

Unfortunately, Marazgali's life in the free command proved extremely unlucky. No hand was there to protect him from total evil and darkness. First of all, he developed an idiotic relationship with the free command's Russian comrades. Lately, many in the prison had been looking enviously at the fact that, thanks to his friendship with me, he'd ended up in a materially better position and was living "like quite a lord." Some were displeased that I'd written a petition for him at a time when so many Russians were forbidden to petition.

"So, that young Tatar snake's better'n us? Does whate'er he wants."

Thanks to various rumors and gossip, this ill will carried past prison walls: it was said that the commandant himself was protecting Usanka and—not without an ulterior motive apropos this—that he could "obviously git you with his tongue"… Petty carping and persecution began. I can imagine that Usanbai's proud heart, enduring these unfair slings and arrows, must have been suffering; I can imagine the savage flashes of his purely Asiatic temper when he was frightened in prison… Hence, I remember one of his skirmishes with The Angry Cockroach over some ill-starred laundry bag. The Angry Cockroach claimed it was his, but Marazgali was showing him a mark he'd made on the bag with his teeth. At first there was a simple verbal duel as both rivals held onto the contested object; but then Marazgali suddenly burst like fire and turned deathly pale… His hands were trembling and he shook convulsively… He made a vivid picture at that moment, with his head proudly raised and eyes glowering terribly… The Angry Cockroach let go of the bag and, mumbling some profanities to himself, backed away… I can therefore imagine how, one day, Marazgali ran with knife in hand at a free commandee who, labeling him a spy, called him the most terrible name for a prisoner… He was just barely restrained and pacified.

Naturally, what he needed to do in such a situation was to distance himself from the Russians and to close ranks with his group of like-believing Mohammedans. In certain respects, the life of a Shelai free commandee was far worse than that of a prison inmate: you couldn't earn a kopek anywhere or in any way, and when it came to eating, there was only the regulation skilly and no tea or sugar, just like in prison; and at that time, official labor quotas were larger and more difficult. Marazgali was forced to be night-watchman for the storehouse containing prisoners' food and possessions. He had to stay awake all night during bitter January and February frosts, and then run errands for the guards all day. The poor man soon wore himself out completely and once more developed a serious cough. To top off his misadventure, bad luck befell him at the beginning of Lent. The malicious and vindictive mare decided to undermine him and so someone, one day, noticing that Marazgali had dozed off at his post before morning, stole several weights from the government scales. Having awakened and noticed the theft, he began imploring the prisoners to return the weights, but the scoundrels showed no pity and even reported their absence to the quartermaster. Precipitating the permission of the commandant, who was still sleeping, he ordered Marazgali sent to the isolator.

At the time he was sent there I was in the mine, but I quickly learned upon returning from work that Marazgali was to be kept under arrest for five days. Every day, via the ward attendants, I sent the prisoner tobacco and sugar, and learned from them that his health had completely collapsed and he was lying down without raising his head and just moaning occasionally. On the fourth day of his arrest I barely managed to persuade the medic to visit Marazgali in the isolator, and even this dubious representative of medicine found it prudent to ask Luchezarov for permission to transfer him quickly to the infirmary. During this transfer I caught sight of Marazgali and hardly recognized him. My poor Fergana eagle, what had become of you?

What a wretched, faded, and indescribably pitiful old man he looked to me! Yellowed, pale, and sad, he smiled and nodded his head at me with difficulty; he could hardly move his feet; his hair was disheveled and damp from feverish perspiration. Even his clothes looked most pathetic: a crumpled little cap, torn cassock, and a red sack full of holes…

He was given a small private room in the infirmary, and I again spent all my free time with him. I admit, from time to time I actually wished him death… What, indeed, could he hope for in life? What else could it give him except more grief, injuries, and losses?

Marazgali himself was obviously worn out, and there was now not a trace of what should have been that youthful cheerfulness and ceaseless thirsting so erased during the course of his illness. But I tried to banish these dark thoughts and harmful wishes, tried all the same to convince myself and the patient that he would not die at this time. And thanks to my speeches, a spark of hope sometimes flared inside him once more; but more often in response to all my convictions, he bitterly smiled and sadly shook his head. He didn't stop coughing blood the whole time. One day, I found him in an extraordinarily agitated state. He'd been waiting, and reproached me terribly:

"Why I not escaped, Nikoliaichik? Why listened to you? Why you persuade?…"

A shower of tears…

Soon afterward, Usan appeared to improve. When the prison doctor, whose next visit (once every six months) we'd long awaited in vain, arrived at last, real hope grew in him, and he, raising himself slightly from the bed, seemed to look at him imploringly. But the doctor—a veritable *katorga* doctor!—barely glanced at the patient and, waving his hand, moved on. I could stand no more and went up to him with these words:

"For God's sake, doctor, see to this boy's improvement… Maybe something can still be done."

The doctor frowned.

"Are you his brother? A relative?"

"No, but this young man's fate is so worrying…"

"It should be twice as worrying, since there's no medicine to give him. If he were in Italy or the Madeira Isles, well then… But, in *katorga*…"

"But won't you examine him?"

"This is… what *is* this? Are you *lecturing* me? Patients *lecturing* an official, an *official!* Mister Medic! What are these unnecessary folks doing here? This isn't a theater, it's a *hospital!* This isn't a *tavern!* The patients need peace!"

I shrugged my shoulders and left.

Spring. Its first heralds were the small, fidgety, velvety things flying round. The sun became warmer. Pigeons cooed on roofs, and squabbling sparrows were joyfully flying and chirping everywhere. Green grass appeared on the hills, and Marazgali began going into the yard to warm himself in the sunlight. He dreamed of home and his mother.

"Nikoliaichik, today I saw," he told me one time, "at night I saw… a sweet Sart girl… Preetky-preetky!"

He even clicked his tongue over the best attribute of the young Sart girl he'd seen in his dream—and suddenly became terribly embarrassed and hid his face in his yellowed hospital gown.

"I soon getting out, Nikoliaichik, soon, thank God! See: I completely well, completely. Only just little bit pain… here… in this spot… Devil knows what hurts there? Heart sick, liver sick? Devil knows!"

These joyous outbursts passed and were replaced by dull apathy and interest in nothing, when even on the sunniest and warmest days I could not persuade him to forsake the hospital and get some fresh air. Then the slightest breeze would frighten him, and neither little birds nor sunshine nor the first flowers (*urgut*[8]) that I brought him from the mine could dispel his gloomy spleen. His outward appearance also soon worsened. His body turned into a veritable skeleton; there was not a drop of blood in his face, the blood played in his lips only at times, and his eyes burned with an especially bright flame and were unusually dilated. He was burning down, like a candle…

Once, I found him studying the hair on his head before a shard of mirror.

Noticing me, he laughed hoarsely.

"Look, Nikoliaichik, look: grayee… Grayee, grayee here, and there, and there… All my hairs—old man!"

"But how old *are* you, Marazgali?"

"God knows. Registered in Margelan sixteen years… Held in Vernyi two years… On march one year… Jailed at Algacha another year… Here another year and a half."

"That means you're twenty-two."

"Yes, twenty-two. Who knows? Mama knows…"

With these words he became grimly pensive.

I had for a while been feeling my own strength on the decline, and foreseeing a terminal outcome and wishing to be near my friend during his final days, I decided on this pretext to sign myself into hospital. The icon lamp was quickly burning out, the oil nearing its end.

During his last days the dying man spoke with me about God and asked, would he go to *begísh*, to Paradise, or to *dzhageném*, to Hell? Would he see his father or brother? Would he see his mother? With regard to the latter, he was very worried, since according to him there is nothing said in the Koran about the fate of women.

On the morning of the last day he was animated yet again, and got up from the bed and began brilliantly describing Margelan, going on about his sweet dried apricots, rice, etc., and even clicking his tongue several times.

"In our parts, Nikoliaichik, there an herb, too: cures any sickness, *any* sickness!… Akh, here no such herb… Just these medicines… Devil knows, nothing helps, nothing!"

And he clicked his tongue again to better express his sorrow over this. Not knowing what to say, I found it somehow necessary to report a bit of news I'd heard, that a *katorga* prison was being built in the Caucasus for young non-Russians who weren't strong enough to withstand Siberia's cold weather. Having heard this, he seemed overjoyed.

"That good," he said seriously. "Caucasus are good."

And, lying down again, he reburied his face in his blanket. I left. Two hours later, the hospital orderly Dorozhkin came to me, smiling:

"What an eccentric that Usanka is! Suddenly he's callin' to me: 'Get me somethin' eat!,' he's saying. 'I want eat a lot right now… Get me more, much more!' I grabbed him some eggs, bread… 'n' he ate three whole eggs 'n' a great big round o' black bread. Now he's lyin' there sleepin'."

I got angry at Dorozhkin:

"You've lost your mind! What have you done? You know black bread can harm him…"

Dorozhkin laughed.

"Harm *him*?! What're you sayin'?! Have you lost your mind yourself?! You know it don't matter if he dies t'day or t'morrow. Give 'im some provisions for the long journey."

I fell silent. Dorozhkin came back an hour later.

"End's comin' soon!"

I grew anxious.

"Why do you think so?…"

"'Cause he's tuggin' at his blanket 'n' snatchin' at somethin' in the air. That's a true sign, you can be sure…"

With palpitating heart I went to Marazgali and, without entering his room, stood watching from the opened door. He was lying in bed with his face to the wall, eyes apparently closed and from time to time actually grabbing for something in the air with his left hand…

I softly called to him, but he didn't respond.

As of evening roll call he was still alive and, suddenly raising himself, said something in his own language.

"How're you doin', Marazgali?" the guard asked.

"It's nothing, I alright," he answered, and lay down again. These were his final words.

Gazing timidly from the door, we watched him breathing for a long time. Weary from waiting so long, I dozed off on my own bed. Dorozhkin woke me around midnight.

"He's gone!…"

"Can it be?" was my completely involuntary shout, which Dorozhkin did not even bother to answer, and I hurried behind him to Marazgali's room. Several hospitalized prisoners were already crowding round the body, trying in vain to close his wide-open, markedly surprisedly gazing eyes. I grew indignant at this hastiness and, after driving away the unbidden trustees and taking an emaciated, matchstick-like pale arm that was dangling from the bed, felt that it was still warm. I looked in his eyes, but they were already gazing insensibly and appeared glassy. Usanbai Marazgali had completed his earthly journey!

Dorozhkin began bustling around the dead man.

I was struck by a singular characteristic in this old vagabond, oblivious to anything sacred and honoring nothing in the world: rather rude and often intolerably pestiferous when dealing with patients, he now revealed with regard to the corpse some strange, almost maternal tenderness and solicitude.

"There now, dear-ie!" he kept saying, as he put a clean shirt on the body. "Now you'll see Margelan 'n' your mother… No one can put you in prison or hurt you anymore!"

Amid the grinding of the door-lock, the medic and several guards who'd now been informed of a prisoner's death entered the hospital with a din…

Marazgali was buried in the prison cemetery, not far from the road along which *katorga*'s mare went to the mine. There was no cross over the grave, and in winter it would get completely covered with snow, but in summer, wild rosemary flowers and the tediously fragrant dogrose sprouted all over it. What do you dream, my poor, kind boy? Have you found, here in this dark grave, respite from your incurable longing for your faraway home? And if so, was it not better that you died when life could not harden you or pollute your pure, beautiful form?…[9]

SOLITUDE

I. IN A NEW WARD; INNOCENTS AND BRUTES

My story has run too far ahead, however, and I should now return to that point when I ended up in ward No. 1 during the redistribution of prisoners. The repressions resulting from the incident with Shah Lamas lasted no more than a month; after this, they little by little weakened again. Kitchen kettles were returned, the deprivation of which had so maddened Nikifor; locking of the wards was again neglected; cards appeared out of nowhere; the headman Iukhorev and other Ivans even managed to get vodka from time to time… Shackles on prisoner's legs and the absence of my books, which I'd decided not to ask Luchezarov for again, remained the sole reminders of the ruination of human existence. However, the shackles were once more soon removed from the miners: in view of repeated accidents in the mines by prisoners in leg irons, the mining administration office, in general extraordinarily humane regarding penal laborers and often siding with them in disputes with prison officials, stated absolutely that penal laborers should walk to the mountain unfettered.[1] Meanwhile, the absence of readings during long winter evenings was felt acutely: naturally, with nothing to occupy their imaginations, prisoners ended up recalling their lives on the outside and, whether I wanted to or not, I heard the most horrible, bloody, and cynical stories. Whether because my own troubled constitution threw a funereal veil over the whole world and forced me to see people's bad sides more starkly, or because of something else, I nevertheless held the darkest notions about my involuntary cohabitants from this point on; the most terrible stories were especially engraved in my memory during this period. One aspect of these stories particularly frightened me: the majority were rather content with their pasts and their crimes, regarded very lightly the spilling of human blood and the destruction of another's life, and wished only that they had had the presence of mind to better cover the traces of their crimes and hadn't been "unfortunate" in evading the hand of justice… I constantly noticed an effort within even the least dissolute not to right themselves and to play the innocent victim. Often, I even gave in to the conclusion that repentance, in that high ideal in which it is understood in the educated world, was a feeling completely alien to commonfolk prisoners. Every fetus is crushed in his soul by the knowledge that he is suffering punishment, that he's being tortured and ripped apart for a sin. Upon first encountering me, nearly every penal laborer, even the most unrepentant, tried for some reason to convince me he'd been wrongly convicted due to the spitefulness of some malicious investigator or witness (most often a female). I eventually got so used to these assertions that I became skeptical of the stories of those who, perhaps, had actually ended up in *katorga* for someone else's sin. I was far happier when prisoners would straightforwardly and unashamedly identify themselves as "robbers, scoundrels, and swindlers." Moreover, such prisoners can be divided into three distinct categories. Some, the most unrepentant, strutted around and boasted as if they had a kind of "quality"; either they were truly embittered to the last degree and exceptional among their own type of people or, by contrast, they were the most worthless frauds, babblers, and braggarts, liars and insolents who disrespected themselves and, having come to regard human life as the same as that of a flea, were ready to commit brutal murder or any other foulness for the sake of a penny or a tumbler of vodka. To top it all off, they were terrific cowards. Trying to emulate great scoundrels and to acquire the glory of these same "thugs," they went endlessly further than they in their radical views toward things: they not only denied all the world's sanctity but offhandedly blasphemed and apostatized; they not only murdered, but actually drank living human blood from a glass; they were happy to flaunt their unpardonable and irredeemable dissoluteness and corruptness at every step. This category of prisoners, the living forms of which I'll now present to the reader, were the most antipathetic and harmful. Petty-souled and intellectually impoverished, they were incapable of that high movement of the spirit that so often distinguished criminals of Semënov's or even Goncharov's type. It stands to reason that this basic character, in his turn, possesses several elements, beginning with openly shameless impudence and cynicism and ending with loathsome duplicity and sycophancy. The same characterized those who stubbornly declare themselves falsely convicted, and so I repeat: such assurances had to be regarded *cum grano salis*.[2] There is not the slightest doubt that forty years ago, in Dostoevskii's time, when Russia was "a profoundly unfortunate country, oppressed and illegally enslaved," when alongside serfdom there still existed twenty-five-year soldiers' widows[3] and, in the expression of the poet, "the people's terror of the word *recruitment* resembled a fear of execution"[4]—undoubtedly, during those times a huge percentage of completely innocent people must have been sent to *katorga*, and still greater numbers were sentenced to less strict measures. In those days, the most horrific crimes were committed by people who were completely normal, not morally dissolute, and had simply been pushed beyond the limit of patience by the abnormal and unfair structure of their lives. Therefore, owing to the spiritual nature of those who were essentially the same as *the people*, Dostoevskii had a certain right, I believe, to idealize the inhabitants of his Dead House, nearly half of whom were soldiers (illiterate almost to a man); but such a right cannot be held by a contemporary observer who has set himself the task of sketching a picture of contemporary Russian *katorga*. It cannot be at all doubted that in this very same forty-year period Russian justice and law, just like lifestyle and behaviors, have made enormous strides forward along the path of humanism and fairness. *A priori*, it may therefore be believed that those more incomparably deserving than in previous days have ended up in today's *katorga* and that the population of present-day *katorga* represents, *for the most part*, the *scum* of the human sea and by no means the Russian people themselves… Actually, a good half of the prisoners I saw nevertheless insisted that they came to *katorga* for the sins of others, and nearly all without exception complained of the severity of their sentencing by an "unfair" trial—and during my close familiarization with their characters, their pasts, and the charges leveled against them, I rarely found a completely unfairly convicted man. In the majority of instances, if in a given case there may have been a mistake or a biased court, then the very same prisoner acknowledged, as did Goncharov, that, innocent in that instance, he had previously committed many crimes that remained unexposed but were worthy of *katorga*. Yet, having admitted this, he would nevertheless complain about his lot, curse all the world's judges and laws, and insist he'd been exiled to *katorga* unfairly…

However, does all this mean that I'm advocating harsh treatment of today's penal laborers, that, having called them "the scum of the human sea," I'm expressing that same absolute contempt towards them as towards the "trash" who serve those who merely toss them away and consign them as far as possible to oblivion? I allow myself to hope that everything I've written about the world of the unfortunate outcasts dissuades the reader from so unfair and incorrect an understanding of my words. Are there really no pearls in the sea's depths? If it be said that the surface of water in a vessel is distinguished by it favorable qualities, then does this really mean that its depths are completely unsuitable for drinking? And, really, is not the principal task of my essays to show what in fact *must* be demonstrated, that the inhabitants of this terrible world, these crippled, benighted, occasionally crazy people, were, like all of us, capable not only of hating, but of loving passionately and profoundly, of falling but of rising, of thirsting for light and truth, and suffering no less than we from all that is a barrier on the path to human happiness?[5]

But we return to our analysis. Do innocents, victims of misunderstandings or judicial errors, exist in *katorga* nevertheless? Theoretically speaking, they undoubtedly exist, though I was personally not surprised to meet those whose innocence I would not vouch for with certainty. What, for example, can I say about the parricide Dashkin, an enormous, awkward fellow with an unpleasant, bestial expression on his ruddy face and brainlessly sleepy eyes—about a man whose intellectual capabilities were positively primordial? He should have been in *katorga*, not wearing chains or entering the free command for precisely seventeen years but, upon conclusion of his term, have been put like all parricides in solitary confinement in Verkhneudinsk Central[6] for the rest of his life… Any prisoner in his place, having no hope to look forward to whatsoever, would have thought only of how "to break loose," to escape or at least transfer to another prison where existence was rather carefree; and finally, having remained in Shelai Prison, he would have been a sty in the commandant's eye, would have behaved impertinently and loafed about and feared nothing. Among other things, Dashkin worked like an ox and was quiet and peaceful as a lamb. A new person who didn't know him at all would probably have imagined that the worm of repentance gnawed at him, that he wanted to soothe the torment of his heavy conscience by taking up this cross. Not in the least! He categorically insisted that he didn't murder his father or at least didn't remember this, since at the time of the murder he was dead drunk.

"I can't say anythin', I myself don't 'member whether I kilt 'im or not," he perplexedly said. "I don't 'member a thing. Or, rather, I didn't kill 'im, but my brother-in-law did, 'cause there's no reason I'd kill my father!"

According to Dashkin, he didn't initially confess at the inquest; but then his brother-in-law, who wasn't a suspect at the time, supposedly persuaded him to confess, saying that in this case the court would treat him easier. The moronic Dashkin believed this and ended up in prison for the rest of his life. Of course, in this very case it's possible Dashkin's conviction was a horrible and essentially tragic error; but it's also possible that Dashkin, knowing full well the prison mass's hostility toward parricides, was lying.

Much more frequently encountered were those cases when a man had been convicted from a simply legalistic and impartial point-of-view that was, by contrast, essentially inhumanly cruel. The most outstanding example of such type was Marazgali's case, which I've discussed above. Our code of punishments is generally too severe regarding escapes, and the administration itself has only recently begun to turn attention to the horrible fact that *to this day* there are people in *katorga* who were completely innocently— from a contemporary point-of-view—sentenced to brief terms *even in the days of serfdom* but who, thanks to frequent attempted escapes, are in *katorga* serving sentences of life and even longer for this purported crime...[7]

But what law can deal with a man like Shemelin, for example, sentenced to twenty years for murdering his own brother, and who actually did this? The law and even people's morality regard crimes like this especially harshly. The worst prisoners often yelled at him and joked in earnestness:

"You're worse'n any of us! You killed your own brother, *Cain!* You deserve the noose!"

The old man, evidently displeased by such exclamations and in his heart reckoning himself infinitely superior to and better than a herd that had been corrupted to its marrow, patiently heard them out in silence. In the meantime, upon hearing about his case, it was essentially impossible to sternly reproach Shemelin. A Russian peasant from a most far-flung and godforsaken place, having grown up as if rooted in the forest among those who, like himself, were of dark and primitively simple mentality, devout, hard-working, fearful, wealthy in patience and endurance, and, lastly, for his part deeply honest, he was incensed by his older brother who sued him for a patch of land and wouldn't return it for anything. This dispute dragged on for seven whole years, now abating, now igniting again like a dying fire into which new kindling is tossed, and it constantly perpetuated the hostility between the brothers. The elder was, apparently, the more courageous and brazen. In fact, having commandeered the land he still permitted himself to mock and "make fun of" his younger brother in public. Shemelin himself said that it popped into his head several times to kill his brother, but each time God stayed his hand from sin. But his patience finally cracked; and when one Sunday his brother, arrayed in his Sunday clothes, was walking to church past his house, he killed him on the spot with a rifle. Shemelin never defended his act and never said he should have done it at a different time, but, on the other hand, he couldn't comprehend the full moral gravity of his crime, and viewed it not as a sin that had to be expiated in the torment of *katorga* but simply as a misfortune that could not be gotten rid of. Silent and for the most part averse to any clashes or arguments with fellow prisoners, he in his heart nevertheless regarded himself a good man and was proud of his honesty. For instance, he loved to tell how, on the road to a way-station, he returned to a market woman a twenty-kopek coin she'd given him as change, and how the whole mare had jeered him for this. During one conversation in the ward about direct and indirect taxes, this primordial intellect distinguished itself more colorfully than the rest. Among penal laborers were experts for whom the theory and practice of state finances were mere bagatelles. One of them, cursing for all he was worth at government costs, poured out facts and figures. The others were avidly listening and agreeing. Finally, the silent Shemelin could no longer restrain himself and sing-songingly drawled:

"Well, you're a-lyin' 'bout this."

"What am I lyin' 'bout?"

"'Bout how much they takes from us. For example, I ne'er had as much in my life as you got in a year."

"What? Ain't you bought yourself a calico shirt or a sarafan for your woman?"

"We ne'er bought *calcos*… Wove what we needed ourselfs. Right now, only fashion we got is dressin' village-style."

"Very well. But ain't you bought matches?"

"Made matches ourselfs… In my time, peasants 'as always made ever'thin' themselfs."

"Oh, you devil's head! Ain't you smoked tobacco? You had tea 'n' sugar?"

"God spared me 'n' I ain't smoked tobacky. But tea 'n' sugar… Ain't heard of 'em 'fore *katorga*, 'n' didn't know what to eat 'em wid!"

"This here's a time-wastin' scoundrel! Look at this pine tree in the forest—such an educated man's speakin' to us! You drank vodka? You paid for vodka?"

"Ain't paid for vodka… Made our own…"

After this explanation the orator spat heartily, waved his hand hopelessly, and moved away from Shemelin; but Shemelin, too, fell silent, in beatific recognition of his own righteousness and superiority, before which his enemies' machinations were powerless. And, in actual fact, you could be moved by the touching simplicity of his physical needs and intellectual interests, not so far from those interests and needs by which grass exists in a meadow, a bird in the sky, a tree in the forest. Did not this psychological simplicity bind him to the "honesty" he maintained in *katorga*, even under the influence of hundreds of corrupting examples and proofs, under the pressure of the importunate propaganda of every dirty trick and swindle? However, to these Shemelin had already made some concessions. Thus, by means of old-fashioned thriftiness and accuracy and having recognized that, in *katorga*, all superfluous regulation items are seized and that, at the same time, several pairs of mittens, puttees, and other rags had been piled up across the road, he threw them among some litter before arriving at the mine, hoping they wouldn't be found. But not only were they found in Shelai Prison, they were taken and piled up for burning along with the litter itself. The old man was very distressed by this, and frequently complained to me that he might have sold them for a good price, indeed, "here some fool got a notion o' draggin' 'em straight to *katorga*!" But how naïve and simple this unfortunate ruse was in comparison to the swindles and trickery of *katorga*'s true "artistes"!

Shemelin was the honest of the honest in Shelai Prison, so honest that all his comrades mocked him and considered him their family freak. He really was a rare exception. What could *katorga* teach such a man? Could it have been anything useful or edifying? Would it not have been better, still fairer, to give such a man his freedom after having limited his punishment to removal from his birthplace? I believe so; but the law, unfortunately, did not act in consideration of any except formal and superficial fairness and so Shemelin, sentenced to twenty years' *katorga* labor, had to spend seven of these years in prison (four years in manacles and all seven with a shaved head) and eleven more in the free command, where he had to perform the same penal labor tasks and submit to the same arbitrary regime. The man's life was definitively and hopelessly broken...

I've already recalled more than once that, in certain regards, I think of prisoners as true children and savages. Although I'm far from the notion of fully developing a corollary between criminals and children, even as foolishly purposeful and utterly depraved, certain similar characteristics nonetheless strike the eye: that same fervent impressionability without deep and lasting impression; that same ineptitude at concealing psychological impulses; that same inconsistency of will, the quick shifts from one to another idea often completely contradictory to the first, and—what was still worse—the thoughtlessness of their very actions too quickly converted from word to deed. It is this inconsistency of will that serves, I think, as the principal reason for most crimes. But is this an unmistakable sign of in-born criminality or so-called degeneracy? Abnormality of social relations, crude upbringing, uncultured environment—these, I believe, are the principal nests of infection. People quite normal and healthy, resembling thousands of other people peacefully living in freedom and with a reputation for incorrigible honesty, are frequently knocked onto the criminal path simply by idiotic specimens inured to seeing blood and all sorts of violence. However, it has to be remembered that children tend to be horribly cruel and indifferent to another's suffering; even Grandpa Krylov[8] said about them that "that age knows no pity." I remember my own early childhood, how I was now and then cruel towards little birds, insects, and other defenseless creatures, and how with curiosity I sometimes attended scenes of shocking violence (if, of course, I was myself not threatened in those instances); in the meantime, having grown up and become an educated man, I cannot calmly abide the sight of blood or even hear about any sort of terrible injury without shuddering and feeling absolutely physically ill. So great is the difference between a child's psyche and that of an educated adult! In these regards, many prisoners are distinguished quite like children by an inability to imagine or feel another's suffering and pain as their own.

Sore spots frequently bespeak brutality... However, it cannot be denied that they are to be met with among criminals and subjects whose natural simplemindedness combines with a particular form of voluptuousness, a cynical brutality, an utter thoughtlessness that nothing can apparently explain... But such true degenerates are exceptions—sick people who necessarily shock but do not torment.

Prior to *katorga*, for example, I would never have believed that cannibals still exist in Russia; yet not only prisoners but representatives of the prison administration assured me there were in Algacha Prison several Russians and Tatars convicted of dealing (?!) in human flesh... On Sakhalin, there are apparently a large number of murderers who've eaten the flesh of their murdered enemies. Even in Shelai Prison there was one vagabond who insisted that he himself had tried meat-pies stuffed with "human flesh" and found them quite tasty... Even if this story was a lie, he was nevertheless quite typical. Another prisoner rather cold-bloodedly told a much more likely, albeit no less disgraceful, story. He escaped with his Kirgiz comrade. Along the way they encountered a young woman and, before killing and robbing her, the Kirgiz cut off the unfortunate woman's right breast and drank a cup of living blood from it.

"How could you let him commit such an atrocity?" I asked the storyteller.

"But what right did I have to stop 'im?" was his shameless answer. "He was my comrade."

"Indeed, God knows! You should have used force to prevent him."

"Ha! Force… 'N' what if he'd o'erpowered me?"

"And why did you murder the woman?"

"It jus' happened. 'Twas her fault. We'd been starvin' for three days 'n' she had money. We shoulda perished? It was then, boys, I saw for the first time how human blood's drunk. Before, I thought only wild animals did this, well, then I saw that our brother also…"

"That's how they still do it!" underscored one listener.

I never saw or heard a story—about a murder or a torture, in all its vile details—make any listener shudder, shout, or express disapproval directly to the scoundrel. On the contrary, the audience was always obviously on the side of the perpetrator, not the victim, and for the best of them there was always some evident excuse in their eyes. And then I had to listen to the whole ward's joyous, cheerful, pealing laughter during stories that chilled my hide and made my hair stand on end… Once, a small and usually quiet little prisoner nicknamed Andriushka-the-Cook related in my presence how he'd murdered his sweetheart. This story had certain superficial characteristics that strongly reminded me of Paramon's story, but in essence there was no similarity between them.

Andriushka lived with his Uliana for three years, and moreover, in his own words, he drank unrestrainedly. Because of this, Uliana finally fell out with him and, grabbing her "threads" (clothes), left Andriushka for another man. Andriushka didn't miss his lover, but he considered the "threads" his, and so after several days he went to his former cohabitant's place to demand his purloined things. A vulgar refusal followed.

"Before, I wouldn't-a paid it no mind," said Andriushka, "but that got to me! 'What?' I'm thinkin'. 'I should pay so this filth can laugh at me?' I'm lookin' round. Sittin' on a bench in the corner is a peasant, her new lover, but there's a big knife lyin' on a table. I grab the knife: 'Ah! So it's you?' I say. 'So he's right here for you, you creature!' and I stick the knife in her belly… Her eyes opened wide… I'm lookin': her arms spread out 'n' she's clawin' 'n' clawin' at me… That's how it was… Ha-ha-ha."

"Ho-ho-ho-ho-ho!…" the ward burst out in response to Andriushka, who was portraying with his face how his victim had stretched out her arms, opened her eyes, and been clawing at him.

"'Where you gonna crawl, you stinker?' I says to her. I gave her some sense from my own hand… She was kickin' her legs 'n' crashin' her head… Ha-ha-ha-ha-ha!"

"Ho-ho-ho-ho-ho!"

My entire body was trembling as I looked in horror at these people, wondering how they could laugh at such things. I clearly remember feeling at that moment as if I were in a madhouse, and I was reminded of a certain criminal theory that had at one time powerfully disturbed me and that acknowledges all "criminals" as people with abnormal mental capabilities.

"How that lover o' hers jumped off that bench! He grabbed an axe from somewhere 'n' threw it right at me! Axe went whistlin' past my ear 'n' stuck a half-quarter into the door. I gathered my wits 'n' attacked him with the knife as well. 'Ah! You don't wanna

live? Follow her!' I cut his guts open… His eyes went wide, too, 'n' bang on the ground…
Ha-ha-ha-ha-ha!"

"What are you laughing about, Andrei?" I could not refrain from saying, still horrified
and shaking all over. "Can people really be killed so lightly and happily?"

The ward hushed at that moment.

"But what's so hard 'bout it?" Andriushka, glaring in surprise at me, for his part asked.
"I myself was thinkin' at first: 'They say, don't ask God to kill someone.' But, in fact, I saw
that stabbin' a man's jus' the same as stabbin' a ram! They're a pair. You stick a knife in
the belly 'n' can't e'en hear it: knife slides into somethin' soft, like into pulp."

Certain prisoners in the ward started laughing again, this time more ignorantly: either
marveling at the stupidity of Andriushka's talk or in sympathy with him. There seemed
a bit of this and that in the laughter.

"Ever'day now, I'm plannin' to stab one of 'em when I leave *katorga*," the raving
Andriushka continued.

"One of whom?"

"Whoe'er shows up. Whoe'er deserves it. Black sheep, white sheep—same ghost…
Priest, nun, or sexton—it's a single class. But most of all, boys, I plan to stab women,
'cause I found there's more stuffin' in 'em… Ha-ha-ha-ha-ha!"

"Well, but what happened then, Andrei, after the murders?"

"What happened? Well, I turned out to be an arrant fool. I coulda run away very
easily, but I went 'n' told the village headman: 'so-'n'-so,' I says, 'I killed two devils,
arrest me.' Well, he bound my wrists. The business happened early in the mornin'.
But by nightfall so many officials had come, it woulda weighed 'n' not swayed a whole
day. But they was afraid to go into the icebox where the bodies was lyin'! No one
wanted to clamber in… 'Andrei,' they said, 'you go 'n' drag 'em outta there.' *Me*! I
crawled in. I see them lyin' there not movin'. I grabbed one by the hair 'n' the other
by a foot 'n' dragged both into the wide open: feast your eyes, esteemed comp'ny!
Ever'one just ran off… 'Them's your doin'?' the assessor asked me. 'Them's mine,
your worship,' I said. 'Don't lose your mind, the trimmin's are very neat…' Ha-ha-
ha-ha-ha! Then I got laid up with typhus for six weeks, 'n' they all came to me, the
scoundrels…"

"Who?"

"Them dead ones… They keep comin' 'n' comin'! I stuck a knife straight through
their guts: get away, you sinners!"

Andriushka-the-Cook was sentenced to labor for eleven years for murder. He told
comrades his story very many times (I heard it at least three times), and each time he
was for some reason seized by irrepressible, almost hysterical, joy and was often ready to
split his so-called tummy from laughter. But in the meantime, this prisoner was during
his usual life far from the worst, was quiet and hard-working, and had not completely lost
his conscience and hadn't washed his hands of honesty. On the other hand, he made an
impression as a daft fellow. Normally quiet and invisible in a crowd, he was excessively
hot-tempered and sensitive to wisecracks. Besides, he loved to embellish his stories and
boast about his former life: hence, if he'd been drinking it was certainly year-round and
without stopping; if he'd killed an elk while hunting it was the size of a house; if he'd seen

a dangerous snake it had wings. The mare therefore treated Andriushka condescendingly and thoroughly disbelieved his stories.

I remember not a few other stories blathered at me and my neighbors with what seemed the most unbridled joy. One day, there was a story connecting the dead to popular superstitions. A certain Sokoltsev, one of the most worldly convicts in Shelai Prison, began a comparatively innocent story.

"Happened on the Lena River. My first time in Siberia. Me 'n' my comrade needed some money or supplies very badly. Here we came at night to a large village; we see on the outskirts an empty hut, but there's a lock on it. 'Well,' we're thinkin', 'clearly there's a storeroom we can rob.' We get the lock off 'n' go in. Absolutely nuthin' in the hallway. 'Stand watch,' I tell my comrade, 'I'll go fumble round in that section.' I light a match 'n' go there. I see sheep carcasses lyin' there… What joy! I'd just gone to drag one by the snout—ah, hell: it's a dead man!… Ten of 'em's there. So, some 'ad been killed immediately 'n' others was waitin' for a doctor. This was in winter. 'Aha!' I'm thinkin'. 'I'll get one o'er on you, I'll give you a little test…' I go to my comrade in the hall: 'Well, brother,' I says, 'the matter's at hand. I found ten sheep carcasses. Go get one or two. Go without a flame, so's no one sees.' 'No,' he says, 'you'll crack your head without a light. Gimme a couple matches!' 'Go,' I says. So he went, 'n' I stood watch in his place. Suddenly, he's screamin' from there like a madman… 'Where're you goin'? Where?' I shout at him. He's shootin' past me to the door without a word! I only saw him noon the next day… I stayed by myself, goin' into every corner, pinched the dead men's shirts, 'n' left."

"So, you don't know what happened?"

"No, we didn't know. There was still some silliness, 'n' they tried to make us responsible. But, on the contrary, it was absolutely nuthin'. We was locked up for months 'n' released to the four winds. Well, they beat us thirty times, o' course."

"But I couldn't-a done what ya said 'cause I'm afeared o' the dead!" said Vodianin, also called Iron Cat, a well-known prison wit and rhymer. "Though a most clever fellow, I'm truly 'fraid as well. I marvel at myself: how I killed 'n' buried me Tatar!"

"But d'you really do that to a Tatar?" someone asked.

"Oh! I did it to a rich lord, brother," the smith answered. "Weren't gonna have mud thrown in *my* face, too. Clean job for a clever guy. Ain't been for that scurrilous woman, no one woulda e'er known."

"What woman?"

"Well, my toad."[9]

"Your wife? Whatta pig! She did that?"

"Sure did, boys, I recall she stuck me in me livin' grave. Sent me to the rock-quarry here."

"Tell the story proper, Iron Cat!"

"Here goes. A little Tatar comes to our place. He's carryin' two hunnerd wares 'n' as much again with him. I say right then to my woman: 'See all the rich things he's got. I'll get half a brick o' tea.' I call the Tatar into my yard: 'Come 'ere, good man, I want somethin' on credit.' My woman leaves, 'n' he's in the middle o' the yard—'n', well, he drags a whole pile o' goods outta a chest. I started shoutin': 'Where d'you go to buy so much? I don't got small bills 'n' you can't make me change.' Like this is worryin' me. 'Eh!' the Tatar's laughin' at me. 'Me have hunnerd silver coins change.' 'Aha!' I'm thinkin'. 'If so, fine. I'll pay you now.' I get a ten-pound hammer from the forge 'n' stand behind him. My woman's barterin' 'n' arguin' all the more. Then I see it's time for this clever chap to do it. I smash him in the head with the hammer! He falls on his side in two seconds. Then I put a noose round his neck 'n' dragged him to the horse shed. Then me 'n' the woman covered up 'n' tramped down every grain of ev'dence; put the wares in a chest 'n' hid it. We decided: soon as night falls, we'll drag the Tatar to the swamp 'n' lower him in the pond. Evenin' came. But I notice the new moon's glintin' off all the shovels. Was impossible to be carryin' a dead body—it'd be noticed. I lay down to sleep again. I wake up— 'n' it's e'en brighter in the yard. God's punishin' us! I spit hatefully 'n' lay down again. Finally, I wake up—darkness. Well, it seemed a long time ago. 'Mistress,' I say, 'we'll carry 'im in a barrow.' But she, the stinker, decided to wonder: 'How can I leave the baby? He'll start bawlin' suddenly 'n' make a ruckus, 'n' folks'll hear 'n' come over. Take him yourself.' I got angry 'n' spit in her braids: 'Alright, I'll take him myself!' I go in the horse shed. Before this, I'd been scared o' the dead. But then I toughened up. I go 'n' get him. Tied his legs to his back 'n' sat 'im in the wheelbarrow… jus' so…"

Iron Cat got on his knees, showing how the corpse was set in his barrow.

"Take 'im to the swamp, through the swamp. Was tough goin' through the swamp. Specially when there was a tussock, my barrow would tip o'er on its side with the corpse. Like so."

Iron Cat toppled over on his side.

"'N' when there was a bump goin' through the bog, my dead man would jump completely outta the wheelbarrow. Why do that? I'd get the barrow 'n' put 'im back in."

During this, the storyteller again got on his knees; watching this vivid presentation, the whole ward broke out laughing.

"Well, it's an *Iron* Cat! Straight onto both sides… He ain't the Cat, but a delicacy."

"I'm goin' onward, m'boys. You go two or three steps—'n' my Tatar jumps out again!"

Iron Cat lay on his side once more, provoking his spectators to unrestrained mirth.

"I fought so long to get through that swamp to the pond. 'Well,' I'm thinkin', 'thank God!' I stop there 'n' go back to the pathway. Throw him in the pond. But the factory weren't op'ratin' at night 'n' it turned out there was little water in the pond, less'n two gallons 'til daytime; 'n', for sure, my Tatar ain't sinkin'! I stick 'im on one side, then the other, but nuthin' doin'. I gotta drag the soggy fellow back to the wheelbarrow again 'n' start pushin' once more. I finally come to a gold minin' pit. The pit's as big as our ward 'n' filled with water. Throw 'im in there, but the pit had rough sides to it. My dead man starts rollin' down the side 'n' hangs up somewheres. I didn't wanna climb down there. Got mad, spat, rubbed my hands, 'n' went home. In the mornin', I went to see Agapov, a certain lucky guy, 'n' talked with him 'bout the goods, where to take 'em 'n' such. Unfortunately, his woman was eavesdroppin' on us. Because I left my Tatar in plain sight in the pit, Agapov's 'n' others' places got searched 'n' a half a roll o' calico got found. Suddenly, he, the dearie, is under arrest. Straight to prison, the outer darkness! His woman got scared 'n' fingered me, sayin' she heard her husband talkin' 'bout the goods to the smith. So, I, a young man, got arrested, too. My woman comes to meet me, tells me when 'n' who's bein' arrested. She said they also arrested Kliukin 'n' found a length o' calico witnesses said the Tatar had that day, 'n' he, the fool, is disownin' it. I'd figured we could use that length. 'Woman, go 'n' hide this at his place.' But then, still another clever chap of ours pecked his way outta the shell with Agapov. A certain hatchlin' soldier agreed to become a husk 'n' take on the murder. We'd already made a deal, like so: seventy-five rubles worth o' money, boots, velvet trousers, 'n' two silk shirts, red 'n' blue. If my woman weren't a scatterbrain I'd 'ave gone free. I'm waitin' for my next meetin' with her. Day goes by, then two, then three, then a whole week. Woman didn't come. Then the investigator tells me, 'Your wife,' he says, 'pled guilty.' Reads me her statement: everythin's there, down to exactly what got said. It's a well known fact women can't keep their mouths shut."

"Whatta stinker! What got into her noggin? Who made her think that?"

"They did, o' course. After the squealer squealed, she fell down at my knees. You see, she thought it'd be better for me if I admitted ever'thin'! What could I do? I cursed 'n' cursed her, jabbed her in the teeth, eased my soul 'n' e'en apol'gized. 'Don't let the children slide, don't let 'em complain after me,' I tell her. 'I'll remove this sin from you, I'll take ever'thin' on myself.' And so: I gave such a statement that the court freed her completely, 'n' stuck me alone with twenty years. Only, that woman turned out to be a scoundrel. I reckoned she'd be faithful to me 'til the grave after that, 'n' would follow me to *katorga*. As the trial's draggin' on she—'n' how—is hangin' me by the neck, 'n' since I pulled her outta the fire she's ne'er come or asked forgiveness. 'Jus' sit there, sweet friend, I got you well in my pocket!'"

"Ha-ha-ha-ha-ha!"

"But, Mikolaich," Iron Cat suddenly turned to me, "how can I make her, the rat, come to me?"

"You want to make her?" I was surprised.

"But, yes. Ain't there a law so's a husband can demand his wife march into *katorga*?"

"There's no such law. And if she treated you poorly, why should you have her? There's no reason to pity her!"

"Would I really pity her? She comes here—she should be beggin' for my cane! Should be beggin' on her knees, markin' my words in advance that I am the Iron Cat. Mikolaich, can you weld together such a little note to her, pretend like I'm bored stiff without her, so's it tricks her into comin'?"

"I won't write such a letter, Vodianin."

"Ha! Why not? What does it matter?"

"It would mean I'd be participating in fraud."

"Can there really be fraud against evil? Would I beat her to death? I'm jus' gonna teach her a little lesson, for mem'ry's sake. 'N' then we'd start livin' 'n' gettin' on again. It's a pity for my children most of all. Now's the time the oldest should be learnin' a trade. 'N' if I went to the free command early, I could be a man again. That'd be my goal… But what am I now? A good-for-nuthin' soul, in a word. I go free, 'n' I'll either take to vagabondage or fall in love with a new calamity. But how can you bring a boy here without a woman?"

I later became convinced that Vodianin was partly right. If he'd had any goal in life he would still be on an honest path. There were certain very good aspects to his character.

To use a word he could have audaciously delivered to a comrade, there was absolutely no hypocrisy in him. He loved his children very much, sometimes recalling them with tears and, not wishing to write his wife, asked through his father-in-law about them and sent gifts. The man's lack of greed was also pleasing to the eye. Working in the capacity of a smith for what for a prisoner was respectable money, he divided it in half with the striker Efimov—something not at all according with the rules for craftsmen.

II. EFIMOV; A PRISON SOPHIST AND MEPHISTOPHELES

Having told about Iron Cat, I'll now briefly describe his striker Efimov. He was a completely different type. Vodianin got along with him as with a fellow countryman; their trade also brought them together. The guards somehow happened to assign them both to the smithy and then, as usual, didn't separate them for several years. It would've even seemed strange had Vodianin and Efimov been assigned different places. They were also placed together even during ward redistributions. They supped from the same bowl together, drank tea together, and split in half all the money they earned. In a word, they seemed bosom buddies. But in fact, it was entirely different between them. Efimov was actually careful around Vodianin, never contradicting him at all and yielding on everything; he just simply allowed him to act like so… Iron Cat gave him half of all his earnings whereas smiths normally gave strikers a pittance and he could have had ten other—and by no means worse—strikers just like him.

For this reason Vodianin, in general a very complaisant and gentle man, did not refrain from telling Efimov to his face bitter truths that, given his pride, he would not have peaceably heard from another. I've said already that his was a nature of a completely unique stamp. He, too, was a native of Perm, and though from a backwoods agricultural locality, also sufficiently corrupted. He entered labor for killing two passing traders. According to Efimov, the idea to kill them appeared all of a sudden thanks to the deep forest in which he encountered his victims. Of gigantic size and strength, he briskly dealt with them and hid all the evidence with utmost care. Suspicion would never have fallen on him, and he was undone thanks only to a purely crazy accident—"false" slander and "false" evidence. A certain woman, having encountered the merchants the day of their murder, testified that she also met Efimov hastily leaving the same woods; but at the time, she had actually seen a quite different man, albeit similar in size. Besides this, during the investigation a shirt was found at Efimov's with a fresh bloodstain that was in actual fact not human but that of a calf… Yet, so much other similarly sham evidence combined to make such an incriminating picture that Efimov, refusing to the end to confess to the murders, was sentenced to fifteen years' *katorga*. This circumstance affected him powerfully. He told me many times that he well knew how unfavorable it was to be a swindler and that henceforth he was going to live only by honest labor.

"Y'know, I thought I hid ever'thin', took neat care of it all, didn't leave a single piece of evidence, but I landed in *katorga*! I'd seen so often that a murder's hardly e'er uncovered."

"But, earlier, Efimov, you were in business with some swindlers?"

"My God, no! Our whole family's honest!"

"Why're you lyin', Efimov?" Chirok turned to him. "Why was your brother sent along the Iakutsk Road?"

"Aha! Chirok's caught you in a trap!" the whole ward, for some reason terribly ill-disposed toward Efimov, cheerfully cackled.

"My brother got sent away for a completely diff'rent reason," Efimov embarrassedly answered, "'n' not for swindlin'."

"I daresay, as a saint?" Chirok maliciously continued to probe.

Efimov was silent; everyone snidely smiled and glanced among themselves. It became clear that only Chirok and I didn't know about this.

"They're Skoptsy!"[10] Iron Cat, who for a long time had been angrily fidgeting on his sleeping platform, could at last not restrain himself. "They'd a whole village o' Skoptsy… His brother went to Iakutsk for this… Only, by some miracle Egrashka ain't been castrated…"

"Pah! Pah!" spat Chirok. "I hate them people… The most oppositional people! Why would I cut my own flesh, mutilate myself? Better to die. Why live if you're gonna… cut yourself? I'm practic'ly an old-timer now, but still hopes I'll go live on the outside again, that I'll be human again."

"Chirok, you think like all the world's people think," Efimov, red as a lobster, shyly defended the Skoptsy, "but they're a special sort o' people… They ponder Heaven, 'cause it's said in the Scriptures…"

"You're damned blasphemers!" Chirok, supporting the general view, hurled at him. "You ponder Heaven? Vermin such as your Skoptsy didn't create the world. They're the most two-faced folk. Filled with so much greed! 'They ponder Heaven…' Pah!… How'd *you* escape ruin?"

"It jus' somehow didn't happen. I married young. Weren't their will that I be taken for the good seal.[11] I'd the desire, o' course, but a demon o'erpowered me 'n' took o'er the village."

"Whatta fool!… A demon o'erpowered him, he says. But where'd the demons come from, if not your sect? I know it well. What you do there, 'n' how you gather for secret pilgrimages!"

"Nuthin' foolish goes on, that's all jus' slander. I've heard them rumors!"

"You would defend your own, o' course. Don't lead me on, brother! I'm from them parts, too. A most foul tribe, the Skoptsy."

"True, so true," Iron Cat once more could not restrain himself, "'n' the castrated 'n' non-castrated alike are the same branded race! They're greedy, they're hypocrites. Jus' look at Egrafa. Y'know, you'd be hard-pressed to find a Yid like 'im with a torch. He wavers like an aspen leaf o'er ev'ry kopek 'n' sits on his money like a dog chained to a barn!"

During these last words Efimov, visibly hurt but not wanting to crank up the argument with Iron Cat, heartily wrung his hands and burned like fire and then ran from the ward. But in his absence they began cursing and giving it to him all the more.

Efimov was indeed a terrible skinflint. On the road, he had run the *maidan*; now, to be somewhat ungrammatical, he ran the calculating of monetary accounts he shared with Iron Cat and stubbornly grabbed every penny. If he happened to buy from the administration some milk or meat on the sly, he never invited his comrade to his meal, and he was visibly ashamed of his own stinginess in the presence of the smith, whose ways were more open and who had a generous heart. Only a weakness of character seemed to prevent the latter from breaking off all relations with Efimov; he didn't terribly like him and often, able to endure no more, sharply denounced him to his face.

Efimov's wife had decided to join him in *katorga*, and had already commenced the way-station journey and sent to her husband for safe-keeping several dozen rubles acquired from selling their possessions. I advised Egrafa to send registered letters to Krasnoiarsk, Nizhneudinsk, and Irkutsk—cities she would be stopping in along her way. Efimov deliberated.

"O' course, nuthin' should prevent me sendin' 'em," he finally agreed, "only, I'm thinkin', maybe jus' reg'lar letters…"

"Reg'lar letters is certainly better," Iron Cat so agreed that at first I couldn't detect the subtle venom in his words. "Three registered letters—y'know, that'd cost twenty-one kopeks… A family could eat for two days on twenty-one kopeks!…"

I actually naïvely began to argue with Iron Cat, showing that it was no good being thrifty when the matter concerned the peace-of-mind of a lone woman with a trio of infants in her arms, traveling to an unknown territory and unknown life along the difficult way-station route.

"But reg'lar letters is much better, Mikolaich," Iron Cat repeated seriously. "In my opinion, reg'lar letters is better."

He suddenly erupted into a loud, smiling laugh that was joined by the whole ward, once again terribly embarrassing Efimov.

Efimov always carried himself respectfully and efficiently; he regarded himself as an uncorrupted and honorable man, far higher and better than all the other prisoners. He was always terribly offended when reminded he'd dispatched two souls to the other world. He regarded these murders as some kind of minor offense, rather like an unfortunate experiment that could have happened to anyone, and believed with conviction that in a different instance he wouldn't have incurred *katorga*. I was also inclined to think that in a different instance Efimov would count seven seconds before deciding to cut someone's head off: he'd not acquired the "benefits" in this profession… However, I never could be convinced that my Evgraf would resist the temptation of a crime if guaranteed he'd never be caught and that it would bring a very big profit.

Among my cohabitants there was one prisoner who for a long time had been attracting my attention. His name was Sokoltsev. More than anyone's, his appearance caught your eye: a thick-set, not very tall brunet of forty, he was distinguished by such good looks as to be an almost completely other type of Russian peasant. In the delicate lines of his face, the straight, almost elegant, traces of his sensual lips, in the subtlety of his matte-pale skin, the velvet expression of his large black eyes, in his marmoreal neck and all his movements, there was something essentially aristocratic that only dozens of well-tended generations unburdened by physical toil can create. But at the same time, Sokoltsev was a simple illiterate peasant from one of Russia's interior provinces who had strayed from the path early and ended up in Siberia. However, according to him, he had been a certain wealthy count's domestic, and this circumstance led to a notion of his actual origins... Among the prison's residents, Sokoltsev enjoyed a reputation as one of the most intelligent prisoners, and was by no means not one of those who were "worthless" and looked their age. His *katorga* term was forty-four years, and the case that earned him this term was one of the bloodiest I ever heard about. Gazing at this beautiful face, hearing this soft voice always speaking so precisely and insinuatingly, I often had difficulty believing that before me stood the very same Sokoltsev who, with a peaceful soul, had committed such things; and at the same time, his terrible thieving exploits were a verifiably incomprehensible history.

Sokoltsev lived in a settlement in Irkutsk Province in the capacity of a worker for a certain prosperous *"cheldon."*[12] The latter was engaged in buying up gold from "plunderers" and those working in the mines. Having one day noticed a pile of almost two poods of gold in his master's house, Sokoltsev inveigled one of his friends in the settlement and, after entering the house at night, they together strangled the master, his wife, and five young ones. Then, having grabbed the gold and available cash, of which there was however very little, they hid them in a prearranged spot in the woods. His partner later went to his place, but Sokoltsev, returning to the house, locked it from the inside, set it well and truly aflame, and, crawling out a window, settled down in the hayloft pretending to be drunk. By the time folks came running, the fire had spread so far that not only was there no possibility of putting it out but also of even getting into the rooms. Somehow, they managed to get into the hayloft, also enveloped in flames and filled with smoke, and to drag from there the seemingly sodden and anyway already singed Sokoltsev. This bestial crime was committed so cleverly that not a shadow of suspicion fell on the worker, who himself appeared to be an injured victim. The murdered bodies were completely incinerated. Someone's evil hand was suspected, but sought for in an entirely different place. To Sokoltsev's misfortune, his comrade was far less discrete and went on a bender, exchanged large bills, attracted suspicion, and got arrested. He was found to have some of the victims' things. Link by link, clue by clue, the judicial investigator reached Sokoltsev himself. He and his comrade were sentenced to indefinite terms of *katorga*, only, the gold could not be found. It remained buried somewhere in the woods, sustaining the condemned men's good cheer and dream of escaping. Sokoltsev's partner, however, ended up on Sakhalin, wherefrom he could not so readily "break loose," whereas Sokoltsev actually managed to hire along the road a husk bound for a settlement, and went in his place to his assigned canton, and from there he immediately returned to search for the buried treasure. "But the mare's impatient," Sokoltsev said about himself, "always wants to immediately catch two or e'en three hares." Wanting to enrich himself with money for a "top fitting-out," he got mixed up in another robbery and murder and was arrested again. Of course, in Irkutsk's prison his guilt was confirmed and he again went to *katorga* under his previous name, only this time for forty years. Here was the primary case that brought Sokoltsev to Shelai mine, the veracity of which could not be doubted. But if prisoners' stories about Sokoltsev and those about himself were to be believed, then this was only a tiny part of this adventures in Russia and Siberia. He was already forty, and his hair was streaked here and there with gray. Unfortunately, in Sokoltsev's stories about himself it was difficult to decide where was the truth and where the invention, where was the serious talk and where the subtle jokes on listeners.

He was a strange man. He didn't belong to those prisoners who pass themselves off as "wags" and "fabulists," but everyone nevertheless knew perfectly well that not one of his stories could be thoroughly trusted. Exceedingly intelligent, Sokoltsev, it seemed, delighted in his own intelligence and superiority over the surrounding herd; he clearly terribly enjoyed defending a certain position against it one day and proving, with no less success, a different, contrary position the next. He was his own sort of prison sophist and Mephistopheles. He seemed to play with his interlocutors like a cat with a mouse and often, having begun an apparently completely serious story proceeding in unison with general views, he, unnoticed by anyone, reached such absurd and ridiculous incongruities that interlocutors' jaws dropped and, gazing at him like sheep, they didn't know whether to laugh or take him seriously… Thus, one day he was most seriously telling how, during harvest-time, thirty-two women had begun soundly beating him for a certain offense, but he then dodged away, grabbed a stave lying nearby, and beat ten of them to death, another ten senseless, and incapacitated several more, and only a very few managed to escape with their lives intact. He told this story with such realistic details, with such lively and at the same time terrible humor, that it was positively difficult to say (especially upon first impression) whether everything was invention or if a kernel of truth hid inside it. When he was laughed at and told once more that he was "fabling," he wasn't the least bit offended and laughed slyly as well—though you couldn't tell at whom: himself or his listeners. Whether for this man's evident inner strength, notorious reputation, or something else, Sokoltsev, regardless of his undoubted "fabling" and "wagging" was, I repeat, regarded as one of the most serious prisoners, as one of those who neither stops nor hesitates in the face of an opportunity.

I myself once heard a story of Sokoltsev's about how he, wandering in vagabondage, hungry as a dog and without a penny, strangled an old pilgrim he'd met and found on her… all of forty kopeks.

"Well, if you're gonna piss out such lies, 'tis proper you should be eatin' like a dog," one of his friends, also a serious prisoner, observed of this. "Clearly, you'll lie less if you need a spot o' tea."

In response, Sokoltsev burst out with his usual velvety laugh, and I was left in a quandary precisely as to whether he'd murdered the pilgrim or had only just now thought this up for effect.

But on the other hand, I heard differently from him more than once. He, apparently, was sincerely indignant towards those vagabonds who, for a kopek, were prepared to commit the most heinous crime, to butcher an entire family.

"I'm a barbarian," he would say in such instances, "a barbarian such as few the world might see; but I simply agree it's better to starve to death than kill a person for their clothes or five rubles. It's another matter if it's outta vengeance, or for a lotta money that some priest suddenly starts blowin' on the road."

Regardless of all his "fabling" and fantasizing about his previous life, among his comrades he took advantage of this very reputation. Listening to Sokoltsev was always interesting; but one of his qualities antagonized me: he was a terrible, refined cynic and his depraved tongue had no rival in the entire prison… He liked in this regard to achieve Herculean columns and often, having begun to discourse perfectly reasonably and nobly, he unexpectedly switched to such vulgarisms and abominations that he scared off half of even his indiscriminating and cynically inclined listeners.

It was clear to each that such a man didn't intend to sit peaceably in Shelai Prison for his indeterminate term, and that a continual concern with escaping or at least transferring to another, more salutary, prison was racing through his mind. I once asked Sokoltsev whether he'd be put in the free command and when exactly he'd gotten a "ticket" (so called is the slip of paper with his term calculated on it that is given to each prisoner). Sokoltsev, laughing, answered that he'd destroyed his ticket as soon as he'd received it, being not even curious as to what was written on it.

"How could you be like that?"

"But what's the free command to me?"

"What's it to you? From there you could get away, but, as you know, it's not so easy from the prison."

"No, the command ain't for me," Sokoltsev answered after some thought. "In my opinion, a spiritual man can get outta prison much easier. Here, you keep a sharp eye out 'n' depend on jus' yourself. But there, whoe'er depends on the free command easily finds hisself done o'er for a penny. Such a man's worth nuthin'."

The answer was fine and thought-out but, as it were, not so easily supported by facts. Prisoners were always escaping the free command, a dozen each summer (even from Shelai's lightly populated command), but, up to then, there hadn't been one serious escape attempt from the prison. The guarding of the prison was actually perfectly organized, and the majority of serious prisoners with hopelessly enormous terms on their shoulders dreamed more of an early transfer to another prison than about escaping Shelai mine. I will devote a special chapter to this topic below, but right now I'll just say about Sokoltsev that, along with all his wit and secrecy there was emerging a certain conniving fellow whom everyone saw was dreaming about the same thing. An outstanding joiner and upholsterer, Sokoltsev always worked in the shop located outside the prison fence; besides him, another two men worked there: the metalworker Zabotkin from the free command and the cooper Kalinchuk from the prison. Having appeared in the shop one day, Sokoltsev gave every sign of being greatly agitated.

"D'you know where my fret-saws are?" he turned and whispered to the young cooper.

"What fret-saws?" he responded in surprise.

"My… secret fret-saws… Seems they all been found. Some bitch has gone off with 'em!"

"I dunno at all. How should I know where they went?"

"I ain't talkin' 'bout you at all. There's only one man could do it. 'Cept for me, only he knew. They were well hidden, y'know. There'll be a report, without fail!"

"Who is it? Could it be Zabotkin?"

Sokoltsev shrugged his shoulders and said nothing.

"What're you sayin'? Is he that kinda man? D'you really mean your comrade, your bosom buddy?"

"That's a comrade for you. Brother, you can't count on anyone these days. If you wanna know, I been suspectin' he's a bitch for a long time."

"Whatta scoundrel! Whatta bastard!" Kalinchuk became indignant, and soon the entire prison knew that Zabotkin had taken Sokoltsev's fret-saws from the shop and that Zabotkin had denounced him. The fret-saws were indeed in the administration's hands. The prison had been suddenly searched and two small fret-saws turned out to be sewn into Sokoltsov's bedding. As soon as the guard entered the ward they went straight for his bedding. There was no doubt about a denunciation. So Zabotkin was abused and it was vowed and sworn that if anything were to cause him to return to the prison his ribs would be broken.

Sokoltsev never said anything, but he appeared to have turned bitter.

It was expected that Six-Eyes would subject him to severe punishment; but for some reason he limited himself to testing the prison grilles during the search and strengthening the night patrol beneath the windows. After this incident, six months passed before Zabotkin really was put in prison for some tricks. Everyone watched with curiosity how Sokoltsev, who had every right to avenge himself, would greet him. But what was the universal amazement when they saw that he not only apologized to Zabotkin, but once again befriended him and began eating and drinking alongside him. For everyone, even the densest, it became clear that if a report had been made, then… *it was at the request of Sokoltsev himself*, who wanted to frighten Six-Eyes and get him to order him sent to another prison; but his cunning hadn't succeeded, and he'd been kept in Shelai mine, only surrounded by a sharper watch. The young and fiery Kalinchuk became terribly and openly indignant toward Sokoltsev for so brazen a deception; what struck the rest of the herd as another minor throwaway joke could terribly embitter a less noticed and respected prisoner. But Sokoltsev was Sokoltsev, and no one dared reproach him with even a word. Everyone hastily tried to forget this incident, but thanks to it, Sokoltsev rose still higher in the eyes of many. For me, personally, it only unnecessarily showed that for his own sake or gain this man would not be squeamish about any methods at all, would give quarter to neither friend nor foe.

III.   DEMONS OF EVIL AND DESTRUCTION

My life in the new ward, in a growing familiarity with those last-named prisoners, those of an apparently simple yet at the same time enigmatic psychology, carried on, long evenings playing out with books or recitations that introduced such intelligence and pleasant animation to life. From time to time the stories got on my nerves, and my cohabitants dreamed up some game in which the smashing of bones and an abundance of noise were possible. A favorite game of this type was "goners," a game, however, completely unlike that innocent pastime that so delighted us all in childhood. Having tightly tied shut the eyes of the wretch on whom the lot had fallen, prisoners circled round with towels and, sneaking in from all sides, unmercifully lashed him on the back and beat him all over (excluding, however, the face), until he managed to catch one of his tormenters and take his place. By game's end nearly everyone had purple welts and bruises all over their bodies, not to mention aching bones and torn shirts, but none of this diminished in the least the universal predilection for goners. "You gets beaten bloody," prisoners said, "—that's your steam bath!" Much greater obstacles proved to be the cries heard by guards who almost instantly came running toward the terrible din raised by the game, and who would start threatening the naughty boys with the isolator and reports to the commandant. The racket then subsided a bit and goners switched to another pastime attracting less attention. There were master acrobats who showed off such tricks that everyone's jaws simply dropped and they vainly tried to do the same thing. For example, Marazgali would lie face-up on the floor and put beneath his head a spoon or a twenty-kopek piece, if such could be found in the ward. Then, arching his spine little-by-little but not touching the floor with his hands, he cleverly got the object lying on the floor into his mouth and quickly jumped up with the triumphant shout:

"Here it is!... Now let another try."

But to everyone's surprise, of all the rest Chirok alone, regardless of his apparent awkwardness and clumsiness, was able to achieve approximately the same thing the dexterous and graceful Marazgali did. Marazgali could also lightly spring from one sleeping platform to another without running, to a distance of over eight feet. No one could do this without running. Chirok once boasted he could, but not reaching the next platform, he nearly broke his nose... It was easy to crack your head, and the audience tried hard to convince me to carry out dangerous experiments. But they soon launched into something else.

"Boys, let's give Chirok some whackin's," Iron Cat suddenly proposed.

"Damn your shameless eyes, what for?" leapt up Chirok, on whom, like poor Makar, all the big-wheels usually dumped.

"Jus' do it, for neither this nor that."

"Do it!" the ward supported Iron Cat.

"No," interrupted Sokoltsev, "why do it for neither this nor that? We'll find some fault, 'n' act completely honestly, 'cordin' to the law. He can be judged."

"Judge 'im! Judge 'im!" everyone dinned.

"Have you lost your minds, boys? I been judged by God 'n' punished by the people. Why this torture for me, an ol' man?"

"Shut up! The chairman forbids you to talk. You're bein' judged! You're accused of still hidin' your soul from Nikolaich."

For my part, I hastened to deny any claim against poor Chirok, well knowing the vileness of the prisoners' "whackin's."

"Don't matter, the ward ain't pard'nin' 'im!" shouted Iron Cat, now hustling with Nikifor up next to Chirok.

"Stop, devils! How'd I hide my soul?"

"But, 'bout that lady… 'bout that lady you told me 'bout at night?"

"Brother kitty! How can you be tellin' such comradely *sekewerts*?"

"Aha, 'sekewerts'… A new fault! Mikolaich, d'you hear how he's sayin' 'sekewerts' again?"

"Whackin's! Whackin's! Give 'im five whacks!"

"I ain't a schoolboy… Guard!"

"Quick, gag 'im! Mikishka, hold his hands… Marazgali, pull off his shirt. Hold his head, this demon's bitin'!"

"C'mon, c'mon!" Marazgali gleefully rushed over to help in the savage game, but I stopped him.

"Don't, Marazgali. This is an abomination…"

"It's nuthin', Nikoliaichik," he pleaded, gazing at me plaintively, "maybe *fife* whacks, not bad whacks."

"Bad, Marazgali, very bad, and unnecessary!"

Having heard me out, Marazgali walked sadly away. But, lying down beside me on the sleeping platform, he couldn't restrain himself, so that he laughed with all his heart along with the booming, puerile laughter, and nonetheless mentally participated in the terrible row taking place on the opposite platform, from where blows and the ill-starred Chirok's muffled cries could be heard.

Whackings consisted of an "executioner" pulling with one hand the skin of the victim's naked stomach and rapidly beating it with the other back to its original position, and "snappin' the buffers." During the lightest blows the skin turned purple after several whacks, but in the case of a serious punishment blood might start spattering after just two whacks.

"One! Two! Three!" Iron Cat was counting off his whacks on Chirok's stomach. "Four! Five! Six!"

"Stop, you scoundrel, you gave him too much! He was sentenced to five, but he got a total o' six."

"Cat's gotta get whacks for this. It ain't fair," insisted Sokoltsev, who hadn't played an active part in the "game" but had from time to time been directing it from his platform.

"No, not whacks, but spoons!" shouted the enraged Chirok.

"Spoons it'll be. There should be one."

"Not one, but six! Jus' like for me!"

"You're lyin', you cunnin' swine," protested Iron Cat. "The five you got was 'cordin' to the law, 'cordin' to the court. I only hit you one extra, so lemme get this if the ward's sentencin' me. I won't go 'gainst society."

And Iron Cat obediently lay down on the platform and hoisted up his shirt himself. Chirok bustled around, running through the ward and finding a spoon… His face radiated like a well-buttered pancake: so excited did he look forward to the thrill of his position… At last, he was brandishing his weighty wooden spoon. Advancing towards the smith's proffered stomach, he swung it, spittle flying onto his arm and shouting: "Take this!" and hit the body with all his might. Iron Cat groaned from the sharp pain and leapt to his feet: his stomach was swollen and blue from the one blow… Everyone started roaring. Approaching the peephole in the door, the guard again shouted:

"You wanna go to the isolator? God's word, I'll report you to the com'dant… Tomorrow everyone'll be distributed to diff'rent wards. Won't be such shenanigans in a one of 'em."

After this everyone quieted down and began little-by-little lying down to sleep. Quiet conversations broke out. The fat man Nogaitsev announced:

"Well, I gorged myself today. Prob'ly gobbled up three pounds o' salted beef 'n' emptied a half-barrel o' pickles."

"Where?" he was asked in surprise.

"I was at the haulage in the gallery. Monakhov's set up a whole storeroom there. Cold there—chilly, a real grave… I snuck right in. Now my ev'ry instinct is drawin' me back there."

"Well, this ain't good," Sokoltsev edifyingly reproved him. "'Cause I know this: if you're an obligin' fellow 'n' are doin' some work for 'im, then it's another matter. But he don't owe you a thing. 'Cause o' you devils there, there's no trust at all in our brother!"

"It's certainly 'cause o' them, the swine!" sounded other voices.

"Y'know it won't e'en get noticed," Nogaitsev tried to justify himself. "So I ate what can't get noticed… Don't matter!"

"Well, if it won't get noticed, then it's good," confirmed Efimov.

Someone began telling about his previous life, about his crimes and the other prisons he'd been in. An argument broke out. The disputants' ideas skipped from one subject to another so frequently they forgot what had initiated the discussion. Having told how he'd uttered: "Grisha! What 'ave you done?" a storyteller who had just vividly described a person's head rolling off his shoulders was now recalling what splendid kasha there was in Tara Prison…

Conversations in the least bit abstract were positively impossible with these people. Some petty, insignificant fact presented by you or one of your interlocutors by way of example dragged them far off track; the object of the conversation being forgotten, true reality with its concrete details and valuations came to the fore. Thus, one day

I began asking who was more likely to be killed in prison: a guard or their brother prisoner? In a moment, a sharp argument erupted: suddenly one participant, having heard another's story about a certain murder in Tomsk Prison, changed the topic by saying that the sympathies of the wards there were not exactly the same as those his opponent was expressing. The latter objected, and the essential matter was so completely forgotten and forsaken that the conversation became boring and I tried to fall asleep. Another time, there was an argument about whether or not the dog is man's friend. Most believed it was. Then, for some reason, a prisoner began narrating his case about how he and a comrade had broken into a certain house, how he had tortured the old master of the house and his old woman, demanding money and tearing up the old man's mouth but impaling the old woman, and, further on, about how during his first stint in prison he got to know prisoners' ways and how he'd then lived in Siberia… This terrible story dragged on for almost an hour, so that everyone forgot about the dog and many had long since fallen asleep. I alone was at a loss, and finally asked:

"What does this have to do with the dog?"

"What dog?"

"You know, we began with whether it's man's friend or enemy?"

"I was jus' talkin' 'bout this very thing."

"How was that about this?"

"Jus' is. I simply forgot to say the dog started barkin' 'n' gave us away… What kinda man's friend is that? If it was my friend, it wouldn't-a ruined me. My comrade 'n' me is killin' the ol' man 'n' woman 'n' the damn thing's barkin'! *Our* dog! We got caught. What kinda friend is that? Certainly, it's an enemy first 'n' foremost."

Souls have been corrupted by such logic and such dark minds' associations.

Sometimes the usual stories developed broad social themes. Here as well I was astounded by my involuntary comrades' savage views and spiritual callousness… among other things, nearly all without exception were distinguished by a terrible hatred for "iron-noses"—nobles, merchants, and bureaucrats (in this strange jargon priests were called "hammerers"). The wildest, most impossibly bloody social reconstruction projects were presented, and depraved theories such as would not be advocated by the staunchest anarchist were propagated!

"Here's what I'd do," shouted the impatient Nikifor. "I'd put a peasant in place o' the masters, lay out some food 'n' give a feast, 'n' make all the nobles 'n' priests plow the soil 'n' feed us like we's feedin' 'em now…"

"Brother, that don't mean nuthin', it couldn't happen," answered the far-sighted Sokoltsev. "Compared with our brother, nobles are an insignificant number, not e'en a hundredth part. How much could they produce, specially from lack of habit? Today's peasants would die o' starvation if they depended on the masters! No, that's not it; brother, here's the method: finish 'em all off—'n' that's the end! That's what Pushkin's Pugachev wanted to do…"[13]

"Absolutely, finish 'em all off, the vermin!" said Chirok, energetically scratching his belly, so carried away was he by the proposal. "'N', really, our folk is stupid! They're countless, 'n' the others is no more'n a thousan', but *they* submit!"

(None of these dreamers, I'll parenthetically note, had even the foggiest notion that the "folk" and they, the residents of *katorga*, were absolutely one and the same.)

"Is that what the punishment'll be," interjected Nogaitsev, "to finish 'em off? How many are they suckin' blood from now, how many are they draggin' by the neck, but all we're gonna do is finish 'em off? Here's what I'd do. I'd kill all the folk, ever'one down to the last person, 'n' leave some o' the iron-noses in the world. Then I'd let 'em try 'n' fend for 'emselves! They'd be singin' then!…"

This unexpected and original proposition instantly stunned everyone. No one found anything to say. Sokoltsev first began chuckling quietly, then the rest joined in.

"That's such easy thinkin' there's nuthin' to say! An intelligent noggin!"

"But I would…," blurted out Bear's Ears, suddenly jumping off the sleeping platform, "I'd kill all the top rich men ever'where in one night… I'd kill 'em all in one night! Then they'd sing!"

"Well, but what would come of this?" I abandoned my neutrality, intrigued by our normally meek poet's bloodthirsty project. "Let's assume you've done the killings… The next day, the sons of the murdered would become the top rich men…"

"But then I'd kill *them*!" roared Bear's Ears.

"Well, but after that?"

"But after he'd robbed ever'one in Raseya!" Chirok answered for Vladimirov. "All the prisons would open 'n' all the rich men would get knifed…"

"So. And after that?"

"After?… What *is* there after that? Eh, Mikolaich! How you talk… You're a good man, I won't argue—good, but you'd get finished off… 'cause you're on their side, the iron-noses. It's your own blood what's talkin'!"

Everyone started laughing at Chirok's unexpected attack against me.

"Where are you drawing this conclusion from, Chirok?"

"You can't fool me, I'm concludin' it now!"

The others apparently agreed with Chirok's opinion of me. I vainly tried to lay out my own views regarding progress, spoke about the strength and power of education, about the uselessness and harm of bloody punishments; in vain, I pointed to the existence of educated people who stood out among those same "iron-noses" and were prepared to sacrifice their own personal future, freedom, and even life for the people's good… My words were obviously being shouted into a wilderness. The idea of any other sort of struggle with modern life's severity and evil, of a struggle by means other than the spilling of rivers of blood, universal conflagrations, and havoc, was utterly displeasing to these others' souls, covered by the dark scales of bitterness, ignorance, and depravity. After each of these conversations I was stricken with unhappy thoughts; and our country's future became terrible and awful…

IV.   NEW STUDENTS; LUNKOV

I was joined in the new ward by every one of the students except the Burenkovs: Marazgali, Petin, Nogaitsev, and Lunkov. A real school formed, with which I was occasionally unhappy. The latter three had specially requested transfer to our ward for learning, seething over, evidently, with a shared zest for science. However, Petin could read and write sufficiently well when he wanted; he even composed verses and was now dreaming of "higher education."

Unfortunately, great curiosity coincided with neither breadth of mind nor ability. Petin, like Sokoltsev, had more than thirteen years' *katorga* on his shoulders (and he'd only just begun), and enjoyed fame as a great "thug" among people who didn't know him. The nickname "Elk," given him for his frequent escapes from prison, was known throughout all of Siberia. However, this was, in essence, hollow… More than anything, Petin did not possess an independent character at all. He was constantly finding himself under the influence of some "suborn,"[14] and within a friendship he ventured the most impertinent deeds, like repeatedly fleeing in broad daylight from under the strictest guard; and left alone in freedom he bore himself in the most ridiculous fashion, going straight home ("went to my mum for some thread"—he joked to prisoners), where he was found and, of course, fell into the hands of the police. Possessing a deep throat, meaty fists, and wishing terribly to play in prison the role of a true Ivan and ringleader, he essentially had the disposition of a calf, was rather slow-witted, sluggish, and somnolent and, for this reason, always followed others' behinds. The "real" prisoners he stuck to didn't rate him highly and often called him "cut-rate" to his face. In his studies, Petin turned out to be exactly like he was in life. He wanted to embrace everything at once; he felt a positive aversion toward sustained work and slow, step-by-step forward progress. Completion little-by-little of a thick book was for him an impossible feat. Nonetheless, he had an exceedingly high opinion of both himself and the other students who had begun with the basics but, owing to their abilities and threatening assiduity, soon overtook and—gazing with supreme contempt—surpassed him.

Incidentally, his ongoing war and rivalry with Lunkov and my other students had actually begun on the road. Lunkov was quite a young chap, twenty-three years old, short, beardless, somewhat round-shouldered, yet pretty as a young woman and sharp in his movements and clever in speech. He was a peculiar character and bitterly hated by Ivans such as Petin. The point is that Lunkov, like Mikhaila Burenkov, despised prisoners and rejected all the norms of prison life the instant they went against his personal views and benefit. But Mikhaila had been secretive and only revealed his individualistic views and dispositions in extreme cases; Lunkov, by contrast, was distinguished by his self-defeating garrulity and candor. Regardless of his puny little frame and weak physical strength, he fearlessly irritated every person's eye by hesitating before neither threats nor boxes on his ears and by not backing down before hand-to-hand fights with the top-most strongmen and daring blades. Within him this courageous disregard for self somehow combined with a sober practicality that was undoubtedly a fundamental aspect of his mind and character; in many respects, Lunkov was what is called fresh out of youth. In another prison, of course, he would have been beaten up and forced into submission, but in Shelai everyone was cropped with the same comb—the giants, the pygmies, the fools, the sages; the very least waste-tub attendant had a voice equal that of the top-most throat and snorter and that, of course, was the Shelai regime's great merit. Petin gazed with malice at his pygmy-rival who successfully completed his reading lessons quickly and boastfully asserted that he would leave him behind. Petin, who proudly named himself and Mikhaila Burenkov "senior students" and all the rest "junior," certainly couldn't allow this. Their amusing clashes were evening occupations.

"Step back, twit, a senior student's gettin' to work now!" snarled Elk, flashing his calf-eyes.

"Brother, why're you snarlin'? You don't scare me," squeaked little Lunkov, moving a bit aside. "Only, science don't benefits you."

"What's this 'don't benefits'? Don't you know that's a noun, twit?"

"I'll learn in my own time, don't worry. But, senior student, why'd you spell 'bright' with an 'e' yesserday?"

"You ass! That was a slip o' the pen. You prison swine, blatherer, piece o' crap!"

"Petin, why are you cursing?" I interrupted the argument. "That's not very nice."

"Ain't nuthin', Ivan Nikolaevich," Lunkov calmly answered. "Let 'im curse. His abuse don't hang on my gate. Specially as I know very well that he himself's a forever resident o' prison 'n' I don't respect such. Y'know, only fools consider his name famous: E-l-l-l-k! But I know better what he really gets by on, this Elk."

"What do I get by on instead? Tell me."

"You get by on the cheap, that's what."

"How'm I cheap, twit?"

"Jus' are. Y'know, I know very well what you was doin' on the outside, what you came to *katorga* for."

"But what'd you come for? What'd you do? You were a knacker. You skinned dead horses in Krasnoiarsk."

"So happened I *was* a knacker, 'n' I ain't ashamed. Only, I weren't rapin' young women, I weren't wrappin' my arms round 'em 'n' draggin' 'em into the bushes. On the road, I weren't gamblin' away the marchin' party's money, like certain other people."

The longer it went the hotter the argument burned, and it sometimes ended in a brawl. The beaten Lunkov would be sobbing with hatred but not want to submit to the impudent Petin. However, even the latter did not have the energy or patience to maintain his impudence and naughtiness for long. He soon lapsed into his usual apathy, slept for an entire day, and abandoned for a long time any studies and prideful daydreams. Such a mood seized him after every serious quarrel. Peace and quiet then returned to the ward. Nikifor had for a long time been reconciled to the notion that his cousin had outdistanced him, and now did not reconstruct earlier scenes of jealousy. All his lessons were now limited to reading.

I've already discussed Marazgali's successes and that these ceased due to his ignorance of Russian words and his loss of interest in grammar. With regard to Nogaitsev, he turned out to be quite a dolt and promised to go no further than to read haltingly. His somnolent and fattened brain was distinguished by a peculiar curiousness, by the way.

"But, Ivan Mikolaevich, do yokels often become pros'cutors?" he suddenly turned to me with this question, having encountered on a scrap of paper he'd found somewhere the word "yokel."[15]

Or else:

"Ivan Mikolaevich! They say Alexei ruled in Russia 'n' there was Dynasty in China … Is this name 'Dynasty' Orthodox or not?"

Like a Gogolesque Petrushka he read with equal enjoyment all books and papers he could lay his hands on.

Faced with my students' similar characters it's no wonder that, except for Mikhaila Burenkov, I concentrated my attention on the diligent and capable Lunkov. Moreover, his past interested me. Thanks to Lunkov's garrulity, our evenings turned into real inquisitions. I was the investigator, Chirok my assistant, Sokoltsev, Lunkov's fellow countryman (from Voronezh Province[16]), a witness, Petin the prosecutor, and all the rest of the ward the gallery, which had become vividly interested in the debate's slightest details. It turned out that regardless of his youth, Lunkov was already a recidivist.

"I jus' stupidly ended up in *katorga* this second time, Ivan Nikolaevich," Lunkov bitterly told me.

"How was it stupid?"

"It was o'er nuthin', it ain't very innerestin'."

"What do you mean 'over nothing'?! You know they say you killed a man?"

"That's so, I killed someone. 'Cause o' him, 'cause o' that swine I hafta suffer the maximum thirty years in *katorga*, 'n' a total o' seven years as a probationer,[17] but now he's sleepin' 'n' it can't matter to him."

"Tell me what happened exactly."

"Ivan Nikolaevich, I can't say I came from Raseya to Siberia the first time for nuthin'. Then it really was for the stupidity of leavin' my father 'n' strayin' off on my own with them people I hooked up with… Well, but that was then—'n' that certainly weren't what did me in, I assure you! It was 'cause o' my char'cter, o' course. My heart, you can see, is impatient; I won't suffer some snorter (he glanced significantly at Petin) bright'nin' up my life. He'd better kill me or I'll kill him!… I was in Eniseisk Province, bein' an exile-settler 'n' tradin' in baubles. You buy up various worthless wares, unnerstand, cotton prints, beads, needles, jewelry, 'n' go to the villages with this basket 'n' earn some bread from the women. Then one day this… man who'd been killed… that is, who *got* killed, came up to me: 'Kolia, lemme go with you to learn how to trade. Though I'm an ol' man, I dunno nuthin' 'bout these things.' I must tell you, I hardly knew him at that point, but I confess my heart didn't go out to him: his look was dark, not good… However, I'm thinkin': What's it to me? Ain't my road, but God's. 'Come if you want,' I tell him. 'I leave Monday.' It was a Saturday. Early Monday mornin', he came to me with a basket on his back, too. Off we went 'n' traveled like so for a week. He'd walk behind me 'n' was mostly quiet. But then he started grumblin' to himself that we weren't followin' the road we should. I didn't pay attention 'cept to say, 'Little uncle, we ain't bound; if you don't like it, go your own way.' He shut up. At that time, I always carried a revolver with me on the road. Didn't travel without it. The day before the murder, we spent the night at the home of a certain widow I knew. We got up in the mornin', 'n' I order breakfast for myself; I'm sittin' down to eat 'n' I invite him, the man who got killed. He refuses. 'Don't wanna,' he says. 'Uncle, why're you so gloomy?' the mistress asks him. 'T'ain't nuthin',' he says. 'Had a strange dream: as if a lot o' snow'd started fallin' 'n' there's logs lyin' on the road.' 'Yes,' answered the mistress, 'that ain't a sleep o' pleasin's.' Why'd he dream such a dream that night? Did his soul really sense somethin'?"

"Well, go on."

"That night exactly, a deep snow started fallin' almost up to the knees. There we were, settin' out on the road. I'm in front, as always, 'n' he's behind. We couldn't manage to get from behind a pasture, 'n' he started arguin'. 'Where're you goin'?' he says. I tell him, to Lesnoe. 'Fool, Lesnoe ain't on this road at all, but o'er there,' 'n' he points to a hardly visible fantasy world, 'cordin' to which peasants glide through the woods on logs. 'You go there,' I tell him, ''n' I'll take my own path.' He grabs me by my basket: 'Why're you so rude?' he says. 'I'm sick of it.' I turned round: 'Lemme go,' I tell him, ''n' don't commit a sin. I'm sick o' you, too. We sure ain't comrades no more. Get away from me.' I started walkin' off. He lets go 'n' blocks my way: 'Go where your elders tells ya,' he says. Then I took out my revolver: '*Here's* my elder! Get outta my way, creature!' He threatened me with his cane, but then I fired… I look—he's flat on the ground: bullet went straight into his left tit… I poked him—he was dead. I dragged him away from the road, covered him with a little snow, 'n' moved on. 'Cept, as I'm goin' down the little hill, I meet a peasant I know: 'Lunkov, was that a gunshot I just heard?' 'I didn't hear nuthin',' I tell him; 'you did, 'parently.' I went on 'n' met sev'ral more peasants. My heart was boilin' so, 'twas bleedin'. Well, I think, I'm sunk now! I had to hide… I sold my basket quick, got someone else's passport, 'n' rolled a hundred versts away from that place. Only, that passport ruined me: the man sold me an unreliable one… I was arrested 'n' brought to the canton. They bring me into a room where the corpse was lyin'.

"'This who you killed?' they ask. I looked 'n' looked at him… He was lyin' there as if alive: little gray hairs in his beard 'n' a tetchy little wound in his chest… I grabbed him by the beard 'n' turned him to the light. Kept on lookin' 'n' lookin'… 'N' just like that, I swung my foot up 'n' whacked him on the chin with my toe: 'I miss you, too, swine!' Well, they grabbed me right there, took me away 'n' wrote up a protocol."

"What did you do such a filthy thing for, Lunkov? Not what you killed him for, but desecrating the corpse?"

"Ivan Nikolaevich, I do nuthin' without my heart. Ever since, when I think 'bout it, I'm tormented 'n' regret ever'thin'. He 'peared in my sleep once… but only one time in all o' two years. He walks over 'n' stands 'n' looks at me… 'Why'd you come?' I ask. He's quiet, just waggin' his beard at me, as if it's accusin' me: 'But, I say, scoundrel, you still laughin' at me?' I grab an axe 'n' go after him. He goes away. Since he 'scaped he ain't come no more. Y'know, it's a desecration of *me* that I got judged so harshly, Ivan Nikolaevich; but would they 'ave given me thirteen years for a full confession?"

"Well, I'll speak my view now," Chirok began upon conclusion of the story, "you're completely lyin'. Not 'bout killin' the old-timer, but you killed him for his *basket*!"

"For his basket, indeed! When they was pickin' him up they found it near him in plain sight: the basket had its goods 'n' four rubles 'n' ninety kopeks."

"You talk! I know you…"

"You know a lot! I can get witnesses 'mong the residents o' Krasnoiarsk 'n' from Algacha 'n' Aleksandrovsk Central. But why go so far? Jus' ask Stepka Cheldonchik here…"

"I'm from Krasnoiarsk, too," Petin suddenly shouted, "'n' can be a witness as well. He killed the old-timer for his basket, o' course!"

"You, I reject," Lunkov quietly retorted. "You're my enemy. You might yet find me in a new murder."

Everyone broke out laughing. Petin didn't have the gunpowder to continue the false testimony.

"But what were you sent to Siberia for before?" I asked Lunkov.

"Before, Ivan Nikolaevich, 'cause of a thing," he answered, breathing deeply. "It's all the same to me, I shouldn't blame fate."

"Well, speak straight, little countryman," commented Sokoltsev, "I can't let you lie now. It's like that time I busted outta Kara 'n' got taken down a little road to Voronezh Jail."

"No reason for me to lie," Lunkov sadly answered. "If I'm lyin', then it's better not to talk."

"Lunkov, were you convicted the first time for murder?"

"What for, Ivan Nikolaevich! Jus' for pranks 'n' other things…"

"What?! You won't dare open up, twit?" Petin, eyes wide open and clenching his fists, advanced on him menacingly. "Didn't you yourself whisper to me in Ward Six you killed a young woman?"

"I ain't countin' that," our defendant coolly answered. "That was a youthful prank 'n' I don't 'member nuthin' 'bout her. Weren't convicted o'er her."

"Nevertheless… how did you kill her?"

"With iron. Kept hittin' her on the temple with an iron cane… Those the trifles you wanna know, Ivan Nikolaevich?"

"Twit, how you do talk, repeatedly, but didn't you say it happened under a bridge? So wheresabout did your cane come from?"

"I ain't talkin' to you, you Krasnoiarsk throat! You know a *lot*—you'll be growin' old soon."

"I know what he killed the girl for," Chirok once more interrupted, "he wanted to rape her but she didn't give in."

"Yes, indeed! I was only thirteen 'n' she ten. You've learned a lot!"

However, Lunkov stubbornly refused to give any details of the murder, and so I learned nothing except that the girl's body was found only after the winter.

"Well, alright. Tell me, what were you sentenced for the first time?"

"Y'see, Ivan Nikolaevich, I was busy in the spiritual sphere"

"'Spiritual sphere'! Didn't you say your father was a cabby?"

The laughter of all the others in the ward was my answer. Lunkov himself was chuckling.

"That is, I… went through churches…"

"…To worship God," Sokoltsev finished. "Our Voronezh, you yourself know, has since antiquity been rich with churches 'n' is famously pious."

Again everyone laughed. I finally understood the matter.

"Ivan Nikolaevich, I need only describe my life to you from the edges," continued Lunkov, adopting once again a serious and even sad look. "My father worked as a grain pourer but also ran a cab stand. At first, one o' my older brothers delivered the fares. He started playin' tricks. Wine 'n' women, you unnerstand. Once, he cut off the horses' tails outta spite. Father really beat him for that. Straight off, some young ladies he knew came 'n' asked for a ride. But the horses was simply spillin' blood. My brother took 'em 'n' drove. The horses was sweatin', blood flowin', 'n' so two o' father's best horses was lost. Ooh, how father beat my brother then, 'n' it's still terrible to recall… Chained him by the hand to a log, lashed him three whole hours with a hame-strap. He'd rest 'n' start beatin' him again. He'd 'ave beat him to death if ma hadn't called a neighbor for help. Well, all the same, my brother didn't reform. He robbed a certain gentleman with another cabby, took a hunnerd silver rubles, gold watches, fur coats, 'n' nice shoes, but they left him alive. Next day, lookouts was posted throughout the city, but they couldn't prove 'em guilty. Only, 'cause o' the watches, father soon realized my brother did it. At first he wanted to take 'em to the police, but ma convinced him not to. He seriously beat my brother again, more serious'n before. After my brother recovered, he left father 'n' began runnin' a little tavern with his sweetheart. Then he got completely messed up 'n' soon went to Sakhalin… Then I started drivin' a cab. Durin' that time ma died 'n' father remarried. Life at home got worse 'n' I, too, got up to some tricks. As you yourself know, Ivan Nikolaevich, a cab is worse'n any other trade for corruptin' a man. You're deliverin' gentlemen nonstop to train stations, hotels, 'n' restaurants 'n' you see how happy people are, them drinkin' well, ridin' round, 'n' havin' lotsa money. Well, o' course, you yourself start holdin' back on the boss's money, drinkin' some spirits, strollin' with the girls… Plus, you see all sorts o' folk. Once, a murder happened in my cab."

"A murder? How so?"

'Jus' so. I was drivin' the well-known townsman Ulitin 'n' a certain lady; both was drunk, o' course. They started quar'lin' 'n' arguin' 'bout somethin'. It was nighttime. He grabs the wrench from my toolbox 'n' bang! on her temple. She gave up the ghost!"

"What did you do? Did you bring him to the police?"

"Someone well-known? Lissen to you, Ivan Nikolaevich! I acted nobly. We took her behind some brick sheds 'n' tossed her in a cesspit…"

"Very noble! Does this mean you now had three souls on your conscience?"

"Lissen to you, Ivan Nikolaevich! What else could I do? It was completely outta my hands."

"But didn't a lotta blood splash on you in the cab?" Chirok for some reason inquired.

"Not a drop. There was jus' blood on the wrench."

"Well, now you're lyin, you're confusin' things. If there was blood on the wrench, *obverously* the whole cab was splashed with blood."

There began an argument about this in the ward. All the worldly ones were experts in this area… The majority supported Chirok; but Lunkov stubbornly held to his position, insisting that the young woman had been wrapped in a shawl and the blood had not gotten out from under it. With difficulty, I persuaded the disputants to cease what was not for me an interesting argument and to return to the story.

Lunkov's "trickiness" kept going further and further; his father began disciplining him as he had his brother, and one fine day he fled as a seventeen-year-old youth from his parents' house and fell in with the gang of a certain "Stepan Ivanovich," a well-known petty thief of Voronezh with whom Lunkov had been enraptured up till then. Stepan Ivanovich was principally occupied in the "spiritual sphere." The very first night Lunkov joined this sphere he became witness to a murder. While unlocking the church's lock a comrade's hand got shut in the doors and he yelled in a voice not his own, and then Stepan Ivanovich quieted him forever with a crowbar over the head and dragged the body to a stream. Several days passed and the same gang, overtaking two traveling merchants outside the city, committed a murderous robbery. Lunkov was the driver during this, and it was Stepan Ivanovich along with a certain Fëdor and three other comrades who shot them with revolvers, and it was on this basis that Lunkov was denying his guilt in the murders:

"Mercy me, lissen to you, Ivan Nikolaevich! How was it my crime? I didn't shoot or strangle 'em with sashes… I just drove the horses… I didn't report 'em, o' course; as you know, 'cordin' to us this ain't a fault but a merit."

When Lunkov spoke about such things in his reedy singsong voice, seriously or even sadly, it was impossible to tell whether this was a type of naïvety and inability of thought or the summit of depravity and dissimulation.

Stepan Ivanovich gave Lunkov one of the murdered men's passports, and it was in this guise that he was later convicted. His current surname was ostensibly not Lunkov but someone else's.

It would be tiresome to relate all the tricky adventures Lunkov participated in during his five months of the free life. It was a peculiar world, and there were peculiar ideals and understandings of honor and comradeship. In a certain village below Elets[18] the gang, consisting of Stepan Ivanovich, Fëdor, and Lunkov, was informed by a woman they'd "placed" in the service of a wealthy peasant and who'd sunk her teeth into him that there was a money-locker in one of three sheds near his house. In a single night they actually found three thousand rubles in the designated spot and "burned" forty-five versts in bare feet getting away from there. They stopped at a ruined cellar outside the city. Lunkov and Fëdor stayed to rest but Stepan Ivanovich went to the city for some purchases. After a certain time he returned drunk with four new comrades, one of whom was a notorious spy. All seven went to a den of iniquity and squandered two thousand over several days. Then they began thinking how to get rid of the spy. They really wanted "to nail" him, but preferred to give him money and send him off with some instructions. The spy hid for a while. Then the den's mistress showed them a church they could make some money from. They visited the church that night, but in a mistaken calculation netted all of forty rubles in money and a hundred in goods. Next morning, the police unexpectedly showed up. During a search of Fëdor's place they found a church paten in his pocket… There commenced an inspection of documents. Everyone's turned out to be genuine; only, they dug up in Lunkov's document four prior arrests he hadn't even known about. Thanks to someone else's sins, he was apparently exiled to a settlement at the same time his comrades were serving simple jail terms.

"But, countryman, what'd you go to jail for a year earlier?" Sokoltsev, who had been thinking about this the whole time, suddenly asked.

"When, earlier?"

"When, indeed. Y'know, durin' that time you was tellin' 'bout when you weren't in Voronezh. I was leavin' for *katorga* again."

"How's that? Well, for certain… you're mistaken, you didn't see me in Voronezh Prison. I weren't there earlier."

"Not there! You still deny it! I ain't mistaken. Indeed, didn't you recognize me first?"

"Ho-ho-ho! You're sunk, dearie!" shouted the ward, delighted that they'd finally caught out Lunkov.

"Let's say I was there… for exactly… jus' a month 'n' a half… 'n' *that* jus' for some nonsense," Lunkov flustered about.

"Why, you don't say."

"Speak up, twit!" snarled Elk.

"Speak, countryman, speak. You yourself boasted that if you're lyin' it's better not e'en to talk at all."

"I was in the prison 'cause o' my brother's case… That is, *not* the Karl Ivanovich case."

"You well know Karl Ivanovich was guilty for the post, but your brother for the priest. I well know you know."

"Indeed… that… Only, Karl Ivanovich was acquitted in that case."

Finally, Lunkov was so pressed to the wall by the general force of Sokoltsev, Chirok, Petin, and me that he told us the following. He was still living with his father when there was a daring attempt to rob almost 45,000 rubles from the post: two postmen were killed on the spot, but the coachman managed to get away with the mail. Suspicion fell on Lunkov's brother and his gang, who were arrested shortly afterwards in the other "case of Karl Ivanovich." Our acquaintance, Lunkov the younger, was held under arrest for two months. The coachman had testified that during the attack "a youth" was sitting and shouting: "Don't tie 'em up, *beat* 'em to death!" The prosecutor suspected that the younger Lunkov was this youth. But during the investigation he portrayed himself as an innocent babe; besides this, the prosecutor's comrade made, in the storyteller's words, the biggest mistake, having told the coachman the surnames of those suspected of the murders. Evidently owing to the collapse of the charges, the case was dismissed. Telling this, Lunkov had not, however, decided to acknowledge that the "youngster" was indeed him, though Chirok straightforwardly said:

"Yes, o' course it was *him*! Him, the rat!"

"You've lived foolishly," I once told Lunkov.

"Foolishly, Ivan Nikolaevich?" he shot back. "Right here, if I was goin' round starvin', in rags, beggin' under windows, then you could say: foolishly! But, for God's sake, I was *livin'!*"

Such a cynical justification perturbed me.

"You still remember God!"

"He intercedes, Ivan Nikolaevich. Y'know, it's said in the Scriptures—here's what I read long ago: 'If God wishes, not a single hair'll fall from a human head.' Them words 'ave been cut sharp into my memory. So, how was my killin' someone a sin? Certainly, God wanted it. Don't be angry with me, Ivan Nikolaevich. I see you're angry. What for! I'm tellin' you the truth… Others fake themselves in front o' you, hide what they are, 'n' you like such two-faces… But there's one thing I do regret, Ivan Nikolaevich. How I was livin' in Siberia 'fore the murder, 'n' a certain little woman made me a proposition: 'Take me away, Kolia! We'll take five hunnerd rubles from my husband 'n' go away.' I shoulda taken her far as Perm, handed her o'er to someone, 'n' gone on by myself… Now, I'm *truly* grievin' a bit about that."

"But what would you have done, Lunkov, if you had gone free? Would you have returned home?"

"O' course I woulda returned. I had a safe place, y'know. I coulda gone straight to my home address."

"To your father's?"

"No, I coulda earlier… I woulda been a guest… I woulda gone to a certain place in Elets."

"Guests are to be treated well!"

"Yes, indeed, Ivan Nikolaevich! I woulda been ashamed to come to my father's without money, with empty hands. 'Where you been loafin' 'bout so many years?' he'd say. 'Comin' back a pauper? Now I'm to feed you!'"

The young rationalist, dampening not in the least, but actually strutting, his candor, directly told me that he wouldn't hesitate to kill a man for a hundred or two hundred silver rubles.

"But if Mikolaich was vagabondin' with you," Chirok once asked him, "would you finish him off?"

"No, what for?! If I went to Ivan Nikolaevich's in the free life, I'd ask 'em for a bit o' money, 'n' they wouldn't refuse."

"Well, but what *if* he refused?"

"I wouldn't renounce him, o' course… But if they teach me to read 'n' write, why should I kill 'em?"

Hearing these words I laughed along with everyone, but in my soul was terrified and didn't know what to think of this strange character, still almost a boy and already so very, so hopelessly, dissolute and lost. The innate fearlessness with which he, young and weak, battled against the prison's Ivan-Herculeses, striking their eyes with mother-truth, is what attracted me to him. If Lunkov's words were to be believed, then during his life in freedom he had idealized prisoners terribly.

"I thought, Ivan Nikolaevich, that if they had one religion, then they'd have one soul they steadfastly maintain for each other in misfortune."

"What kind of religion is this?"

"Such that all swindlers is judged the same… But from what I've seen, they're all worthless creatures. Give him some tea today, 'n' you're his best friend; but you don't give it to him tomorrow, 'n' he's cursin' you first thing in the mornin'! They're the most worthless 'n' mercenary folk, Ivan Nikolaevich. All their laws 'n' regulations ain't worth a brass farthin'. I've since decided not to respect 'em 'n' to go counterwise in ever'thin'. I don't have any pity at all for them worthless creatures. I'm good only to those who're good to me; 'n' I pity only those who pity me. 'N' I ain't afraid, Ivan Nikolaevich, that with my heart I'll be destroyed by the leadership, or that I'll disembowel my own brother sometime or will myself be done in at his hands. I well know these various throats 'n' snorters hate me; but I ain't scared of 'em. Let 'em kill me—I ain't gonna run to save my life. Maybe I'd e'en be glad if someone stabbed me to death. Let 'em! Comin' to harm ain't terrible… Here, I could get the rope from the court—this I wouldn't wish for… I still don't wanna leave the wide world! If I don't fear the rope, I should really suffer? I shoulda been alone a long time ago, 'n' not paired up."

"Lunkov, this means you very much want to live?"

"The desire's there, o' course, Ivan Nikolaevich. How much o' the wide world do I still gotta see? Well, but all the same, prob'ly had I known two years ago I'd been fixed by God to die, I wouldn't-a wasted time then… I wouldn't-a had to put up with these two years… By myself, I woulda pulled off such a job that I'd prob'ly be off on my own not for fifty, but a hunnerd years! My name woulda become famous!"

"What was it you were going to do?"

"Not worth talkin' for no reason, Ivan Nikolaevich. I'll just tell you one thing: my job woulda been not on *that* half [Lunkov nodded his head toward the door's peephole], but on *this*, right here [he enigmatically rapped his knuckles on the table]. 'Cause I don't so much blame *that* half. O'er there, I don't have e'en any malice in the least, but *here*… Here, I find most o' the blame!"

Lunkov never wanted to explain for me all the reasons for his hatred of the prison masses; I could only guess, based on certain hints, that he'd been unable to forget a number of other offences or to forgive a prison ringleader's unfair accusation against him of one of the lowest vices which, in prisoners' eyes, assigns a brand of ineffaceable disgrace to each one guilty of it. To his misfortune, Lunkov, as I've already said, had a young-looking, femininely pretty little face, and in the dissolute herd's eyes this accusation had plausibility. *Katorga* generally knew neither mercy nor compassion toward victims of this sickening vice, and, by contrast, it regarded not only with indulgence but even respect those of its brethren who took advantage of their weakness.

"In prison, I gotta suffer, Ivan Nikolaevich," said Lunkov. "I'll try to endure ever'thin'; but I'll surely persuade two, if not three, when I break free! Word of honor, I'll persuade 'em! I'll e'en pour out a cup of his blood 'n' drink it straight off 'fore I kill the stinker!"

Lunkov regarded not only without rancor but even a kind of sentimental affection certain of those same prisoners. Several men who like him stood off to the side of general prison life, and one sick old fellow countryman in particular, were actually his bosom buddies. For a long time this seemed exceedingly strange and incomprehensible: given such hostility towards the prison's law and traditions, how could Lunkov take on the role of selfless sister of mercy toward everyone sitting in the isolator? No one with great courage and stamina looked after those he sure did not need, and no one with great cunning gave them all they required in front of the sharpest-eyed and smartest guards. Iashka the Marmot often fell at a venture, but Lunkov conducted his business artistically, absolutely loving and playing his art… I soon noticed, however, that his activities were partly motivated by that same hatred and contempt for prisoners' opinions and decisions. He took care of decidedly anyone who simply sat in the isolator, discriminating not in the least between whom the collective liked and whom it hated. Thus, once there was a free commandee in the isolator whom everyone had labeled a spy and decided to give nothing to. Lunkov demonstratively attended to him even more and with greater zealousness than for anyone at any time.

"Ivan Nikolaevich, I dunno why I do it," he explained his conduct. "The little mare is talkin' either fairly or falsely 'bout him. Don't matter to me. I seen a lot in prisons, how God knows fully innocent people are accused 'n' e'en more often murdered! He's bein' punished by the authorities; so why should I, a wretch like him, torment him, too?"

For all the contradictions and muddled ideas that hampered Lunkov's reasoning and views, there lurked inside him a kernel of something seemingly good, honest, and separate, a kernel perhaps barely noticeable beneath the dark shell of depravity and crudeness but nonetheless having endowed him with a kind appearance, endowed him with a comforting uniqueness among the truly worthless and hopelessly dissolute herd. Most prisoners terribly hated and cursed Shelai mine; Lunkov, on the other hand, was one of the few who complimented it. He conveyed contentment at precisely what Petin, Sokoltsev, and Semënov were instead indignant: that, compared to other prisons, it was stricter at this mine, that each member of the collective had a voice equal to everyone's, and this was why the stealing of general possessions did not happen and the food was better. Also, he didn't like cards and preferred a book instead.

Such was the second of my favorite students. Did his studies advantage him later? Or did he die? I give omens for these questions, to which I myself have not the strength to provide a definitive answer.

V. SAKHALIN DISTURBANCES

With spring's arrival, dark rumors circulated among *katorga* prisons about a forthcoming transfer to Sakhalin Island. Prisoners were deathly worried. Some feared like the death penalty just this terrible island's name; for others, by contrast, it seemed to symbolize a secret hope of resurrection… It was said that this time, all vagabonds disguising their backgrounds, anybody who'd been twice convicted, anybody who'd escaped from *katorga*, and, lastly, anybody who'd committed some kind of violation in prison, would be sent there. These categories accounted for a huge portion of the prison population, and everybody was understandably anxiously awaiting the resolution of their fate. Strictly speaking, no one knew anything for sure about Sakhalin, this infamous "Sokolin" island. Some insisted it was a living grave from which no one ever returned; horrors were told about *katorga* jobs in coal mines, where work had to be done on your knees and in water up to your neck… Others, by contrast, laughed over such fears, portraying Sakhalin as some kind of earthly Eldorado: according to them, the longest-sentenced prisoners were immediately set free to the four winds; there was almost no official labor; prisoners were given tools, cattle, and even money for establishing homesteads; and if this weren't enough: each man was allowed to choose a wife from among dozens of rows of female penal laborers… For those for whom all these blessings weren't sufficient, there would always be the possibility of escape. The names of dozens of prisoners at Zerentui, Algacha, and Kara who'd supposedly escaped from Sakhalin and were praising it confirmed this. Ultimately, no one knew whom or what to believe. Short-term penal laborers, as well as residents of Transbaikalia who dreamed of returning home upon the conclusion of their sentences, were, needless to say, those most frightened by Sakhalin, falling into despondency at each new rumor of imminent transfer. The hopelessly long-term ones, however, dreamed of getting onto the roster of transferees: they would have been ready to go beyond even Sakhalin to the very ends of the earth, if only they could break free of the walls of Shelai Prison, which for most seemed worse than death. "Changing your fate," changing at any cost and in any way, was their primary and most treasured dream, allowing them neither sleep nor rest. None of these dreamers liked or was able to imagine the distant future. Sakhalin, even if it were to turn out to be a terrible thing, seemed almost as remote as life after death, but in the meantime, imagination portrayed the march-route there as an easygoing life, with *maidany* and card games with the populations of new prisons through which it would be necessary to pass, with many new people, meetings with old acquaintances and comrades and—who knows?—perhaps fortunate circumstances that would again bear a dead man into God's world… The dreams of long-termers with wives were especially fervent. The opinion (right or wrong, I don't know) that, not only on Sakhalin but in most other *katorga* sites, married prisoners were not kept in prison even during the probation term but almost immediately released to the free command, on the understanding that married prisoners very rarely escaped, predominated among prisoners in general. In any case, there was no such arrangement at Shelai mine. Six-Eyes treated the married just as strictly as the bachelors. They were allowed one meeting a week with their wives, under strict observation by guards; they weren't allowed foodstuffs from outside (except that it was possible to eat during their meeting), and no one had any hope of entering freedom earlier than the conclusion of both their probationary and correctional terms.

"Don't dream of it," Staff Captain Luchezarov menacingly announced one day during evening roll call. "You're all the same to me, and I'll release no one before his legal term. And if I don't release you, then God Himself can't get you past these walls!"

In the meantime, most of Shelai's married men had hopelessly long probationary terms, and since all believed that other prison commandants treated husbands better, it was understandable that they yearned to free themselves from Six-Eyes's talons. The situation for some of them actually inspired sympathy. The young Pole Musial had received twenty years for murdering his wife's stepfather, who had exasperated him with a string of injustices, deceptions, and criticisms over many years. Musial was a simple Polish peasant, his primitive intelligence and moral innocence strongly reminiscent of the Russian Shemelin. If Musial's story was to be believed (and there was no reason not to—the story was so simple and close to reality), most Russian prisoners, faced with his father-in-law's disgraceful deeds, would have immediately and without hesitation done what he did only after several years of the most asinine patience. Juzefa herself, Musial's wife, prompted her husband to wreak vengeance on the offender. After Jan was sentenced for the murder she, having left her young children with relatives, followed him to *katorga*. On the way, still another daughter was born to them, the pretty Kasia, whom I sometimes saw during their meetings. For a man such as Musial, still entirely morally intact, truly deeply connected to his family and wife, and who'd committed his crime partly out of love for them, I could have a heartfelt desire for a quicker release to freedom. He suffered much, and to my eyes, his encounters with his wife were a terrible drama. Jan was neither bright nor jealous, and the beautiful and hearty Juzefa presented such a tasty morsel not only for free commandees but the Cossacks and guards themselves, that a whole series of the darkest intrigues and dirty tricks was inevitably mounted against the young couple's good fortune. Juzefa was hounded by dozens of seducers, and only her peasant woman's innocence and Catholic piety saved her; rare would have been the Russian woman who could endure such a test as befell her... One filthy rumor after another arose beyond the prison walls and through the mouth of the malicious mare, always avid for the suffering of others, and reached her husband's ears. For a long time he just laughed, believing in his wife as in a saint. Slanderers and scandalmongers of all kinds sharpened their imagination and ingenuity: they said that Juzefa was living with a Cossack officer, then with one of the guards, then they named a somehow wealthy resident of the free command. They presented the most realistic details, dreamed up the most believable scenes and supposedly overheard stories... Suspicion at last began to take root in Jan's heart... To top off the mischief, at one of their meetings a guard, who had for a long time been grinding his teeth over being spurned by Juzefa, intercepted some innocuous note she planned to give her husband, and Six-Eyes punished them by forbidding meetings for five months. Only an enemy could have done this. The slander became still more shameless and daring, and the wretched Jan lost even the capacity to trust her, and was from then on enflamed by jealousy. Many well-wishers tried in vain to calm and persuade him not to believe prisoners' rumors and fabrications; he himself now turned into an accuser and publicly and loudly used such words against his wife as would have earlier caused him to beat over the head anyone who said them. Encountering her at times outside the prison, he cast a fierce look, and in the convoy guards' presence threw vulgar insults at her. Still innocent, Juzefa was for a long time at a loss, and in response to the undeserved insults simply sobbed grievously; but soon she, too, got angry and began replying to insults with insults. The little mare, witness to such spousal scenes, chortled happily in celebration of its victory. As it turned out, upon the end of the five-month punishment Juzefa herself did not want to meet with her husband. Family peace and future apparently forever broken, Juzefa was now ready to go with little Kasia back to Russia…

Simple chance prevented this calamity. Shelai mine was being visited by the superintendent of Nerchinsk *katorga*, and completely unexpectedly, Musial turned to him with a statement of his pitiful situation. Regardless of its comically half-Russian text, it was expressed so powerfully and movingly that the supervisor, having right there asked Luchezarov about the prisoner's behavior and learning that his probationary term would be ending in several months, ordered him released from prison immediately. The mare saw Musial off to freedom with laughter and spiteful prophesies about what awaited him there…

But all these prophecies fortunately turned out to be nonsense; to reciprocal satisfaction the misunderstandings were explained during a personal meeting, and the young couple took to living in their previous concord.

Of all the married men the tailor Bulanov, who had a large family on his hands, pitied himself the most. He was indeed a foul person, hypocritical, vain, always on guard, with cunning, roving eyes and a saccharine smirk on his lips. He'd lived not at all poorly in his own house, wanting for nothing, but nevertheless came to *katorga* for murdering three people during a robbery. He told the details of this evil act with shocking cynicism, without speaking directly, however, about his part in it; though this was obvious, given his cunning grin and the cold glint in his cutting gaze.

"I ended up in labor without bein' guilty," the crafty Mordvin sang in such instances. "I was sentenced indeterminately without makin' a confession, y'know."

A skillful tailor, he made clothes for all the local commandants, including Luchezarov, and had a fair income; his wife was apparently a practical person and also able to make a bit of money. Nonetheless, Bulanov desired with all his soul to get out of Shelai mine, and continually dreamed of a "transfer": he'd been in *katorga* for all of just two years, and another nine years of just his prison term remained ahead for him.

But none of the husbands bore himself as stubbornly and with such consistency as a certain Diudin, who (in the capacity of a lifetime recidivist) carried round his neck a probationary term that alone was fifteen years. He was a strange fellow, whom nature had invested with the ability to work his tongue until he drove you mad. Unfortunate was he who revealed the slightest interest in speaking with him: for it was then impossible to stop hearing his stories! During these, he always spoke with strange affectations and turns of speech in which a pretense to illumine his education and European gloss was evident. So, according to him, he "once attempted to take the life of the Austrian national Baron Rozenwald"; he was always on "friendly terms" with all the ladies and gentlemen he'd lived with in Russia and abroad; if, during an argument, some prisoner began saying something patently absurd, Diudin shouted at him: "Well, boy, you've now reached the *apogee of ridiculousness!*" In his neighbors' faces he poured forth like pearls the names of barons, princes, and counts he knew. It was understandable why prisoners terribly disliked him, and it was a rare day when Diudin was not abused, argued with, or even hit.

"Diudin's found an adventure again!" the mare would say, hearing a row somewhere that he was responsible for.

Whereas any other married man cringed before the administration and "lashed out at it with his tongue," Diudin, who also, needless to say, did not shy away from this, soon managed to get all the guards against him with his indefatigable stupidity, incessant chattering, and passion for "dawdling." He was forever landing in some "adventure": here he was, illegally bringing into the prison from a meeting bread loaves and tarts while a "good" guard was on duty at the gate, and was subsequently caught by the "bad" duty officer inside, thus leading to his first misfortune; here he was, carrying on an argument and even getting face-to-face with the cooks or launderers; here he was, finally, spreading gossip about guards' wives that reached the latter's attention and led to chaos outside prison walls… No kind of penalty, not even deprivation of meetings with his wife, could correct this foolish man. Absolutely every evening roll call he engaged Six-Eyes himself in endless debates, turning to him with requests and demands and simply any sort of nonsense. Even the brave staff captain's magnificence was for him an insufficient scarecrow, and so he'd finally begin waving his arms and legs, but they still hardly got Diudin noticed, nor did he gain success by opening his mouth wide so he could commence his spate of words… As it turned out, Luchezarov himself began pleading for Diudin to be transferred to another prison.

Short-termers found themselves in a completely different situation: for them, there was every reason to serve out their punishment in the nevertheless strict Shelai Prison, if only to be settled in Transbaikal District and not on terrible Sakhalin. Among us was a certain Transbaikalian peasant, a vagabond concealing his identity, a runaway soldier sentenced "unqualifiedly" for simply having concealed his "birth names"; his four-year *katorga* term was ending that summer but, all the same, it was possible that he was going to be removed to Sakhalin. Understandably, he feared the wait more than he did resolution of the transfer rumors. It was said that the entire healthy population was being resolutely "swept up" from Kara, Zerentui, Algacha, and the other big mines, and only cripples and the infirm were being left in place; even those who'd already completed their *katorga* terms but had simply been unable to get assigned to a canton were being removed to Sakhalin.

But in Shelai mine there was a certain fellow who cowered most of all; he'd grown pale, thin, and met with and distorted everything as if hoping that, in such way, he'd go unnoticed and be left in peace. This was none other than our old acquaintance and friend Kuzma Chirok. He soundly recalled his story with the sheep dog, and though he insisted that his escape hadn't been entered into the written record, since it was a simple absence, in his heart's depths he didn't believe this… Poor Chirok even lost sleep and appetite. And malicious jokesters who soon discerned his disquiet took advantage of it and began to unceasingly weary him in all sorts of ways.

"You're obliged to your Lukeika now, absolutely obliged!" they droned at him day and night.

"What're you sad about, pal? Your sister 'n' blessed brother-in-law is waitin'."

"You all go to the Devil, you lousy creatures, vermin!"

"Whate'er are you snarlin' 'bout, Kuzma Aleksandrych? Or don't you believe in your good fortune? Surely, this matter can be straightened out. We got learned men. Nikishka, compose a petition that says 'Kuzma Chirok, suff'rin' eight years o' dif'cult sep'ration from his only sister Lukeria Aleksandrovna, most humbly asks Your Excellency'—or sumpin' like that… 'to be reunited.' But this is why he wants to be removed to Sakhalin Island, where she's gotta stay with her husband Semën Pelevin 'n' the kids. Sit down, brother, I'll scratch out the *dikatation* with my own hand."

"Yes! Nikishka'll write it… A learned man's been found!" scornfully bellowed Chirok, noticeably upset over the fact that a piece of paper was being unrolled before him and a pencil sharpened to a fine point as the semiliterate Burenkov grandly sat down at table.

"I'm-a gonna write!" Nikifor urged him on, spritely beginning to form some rather astonishing hieroglyphs. "Petition. That's followed by a period. Sister Lukeria. Sokolin Island. Signed Kuzma Chirok. It's ready!"

And he began ceremoniously composing an imaginary petition. Chirok now lost control.

"Oh, the rats!" he screamed. "They're really goin' under the lash!"

He tried to leap from his spot and run to grab the paper from Nikifor. But he couldn't break free and Nikifor, having run along the sleeping platforms among reclining prisoners' heads and legs, fled past Chirok and burst out the door into the yard to be pursued by him. They ran around the prison several times. The fleet-footed Nikishka was at that moment barefoot and in just his underwear and, notwithstanding the snow still in the yard, flew like the wind; Chirok, wearing heavy boots with fetters and a sheepskin jacket, looked clumsy but turned out to be a remarkable sprinter as well. He almost caught Nikifor two or three times, but each time he cleverly dodged away and finally completely eluded and hid from Chirok, who was panting and snorting like a steam engine. Two minutes later Burenkov came up to him.

"You rat, where's the petition? Give it to me!" the still gasping Chirok, coughing, swearing, and spitting, confronted him.

"I threw it under the gate," answered Nikishka. "Let the guards find it."

"Are you lyin'?!" screamed Chirok, either jokingly or in utmost fright, and began to scold and even punch the placidly smiling Nikifor like nothing on earth.

The guards soon learned about these jokes and Chirok's comical fear of Sakhalin, and one time, one of them came to our ward and, with a serious look, read off a list of prisoners who had supposedly just been designated for removal to Sakhalin; included in it was Kuzma Chirok. The latter turned completely pale and began shaking like a leaf… The joke had now gone too far and someone, taking pity on him, hastily explained to Chirok that the sentence against him had been concocted. His indignation was boundless, yet at the same time, the mare was once more in rapture.

One beautiful March day, an electrical spark seemed to flash through the prison: a rumor went round that a list of thirty men designated for removal from Shelai mine to Sakhalin had at last been received. Everybody went instantly quiet, as everyone seemed to go deep within himself, only occasionally conjecturing in whispers to each other as to which thirty men might be, in the opinion of some, the unfortunates, and in the opinion of others, the lucky guys. Waiting for that evening's roll call was difficult. You could have heard a fly buzzing, so quiet was it when Luchezarov, having himself appeared at roll call, full-throatedly announced after prayers that in exactly one week all thirty residents of Transbaikal District, including the Burenkov cousins, would be removed to Sakhalin. Diudin alone had somehow managed to worm his way into this category, even though he did not at all belong to it.

For most, this announcement was a clap of thunder from a clear sky. Some heaved a deep sigh of relief, others almost shouted in horror, and still others swore in disappointment. "Mister Com'dant! We're family men, y'know," Nikifor pleaded, "wives 'n' little children… They can't get along without us… 'N' the end o' my term's almost here."

"'N' how come we can't go? Y'know we was askin' to!" long-termers were yelling.

"Silence! By what manners are you all speaking at once? Wait, while the commandant explains. No other categories are demanded for Sakhalin this current year. Trust me, I would be happy if many of you were to transfer. I sent a list of all the artists who are not welcome in my prison, but, unfortunately, they're only taking Diudin for now. With regard to short-termers and family men like the Burenkovs, their situation is truly sad. But there's nothing you can do: it's the law! You must submit. Before it, I'm no different. I can only recommend this to you: immediately telegraph your wives to get ready for the journey. You'll be going to Ust-Kara and will probably be there for a long time, and they can catch up to you there."

"But if there was tried, Mister Com'dant," the short-termers timidly said, "if a telegram was tapped out to the gentleman gov'nor?… The children, it could be said, the little ones, the sick wives… Maybe he'll deign to stop it."

"It would be a wasted effort. The law can't be changed: residents of Transbaikal District must be settled on Sakhalin."

"He could be asked all the same, Mister Com'dant."

Luchezarov shrugged his shoulders:

"Perhaps I'll try. Guards, take the prisoners to their wards."

In our ward, we couldn't sleep until deep into the night. Chirok surrendered to a mindless joy and began joking with everyone, getting up and cackling venomously at those for whom a pit had been dug, and who were composing anonymous letters and petitions and suddenly falling in love with misfortune. Nikifor and Mikhaila were utterly crushed… Petin, Nogaitsev, and Sokoltsev, having dreamed of Sakhalin, were more disconsolate than anyone, and began concocting new plans to break away from Six-Eyes and his prison.

The following day, the Burenkovs sent to Troitskosavsk a telegram for their wives. Another pair of those designated for removal sent a petition to the governor by telegraph. I don't know if Luchezarov forwarded this petition, but four days later, he briefly informed them that a reply had been received… The Burenkovs were greatly agitated, having not heard an answer from home for a long time. Nikifor candidly announced that if his wife refused for some reason to follow him, he would be a lost man.

"I'll run straight from the road 'n' declare myself to her… 'Ah, you bitch,' I'll say, 'you was thinkin' to send me to Sakhalin so's to cut loose? Wanted to go live as you please? No, you ain't tryin' that with me. I'm right here. You can't keep me in chains.' Y'know I will, boys, 'n' that's a fact… If I makes up my mind, then I'm a man on fire! Then I ain't 'fraid o' nuthin', not people nor God Hisself. If I take notice of her faithlessness or some monkey business o'er there, then I won't be doin' a lotta discussin': the low-life's head'll be gone! You'll know us, Sokolinites! I'm-a gonna kill her, 'n' I'm-a gonna kill the little ones, too. God don't give father good luck, there won't in the whole world be such a blackenin', such unfortunates…"

"Enough, Nikifor," I interrupted, "you can't believe what you're saying. Your wife will of course follow you through fire and water."

"That's prob'ly true… It should be thought she'll go, Mikolaich… Tomorrow'll be five days since the telegram got sent, but there ain't no answer."

"That still means nothing. Better you tell me how you got married: did your fathers arrange it, or what?"

"We's eloped, Mikolaich… That's often the way 'mongst us, us married ones. You 'member the dif'rent novels you read 'n' told to us? I daresay you thought this dif'rent love goes on only in your life, but that us simple peasants live like cattle? No, brother, we got the same things goin' on… I'll tell you 'bout it, if you wants."

VI. NIKIFOR'S ROMANCE;
THE SEND-OFF

"Our two families—mine on my father's side 'n' Nastkina's on her mother's side—had the most terrible emmity for each other"—thus Nikifor began his romance. "Our fathers 'n' mothers would grit their teeth 'n' couldn't look calmly at one another… I can't talk 'bout it well 'n' truly, 'cause I was still tiny when it first started. Only, us children copied the grown-ups, o' course. I twisted into pretzels so's not to admit my love for Nastka… I'd catch somethin' somewhere 'n' stick it in her hair, then rub dirt in it. Only, she'd never cry, 'n' just angrily defend herself without really tryin'… Also, I'd hold her down 'n' bite 'n' throw crap all o'er her… Well, needless to say, only after all this was o'er did I lay her out. Also, she never wanted to complain, to never tell her mum 'n' dad that I was beatin' her, 'cause then none o' my elders woulda let me off the hook, what with the adults livin' in emmity. Nastka was scared o' me: she'd see me, scream 'n' run… She'd run 'n' run, fall down, get up again 'n' run as absolutely fast as her legs would carry her. I was a little barbarian, y'know, just ask Mikhaila. He 'members. He pinched my ears more'n once. Well, o' course, as Nastka 'n' I grew up we stopped fightin'—it's shameful now… 'N' Nastka didn't try runnin' from me: she'd just walk past without lookin' or battin' an eye… We was perfect strangers. She'd go past like a tsarevna. She'd flirt with the other youngsters, my comrades, 'n' make all kinds o' jokes (we youngsters behaved like grown-ups, y'know, specially the wenches), but I certainly weren't for her. I'll say yet again I was a tiny demon… No-no! She'd just glare at me hatefully with burnin' eyes! Then I took offense 'n' started gettin' angry. One spring (I was already sixteen), I'm ridin' a horse 'n' I see Nastka 'n' her mother goin' somewheres to visit neighbors. It was a holiday; both was really done up, flashily dressed… But the street was muddy, muddy—God knows you coulda drowned in it. How my cruelty bubbled up inside me! I snapped the whip on my horse 'n' galloped past 'em: they got spattered in mud from head to toe! Young ladies, kids, chaps standin' round, started laughin'… Nastkina's mother screamed: 'Catch that villain!' Where'd I go? Weren't a trace o' me. After that, we didn't meet for a long time. I myself had somehow got ashamed: I'd see her somewhere but walk off to the side. 'N' if we couldn't avoid meetin' somewheres at a round-dance or a youngins' get-together, then I'd try not to look 'n' would court the other girls. 'Cept, she busied my heart from then on… She was a proud wench to say nuthin'. Mikhaila here knows she didn't vent her anger… It's actually funny to say it: I'd really see her in my dreams, embrace her 'n' call her tender names… Honest to God, I ain't lyin'! But come mornin', I'd wake up an angry fellow 'n' wouldn't look at her in broad daylight. Well, in a word, this is comin' outta me letter by letter, like in them novels you read, Mikolaich… Now here she is, my sweetheart, 'n' that's for sure! I gotta say, straight out, that I've begun pinin' for Nastka. I'm thinkin': certainly, she'll agree to come if I ask her to; maybe she'll agree to get married. But then again, I'm goin' outta my mind: I imagine she really hates me 'n' can't forget how I beat her when she was still a little girl, 'n' how later I embarrassed her in front of everyone by spatterin' her with mud. In my mem'ry she's tough, owin' to so much pride, 'n' never complained to me when she was little, 'n' she e'en rarely cried. One time, I was comin' home from huntin'. I'd gone out in the spring for ducks. I'm strollin' beside a stream, 'n' from behind the bushes I see Nastka washin' linen on a raft. My heart was poundin', for sure… I twisted my moustaches (though my moustaches had only just started sproutin'), put my rifle o'er my shoulder, 'n' walked straight o'er towards her.

"'Greetin's, Nastasia!' I said.

"I was appealin' to her for the first time in my entire life. She was suddenly frightened (see, she hadn't heard me 'proachin') 'n' e'en dropped her flail…

"'Oy,' she said, 'how you scared me, Nikifor!'

"Lettin' out my name by chance, she bit her lip. She went quiet 'n' began wringin' the linen. I stayed right there.

"'Nastia,' I asked, 'are you very cross with me?'

"She didn't answer.

"'God knows,' I said, 'I'm humbled 'fore you, I'm humbled for ever'thin'"—(I was talkin', but it was like someone had hold o' my throat)—'forgive me, Nastasiushka!'

"She didn't look, 'n' kept on wringin' the linen.

"'Why should I be angry?' she said. 'We gots dif'rent ways, but there's nuthin' to sep'rate us.'

"'There's really nuthin'?' I asked. 'You're sayin' right now you're not cross, but you can't e'en look at me.'

"She shot me a look—'n' started laughin'… She laughed so, it was like ever'thin' inside me was laughin', like there was sunshine lightin' up my soul, it was so bright.

"'Ain't what I'm seein' been spelled out to you?' she said.

"I laughed, 'n' moved still closer.

"'Nastia,' I said, 'Now I can't live without you. Will you marry me?'

"She laughed all the more.

"'This is what you imagine! You beat 'n' offended a little girl, 'n' not long ago e'en humiliated her in front of all the folk, but now you wanna marry her. What's this, have you really fallen in love with me?'

"She had her hands on her hips, lookin' at me with burnin' eyes, 'n' was roarin' with laughter. I was seein' stars, 'n' I grabbed her 'n' tried to embrace her… She pushed away 'n' got so angry she turned completely dark…

"'Whattabout me's gotten into your stupid head? You reckon you can take a stroll with me? Know this, Mikishka,' she said: 'I can't see you like I can't see my own ears! You'll never have me! I won't be deceived for anythin' in the world!'

"'But ain't you 'fraid I'll kill you?' I asked. 'Should I kill you 'n' me right now?'

"'N' I took the rife off my shoulder…

"'Shoot,' she said, 'I ain't 'fraid e'en if you shoot right now!'

"She folded her arms 'n' stood there. Right then I burst into tears, couldn't take it, 'n' ran home.

"After that, I left for the mine. I panned so much all summer that I don't know how my back didn't break. Me 'n' the lads was lucky: we panned a lotta gold. O'er jus' some six weeks my portion came to a thousand rubles—'n' I began struttin'. Drank without stoppin', brawled, whored, 'n' threw my money round like woodchips... I covered the road 'tween shop 'n' tavern in rich calico prints: said I didn't wanna walk in mud! Rumors reached our place: 'twas bein' said Mikishka was completely lost 'n' worthless. But I tole all the boys who was goin' home: 'Go to my relatives 'n' friends,' I say, ''n' ask my friends 'n' comrades if they 'member me badly! They won't see me no more! I won't live in the wide-open world. I'll jus' blow the rest o' my money here.'

"I was a case indeed, boys, 'n' foolish notions was comin' into my noggin. One mornin', I spilled out into the middle o' the street, ragged, filthy, covered in blood, the Devil's very own... Pockets completely empty, 'n' I didn't e'en have a coin purse. Barefoot; splittin' headache. Well, I was thinkin' at the time: the stone's round my neck, 'n' I'm goin' to Father Chika!...[19] I'm thinkin' this, planted in the middle o' the road. It was real early. Not a soul in the street. Sunrise comin' up from behind a hill. God's world is brightened by such a joy... 'N' I 'membered Nastka again... It was like I heard her words: 'How you frightened me, Nikifor!' It was like I was seein' how she'd looked at me 'n' laughed...

"'Oh!' I was thinkin'. ''Fore I die I'll go 'n' see her once more 'n' bid farewell.' In that very condition, as I was, I got on my feet 'n' covered no less'n fifty versts on foot in one day. I entered the village—it was already evenin' in the yard 'n' ever'one had gone to bed. I went straight to their garden 'n' climbed a little mound leadin' up to Nastkina's window. I saw the window was open 'n' she herself was sittin' there in just a blouse. I, the Devil's own, covered in sweat 'n' dirt with bloody feet, 'peared 'fore her like a apparition... She tried to scream 'n' backed away from me; I tried to reach out to her.

"'Don't scream, dear,' I said, 'don't get scared, I only came to say farewell. You can't look at me, a villain, but I'm with'rin' o'er you 'n' don't wanna live without you... Just look one last time at me... The stone's round my neck—I'm goin' to the water... Forgive me!'

"I tried to leave. But now she was lookin' at me 'n' wouldn't let me go...

"'Stop,' she whispered, 'I'll tell you the God's honest truth. I myself will die without you... I was thinkin' you was already no longer in the world 'cause o' hateful me, 'n' that I would kill myself as well!'

"'Oy, really? Does this mean you'll marry me?'

"'I'd follow you to the ends o' the earth! E'er since you pounded 'n' humiliated me as a little girl I've thought only o' you, Mikishka.'

"We decided to elope that very moment, 'cause we knew our parents wouldn't give their blessin'. So that's what we did, as Mikhaila here 'members. But later, after the deed was done, the old folks softened, y'see. The former *emm*ity ended 'cause o' the peace made 'tween me 'n' Nastka. That was a fortunate patch o' time, Mikolaich! You unnerstand, I wanted to learn to write so's I could describe my life to you!"

Nikifor had said all this with great forcefulness, striding throughout the ward with hands folded behind his back and fire in his pale blue eyes. A rather noble glow illumined his entire face, framed by long blond mustaches, and rectified his tall, bony frame.

"Look how you've fallen o'er a woman, you rat!" Chirok, who had listened attentively to Burenkov's story, laughingly observed. "He's still gotta write it down… What should he write? You was a fool—then 'n' now: you decided to drown yourself 'cause of a wench! You still dunno how they are, the creatures!"

Sokoltsev, Iron Cat, and others picked up on Chirok's words and elaborated upon them, dispelling little by little the charm of the simple and moving romance told by Nikifor. But he, it seemed, was paying no attention to his comrades' cynical comments and jokes, and continued walking about the ward deep in thought. With unwanted bitterness, I reflected upon how fate had unfortunately turned this man away from a nature so open and kind.

"Now you see, Nikifor," I said to him consolingly. "How could you doubt that such a wife would ever change?"

"There's certainly no doubt about your woman, Nikifor," added Mikhaila. "Nastasia is an utterly exceptional woman. Just take my woman—she sure is a snake in the grass. She, I know, will refuse to go. I was a fool to agree to blow my money on a telegram! She's now probably joyous as a sectarian that they're banishing me to Sakhalin: her dear man can't escape from there, she's saying! Well, I sure can't start bawling over her, too, and I won't be humiliating myself!"

"But, Mikhaila, did you take your wife like Nikifor did?"

Mikhaila laughed quietly. Nikifor answered for him:

"Mother made him get married… He was livin' with another before… All the wenches marveled o'er him, too, 'cause he was a good-lookin' lad 'n' behaved well."

"But did she marry him freely? Maybe she'll go?"

"If she didn't go at first," Mikhaila himself answered, "now she won't go all the more. Sakhalin! A mysterious land! Y'know, there's people with dogs' heads living there— various old women say—so why would you go away to those barbarians? God's sunlight doesn't shine there, it's night all day long… She married freely, you say? Ha! At that time, y'know, I had money, my hands weren't tied, and the blood danced in my face… But now I'm almost an old man already, and if'n I was on the outside, I'd probably even have to dance for my gifts o' bread…"

"What Mikhaila's sayin' is true," added Nikifor. "What kinda folks is women? You leave their sight—they go outta their minds. Even scurrilous ol' womens start talkin' you down. Don't you e'en know our old women, Mikolaich? Hags' hags—'cept without the tail… Here's why I'm 'fraid Nastka won't foller me… But then take Mikhaila's wife: if she decides not to go, then ob*ver*ously she'll convince mine it's no shame to be alone!"

I've copied down the Burenkovs' conversation of how they would leave and start living on Sakhalin. However, with regard to Nikifor, he was a man of the moment, of circumstance and strange influences, and had he only begun bowing and praying, he no longer would have played the swindler and his words would have lost all meaning whatsoever. I could only wish for him with all my heart that opportunities salutary to an honest existence would create new conditions in his life, and that the first of such salutary conditions would be, in my opinion, concern for his family and a life in common with it. Nikifor himself well understood that he was a man of the minute, and during those days before parting he spoke about himself simply ridiculously, though with an anecdote characteristic of him.

"One time, Mikhaila 'n' I'd left the mine 'n' come to a wide stream where, howe'er, there was a ford. I took my shoes off 'n' undressed first, 'n' tole Mikhaila: 'I'll carry you on my back, don't undress.' I said this seriously, thinkin': I can really carry him. Without thinkin', he believed me 'n' got on my shoulders. I went thirty steps from the river bank, stepped into the deepest spot, 'n' changed my mind. 'Know what?' I said. 'I'm stuck.' 'Well, so what,' he said, 'get back somehow.' 'No,' I said, 'I'm stuck, I can't carry you further. I'm sittin' down.' 'N' so I started sittin' down in the water… How he was shoutin': 'Are you an idiot, Mikishka?' But I didn't care 'n' sat down. I got out from under him 'n' went back to the bank. He's layin' there in broad daylight like one helluva devil: water streamin' through his clothes. I'm on the bank laughin'! Ever since, when Mikhaila talks 'bout me, he can't let go o' the idea of my thirty steps…"

Mikhaila's words held inordinately large weight and meaning, and it didn't seem to be simply a "tone" in his mouth when, for example, he said he'd begun the criminal life more out of anger than gain. According to him, he was already a married man when his mother, encouraged by his uncle's hostility towards him, insisted that the village publicly thrash him with birch rods. At that time he'd not taken on any large violations, but the uncle persuaded the foolish old woman that her son might eventually go bad if his reins were slackened. With an indignation building even now, after fifteen years, Mikhaila told how he was shamefully punished before all the folk and how he wanted to kill his uncle and mother for this, and how the latter then repented of her crime but it was already too late; her son had become bitter and plunged into dissipation… Anger toward the fellow villagers who offended him and afterward bore him no small grudge was so powerful in Mikhaila that he fled to avoid an unfortunate turn of events in the life of the village, and promised to make short shrift of them at his own choosing.

"I'm now of two minds over what I do," he characteristically answered my questions, "I haven't made much through crime. I'll tell you straight out that I haven't made much, and it wouldn't be hard to let go of those trifles. Mikishka here knows me well: if I decide to, then I'll do it. People, comrades, won't lead me astray one bit. But then I get a different notion: I'm creeping up on old age, and if I'm all alone, who and what will I live for? Especially if the living is poor? It's just that I can't promise you anything more. I'll look—and see that I decide something and then write you."

We had devised an entire conspiracy with regard to our correspondence. On no account would Luchezarov pass on letters by the Burenkovs that were addressed directly to my name: according to regulations, prisoners had the right to correspond with only their closest relatives. In view of this, we agreed to communicate with each other through a round-the-world route: Mikhaila would write to my mother in Russia, whose address I wrote down for him in the Gospels.

Only on the fifth day of wearisome expectation were the responses finally received from their wives. Because of illness, Mikhaila was staying in the prison and Nikifor and I, having returned from the mine, found the telegram he had already opened ten times.

After laughing venomously, he gave the paper to me, and in it I literally read the following: "Sweetheart, don't get angry, I can't bring the children there."

My heart painfully clenched and for a minute I found myself as a loss for a single word of consolation… Nikifor's spirit immediately fell and became despairing. The next day, his depression gave way to an upsurge of reckless gaiety and pure prisoner's dash. He twirled his long mustaches, paced about rather peculiarly, "like a stroller," and from his lips pointedly fell the words: "We, the Sokolinites"… He tried not to discuss his wife, but referred to women in general with unending contempt… But I distinctly knew that this was his mood and no more than a momentary fit, and after he'd had a chance to cool down he was, on the eve of his departure, already trying to convince us there was nothing foolish in the telegram and that his wife had said nothing directly about a betrayal; that her position as a mother was actually terribly difficult: having just received as if fallen from heaven a telegram about removal to Sakhalin, she would have needed true heroism and an almost equal desperation to immediately grab her little children and set off with them on an unknown path. I persuaded Nikifor that a similar letter which his wife would receive any day now would give her a better chance to evaluate and think about this trip, and convinced him that he would unfailingly get a favorable answer in Ust-Kara. My words were obviously a real balm for Nikifor's pained heart, and he once more cheered up, although Mikhaila, though he didn't argue, was manifestly skeptical… However, both exchanged frank words, tried over the course of the year to avoid going to extreme measures, and looked forward to when family matters would become definitively clear.

Regarding the cousins' relationship to each other, the breezy Nikifor, softened by the misfortune that had simultaneously befallen him and Mikhaila, actually seemed to forget his former hostility toward him. Mikhaila's name was now hardly gone from his lips: he expressed in every word and look toward him a purely fraternal affection, and a bystander would have thought that no black cat had crossed between them and that you couldn't douse their friendship with water; it clearly never entered his head that they would not be going down the road as brothers and comrades. For this purpose he readied all sorts of little sacks and bags and bustled about so much, it was like he'd undertaken to provision with utmost complexity and precise economy an entire family. But Mikhaila remained stubbornly silent, and obviously had none of Nikifor's expansive and sentimental enterprises in his mind. Having noticed this, I soon called him aside and asked why he seemed angry toward Nikifor.

"I'm not angry, Ivan Mikolaich," Mikhaila answered, "it's just that I've firmly decided: I'm not traveling with Nikishka in comradeship."

"How's that? Why's this?"

"Here's why. I know his and my characters well. In two days his goodness will have had enough—and there'll be no pain. Like before, he'll get known among the various gadabouts and will be in the card games and our union will go bad, and as long as I live I won't like this. So it's better not to fool each other from the start, and to travel separately."

For a long, a very long time, I tried to prevail upon Mikhaila to consign to oblivion all previous tiffs, old scores, and slights and, in view of their common misfortune, make one final effort at a shared life with Nikifor. Obviously from a desire only to please me, before whom he considered himself forever indebted, he finally agreed to have another try with Nikifor…

At last, on 25 March, the holiday of the Annunciation, a clear sunny day, the Sokolinites set off toward the gates and were bid farewell by positively the entire prison. I kissed the Burenkovs with all my heart…

Unfortunately, I know nothing of their subsequent fate. My mother never received from Mikhaila any letter whatsoever. Prisoners explained this by saying he probably escaped during the march. Some actually insisted they'd heard about this, and even passed on in detail that within a Sakhalin party there was a huge escape attempt "at hurrah," and that Nikifor Burenkov was among the many killed but Mikhaila managed to get away… Was the mare telling the truth or a lie—and how could you know which to believe?

VII.   ESCAPES AND FIRST BLOOD

In early May there came by some path from Pokrovskii mine to the Shelai free command a sensational rumor about a certain prisoner's escape through the mine works. This rumor soon reached every corner of the prison and greatly excited its entire population. Conversations solely concerned the clever fellow Krasotkin (so the escaped prisoner was named). Many were surprised that it had not occurred to anyone earlier to escape through the mountain.

"'Twas known earlier," almost anyone with whom I discussed this topic now told me, "that somewheres on the other side o' the mountain, where there's no guards, there's a way out. Y'know, the works go for fifty versts, 'n' you can get lost… Here's your woods: then you go straight, then right, then you turn left, then you go down, then you climb up again… The corridors go dozens o' dif'rent directions… There's only a certain one—'n' it goes terribly far. Many other works have been abandoned for years now, 'n' it's strictly impossible to go there; the supports are all rotten—'n' there's a fear they'll fall 'n' crush you… 'N' in the other places there's water 'n' ice."

In a word, most nonetheless insisted there was an exit on the other side and that a man might emerge still breathing. But one day the poet Vladimirov, having heard several such dissertations, suddenly stood up from the sleeping platform and boomed categorically:

"They did indeed escape earlier!"

"When'd they escape? Who escaped?"

"Indeed, they escaped here! Only, they didn't wanna completely leave, 'cause they had families, but they'd found a way. The Pole Nijas 'n' the yokel Egoza found one once. They'd gone lightheaded in an icy corridor 'n' got lost. Suffered so much horror, they said 'bout it later… They climbed up an icy ladder, barely alive. Chilled to the marrow, soakin' wet… Then they suddenly came to an openin'… They got out 'n' saw a forest around 'em, but the mountain had been left far, far behind! So they coulda gone, if'n they'd wanted. Only, they didn't wanna, 'cause they was married, 'n' they went to find the Cossacks. At first, they weren't gonna let 'em go to the mountain, but later, as it was explained, it became a dif'rent matter 'n' the convoy got scared 'n' simply marveled at 'em!"

"Maybe you dreamt this, Bear's Ears?" Sokoltsev laughingly asked.

"Why a dream! Ask the yokel Egoza or Nijas."

"How can I ask 'em now, since they went to the cantons a long time ago? But they themselves tell you this?"

"Not themselves… Others all heard the same thing… They coulda gotten away if'n they'd wanted! Only, they didn't wanna, 'cause…"

"If they wanted! No, we better wait 'n' learn which way Krasotkin escaped, 'n' then we'll believe you. No, old chap, if there was ways outta the mountain, the administration would know 'bout 'em better'n you 'n' us, 'n' they wouldn't be left unguarded durin' work times. That's what I think."

Goncharov, Iukhorev, and other experienced and worldly people shared Sokoltsev's skeptical view. This view turned out to be correct after a certain time, when other, more trustworthy news came that Krasotkin hadn't escaped at all and had only tried to stay in the mountain, but after two weeks had to turn himself in to the authorities due to his own stupidity. Sokoltsev himself brought this news from the workshops, and told the following to the crowd gathered round him:

"If there was someone else in Krasotkin's place, he certainly could've escaped. I know him well, 'n' when I heard 'bout this the first time I was thinkin' to myself that Krasotkin couldn't 'ave pulled off such a thing. He didn't dream it up hisself, but the boys tole him 'bout it, almost forced him to do it, 'cause they felt sorry for the dear fellow: he's quite young, but is carryin' forty-five years' labor on his back. So *they* dreamed it up. Durin' work-time they hid him in an ol' works, in a splendid spot only two or three men in the whole prison knew 'bout. They'd hauled some provisions there earlier, so's he could stay for three or e'en four days. They covered the spot up with rocks 'n' went away. Work was over 'n' it was time to go to the prison. The Cossacks counted the prisoners twice—what the hell? One ain't there. *Jus' ain't there.* The alarm sounded. Cossacks runnin' all o'er the mountain—couldn't find nuthin'. All the same, they decided not to take off the prisoners' shackles 'n' to wait: maybe he was hidin' somewheres, concealin' hisself—sooner or later, they said, he's gotta turn up. The sentries crossed themselves 'n' swore that no one had slipped outta his chains. If the mare'd been behavin' proper, but most importantly, if Krasotkin hisself had been watchful, this all wouldn't-a been a disaster, but the boys was rambunctious 'n' so they hadn't taken off their chains 'n' they posted a lookout for two or three days. Durin' them days he had to sit quiet 'n' keep a sharp watch. The first night a whole comp'ny o' Cossacks with lanterns went into the mountain 'n' rummaged 'n' searched ever'wheres. Found nuthin', o' course. They stuck round for two more days, then presto—they left their posts. They decided the watchman musta removed his shackles 'n' let 'im go. Krasotkin coulda taken to his heels right then—our boys whispered to him that the search had backed off 'n' the path was clear. He had ever'thin'—civilian clothes, money, passport. But he, that demons' offspring, chickened out! This is why three days was wasted. 'N' then, see, the provisions that'd been stored for him ran out. They'd have to swipe 'em from the prison ev'ry day. They came to work in the mornin'. Well, they're thinkin', now he musta left. Lo 'n' behold—he's still lyin' there. 'What the heck are you doin'? D'you wanna perish here?' 'Honest to God, boys, I'm leavin' tonight. I woulda left last night, but the guard turned out to be there again.' Here was a cowardly loafer! But he was still a young chap, 'n' could work for forty-five years in *katorga*. 'N' then a shudder passed through the mare... At first, only four trustworthy people knew 'bout the feller; the large portion, like the administration, thought Krasotkin was long gone—so go catch the wind in a field. But then some bitch noticed 'em bringin' 'im food in the mountain 'n' muttered to hisself, or rather, to someone else, 'n' pretty soon the whole prison knew Krasotkin was lyin' in the ol' works. Yes, the whole prison knew—'n' the guards 'n' the convoy knew. The alarm sounded again, 'n' guards was posted 'n' shackles put on: ever'one was thoroughly searched, so's they couldn't bring him bread… That was it! They were such clever bastards: they poured ash in the corridors 'n' stretched threads 'cross 'em… They was thinkin': if he moves durin' the night—goes to drink the mine water or tries to run away—he'll leave traces leadin' straight to 'im. They started pokin' round day 'n' night. Once, they e'en played a sort o' trick. The Cossacks didn't herd the prisoners to work, but picked up the hammers 'n' augers in their stead. Started poundin' in the mine as if real work was goin' on. Well, Krasotkin guessed it was a trick 'n' didn't come out. Howe'er, the poor man was suf'rin' durin' them days. One day (a lad told me later), durin' a search, two Cossacks came to the very place where he was lyin' under the rocks. There was a noise 'n' they started smashin' away. One says to the other: 'If he's there, we'll stab the bastard right now.' His soul died right there: here they was, 'bout to find 'im! Suddenly, lucky for him, others somewheres far off started shoutin': 'Here, he's here!' How the spooks ran o'er there… So, the danger passed. Howe'er, his situation was turnin' bad! He could get only a tiny bit o' bread, 'n' not ev'ry day. Couldn't move round at all. It was dark in there, air was stuffy… His legs started swellin', scurvy broke out. A dif'rent clever fellow woulda jus' had a smoke right there![20] He woulda done it regardless! He would've attacked the night watchman straight off, caught 'im as he was standin' there pickin' his teeth 'n' gawkin' at 'im, 'n' finished the damned spook off! But Krasotkin could only go round 'n' round 'n' simply couldn't make a decision. Once, there was such laughter goin' on, he went out… Indeed, he popped out so unsafely that the watchman saw, shot at 'im, 'n' shouted! Cossacks came runnin'… they was on his heels. After that, he was utterly scared, stopped crawlin' out from his burrow, 'n' fell ill. He was thinkin' death was sure a-comin'… Once, he was lyin' there in this way, 'n' suddenly heard someone comin', smashin' through the rocks. Little pieces o' rock was fallin' down… This person was gettin' very close, 'n' the darkness became absolutely bright. It was as if there was a man standin' in front o' him—neither tall nor short, with a small gray beard. 'You here?' he asked. 'Here,' answered Krasotkin. 'Wanna eat?' 'Sure do,' he said. 'But is you cold?' 'Ever'thin's numb with cold.' 'Well, wait a bit,' he said, ''n' stand up real gentle.' He said it was like he'd fallen into the earth 'n' couldn't be seen. But it was actually easier for him to get up now: it was as if starvation was pullin' his body outta there…

"Next day ('twas now the *nineteenth* day!), Krasotkin explained to the boys straight out that he couldn't take no more, 'n' if they couldn't come up with a way to get 'im out alive, then he hisself would walk out 'n' let 'em shoot 'im. What to do? Mare told the senior guard (a good soul, they say, a fellow who helped our brother): such 'n' such a fellow, they said, was close to death 'cause the Cossacks had beaten him non-stop, 'n' as he'd only just turned up, they was mighty angry; show some Christian mercy 'n' help 'im out. Naturally, he went with the boys to the mountain, dressed Krasotkin in civilian clothes, 'n' took him past the unnoticin' Cossacks. Whoe'er's been in Pokrovskii knows the mine there is right beside the prison 'n' the picket line circles far, far out… As they came to the gate, there was jus' two young relief sentries tryin' to grasp what was hap'nin'. They started runnin' around here 'n' there like madmen, grittin' their teeth 'n' not knowin' what to do. 'Lay one finger on 'im,' the senior guard shouted, '…'n' you will strictly answer for it!' The relief sentries flew to the guardhouse, 'n' out came all the guards with rifles. They woulda instantly murdered Krasotkin without a second look, but at that very moment the duty officer managed to open the gate 'n' drag him into the yard. So, the Cossacks was left lookin' stupid, 'n' were just pokin' their rifles through the grate 'n' cursin' to no end. Y'know what beasts they are!"

"Ev'ry one o' them damned spooks should be crushed," insisted the listeners, profoundly excited by Sokoltsev's story.

Krasotkin was getting it hot, too. There'd been complete disappointment. Although the notion of escaping through a mountain's works didn't make any sense in tiny Shelai mine, where the large works of olden times were located far from the current ones, in a prisoner's heart that had been swollen by this story the most cherished feelings, the most sensitive strings, were being touched… Going into that spring it was swollen to its furthest extent; beyond the high prison fence, beauteous hills were greening and flowers and trees sweet-smelling… Everybody was thinking about freedom and about life, and each man's heart ached torturously… But escaping Shelai Prison—so vigilantly guarded against by Six-Eyes—was not easy, and the most audacious daredevils preferred to await propitious circumstances and dream of preliminary transfer to other mines. But to make up for this, there were from the beginning of the summer numerous escapes from the free command, over which there was practically no surveillance.

First off, Luchezarov's own chef and cook got away. Luchezarov organized a posse of several guards and Cossacks to go after them; but a three-day search turned up nothing, and the pursuers returned empty-handed. The excitement these initial escapes caused in the prison had hardly died down when a prisoner, a former favorite of Luchezarov whom he'd employed as a clerk in his office, disappeared. The escapee, who among other things walked off with Rakitin's wife's sister, a girl of fourteen, had been sent to *katorga* because of *his* sister. This time, the brave staff captain, having gotten information from a prisoner about where to go to find the fugitives, led the chase personally. Upon leaving he allegedly boasted that he'd bring the clerk back dead or alive.

"Geez, whatta viper!" prisoners said to each other. "Why don't they look at other mines to find them whats escapes from free commands? The com'dant ain't gonna answer for this, y'know. E'en if you scatter yourself to the four winds, dearies!"

"'Cause he's a six-headed snake," the half-wit Zhebreek orated, "'n' our brother's like golden kasha to him. We're like his blood-brothers, we's so valuable to 'im! He can't sleep peacefully without us. He won't let go of one prisoner in his whole life. He starts with'rin' away if someone's term is comin' to an end, 'n' his belly swells with joy if someone gets longer. Why didn't he let us go to Sakhalin? Didn't wanna. Now I know he didn't wanna. He hisself chases after 'scaped prisoners—'where is they?' How can a noble commander take an innerest in such trifles? Well, let him amuse hisself, drainin' our blood, let 'im! Someday, his time'll come… Now I know it's comin'! It's-a comin'!"

And raising an arm, Zhebreek solemnly pointed a finger to the heavens.

Luchezarov's boast, however, turned out to be in vain. He and the Cossacks had to follow the thoroughfare, but the fugitives were able to bypass it through the taiga, having before them dozens of roads and just laughing at him from afar. On the other hand, further along the way, where thirty to fifty versts from Shelai's hills the path begins dropping toward Chita and the farther steppe, Cossack villages proliferate. Getting past these was incomparably more difficult, and only a few of the several hundred fugitives who came from all of Nerchinsk's mines each summer managed to break through the *katorga* zone's border. Most ended up in the authorities' hands once more. However, Shelai's fugitives would be fortunate if, after being caught, they got assigned to a different prison.[21]

Six-Eyes returned from his unsuccessful chase angry and dark as night. The mare privately rejoiced. Escapes from the free command continued nearly every day; only those who were married or whose terms were coming to an end remained. At that time, Luchezarov allegedly received an order from senior command about the excessive costs of administering Shelai mine and whether new expenditures he supposedly partially paid for out of his own pocket would be reimbursed. I don't know whether this was true or imagined, but such rumors were pointedly used to explain the change noticed in Luchezarov that spring. Regardless of all the thunder and lightning in the speeches he directed at prisoners, he had until now presented himself as a man—albeit menacing— capable of restraining himself strictly within the law. Even after the insult he'd received from Shah Lamas he apparently hadn't surrendered to personal bitterness and limited himself to using the isolators, bolts on the wards' locks, and verbal threats; now, a completely new, previously hidden trait suddenly appeared in the brave staff captain's character—the purely Russian ability to be "fussy." He'd been showing up in the prison very rarely as of late, but time and again there were rumors of his adventures on the outside. There, so it was said, he ranted and raved. First of all, his frustration with prisoners who had dug a ditch outside the prison came to be learned about: he'd given them incredibly large quotas, almost fifty square feet per day per man, forgetting that convicts are not paid laborers who have better food, more physical strength, and high spirits. After several days of such work even the strongest were exhausted. Little Lunkov's comrades had to drag him by the feet out of the clayey ditch: boots got so stuck they had to be exhumed with iron shovels… Not having completed their quotas, their following day's ration of meat and bread was less, but they had to work all the same. This situation made all the more apparent the "worthlessness" of loud-mouthed prisoners and that Ivans' reputations were brave and courageous in words only. When the matter came to a head they were quieter than water, lower than grass, and, like oxen, popped a tendon just so the terrible Six-Eyes wouldn't get mad. But to make up for this, the unwelcome Lunkov showed once more he was no coward. Having completely worn himself out one day, he cursed the officer assigned to him and was put in the isolator. Six-Eyes ordered him put in manacles for a month and tried by the court. The same fate soon befell another of my friends—the fat man Nogaitsev. During those days the isolators weren't empty. According to rumors, Luchezarov was raging within his own house and making short work of his maid with his own hand. Several guards, who in general were more scared of him than the exiles themselves were, were also subjected to dressings-down, fines, and even dismissals. In the prison, if it was believed something terrible was going to happen, the menacing commandant's appearances at evening roll calls were met with trembling expectation. Everybody cowered just as if they were expecting a blizzard…

Indeed, after returning from the mine one day, we heard something else that made us wince: inside the prison yard and even the hospital could be clearly heard the harrowing cries of Luchezarov's driver, the Kirgiz Salmanov, being brought back to the free command after having been punished with birch rods. Not long before, Salmanov had left for freedom; a big, awkward chap of enormous height, with a shapeless, pock-marked face and a voice resembling the roar of a bear in the taiga, he was an extremely good-natured and honest fellow. Even prisoners who disliked Kirgiz were surprised to hear that such a man was involved in the theft of a pair of regulation horse collars. It was later made clear that the offender was a different prisoner who had already completed his term but was still living in the free command and awaiting assignment to the countryside. This would have become clear that very day had there been the slightest peaceful investigation of the matter; but Luchezarov hurriedly gave himself in to the first violent flash of rage and instantly ordered Salmanov caned beneath his chancery windows. The Cossack executioners beat him fiercely and mercilessly. After thirty strokes, Luchezarov came onto the balcony and asked the driver where he'd put the collars. The wretched Kirgiz threw himself on his knees but could give no answer since he himself knew nothing. The brave staff captain, having ordered the punishment to continue, returned to his office. After another thirty strokes he came out again and posed the same question and, receiving no answer as before, signaled to the Cossacks once more. This brutal scene continued four times in a row, and Salmanov himself later told me he received a total of one hundred and thirty-four strokes, even though, according to "regulations," a local prison administration had the right to give only one hundred strokes. After this the bloody Salmanov was taken to the isolator, put on trial, and, after a month, sent to a common ward. Fortunately, his innocence soon became clear, and he was released once more to the free command. The good-natured and cowardly savage dared not complain about his unauthorized punishment, and the incident was consigned to oblivion. For Salmanov, as for all the rest of the mare, only the physical pain that accompanied barbaric torture was important: the pain went—and so was it worth thinking about? But I didn't feel that way… It seemed that the better part of my soul had been defiled and blackened, that this time I'd been burdened with a cruel and unforgettable injustice. I had managed to discern an incorrect formulation of various problems, an excessively formalistic understanding of the law and so forth, in all of Luchezarov's earlier behavior and the whole of his system for administering the prison, but now his true reality, that Russian serf owner's reality that no European gloss, no system or regime of the latest self-devised notions had so far destroyed, was for the first time revealed to me in all its brightness and beauty…

For a long time afterward I could not look at Luchezarov's corpulent physique without shuddering. But, alas, this was not the worst that I was fated to live through in Shelai Prison!

VIII.   THE WAGGER AMUSES ME

Just as sunshine cannot exist without darkness, and night without daybreak, so in life the gloomy and sad almost always stand alongside the comic and amusing. Several days after the story involving Salmanov had raced throughout the prison, Rakitin allegedly bit his wife half to death in a drunken state; had it not been for a neighbor who immediately ran for the senior guard, the woman would have met her end… In the evening of that same day our ward's padlock growled, the door opened, and Rakitin appeared with his things on the threshold.

"Our complerments, ol' men!" he turned toward the prisoners with cheerful familiarity.

The mare broke into gleeful laughter.

"You got into trouble, dearie! A bit too soon! Well, brother, tell us, what for?"

Rakitin then began pouring out such rubbish that it was absolutely impossible to understand a thing. He tossed into one heap a clandestine trade in wine, of which Six-Eyes supposedly suspected him, his sister-in-law's escape with the clerk, a connection between Marfa, his own wife, and this same clerk, and the Devil knows what else.

"But is it true you bit your wife, Rakitin?"

"Nibbled on her some, Ivan Nikolaevich, 'tis true, that's true. But how could I not bite the creature? Y'know, they was screwin' my little head around! They'd been ready to toss me into prison for a long time, y'know!"

"They, who?"

"*They*, is all: the wife Marfa 'n' Domna, my sister-in-law who ran off with that clerk. If you could know what they'd been doin' to me, how they upset my little heart… Simply boiled the blood in my veins!"

"What exactly did they do?"

"Ekh! It'd take all night to explain—'n' I ain't gonna tell it all. Domna is all of a fourteen-year ol' girl. No mother or father—a complete orphan. Since she was a baby I sheltered, fed, dressed, 'n' nursed her. But should I expect any gratitude, Ivan Nikolaevich? I warmed that wicked snake on my breast! So much cunnin' 'n' deception was lurkin' in her, that low-down, you wouldn't e'en believe. One time, when I was still in prison, I ask Marfa what Domna's been doin'. 'Domna's mostly busy with her readin's,' she says. 'Always sittin' in front o' the Gospels.' True, our Domna was literate. Well, that's good, I'm thinkin'. Here I go free, Ivan Nikolaevich, 'n' I see: Domna's truly sittin' at her readin's. 'Little Domna,' I ask, 'what're you readin'?' 'The divine word, brother,' she answers. Right then, I shoulda looked at that little book, 'cause you'd already taught me to make a bit out, Ivan Nikolaevich. Well, there just weren't enough time. Y'know, it was playin' round in my head in a circle —could I 'member what I'd learnt? Well, but when she was 'scapin' with that scoundrel the clerk—may *cheldony* rip his guts out!—I snuck a peek at her little books. 'N' what kinda books you think I saw, Ivan Nikolaevich? They was all 'bout love, yes, *love*… All the very things that's the absolute worst for girls to read was written down! Seems that clerk was bringin' her various romances he got from the guards 'n' Monakhov. But what arrows she shot at me: it's the divine word o' the Gospels 'n' Bible, she says! Here's the backwardness of our little fool! For sure, if my Kolyvansk birch basket has nuthin' but free time it won't stay empty! Now I wanna study under you straightaway, Ivan Nikolaevich, I wanna get deeper into science!"

"Why did Domna run away from you?"

"I don't blame *her*, Ivan Nikolaevich, 'cause the girl's mind's still babyish, as much as I do *him*, that bad seed, that Dormidoshka-snake.[22] He's my countryman, y'know, 'n' we was bosom buddies until the last hour our friendship broke… You won't believe this, Ivan Nikolaevich [here Rakitin lowered his voice to a whisper]: y'know, I'm really… Egor Alekseev, not someone else, 'n' I helped him to escape! Durin' the march I dried myself into his husk 'n' gave him the others' provisions… But he—'n' here's what a burden I'm under—lures the girl into vagabondage!"

The prisoners broke out laughing.

"So why're you sorry for her?" asked Chirok. "Or maybe you yourself was targetin' her? Ain't she your relation? She's gone—the hell with her, may her lips fall off her face! Specially if'n she's such a deceivin' reptile!"

"You're a crank, Kuzma, truly a crank! 'N' how you'd start singin' if the stinker took off with your crappy boots, weasel-skin jacket, 'n' twenty rubles… It's shameful, y'know! It's *my* bloody money!"

"Well, don't lie 'bout this. What'd they take from you? I daresay Marfa was dealin' in vodka, not you."

"It's all the same, brother. As is written 'n' said, a husband 'n' wife makes a single Satan. How could I not wanna tear that stinker's head off?"

"But, all the same, Rakitin, I don't understand why you bit Marfa."

"'Cause, Ivan Nikolaevich, she—that low-down—prob'ly knew 'bout her sister's plans to escape. Without that, there's no way it coulda worked. I'm the gov'ment's man 'n' find myself at work morn to night, but she's home all day, y'know."

"So, according to you, Marfa participated in the theft of her own things and money? Wonder*ful*! Indeed, she could hardly have agreed to her own sister escaping with a hard labor vagabond: it's clear he might rape, rob, or murder her. They say your wife's an intelligent woman."

"Ekh, Ivan Nikolaevich! You can't 'member nuthin' 'bout our life, 'n' you dunno nuthin'… It's well known you're always ready to defend the snaky sort!"

"Very good, Egorka! You've bit Mikolaich well!… For once, you spoke the basic truth… All them creatures should be strangled, strangled without exception!"

"They certainly should," said Rakitin, encouraged still more and banging his fist on the table. He was very glad that the sympathy of prisoners who had not long before been laughing at him was apparently turning his way.

"I mentioned afore, Ivan Nikolaevich, that it wouldn't be long 'fore I had to bust her head 'cause o' such tricks. But I forgave ever'thin'. Didn't I see, for instance, how she was havin' a love affair with that very same clerk? Our lily-fingered so-'n'-so Dormidont Ivanych 'n' that bitch; this Dormidont Ivanych needs to be given some fun… For me, for the husbandly kind, I couldn't let his type go! But did Egor Rakitin rub dirt in the Dormidoshka's face? No, that wolf's skin don't wanna live with her 'cordin' to the law! It's well known that forbidden fruit's more enlight'nin'!"

"But how can you say you waited to break off being friends with him until the final hour, Rakitin, if you just said your wife was going after the clerk? If you noticed he was going for your wife…"

"What're you suggestin', 'n' how can you let yourself say this 'bout Egor Rakitin? Is he an errant fool? No, Ivan Nikolaevich! There's a little somethin' in this noggin, too… You've known me so long, 'n' yet you still don't *know* me! D'you think I can't pretend to be a scientist? I sure can! I can get into the Devil's soul with butter, if I want. Didn't I say from the first I could see through all their tricks? I should be glad that he, my miserable family, 'n' my life's gloom is all goin' away!"

"Well, but why did you bite your wife with your teeth, and not thrash her another way?"

"I taste more, Ivan Nikolaevich. Sink your teeth into livin' meat—it's like ever'thin' freezes! A most beautiful thing. Y'see how my teeth is even, like they're young, tetchy, still growin' egg-whites…"

And beneath the ward's deafening laughter Rakitin earnestly opened his mouth and showed me two rows of dazzlingly white and veritably small, sharp teeth.

"If she hadn't been taken from me, I woulda drank that stinker's blood, 'n' I coulda shown what it means to cheat a husband 'n' destroy his property!"

"What do you think you're going to do now, Rakitin?"

"Now, Ivan Nikolaevich, my little head's already sorry, o' course! Now, Six-Eyes is gonna lemme rot in prison. There's one thing left: rippin' her guts out at our very first meetin'."

"But wouldn't it be better, Rakitin, to ask for Six-Eyes and your wife's forgiveness and to go free again? You were probably drunk, right?"

"Only in one eye, but not a snowflake in my other… But I should humble myself? Should humble myself 'fore a woman? Mercy! Egor Rakitin should start beggin' to go to the free command again? Not for anythin' in the world. I'd rather get my livin' hide tore off. You yourself know, Ivan Nikolaevich, I'm no tail-wagger 'n' no linguist, but a genuine sort o' prisoner. You'll see: Egorushka will stand 'fore Six-Eyes rooted to the ground like a stump, 'n' won't say a teeny word in his defense. I'll jus' bury my little head in my tempestuous breast 'n' let mister com'dant treat me to his own mercilessness! The power's theirs!"

And during these words he assumed with such comic sincerity the visage of a forlorn knight that everyone started roaring with laugher again.

"Ah, you wagger!" the prisoners said over and over.

But the wagger didn't let me fall asleep until late in the night, first lapsing into his bellicose and impassioned mood, promising to kill his wife and to stand tough as a stump beneath the blows of encircling enemies, then adopting a mournfully plaintive tone and losing himself in complete melancholy and despair...

The following day during evening roll call, Six-Eyes himself appeared in the prison. The ominous silence that he maintained during roll call made everyone tremble still more. However, it seemed that everything was going to turn out all right. No one had appealed to him with any request during his tour of the wards. Except for Rakitin, who to my utmost surprise bounced up behind him like a spring and, as Luchezarov was preparing to majestically sail from our ward, suddenly moved in front of him and said in a sugary, melancholy voice:

"Mister Com'dant!"

"Stay in place! Don't move an inch!" shouted the guards.

"What do you want?" Luchezarov asked quietly, without emotion.

"Mister Com'dant, show Christian mercy! Since I'm the father of a family... 'N' my health's very weak..."

"What do you want?" the commandant raised his voice.

"I been assigned to the prison."

"I know. What do you want to report to me?"

"For God's sake, it ain't *fair*, Mister Com'dant... For God's sake, I dunno what *for*!"

"But I know: it's for torturing your wife. I will not allow atrocities on the part of prisoners under my authority."

"'Twas a family matter, Mister Com'dant... You yourself unnerstand: how can a husband not teach his wife or child a thing or two sometimes? Specially if they been naughty..."

"You are amiss in teaching the way you've taught. I myself saw the black marks on her body from your teeth. Under me you will pay, lad, for such teaching!"

"Be gen'rous 'n' forgive me, Mister Com'dant!"

After flashing his eyes angrily, the commandant hurried on his way. Behind him and his retinue the door slammed loudly. Rakitin stood utterly dejected, thoroughly confused... Prisoners began teasing him.

"How could you vow to Ivan Nikolaevich last night that you'd rather have your livin' hide tore off—but stand there beggin' Six-Eyes's forgiveness? You should be slapped good, wagger!"

"Ech, you, my own boys!" answered the quick-witted wag. "What was I afore Six-Eyes? A worm—in a word. If we show a brave face, don't people get hoisted by their noses 'n' beaten? Besides, I'm a family man... There's the wife, o' course—the hell with her! I shouldn't cry 'bout her... But whattabout my little son, my own Keshenka? How I think 'bout 'im, that he's alone there, my sweetheart, 'n' as you may believe, Ivan Nikolaevich, he's sharp'nin' his own teeth! God's word. Whatta trickster, y'know! Lies down beside his mother—won't fall asleep for anythin' in the world, can't wait for little daddy. I gots a wart on my chest. So he, you unnerstand, pulls this wart all the time. Pulls 'n' pulls—'n' he falls asleep that way."

After that evening Rakitin fell into a gloomy mood. His songs, jokes, and quips disappeared. During all his free time from work he wandered about the prison like a lost soul, evidently not knowing where to go. He lost sleep and appetite; he couldn't talk about anything else except the punishment facing him and what form and way it would manifest itself. Many intentionally frightened him with an extended term of *katorga*, the birch rods, and so on. I soon noticed that Rakitin began passing secret communications to his wife through Sokoltsev and other prisoners who worked outside the wall close to the free command. One or two weeks passed and Marfa, having forgiven the assault, appeared for a meeting with him… Rakitin was joyous again. That evening, he was already singing dithyrambs to his wife and started in with his usual candid revelations, insisting she was as lovable as a kitten, a true beauty in his youth, and was a trustworthy wife and splendid woman possessing only two flaws—age and stupidity; all his indignation was turned toward Domnushka and the evil clerk. For her part, Marfa, who had clearly not for the first time been nibbled by the teeth of an obliging little husband and had endured this means of punishment as being as natural as any other, began pleading for his release.

IX. A MASSACRE OF WOMEN AND INNOCENTS

Six-Eyes continued to rage. Releasing Rakitin to the free command had been a kind of fortunate accident, against the grain of all his politics that ill-fated summer. Prisoners, guards, and even Cossacks, who weren't under his direct authority, suffered each day in unimaginable fear. To my surprise, Zhebreek, who loved to prophesize and predict, neither exulted nor resounded but went about sadly and silently the whole time. Once, I took it into my head to talk with this madman about the unhappy times that had befallen the prison. In response, Zhebreek merely glanced at me sorrowfully, shook his fire-red goatee, and, after mumbling: "What're we still waitin' for!"—grandly walked off with tiny, uneven steps…

One day, I didn't go to work because of illness. Suddenly, a breathless Chirok rushed into the ward and explained that one of the guards the prisoners loved least, who went by the nickname Snake Head, was destroying a nest of bee-eaters beneath the prison roof. In Siberia, a species of swallow with large, ill-shaped heads and loud voices similar to the chitter of grasshoppers are called bee-eaters or martins. These harmless and sweet creations, returning each spring to the sad, cold north and constructing their nests beneath house windows, offered the prison's residents enormous comfort with their restless solicitude and ceaselessly joyous chatter and chirping. All prisoners loved these birds and protected them. If they came by a scrap of cotton wadding, they tore it into little pieces and, after tossing it all over the yard, followed with animated curiosity as bee-eaters snatched and carried them to their abodes. Wrapping up a stone in wadding, they amused themselves as a bee-eater, unable to extract the booty, tried lifting it into the air and letting it fall to the ground, and tried lifting it again… If the stupid birds no longer had the energy to instantly dart out from their rooftop nests, they carefully took to building for another suitable family, since knowing whose was theirs was difficult. The swallow, as it were, abandoned chicks and drove them away. Then a soft-hearted soul from among the prisoners would appear, his maternal sympathies evoked, and raise the deserted orphans on cockroaches and flies.

Understandably, given this, the prison was excited after hearing word of the misfortune befalling their beloved birds. I went with others into the prison yard. Snake Head was indeed stalking around the buildings with a long pole in his hands batting ill-fated bee-eaters' nests. Unhatched eggs fell to the ground from some, naked hatchlings from others; having fallen, they were immediately bashed, and most were already distorted by terminal spasms. Only a few nests had feathered chicks, but they still couldn't fly. The compassionate among the prisoners tried as they fell to catch them in their hats and carry them off, hoping somehow to feed and water them. Others laughingly turned to the guard and asked why he was carrying out his massacre.

"Com'dant ordered me," answered Snake Head, swinging the pole at another nest, "he noticed the debris in the rafters 'n' said it shouldn't be there no more."

"Other measures could have been taken against the debris," I intervened, "for example, ordering the cleaners to sweep the rafters every day."

"That ain't my business," Snake Head answered, "I jus' do what I'm told."

"And if you was told to beat your head 'gainst a wall," observed the headman Iukhorev, "or murder us, would you do that? Ever'thin's gotta have a reason, Vasilii Andreich."

"If I wanted, I could punish you for words like them, Iukhorev. The com'dant ain't gimme such an order. He's a human bein'."

"But is this order humane?" I asked. "Aren't chicks living beings? Look how many you've knocked out! There's probably several hundred such nests all around the prison, with whole thousands of chicks…"

The mare supported my words with loud grumbles. The guard became embarrassed.

"What can I do?" he beseeched. "D'you think I enjoy carryin' out this job? I myself is suff'rin' for it."

"Suggest to the commandant that in two weeks the chicks will be fledged, and then, if need be, the nests can be destroyed."

"'Suggest this'—no, thank you very much. He'll tear me to pieces worse than e'en the prisoners."

"I'll go 'n' suggest it after a spot o' lunch," announced Iukhorev.

"Well, that's splendid," Snake Head relented. "I'll wait till one o'clock. What's it to me! I'm e'en glad to."

After setting off from lunch for Six-Eyes, Iukhorev actually had an interesting conversation about the bee-eaters with him. This intelligent and imposing brigand was able to speak completely pathetically… Luchezarov quietly heard him out and laughingly said:

"Aha! They've been thinking a bit too late. In *katorga* they've begun acquiring *compassion*? While free, they butchered families, set little living children on fire: there is such an artist among you… Don't you remember you yourself chopped up more than one person?… But you pity the chicks there!… Nonsense, nonsense, and hypocrisy. Kindly tell the guard that I order all nests destroyed by evening. I myself will be coming at roll call to see."

Iukhorev necessarily fell silent, and after lunch the monstrous slaughter of innocents resumed. The mare limited itself to spitefully discussing Six-Eyes's response in front of Snake Head.

"'N' I thought *I* was the barbarian," Sokoltsev said, noting the sobriquet Luchezarov had for his part given him, "such a barbarian as was rare in the world. But I ne'er committed the same barbarity as you 'n' your com'dant. I'll kill a fly only outta extreme necessity, but in no way a hatchlin'. 'Cause, 'cordin' to my unnerstandin', it's less a sin to kill a man than it is God's innocent creature—the swallow. O'er time, a baby might turn into a top-rate barbarian, but a swallow could ne'er harm *any*one."

This philosophy of Sokoltsev's, entirely harmonious and illustrated with examples, was heard with great sympathy by the prisoners gathered in the yard; but it did nothing for the swallows: they fell and perished under Snake Head's relentless blows. Whole dozens of adult bee-eaters flew with beseeching peeps around their dear hearths but were unable to do a thing. Only after two hours did Luchezarov himself curiously gaze at the prison and, seeing with his own eyes Snake Head's work, order the bloody carnage to stop. In this way some one hundred were spared destruction; but the main business was done. For a long time, most of the small corpses lay scattered throughout the yard, summoning forth bitter memories…

At approximately this same time another unfortunate incident occurred. Having just returned from the mine, I was extremely surprised to discover that our ward No. 1 had been subjected to a strict punishment for a whole month: put under lock and key, in manacles, and deprived of tobacco, our own tea, and meetings and correspondence with relatives; the ward's headman, moreover, had been put in a dark isolator for a week. Like the rest, I was subject to all the ward's regimens. It turned out that that morning, Six-Eyes himself had come to the prison with a search party and noticed that one of our ward's door-hinges was rather loose. He immediately ordered a prisoner to grab a crowbar and pry the hinge off. One after another, several prisoners tried to do this, but couldn't.

"You don't do it that way," a guard then interjected after grabbing the crowbar, and he began twisting the hinge like a screw. It was actually pried off in this way. Having ordered the hinge brought to the smith and forged anew, but the ward put under arrest, Luchezarov stalked off in a rage. Everyone was bewildered. The matter became clear only during evening roll call: standing before prisoners' ranks, the senior guard announced to Shelai Prison an order in which it was mentioned that during a search conducted by this same guard, the door-hinge for ward No. 1 was proven to have been "pulled out," and that this undoubtedly showed an escape was being planned. Upon hearing this order everyone's jaws dropped—it was so unexpected and surprising! Having been condemned and stunned, the mare, as usual, resigned itself to its fate and did not even contemplate protesting against the reason for this clear injustice; but, I confess, I was disturbed… For me, it was all the harsher and worse that one of the designated punishments (deprivation of correspondence) affected specifically me and only me, since most other prisoners wrote letters no more than once a year… Having closely inspected the place on the inside of the door where the old hinge's corner should have been, I noticed it was smoothly covered with paint like all the rest of the door: this clearly proved that an angled corner for the hinge had never existed and it could not have been premeditatedly removed at all. Furthermore, prisoners and guards knew perfectly well (and this was anyway easy to verify) that the door-hinges in many other wards were exactly just as loose as ours, evidently because they had been poorly affixed during the prison's construction. Now, I won't say that plans to escape through the doors of wards locked in from all sides of the corridors where a guard was constantly in attendance would be absolutely insane, and that to carry out such insanity might only be an intentionally malicious desire to create a pretext for new cavils and oppressions. But what an extremely unfortunate and stupidly chosen pretext… Similar meditations disturbed and vexed me. First thing on Sunday, I demanded the complaints book and wrote in it a statement about the injustice perpetrated against me and the entire ward. An immediate result of this statement was that three days later, our headman, by law the person most directly responsible, was released from the dark isolator to the free command… This should have put into greater relief the senselessness of our arrest. Six-Eyes seemed to be telling us: "I myself know that my accusations are stupid and unfair; but you will remember day and night that I do what I want."

Exactly six months after this incident, when everything had been nearly forgotten, it was ceremoniously announced at evening roll call that Nerchinsk *katorga*'s commander[23] had taken no action concerning my complaint against the allegedly illegal punishment for prisoners' loosening the door-hinge.

Our ward was still under arrest when the administration sent over the sentences for Lunkov's and Nogaitsev's refusal to work and for insulting the guard: as the most guilty, the former was, "for bad behavior,"[24] deprived of a sentence reduction (which equaled a year of *katorga*) and subjected to a hundred birch blows, but the latter was sentenced to a month's incarceration in a dark isolator and fifty birch blows (decisions presented as coming from prison wardens' reports usually come from the administration). Lunkov was actually beaten right off in one of the isolators' little yards, but Nogaitsev was secluded in an isolator; when he emerged from there, the storm had already passed—Luchezarov was once more in a humane mood and the birching was forgotten.

During these same days, the brave staff captain waged a persistent war with the *katorga* women located in the free command. A women's prison did not exist at Shelai mine, but for the fulfillment of certain purely female labors it always had several female penal laborers, often sentenced indefinitely, who in the absence of a prison lived in freedom. In recalling the march to Siberia, I mentioned that a female criminal penal laborer was in most cases simultaneously a prostitute. The concentration of an overwhelming number of men, prisoners, and Cossacks before the almost complete absence of the female element meant that these five or six female convicts in Shelai's free command were, in the literal sense, communal women… Debauchery reached astonishing proportions. The shamelessness of certain of these shrews, always nearly intoxicated and fearing no sort of punishment, attained a kind of cretinism. There may have been only two ways the openly public displays of disgraceful ugliness could have been abolished: either by increasing the number of women or banishing beyond Shelai's borders those on hand. Luchezarov tried to find a third way: he believed in celibate repression and strict punishments. During that fateful summer, he guarded prisoners' morality especially vigilantly, and every day sent entire batches of free commandees and the women themselves to prison isolators. In the latter case, regardless of guards' shouts and threats, the mare secretly ran around and darted to and fro beneath windows from morn to night; told pleasing stories and traded compliments, albeit not taken from Goppe's *Good Manners*,[25] of course; and secretly brought to the isolators meat, tea, sugar, and tobacco. But purely platonic love could understandably not satisfy the prison's lady-killers, or "lovers," as they called themselves in prisoner jargon, and soon there were openings to all the prisoners' cleverness, cunning, and daring: audaciousness and resoluteness was really needed, you know, and they weren't scared of being punished for getting caught red-handed…

Among the convict women, there was a certain Laïs[26] who had till then been less debauched and shameless than the rest, but now she primarily suffered the thunder and lightning of a Luchezarovian rage. Luchezarov was at a loss as to why the previously meek and quiet Elenka had suddenly turned into an impudent vulgarian, whom even nearly daily visits to a dark isolator did not render submissive and well-behaved. It didn't enter his head that at that very time when it seemed only terror reigned, directed against prisoners by his strong measures the isolators, manacles, birch rods, sentence reduction cancellations, etc.—that during these very days the prison, *his model prison*, had turned into a den of iniquity and that his own measures were making this happen! What would the brave staff captain have felt, what would he have said, had he once dreamed that his hated "artists," after placing a stirrup in the yard, climbed over the isolator compound's fence, penetrated the "secret" corridor, and went through one of the isolator's skillfully dismantled wooden walls[27] for a private tryst with Elenka Zonova?[28] He would probably have lost his mind or died from an apoplectic fit…

Thanks to her sojourn in the isolators, this *katorga* sylph managed to acquire and carry into freedom several dozen rubles! Such was the "lovers'" cunning that ultimately there were hidden passageways connecting even separate isolators, so that the tractable Elenka carried on her work day and night, and for prisoners, ending up in an isolator became not a horror but a truly desirable thing. When guards subsequently discovered these hidden passageways they went into a fright and, having decided not to tell Six-Eyes about them, forced prisoners to cover them over during a remodeling of isolator buildings ordered soon thereafter by the authority himself. Only much later did I myself learn of my cohabitants' romantic escapades, and I was for a long time perplexed by what all the whisper-laden, enigmatic bustling and mysterious barbs about Chirok *et al.*, *et al.* meant—so improbable was what I've just told. Luchezarov, despite my suspicion and supposition that he believed his thunderous rage the sole means of correcting prisoners' immorality and curbing their lust, nevertheless continued among other things his undignified behavior against the women.

One beautiful day, a rumor circulated throughout prison that Six-Eyes had sent Zonova and free commandee Kalinkin to court for indecent behavior in front of a guard's children. One child was two years old, the other three. In addition to their being witnesses, the little informants must have been getting a fine upbringing if they were able to understand such things… An order came from the administration: Kalinkin would finish out his sentence in the prison, but Zonova would be subjected to one hundred birch blows. For a long time Luchezarov did not publicize this order and, having put Kalinkin in prison, apropos Zonova he sent her straightaway to an isolator but undertook no further measures. In the meantime, her *katorga* term ended; the convoy that was to deliver her to a settlement had already arrived, and it was perhaps hoped that the vicious order wouldn't be carried out. However, hope was this time betrayed… Early in the morning, Zonova was taken from the isolator and, not far outside the prison gates, savagely punished. The executioners were Tatar convicts, and as is said, they have a hatred for their victims; and the senior guard who attended the punishment, ordering them to beat her still harder, spat in her direction torturous wisecracks that cannot be put in print.

I well knew this woman occupied the lowest level of moral degradation, and that in normal times there was probably inside her a shamelessness no better than in the lowest prisoners; this I knew—however, I could not escape the notion that they were caning a *woman*, and spitting into her face what a person will say to a person but not a cow. Indeed, who can guarantee that in that terrible moment of torture there did not stir even within this fallen soul the sensation, until then muffled by ignorance and depravity, the sensation of a woman oppressed?…

I immediately thought this when I noticed that, right after the punishment, Elenka's convict girlfriends, wretched and ruined creatures just like she, gathered round her and for a long time wept silently…[29]

X.   A CURIOUS CONVERSATION

Two weeks after this event, I was unexpectedly suddenly called to the prison office. Behind a broad writing table sat, his entire face beaming, Luchezarov, stolid, ruddy, and evidently pleased with himself in the full light of morning. I silently bowed.

"A small parcel has again arrived in your name," the brave staff captain politely announced, "be so kind as to open and take from it everything safe and intact. And, incidentally, I wanted to ask you… to personally ask: how is your health?"

I dryly answered, what might be the reason for such interest?

"You see," Luchezarov rather awkwardly responded, "a certain person in Petersburg inquired of me about this…"

"In Petersburg?" I was still more surprised. "In Petersburg only my mother could be interested in my fate, but I am already in correspondence with her."

"No, there are, indeed, other persons… There's at least one personage—mark this: a high-ranking personage!—asking me to telegraph him about your health."

"I don't understand anything. Please explain."

After a moment's hesitation, Luchezarov gave me a telegram. I read: "Telegraph health of N.[30] Relatives worried." An unrecognizable signature followed. Greatly agitated, I shot Luchezarov an inquisitive gaze.

"Why are my relatives worried? Why did they turn to a stranger, and not telegraph me personally?"

Gloomy suspicion flashed through my head. I recalled that my birthday had been three weeks ago, a day which, in freedom, my family would have celebrated; I even remembered anticipating a congratulatory telegram that day. Then, laughing suddenly over my dolorous feelings, I forgot about it; but now my suspicion quickly turned to certitude.

"You had to withhold a telegram from my mother?" I anxiously asked Luchezarov.

"I confess I did have to do this… Actually…," he hastily began saying. "But… you see. Don't blame me. I could not give you that telegram as a result of my old training (of course, as I remember it)."

"Why?"

"Because… it seemed suspicious to me."

"Suspicious? My mother's telegram?"

"Yes. Needless to say, I see right now that I was mistaken, but at the time…"

"For God's sake, what was in the telegram?"

"It asked about your health and sent congratulations."

"Is that all? But the congratulations was for my birthday… Was that what you found suspicious?"

"Yes! Why wasn't it mentioned exactly what you were being congratulated for? Some two words were left out…there was twenty kopeks… and none of this would have happened!"

"Was there a prepaid reply with the telegram?"

"Yes."

"But you didn't answer yourself?"

"No!"

"But you could have at least told me a telegram had been received that wouldn't be given me! I honestly don't know how to describe your conduct. What must my mother have thought, not receiving a reply? Just imagine how many authorities she turned to before finally reaching a sympathetic soul."

"Yes, this is true, true. It's the bitter truth. I wasn't thinking at the time; I truly was to blame. We'll correct this mistake with dispatch. I'll telegraph the dignitary who's asking… Tell me: what exactly should I write?"

I warmly answered that the dignitary meant not the slightest to me, that he'd not addressed me, and so he might respond to him as he wished.

"Nevertheless… I'll write: healthy, cheerful?"

"I repeat: write what you please. I'll send my own telegram to my mother!"

"Beautiful, beautiful. Here's some paper, sit down and compose it right now. Here's a form for the telegram. I always have them. Write, please, and I'll bring it to the station immediately. I can see you're very distressed. Such an attachment to one's parents is rare these days, and I find it very touching."

These free-and-easy words, redolent with callousness and smugness, exasperated me once more. I again burst out with bitter reproofs.

"You may persecute, insult, torment me"—I said, shaking with nerves and tears in my voice—"me, a person with hands tied… But by what right and for what reason do you torment people guilty of nothing—my mother, my relatives?"

For a minute, Luchezarov appeared lost and, red as a peony, knew not what to say or do.

"I, clearly, am not tormenting or insulting you," he babbled, "quite the opposite…"

"You say this with a clear conscience?" I continued my attack. "You didn't humiliate me during the door-hinge incident? How have I figured in all the unfair clampdowns and carping you've directed at prisoners? Do you suppose that I watched with indifference from the prison the outrage committed against a woman and the flowing blood?"

"I can see you're greatly distressed and don't know what you're saying," answered Luchezarov, lowering his voice to an almost confidential whisper. "Out the door, old chap!" he loudly addressed the armed watchman who was standing there. He obeyed instantly.

"You are completely correct in faulting me for my attitude toward the prisoners," he began exculpating himself. "What concern of it is yours that I might single you out from the general mass? I don't even have the right to. During the door-hinge incident, for example, I even let slip from personal view that you were located in that very ward."

"But have you until now sincerely believed you were right in that matter?"

"You see, you're passing judgment as a private and partly rather interested individual… It could be said you've suffered… You're not in a position to thoroughly interrogate the position of a person in charge over such… such a complicated institution as a *katorga* prison. I doubt you'd even be able to fully acknowledge what these gentlemen artists have been arrested for. You simply have not had the experiences in life for this… you're too innocent! To keep them in check you have to be able to be terrible, you must use harsh measures from time to time!"

"But evenhanded measures all the same…"

"Of course, of course. As is possible… Do you know, for example, that this spring I received information about preparations for an escape, and that one of these artists is located right in your ward?"

I remembered Sokoltsev's fret-saws and, smiling inwardly, kept my silence. Fixing upon me a triumphant gaze, Luchezarov went on:

"To resolve the issue was not as easy as it seems to you. A warning was needed. I know the *katorga* world well, for ten years now, it's been my misfortune to maintain an acquaintance with these prisoners. But I confess to you: I took over command of Shelai mine with the most optimistic dreams, with a belief in man, even the disgraced, with the hope that mere threats and typical punishment measures would be enough to correct and restrain him… Believe you me: I have said with sincere and complete conviction… in front of the ranks, I've said… that I don't want to resort to corporal punishment. And it shouldn't come to that!"

"And yet, have you not however resorted to it? You've done what cannot be remembered without burning shame—you punished a woman!…"

"What are you so overwrought about?… Don't you know what kind of woman she was?"

"It doesn't matter. It's not important *what* she was, but that she was a *woman*."

"But what was there to do? I saw how all other means available to me by law were powerless, how this creature's depravity and impudence had become impossible, and in any event the primacy of authority had to be upheld."

"And birch rods, you think, upheld this? In whose eyes? Don't you know that any prisoner prefers a small serving of birches each month over difficult seclusion in an isolator?… Or, perhaps, it's in the eyes of the educated world? Are you saying you want the Russian and foreign press to connect your name to such incidents as the desecration of a woman? Perhaps not? You've succeeded only in smearing your own name!"

"Enough, enough. This conversation is over. I'd like to see someone dare to smear my name!"

"I didn't intend to offend you, but only to open your eyes to the real state of things. Corporal punishment, in my opinion, might corrupt uncorrupted people, completely humbling their feelings of human worth and forcing them to lose the last cinder of shame."

"It's possible you're right, of course. I acted in a fit of despair. All my good intentions towards others have only suffered ruin, and all I see around me are black ingratitude and baseness. In my place, God Himself would lose patience! In each case I acted on the basis of the law. I didn't go beyond the boundaries of legality. What's to be done if our laws are still imperfect! Most of all, however, it grieves me that I caused your mother such trouble. Is there anything I can do to make amends for my mistreatment of her?"

I shrugged my shoulders in silence.

"Nothing, really? Think… Don't you want me to send her your telegram?"

"That's not necessary. Kindly cancel today's telegram. That will be sufficient. What was done can't be reversed. Let's just hope similar… misunderstandings don't happen in future."

"Yes, exactly, misunderstandings! That's the word… It was all a sad misunderstanding!"

Having taken my leave, I bowed and hurried to the prison, full of grievous feelings and thoughts for mother, about what my poor old lady must have been suffering these three terrible weeks. Later, I received from her a letter in which was written all her anguish, a letter that tore at my heart… I don't know whether the brave staff captain felt any pangs of conscience, but after the above conversation, it once more became easier to breathe inside the prison: for a time, the hiss of the birch rod, confinement in the isolator, and sentence reduction cancellations ceased.

XI.   HITTING BACK

Summer, with its abbreviated nights and lengthened workdays, was always a more difficult period in the lives of Shelai mine's residents. Especially difficult was the work in the ditch about which I spoke above. I personally happened to experience the delights of gardening. The word "garden" usually conjures up the notion of comparatively easy and, in the main, enjoyable work in the open air, useful for increasing physical strength and stimulating the appetite. But let the reader imagine for himself that he, tired from not having had a good night's sleep, has been hauled to his feet at three in the morning, shackled and surrounded by the bayonets of armed guards, and forced to dig with a blunt iron shovel into hard—seeming to at times consist of stone—soil. If you don't complete the immensely large quota that's been assigned, then you'll be pleased to dig "from bell to bell," that is, until seven in the evening. Prisoners who've been standing want a smoke, and settle themselves down to rest. Two minutes pass—and the guard "standing on your soul" is already shouting it's time to get back to work. One or two words of objection— and you're threatened with the isolator.

Meanwhile, the sun is climbing higher and higher. Prisoners are all impatiently gazing at the heavens in the hope that the blessed dinner bell will soon sound. They finally ask the guard the time, and receive the answer: "Half past ten."

"Lord! There's still a full hour 'n' a half to go!"

The sun gets hotter and hotter, sweat begins streaming down face and neck; feet are tired from pressing down on a shovel that goes poorly into the soil… And suddenly an order rings out:

"Attention! Caps off!"

Everyone freezes in fright, throws shovels to the ground as instructions require, and hurriedly bares their heads. Only then do they timidly look around and see, approaching with cane in hand, Six-Eyes.

"Caps on, resume working!" resounds his shout, and the prisoners, having quickly covered their heads, pick their shovels up again. In the commandant's presence, the work is carried out more zealously than before. Luchezarov walks around. He knows everything, is the expert on any kind of job. If his word is to be believed, he has been a gardener, a farmer, a horticulturalist; he knows metalworking, smithing, carpentry, stove-setting, road-building… He left behind in Chita his own handmade bookcase and a wagon with some unusually smartly built wheels. He loudly asks a guard about the quality of the given soil, and for some reason tells him about an incident from his own life, somewhere in the gold mines. But amid this talk Luchezarov's roving eyes are wide open and he does not fail to notice Petin, that he has to push deeper with his shove, and Nogaitsev, that he's being lazy.

"Give me your shovel, I'll show you how to dig."

He takes the shovel from Nogaitsev's hands and tries to push it in with his finely polished boot. The brave staff captain's corpulent figure strains, stresses, and turns red, but all in vain; in vain, panting and wheezing, he heartily pounds his foot on the shovel: throwing the shovel to the ground, he doesn't want "to show how to dig."

"Soil's full o' rocks, Mister Com'dant," Nogaitsev takes the liberty to mention, "the assigned quota's too big."

"You like to talk nonsense, fella!" the unflappable Luchezarov angrily responds. "The reason is simple—the smith poorly sharpened the shovel. So it is: the edge is a pancake's pancake! The scoundrel must be loafing about as well. Who's doing our smithing today?" he addresses a guard with this question.

"Vodianin!" Snake Head gallops over, delivering a salute. "Efimov's the blacksmith's striker."

"Aha! I'm familiar with these artists… I'll go see them for myself, and watch."

And Luchezarov, dissatisfied and gloomy, stalks off in the smithy's direction. Everyone heaves a sigh of relief.

"We need a rest, Vasilii Andreevich," the workers say, and, not waiting for permission, immediately sit on the ground and begin smoking. But at that very moment comes the dinner bell, and with a joyful racket and buzz they jump up from their spots, form ranks, and leave for the prison. In summer, the dinner bell is separated from the next bell by a three-hour rest period. This is the time of most intense heat, when the ground gets as hot as an iron skillet, when your burning head is splitting from incessant pain and your tired legs can barely move. Good to him who possesses the fortunate ability to sleep during the day, whose nerves aren't going full-tilt, whose gall isn't bubbling over, and whose soul isn't nearly howling from pain! That person collapses on the sleeping platform as if dead and lies without stirring these three hours, without memory, without cognition, in a dreamless sleep. But this midday rest refreshes little. You awaken with a terrible pain in your temples and eyes inflamed from having gazed savagely into the light. It's two o'clock in the afternoon; still resounding in your ears is the sound of the little bell that aroused you. The sun is even higher and mercilessly scorches you with its annihilating rays. Again you must work, work to the full until seven o'clock in the evening, under those same bayonets, under the same menace of guards and Luchezarovian shouting, work so that, having fallen into the sleep of a dead man for a brief summer night, you can arouse yourself next morning for a similar torturous *katorga* day… No, I cannot recall the gardens of Shelai Prison without shuddering all over!

When, in mid-June, the planting of cabbage and other vegetables was completed and our group of workers was again sent to the mine, I always joined in with joy and relief despite the fact that summer labors in the mine carried their own thistles and thorns. Inside the shafts, it was as cold as an icy grave; due to ice-covered ladders and walls overflowing with water, you hit yourself in the neck with the augers and your boots filled with water. Planks happened to have been laid down beneath you for the boring, but were soon floating in the constantly flowing water. Then you had to climb out above so that several kibbles' worth of water could be pumped out and you'd be able to bore ahead for a new founding. Darkness, cold, water, arms numb from exhaustion, body shivering all over… You climb out, as it were, from the bottom of a gloomy well to the outside world, where around you is so much azure, warmth, and sunny brightness, where a fragrant larch grove rustles and greens nearby and, farther on, hills rise in a beautiful semicircle, covered almost entirely in lilacs and seeming to bleed the wild rosemary flower—and amid this vision of the splendor of nature triumphant the bile turns in your soul and your indignation boils! Indignation at this unresponsive, soulless beauty, able with just a flower to rejoice in the face of enormous human misery and torment, before living memories of the tears—and maybe even the blood!—shed there.

> The mountains beyond mountains
> Know well the clouds,
> Sown through with woe
> And soaked with blood…[31]

"Ekh, what I'd give now for a free day to settle down 'n' eat!" one prisoner dreams aloud while staring at a monastery's plump swine and suckling pigs running across the foot of a hill. "Then we could prob'ly bust through seventy feet o' this rock! But what can you do? We ain't strong 'nough!"

"Whatta crank! May I ask how you can work with a belly fulla nuthin'? Let his fat belly sit in the 'slator, I can bore forty feet more'n him. Damn his soul! I'd rather collapse in the sunshine, 'n' at least be warm."

"Indeed, freezin' in Six-Eyes's broth," continues the first, "yer stopped from gittin' a free meal in yer belly. S'posed to be, 'tis said, a *katorga pre*gime for youse… At that *katorga* prison… So bust yer damned eyes! Why ain't they sayin' this in the other mines? Why they bringin' all sorts o' grub to 'em? Were there money, you could buy what you wanna to yer content! Milk, pork, lamb, berries, whate'er you can 'magine. What harm's some grub? A man can only go on if'n he's full."

"Grub?! Makes the blood pure, brother, excitement 'n' froth. Fer instance, if'n a fellow gets five pounds o' good meat at one sittin' so's to get o'er the hump, much of his health'll go into his bones!"

"But didja hear what they say? Seems the new governor'll be tourin' the mines… We could make a complaint!"

"I heard the rumor; but is it just prison *bumó*?[32] Someone let it drop, 'n' they believed 'im. But *this*, o' course, should be complained 'bout."

"Don't complain, but simply-dimply ask for a little transfer! Let 'em send us to the ends o' the earth, so long as it's away from this-here garden!"

Such were typical prisoners' daydreams. A good half of Shelai Prison's population would have at the merest opportunity relocated with joy to mysterious Sakhalin, to Khabarovk,[33] Kara, Zerentui, Kadaia,[34] anywhere whatsoever, so long as it was farther from Six-Eyes, with his "food regime" and nauseatingly boring routines prevailing in a prison where there were neither games, nor songs, nor *maidany*, nor anything that brightens the soul of a hopelessly long-term prisoner. The majority, of course, grumbled only on the sly, concealing from themselves their dreams of transferring to other prisons: what else could you do, since it was useless to request a transfer? But there were a dozen such fellows who couldn't do just that, and they decided "to hit back"… They'd been encouraged by the example of Diudin, who so successfully pestered Six-Eyes that he himself petitioned for his dispatch to Sakhalin. They thought that if they could only be as annoying, the same would be done with them. The first of those who followed this path were a certain Komlëv and our previously encountered Petin-the-Elk. For a long time, they had expected to separate from Luchezarov in peace, and during nearly every evening's roll call appealed to him with a request for transfer to Sakhalin. Luchezarov, having several times answered that he could do nothing about this because he had no authority at all over Sakhalin, soon stopped listening to all such requests. Then Petin and Komlëv, having formed an alliance between themselves, embarked upon systematic repulsion by way of incessant arguments with guards, calculated laziness, refusals to work, and so on. Here, from a prisoner's point-of-view, the hidden cost to both allies turned out to be the biggest relief. Luchezarov responded to the refusers' initial tricks with the usual answer—the isolator. The allies did not let up and continued following their line. Then, Komlëv was immediately informed of the cancellation of his sentence reduction.

"So what!" said Komlëv. "I spit on their reduction!… Forty-two years since my birth, but I'm carryin' thirty-five years' *katorga* round me neck. How much can I live through 'n' still be young? What's it matter to me if'n they slap another five or ten years on? Let 'em slap on a *hunnerd*—don't matter! This brother won't be included in no free command or manifesto, so me own freedom's gonna cost me. I'll give *myself* a manifesto!"

"Do you mean you'll fight back like before?" I was compelled to ask Komlëv.

"But how else?" he answered, as if surprised.

"Well, but if… Six-Eyes imposes other measures?"

"A floggin, you mean? I well know it's now up to him to give the lash or rods. Let 'im indulge that way to his heart's content! What kinda prisoner would I be if'n I feared the lash? I ain't gonna be that kinda prisoner. If I ain't scared o' *katorga*—nuthin' in the world can scare me!"

These words were said in the way characteristic of all Komlëv's speeches and actions, simply and with an absence of any bravado, yet at the same time with such inner strength and energy that, I confess, I fell in love with this man. Throughout the entire episode of his "resistance" he maintained the utmost simplicity, without that defiant noisomeness that distinguished the behavior of his friend and ally Petin. The latter, when refusing to work, each time considered it necessary to shout, gesticulate, and threaten with words and signs. Komlëv, by contrast, very coolly laid down on the sleeping platform waiting for when the orderly, like a wild beast, ran in to order him to work.

"Komlëv! How much longer do we gotta wait for you? Ever'one's lined up 'n' standin' under the gate, but certainly not you. Get yourself together right now!"

"Whereto?" slowly, evenly, without raising his voice, Komlëv asked.

"Whaddya mean 'whereto'? You're bein' told to go to work."

"I ain't a-goin' today!"

"Whaddya mean 'ain't a-goin'"? Is you really sick?"

"No, I'm fine."

"So this is what you're gonna do? You taken a notion to joke with me, or do you wanna go to the isolator?"

"The 'slator—so it's to the 'slator. Let's go," he—rising from his spot—answered with an even voice and left for the isolator.

Such was not the Elk. Regardless of his noisomeness and outward passion, it was clear he was far "beneath" Komlëv; prisoners and guards recognized this. Petin himself did not hesitate to underscore this with facts. While Komlëv unbendingly and tirelessly continued driving down that line, demanding transfer to another prison, refusing to work, and fearing not even the prospect of the lash and rods and thus instilling in the authorities genuine respect and fear of him, Petin, in the most critical moments when things came to a serious turn, each time became cowardly and backed off: he was terribly afraid of the lash and rods… Therefore, his behavior was not at all consistent: first he was loafing and acting rude, settling stupid scores with the guards, next he had turned into a zealous laborer and quiet, submissive prisoner. The authorities saw he wasn't a danger and could always be stricken with fear.

Our old acquaintance Semënov was also one of those who dreamed of breaking away sooner from Shelai mine and, like Komlëv, would not tremble before any of Six-Eyes's terrible measures. But he had less than a year before his release to the free command and he carried himself extremely restrainedly and prudently. Nonetheless, and absolutely surprising to everyone, though most of all to Semënov himself, his story got carried away and positioned him in the authorities' eyes as one of Shelai Prison's most dangerous and unwanted residents.

The summer nights were terribly brief. Roll call was at eight o'clock in the evening; in case of Luchezarov's presence, it lasted no less than an hour and you could fall asleep no earlier than ten. At half past four in the morning there was already the guard's whistle calling you to get ready for another roll call. As it were, the exhausting work with bad food turned prisoners into savages with heavy eyes refusing to look at the light, with pain in their temples, with aches all through their bodies. But on his duty day the guard Bezymënnykh, who hated prisoners with all his heart and loved to play "dirty tricks" on them at every turn, abbreviated even this insufficient time for sleep. Even when it was still completely dark, at two or three o'clock at night, he'd walk beneath the wards' windows, pound his fists or keys on them with all his might, and, having woken everyone, shout in an inhuman voice:

"Headman! Lamps out!"

Semënov was at that time a ward headman, and one time, was sleeping so soundly that he didn't hear even this hellish pounding. After twenty minutes Bezymënnykh went to the door's window and, seeing that the lamp had still not been extinguished, began drumming his fingers on the pane and yelling Semënov's name. But, as if murdered, he continued sleeping the sleep of a young warrior. The other prisoners, cracking jokes from beneath their cassocks, feigned sleep as well and didn't budge.

"Well, alright, I'll show you, scoundrel!" Bezymënnykh said, losing his temper and stalking off.

When morning roll call came the prisoners for some reason forgot to warn Semënov about what had happened, and Bezymënnykh ordered him to the isolator without any explanation. Having suspected nothing, the stunned Semënov silently obeyed, but when he reached the isolator and realized, instead, that he was being taken advantage of in the absence of witnesses, he attacked his enemy with clenched fists and a terrible oath. Bezymënnykh narrowly escaped and barely managed to close behind him the bolt on the door to the isolators' corridor. He ran to the senior orderly to report on Semënov's attempt on his life. A convoy instantly showed up at the isolator. Semënov was manacled and put in strict solitary confinement. We hoped that this incident would turn out well for him… Semënov's bosom buddy, the headman Goncharov, became gloomy and pensive.

"Now the free command's lost Petkin," he sadly told me. "Free command's lost 'im— 'n' the poor chap's lost it! If they slap 'im with several more years, then Bezymënnykh won't be a resident o' the wide world no more… Petka won't let hisself forget such an offense!"

Semënov sat in the isolator for over a month, readying a most grievous decision about his fate.

But what was the universal surprise when one fine day an order came from the administration—having taken into account Semënov's punishment of a hard month of seclusion in the isolator, it transferred him as well as Komlëv to Zerentui's *katorga* prison. Abandoning that very day his hated Shelai mine, Semënov must have crossed himself with all his heart, and the comrades left under Six-Eyes's control began with as much heart to envy his "luck." Toward Komlëv they were silent, for in all eyes he was not simply a lucky guy: he'd conducted a long and persistent battle for what he eventually achieved, had been ready to imprint his somber and tough resolve with his own blood, and, far apart from all those who dreamed and boasted about fighting back, had realized within himself the strength and ability to do just this. More than anyone, Elk felt ashamed of himself. He'd been cruel and gloomy, had ruined his heart, and vented his spite in verbal and pugilistic encounters with Lunkov and other prisoners weaker and smaller than he and lacking his cheap arrogance and dash.

But there existed still other types of rebels. I've already discussed, for example, the masterful plan concocted by Sokoltsev and the misfortune that befell his first effort. Each acted according to his temperament and abilities. Hence, an entire group of prisoners contracted various terrible, hopeless diseases that rendered them incapable of any kind of physical labor and, so they thought, made them sooner able "to fly" to the free command or at least end up in an almshouse. In any *katorga* prison there's always a certain percentage of those shamming a limp, the uselessness of an arm, constitutional weakness, or the suffering of all possible ailments. However, it's not as easy to dissimulate as it seems at first sight. Neither guards nor doctors are such major hurdles for these sick men as is the mare itself; in its midst, each chronic patient freed from work immediately gives birth to envy; suspicion, gossip, slander, and systematic spying begins against disfavored comrades (disfavored by nearly each and every one) suspected of shamming an illness. Some note that today he's limping heavily on a foot different than the one yesterday, others see how at night the shamming sick man, supposing no one is watching, or having forgotten his limp because of sleepiness, stands and moves about as if healthy, hobbling on neither this nor the other foot… Soon, similar such suspicions, often completely erroneous, turn into absolute certainty and a dark rumor reaches the administration through unknown channels. Actual and shamming "dependents," regardless of illness, begin to be found at fault and are forced to work… Life will soon become hard for those truly disabled, who through misfortune manifest no signs of illness before ignorant eyes: they have both arms, both legs, no gaping wounds or disgusting scabs. Only such signs are recognized by the mare, and the majority of medics are in concert with it. Everything else—cough, fever, migraine, weakness, rheumatism, heart pains—all this can simply be faked! In Shelai Prison there were, among others, two special reasons increasing prisoners' hostility toward the chronically sick and weak and those who didn't go to work. Owing to the prison's small size and comparatively insignificant quantity of prisoners the meat ration was not, as in other prisons, separated between workers and dependents but was issued altogether. On the other hand, the infirmary was dark and small and could accommodate only a limited number of patients. Given the combination of all these reasons, a prisoner who decided to knock off work on the basis of a feigned illness had to possess a tolerable reserve of bravery and artistry. Among such daredevils and artists old man Goncharov was number one.

Having spent several weeks in the infirmary thanks to a truly serious illness, he soon began complaining about a constant pain in his legs, then he went lame, and finally he just "sat" on the sleeping platform... The latter circumstance overlapped with Semënov's abdication from Shelai Prison. There were no clear reasons at all for his strange affliction; although a physician visited now and then he, too, could not in all honesty verify fakery; the patient's age, his powerful, leonine head of imposingly graying and long-growing hair, made no small impression, of course... In the end, they threw up their hands at Goncharov and discharged him from all labor. At first, prisoners believed him. But time passed and, without speaking openly in front of Goncharov (so afraid were they of his physical strength and malicious tongue, sharp as an axe), many began suspecting him. In time, these suspicious quarrels reached the individual; Goncharov then lapsed into a melancholy, weepy tone previously very uncharacteristic of him. He bitterly recalled the good old days when he had his legs and strength, when he answered every insult with a hundredfold insult, when enemies trembled before him and he had money, associates, and friends... Listening to such complaints and reproaches against fate, I sometimes felt my heart turn grievously out of compassion, and my own suspicions melted like wax. I saw in Goncharov a truly helpless, unfortunate old man whom nobody could defend harming. I often happened to stick up for him, parrying prisoners' savage (indirect, of course) assaults. Much was my surprise when one day, Goncharov himself had a friendly discussion with me about his illness.

"Where's my Petka gone?" he began, sighing. "Ech, Ivan Mikolaevich! If they'd let me into the free command... I could go straight to Zerentui 'n' be havin' a reunion with 'im."

"With your legs, how could you go so far?" I asked in surprise.

"Well, is they really gonna hurt forever?" answered the old man. "They'll get better, honest to God. Specially if I'm on the outside. I can earn a lot there, I know a lotta trades: I can make shoes 'n' clothes, I can weave baskets 'n' scorch coal... Freedom 'n' a free man's food...Mikolaich, that's the stuff, I'm tellin' you," he suddenly began saying in a conspiratorial whisper, "there's nuthin' for me to hide from you. You ain't our brother mare, y'know, you won't hurt me. They're reproachin' me that I'm pretendin', see, that I'm takin' their workers' rations... Saddened me at first, deeply saddened me to hear these reproaches, 'cause my legs was really hurtin'… Well, but now I'm really *mad*! Now, my legs is for certain better. I can e'en say this now: I'd be able to work no worse'n any of 'em… Only, I'm thinkin' to myself: what's it to me? Why should I care if there's more for 'em? What if I start workin' like a bull, strainin' the life outta me, earnin' the administration's favor so's they hang a medal round my neck? I should just go to the free command, Mikolaich, 'n' y'know they's let a sick man go sooner, 'cause inside the prison I'm a completely useless man for Six-Eyes, but there, on the outside, I can make myself useful: guard a storehouse, scorch coal for the blacksmith. This is what I dream 'bout, Ivan Mikolaich. Well, 'n' then, o' course, I'm not their lodger! Shelai Prison won't hafta support me no more! Petka's goin' to the free command soon: we'll make a pair—'n' sorry, mother-*katorga*, forgive us, father-Baikal!…"

Of course, I piously kept Goncharov's secret and felt a deep compassion when his cherished dream came true in September, when Luchezarov expedited his term and assigned him to the free command as a storehouse guard. Thus I concluded that the old man would stay only through winter and enter General Cuckoo's service at the beginning of spring. But, to my surprise, this happened much earlier: he ran away in early October, just as they were issuing prisoners their warm "rags": sheepskin jacket, trousers, mittens… Shelai's administration was terribly indignant at the cunning old man who so adroitly managed to pull it off: yesterday he was still groveling on his knees, today he's absconded into vagabondage! Apropos the fugitive's stupidly chosen time of year, which would undoubtedly soon deliver him into the hands of justice, the guards loudly rejoiced.

"We'll show 'im then! 'N' when he really gets sick—we won't trust 'im!"

"Don't know what difficulty possessed that gray devil to leave right *now*," the mare said amongst itself, "forest is bare, there's no cover, it's hard to find provisions, 'n' it'll be gettin' cold… Looks like the snow'll be pilin' up for days!"

But, hearing such talk, old, world-wise prisoners just chuckled into their beards.

"Now's the time to go!" they answered my questions. "Y'know, Goncharov sure ain't no fool… He hisself is a *cheldon*, a Siberian… He ain't gone fer nuthin'! No folks in the fields now, 'cause ever'thin''s put away, the roads is busy 'n' no one'll bother 'im. Soon now, the lads'll be returnin' from the mines—so again there's less suspicion 'bout an unknown man if'n there's a respectable old-timer leavin' the mines s'well…"

But despite what the experienced people could say, it nevertheless seemed strange to me that such an intelligent man as Goncharov had chosen such a late date to escape: August and probably part of September were still suitable times for vagabonding, but October not at all. Something involuntary and compulsory emanated from such an escape…

And, yes, first there arrived in quick order an indistinct whisper throughout the prison: there'd been a murder in one of the big mines' free commands, after which several men escaped. Named among the fugitives was Semënov… It was being said that Zerentui's prison warden, finding himself in a dispute with Luchezarov over Semënov's transfer to him, immediately released him to the free command in a fit of pique; there, in an argument over cards, Semënov knifed a Tatar and escaped with the pursuit hot on his heels. All the same, I was at a loss for some time about this escape's relationship to Goncharov's escape, but soon other news reached my ears (confided, moreover, in greater secrecy): after his crime, Semënov had fled to Shelai mine and was hidden by his countrymen and friends Goncharov and Rakitin for several days... I came to understand everything after this. In the presence of the bosom buddy, practically a son, to whom he'd willingly/unwillingly run, there rose up in the old taiga wolf an irrepressible thirst for blood, a willfulness that could not be controlled by any kind of sage advice... Bedazzled by a dream of home, family, and probably by a circumstance—and this, irrespective of his years and the approach of cold and winter—he, having tasted another draft of the vivifying liquid, readied himself for the roadway and daringly proceeded to confront all the dangers and adventures of vagabond life...

Whether the fugitives fell into the clutches of Transbaikalia Cossacks, lay their stormy heads down beneath savage Tungus' bullets, or safely went beyond the "Holy Sea" (Baikal)—of this, I have no information whatsoever. I believe, however, that both did not give up their lives and freedom cheaply to whomever challenged them!...

XII.   SHELAI'S GUESTS

The rumor about a new governor turned out to be not simply a prisoners' "*bumó*." Within the prison, activities commenced for the arrival of the distinguished guest. Even the brave staff captain, having put on airs that he who was cast into his mine always be ready "for a visit by the Sovereign Himself" betrayed marked signs of nervousness and excitement; it is well known that a new broom always cleans better, but, in the main, only God knows the morals and tendencies of the new lord of the realm… True, he didn't demean himself by personally entering or inspecting all the trifles and hiding places of the prison's inner existence, but the guards had evidently been given strict instructions. For entire days, from morning to late at night, they rummaged through the building's nooks and crannies, raising every speck of dust and bawling out prisoners for the smallest derelictions toward cleanliness and tidiness. The floors, earlier washed twice a week, were now scrubbed and washed throughout the day, and after cleaning were stained with ocher, which gave them a truly beautiful look, though, on the other hand, after drying out, it soon turned into a fine powder that when swept made everyone cough and sneeze. And the wards' headmen swept nearly every half hour…

Having appeared at one of the evening roll calls, Luchezarov turned to the prisoners with the following speech:

"This is it! You've probably already heard that within days the new military governor shall be here.[35] You will attend to the whistle, which will be blown by the guard on duty, and you will observe order and cleanliness. Later, you will not bother the governor with ridiculous requests or complaints. I know that you love to talk with every new commander: they say that to buy isn't a success, but to barter may be… I will punish absurd talk. Each person who wants to speak should today, when I tour the wards, confer with me beforehand. I'll decide if you have a sensible or a stupid claim. Moreover, a certain foreigner, traveling with a religious aim—a preacher—will be visiting our prison tomorrow or the next day. Concerning your appropriate behavior towards him as well, don't think of appealing to him with any requests. Bite your tongue. He's simply a private individual and has no official authority whatsoever. There is something I'll tell you. The wards smell disgusting. It's no mystery. I cannot at all stand behind Nogaitsev during prayers… You're completely incapable of controlling yourselves. It is nonsense that bread and cabbage cause flatulence, nonsense! I myself eat black bread and love cabbage soup… You can always control yourselves, but you just simply don't want to!"

Having delivered his homily to the prisoners, Luchezarov began touring the wards. Almost everywhere, they appealed to him with requests to speak with the governor. In our ward, the first to approach were Petin and Sokoltsev.

"What do you want to say?" Luchezarov darkly asked them.

"To request a transfer to Sakhalin, Mister Com'dant."

"What for?"

"There's no way, Mister Com'dant, we can finish out our sentences in this prison, it's too strict. What with thirty 'n' forty years *katorga* on our backs."

"But will your terms be reduced on Sakhalin? You're talking nonsense. There's no use making such stupid requests. Even if the governor took it into his head to satisfy them, you yourselves would regret it: Sakhalin is ten times worse than Shelai Prison; besides Transbaikalia's residents, only especially serious criminals are sent there as a form of punishment."

"All the same, Mister Com'dant, let us lodge our request."

"Lodge it, if you like. Just know that it won't be met. Lunkov, what are you fidgeting over?

"Mister Com'dant, I'm… since I ain't bein' fairly punished, then… lemme make a request."

"To complain?"

"Hm… Yes."

"I don't advise it. You insist that you're being punished unfairly, but I think it's completely fair."

And with these words Luchezarov moved on to the other wards. This evasion continued for over an hour. Everywhere, other mine laborers applied for Sakhalin, and all were rebuffed. All the same, and however angry Six-Eyes got at them for this, there had ripened in many a firm decision to speak with the governor. The next day toward evening, the foreign preacher and his interpreter suddenly showed up, accompanied by just the senior guard. Luchezarov wasn't home—he'd gone off somewhere. A tall, crooked old man with a gray beard, in a black frock-coat and with a pile of bibles under his arm, he began walking around the ward and reading to the prisoners a German sermon the interpreter translated word for word into Russian:

"This book is a great book, and is just as necessary for the peasant as for the emperor. The teachings included in this book are profound. They are not only profound but also extremely practical and useful. Sincerely believe in and ask of God, and He will fulfill all requests and desires."

The preacher had just managed to deliver these words in our ward when a deafening command of "Attention!!" ripped out and Luchezarov, in all his radiance, flew in along with heavily breathing guards. The foreigner became confused and fell silent.

"Commandant of Shelai Prison, Staff Captain Luchezarov!" the brave staff captain introduced himself.

The old man gave his name, bowed, extended a hand, and quickly pulled from his pocket a paper testifying to the goals of his travels and permission to visit *katorga* prisons. With a naïvety approaching wittiness, prisoners later said that Six-Eyes, as soon as he appeared, had demanded the foreigner's "pa*ch*port."

"There's a good man!" they said about him, with neither laughter nor real admiration.

"He don't respect no one. He'll prob'ly give the gov'nor hisself twenty pegs!"

"Very well," Luchezarov, having returned the old man's "pachport," said after several awkward seconds of silence, "you've already spoken to them?"

The old man, having understood from the interpreter the sense of the question, nodded his head in agreement and began to distribute his books to the prisoners, first asking whether or not they were literate. But everyone identified himself as literate, even those who knew only the alphabet. After this the visitors left for the other wards, where a loud "Attention!" boomed upon entry to each. The foreigner probably didn't very much like sermonizing under such conditions. He moved on hurriedly, and from all sides the prisoners amused themselves by judging and putting him down. Unfortunately, I heard among these judgments not a single glad word about his visit or what he said. They only talked about his appearance and his clothing.

"If'n I met such a goose on the road," boasted Andriushka Povar, "I wouldn't be 'fraid to take ever'thin' 'e had at the first word, 'is watch, 'is frock-coat, 'n' 'is money!"

"Should be able to find a bit o' money on 'im," the others underscored.

"But could he give us a tenner? I say, boys, here you is cookin' me quite a dinner. For sure, he's miserly."

It was difficult to hear such talk, and sickening to think that this old man, perhaps sincerely believing in his mission's blessedness and significance and having dreamed, out of a pure heart, of igniting within these people's spiritual darkness a spark of that God-given light burning in his own heart, had traveled thousands of versts for just these results… But on the other hand, who was to blame? They or certain others?

For most prisoners, the beat-up bibles they received had none of the significance the preacher gave to them, and they used them for rolling cigarettes and other, still more reprehensible, uses…

Finally, the day of the governor's anticipated visit arrived. From early in the morning, in unusual excitement, guards and orderlies in their papakhas, ceremonial uniforms, and white gloves, ran through the prison and gave prisoners their orders. First of all they ordered floors washed and painted with ocher again, after they'd been washed just the day before. After they were washed a new task appeared: could they be dried? All the corridors' and wards' doors and windows were opened wide… All the same, they fretted by the minute and rushed to see how the drying was going. The day was windy and overcast. We ate lunch and relaxed; there was neither sound nor scent of the governor. The unusual psychological strain made everyone weary. At last, as the laborers were returning from the mines, word flew around that the news had been announced from the station:

"Get ready!… He's comin'!…"

Everyone again became worried and nervous. The governor arrived an hour and a half later, and then the prisoners were finally ordered to prepare themselves in the wards, to put on their cassocks and assemble themselves… A truly piercing whistle sounded from the gates: we came to attention. Only the boldest still stood in the corridor and looked at the door where the commander's retinue should appear. Lunkov and Petin acted as the spies from our ward. From there, they sent one "telegram" after another. The initial news was that the governor was a tall man with a red beard and gray eyes; according to later reports he was small, fat, and black-haired… The "telegrams" about Six-Eyes's appearance were similarly contradictory. Lunkov reported that he was pale and "not himself," propping himself up like a general and holding his arm in a salute—by all indications he was being severely reprimanded! Elk, who was in love with Luchezarov's military bearing, insisted on the contrary, however.

"You blatherskite! Dirty scum! Why're you lyin'? Six-Eyes looks like a hero's hero. Where else will you see such an artist? Is he really a staff captain? He could pass for the field marshal hisself!"

"Your Six-Eyes is still green. We got a certain individual in Voronezh: he could out-do all of 'em! His mustaches is jet-black 'n' he walks jus' like someone from Iroiskii…[36] Whatta lard-ass!"

"Blockhead, whaddya you know? You got somethin' in yer head, but nuthin' on yer mug."

"But what does he know, your Six-Eyes?"

"Knows how to keep your brother in fear, 'n' how to cancel his reduction, 'n' how to give a floggin'… He don't fear God Hisself!"

"Stop foolin' yerself! He might scare you good-fer-nuthins, but we ain't scared. I'm gonna give a complaint to the gov'nor, but you'll be standin' there neither live nor dead."

"Blockhead!"

"Jus' shut up, you devils!… Now you gotten it in your heads to pour on the syrup. They're comin', y'know!"

"They're comin', they're comin'!" the heralds who'd been standing in the corridor came running as fast as they could.

Everyone came to attention, cleared his throat, and stood straight—as if having swallowed a full poker.

"Atten-tion!!" ordered the guard, and in the ward came: the governor, his adjutant, the *katorga* director, Luchezarov, the constable, the procurator, and many other persons of high and low standing. The governor turned out to be a man of average height, middle-aged with a graying beard. He walked around the serried ranks of prisoners, looked each fixingly in the face, and then, having turned round, asked whether anyone had a request or grievance. Luchezarov identified Petin.

"What's the matter?" asked the governor, approaching Elk.

"Your Excellency, please show some heavenly mercy."

"For what, exactly?"

"Send me to Sakhalin."

"What do you want this for?"

Petin fell silent.

"His term is very long, Your Excellency," interrupted Luchezarov, "and so he's hoping, basing himself on prison rumors, that he'll immediately be given his freedom there."

"You're very much mistaken, dearie," the governor said, "the law is always one and the same. Indeed, I still don't know the arrangements here. Do I have the authority to do this?" he turned to the *katorga* director. "Is this something you can do?"

"Requests are acknowledged from time to time, and then a list of healthy and suitable folk is produced toward springtime. Usually, only inhabitants of Transbaikalia are sent."

"So, you see, dearie," the governor turned to Petin, "this is hard to do. However, if there's a request…"

"Your Excellency," Nogaitsev, who had not informed Luchezarov of his desire to speak with the governor, suddenly piped up. The brave staff captain actually jumped with surprise and, having knitted his brows, revealed a surprised look.

"Your Excellency," Nogaitsev bravely continued, "send me to Sakhalin, too… Be so kind… Show such a kindness…"

"Show you a kindness? See, this is what he wants!" laughed the governor, turning to his retinue. "Well, why do you want to go to Sakhalin? Because it'll be so good for you?"

"Yes, indeed, Your Excellency! It means I'll be stuck on the coast."

"You mean you want to be near the sea?"

"Indeed. It means, with water all round, ain't nowhere to disappear to… Then I could stop bein' confused by the wide world."

"Confused? Seems I'm getting confused staying here. Does anyone else have anything?"

Luchezarov indicated Sokoltsev.

"I'm also askin' for Sakhalin… Their prisons is only half-full with such… travelers."

"Aha! And what of their behavior?"

"It hadn't been especially idiotic until now," Luchezarov warmly shouted, flinging a sideways look at the prisoners.

"No one else has anything to declare?"

"Your Excellency," spoke Lunkov's childishly squeaky little voice.

"What is it?"

"We're gettin' worn out here with too much work… we're gettin' unfair punishments…"

"Be precise about this."

"We're diggin' a ditch… We got very large quotas… I can't finish… My reduction got cancelled 'n' I got a hunnerd birch blows…"

"Is this true?" the governor turned to the *katorga* director, having at the same time laid his hand on Lunkov's shoulder. Something soft and sympathetic toward this kind prisoner, still nearly a boy, appeared to flit across the old general's face.

"He's lying, Your Excellency," the brave staff captain jumped in, "the gentleman director well knows that he was punished not for poor work, but for assaulting and wounding a guard."

The *katorga* director supported these words.

The governor removed his hand from Lunkov's shoulder and asked him:

"Why do you lie, dearie? This isn't good."

The flabbergasted Lunkov was silent. The governor, obviously discontented, went out—and with this continued on to the other wards.

My cohabitants crowded together in a group to whisper about what had happened. Lunkov and Petin had quickly gotten frightened and began criticizing one another. Petin was calling Lunkov a blockhead for not knowing how to vindicate himself.

"When it starts rainin', keep yer trap shut! Suddenly, a great idea pops into his noggin! Ooh, you blatherskite, you bigmouth… Now you'll pay for it, you dirty sod!"

"I'm a sod, but what about you, the great Hercules, 'The Elk' by name, how come you didn't know how to make your case? You couldn't explain why you wanna go to Sakhalin…"

"You ass! Idiot! Why should I explain if the com'dant hisself held the grease for me? So! Now do you agree that Staff Captain Luchezarov was a hero before us all? What kinda governor was that? No portliness, no bearin', nuthin'… Just a little stout, at best! A blush on his face… 'N' there was that carefree attitude!"

The argument was getting hotter and hotter and had started turning from whispers into a racket, when suddenly word came that the governor had already left the prison. Everyone then ran from the ward to the corridor, where the entire prison was gathering and communicating the news. It turned out that in almost every ward two or three men had asked to go to Sakhalin, and that in one of them the governor said to the director: "Well, send them off at springtime!" There was compete rejoicing.

"But I heard dif'rent," suddenly explained the cobbler Zvonarenko, chief of the prison heralds and known as Leather Tack, "I heard the director tell the gov'nor in the corridor: 'There'll be a list for next spring straightaway.' But he answered: 'Let 'em keep hopin'! Anythin' for peace 'n' quiet.' So, now you're hopin' they'll send you to Sakhalin!"

At first, this news acted upon the dreamers like a tub of cold water; but since they wanted to believe in something that promised hope in life, in the next moment they didn't believe it any more than the generally positive news that had already been delivered. Leather Tack was so nonplussed that a choice swear word reared up in him, but he was just able to bite it off. The business almost ended in a fight. It was cut short by new information that Lunkov and Nogaitsev had been taken to the isolator.

"How? What for? Who ordered 'em jailed?"

"Six-Eyes. For untrue 'n' unauth'rized speakin'."

In an instant everyone went dumb.

"Well, now Six-Eyes'll give it to 'em," each man thought, "they'll 'member to watch out!"

XIII. NIGHT

Night. More than two hours have passed since a drumming battle in the Cossacks' barracks; all conversation has long since ended, and my neighbors are lying beside each other, some on the platforms, others the floor, lost in deep sleep. It is deathly still in the ward and prison corridors; from time to time only the guard steals up with feline steps to the door's window and, after jingling his keys, retreats. Someone snores, another turns on his side, muttering or moaning in his sleep, shackles clattering—and once again all is quiet as the grave... The lamp, hanging on the wall, now and then reedily sings in a mosquito's voice—and once more dies away, having become specifically afraid of its own artificial song. But I am still awake, alone among the multitude of living bodies spread around me, and a terrible melancholy gradually takes possession of my soul, raising it like sea breakers, wave after wave, with a quiet but utterly powerful growling and grumbling...

"Greetings, familiar guest, child of prison insomnia! I know, today you will again trouble me right up to morning's light, again torment my nerves, body, and soul... Mythical Proteus,[37] how you change shape and form, how your instruments torture! Killing boredom, a monster with icily embracing and bottomless black pits instead of eyes; the feeling of wearisome solitude, because of which you want to cry, cry and shout without hope of being heard by anyone; fear, raising the hairs on your head, running like frost through your body...

Dark thoughts unconsciously emerge one after the other from such depths in the brain, and before your eyes passes like a funeral procession pictures of the past, the sweet, dear past, which—alas!—cannot be resurrected. But the terrible, difficult, accursed past, forever alive, is always standing there at the head of the bed with all its mistakes, lapses, offenses...

However... what is this strange hallucination? Where am I? What are these corpses doing lying near me—to the right, the left, and there, beneath my feet? No! Someone is moving... Yes, yes, I remember... I am not being controlled by a terrible nightmare, I have only to shout—and these corpses will spring to their feet, clatter their shackles, and, as specters, will talk, move, and fly through the night... But why? They really are the living dead to me. What could blind the eye to this bitter truth? I am alone. Alone like a boat on the ocean, like a blade of grass in the forest, alone, alone! I have no comrades here, even if I desired one among these poor people, even if I wanted to pour out part of my soul to them; there is no heart that would beat in time to my heart, no arms upon which I might credulously lean "in times of my spirit's travail"[38]... Woe, woe! How did I fall into this stinking pit, over which is borne the breath of debauchery and criminality?...

What is there in common between me, who aims for the world's heavenly heights, and the world of ignoble ignoramuses, of mercenary killers? Blood, blood surrounding, skulls beaten to smithereens, slit throats, hanging necks, bullet-ridden chests... And above all this horror hover the shades of the murdered searching for their murderers, poisoning their dreams with black visions...

How my soul has been tormented... How I've tried to hold onto a kind of egalitarian philosophy... How terribly I should want to rest upon a close, familiar breast! To have nearby my own comrade thinking the same thoughts, experiencing the same feelings... Akh, how we could talk—

About Schiller, about glory, about love![39]

It has been all of two years,[40] but so long ago, it now seems to me, I was torn away from everything in the educated world. What has happened there these two years? Perhaps the entire physiognomy of the political world has changed; the great burning questions that even then seemed to me so untimely, so remote, have risen to the surface and stood in line... Mighty life rammed in its key, and the bright waves of an unprecedented world splashed away... Were I thither, were I sooner thither, to share all the rapture, all the labor and earnings of my brothers, to be among rows of simple, modest workers and, if necessary, to perish with them for the sake of progress and the good of the people!

But perhaps this: a dark cloud of stagnation hangs over Europe... The best warriors have left the scene and only petty, pecuniary midges and bugs are bustling about. Were I thither, all the same, were I thither! To suffer and perish there, on the outside, with everyone!

But what is going on now in science, literature, our nation's letters, poetry, art? I chocked them up to hard times when the great epoch's last Mohicans departed the arena and, "in the cathedral of truth, the blessed cathedral of the word,"[41] the petty, third-rate literary "herd" began raising its voice. O, does the abomination of desolation really now rule there?! No, no, it cannot be! Bright new stars have flared, fresh streams have surged powerfully, hale chiefs of the world and of truth, not having perished without a trace thanks to the work of so many generations, have appeared. A mighty poet, heart beating with mysterious power, has appeared, a glorious artist has arisen, verbalizing in a great novel everything that...[42]

Lord, Lord! To vegetate in this pitiful lair and to know nothing, to not find any feasible assistance... To die here, perhaps, in this tortured world of outcasts, to die forgotten by all, with a mark of universal contempt on my forehead, with a moan of helpless despair and damnation in my heart, unknown—to anyone!...

Akh, sleep, restless heart! Silence, insane thoughts!

July–August 1893
Akatui Prison infirmary[43]

NOTES

Introduction

1 *Zapiski iz mertvogo doma*. This is often less accurately translated as *Notes from the House of the Dead*.
2 Several categories of exile were abolished in 1900. However, following the Revolution of 1905, the government used both legal and extra-judicial measures to once more expand the numbers exiled to Siberia and other parts of the empire.
3 P. F. Iakubovich, *V mire otverzhёnnykh: Zapiski byvshevo katorzhnika*, t. I–II (Moskva, Leningrad: Izdatel'stvo "Khudozhestvennaia literatura," 1964). Comparison with the 1896 edition shows that this edition was not bowdlerized in any way.
4 It does not form a part of *World of the Outcasts*, and will mainly interest readers curious about Iakubovich and his times.
5 Michel Foucault, *Abnormal: Lectures at the Collège de France, 1974–1975* (New York: Picador, 2003).
6 Cesare Lombroso (1835–1909) argued that criminality was an in-born trait and that criminals could be distinguished by physical features.
7 Sources for this introduction include: B. Dvinianinov, "P. Iakubovich i ego kniga o katorga," in *V mire otverzhennykh* (1964), 3–20; S. Vengerov, "Iakubovich Pёtr Filippovich," in *Russkii bibliograficheskii slovar'* v dvadtsati tomax (Moskva: TERRA–Knizhnyi klub, 2001) 17: 420–23; "Iakubovich Petr Filippovich," Khronos, Biografii, online: http://www.hrono.ru/biograf/bio_ya/yakubovich_pf.html (accessed 4 December 2012).

In Place of a Foreword

1 In this context, exiles who have escaped their assigned locations and are roaming throughout Siberia.

On the Threshold

1 Epigraph to Nikolaevich Alekseevich Nekrasov's (1821–1877 old style; 1878, new style) poem "Blagodarenie gospodu bogu…" (Glory to Lord God…). The poem portrays the Vladimir Road along which prisoners perished on their way to Siberia.
2 Iakubovich describes here the conditions especially of the route between Krasnoiarsk and Irkutsk in 1887. The Transsiberian railroad was begun in 1892, though the portion covering Iakubovich's original march route was not completed until 1899.
3 Iakubovich was held in the Peter-Paul Fortress's Trubetskoi Bastion for two years (1884–85), and in a detention center for another six months.
4 The executioner (*palach'*) typically doubled as prison barber.
5 After the 1860s, part of the journey into exile came to consist of barge travel along Siberia's riverine network.
6 Stenka Razin was a quasi-mythical bandit and rebel from the seventeenth century.

 7 Excerpt from a poem by Anton Antonovich Delvig (1798–1831), "Ne osennii chastyi dozhdichek" (No Quick Autumnal Shower, 1829).

 8 City in Western Siberia where the exile administration processed incoming deportees and assigned them for redistribution throughout Siberia.

 9 Respectively: Ivan Postradavshii, Pëtr Poterpevshii, Semën Mnogo goria videl, Khvostom na goru, Makhnidralov, A ia za nim, Nepomniashchii tridatsii dvukh let.

10 Respectively: Almazov, Brilliantov, Lvov, Orlov, Sokolov, Burin, Vetrov, Skobelëv, Gurko.

11 "Neither honor nor conscience."

12 I.e., not a very salutary place.

13 Iakubovich actually writes that this is the Siberian word for locust (though in Siberia, *kobylka* more often referred to a dragon-fly, which word also colloquially signified "a flighty girl"). However, linguist V. I. Dal´ gives *Cicada* (as well as dragon-fly) as but a secondary meaning, and notes that *kobylka* generally meant "filly." Indeed, *kobylka* comes from *kobyla* ("mare"). Siberian prisoners also called the execution bench on which they were stretched for floggings the *kobyla*. Vlas Doroshevich, in his 1903 book on the Sakhalin penal colony, argues therefore that the entire prison population's collective self-referential use of *kobyla* derived from its association with the executioner's bench. Hence, kobyla was a metonym signaling both "those who are collectively beaten" as well as "those who ride the mare." The former interpretation emphasized the prisoners' victimization; the latter put a sexually-dominating twist on this victimization. The diminutive *kobylka* seems to have functioned similarly. Even though (*contra* Doroshevich) Iakubovich suggests it was used to refer pejoratively to only a portion of the prison population, his use of the term increasingly accords with that of Doroshevich later in the book. For this reason (and to avoid confusion due to any comparison with my earlier translation of Doroshevich), I've elected to elide what I see as Iakubovich's misconstruction and to translate *kobylka* as "the mare" here as well.

14 Black market concessionaries.

15 *Kormovye* (*den´gi*). Exiles received an allowance with which to purchase food from peasants along the march route.

16 Large-scale deportations to Sakhalin began in 1884.

17 This is why it's every fugitive penal laborer's dream to be arrested no closer than Shadrinsk [on the Siberian border in Perm Province]. [Author's note.]

18 The free command was a minimal security village just outside the prison to which certain prisoners were assigned. It released the burden on prisons while at the same time ostensibly promoted the colonization of Siberia. However, escape from free commands was rife.

19 In what follows, Iakubovich actually ends up describing typical situations, rather than a day.

20 Of course, criminal prisoners cannot simply "bribe" anyone who comes along, as one of my critics has supposed, but simply use the more practiced, expert, and stronger among them. It should generally be noted that under the impression of dated figures in [Sergei] Maksimov's *Sibir´ i katorga* [*Siberia and Katorga*, S-Petersburg: 1871; 1900], the public has a completely erroneous assumption of the wealth among parties of criminal prisoners. I doubt that before arriving in Moscow they were anywhere in Russia endowed with such enormous offerings [as Maksimov states] (and possibly squandered this money there, passing it quickly into the hands of officials, fellow criminals, black marketeers, or card-sharps), for the fact is, most prisoners within Siberia's borders were literally destitute. In Western Siberia, alms are still given, even generously, though almost exclusively in the form of foodstuffs. [Author's note.]

21 From the verb *zhiganut´* ("to lash"). This is a category of prisoners much-discussed by Doroshevich, who characterizes them as those who had lost so much at gambling (including their foraging money and rations) that they had to debase themselves with all sorts of servile acts in order to survive.

22 For example, in certain places in Transbaikalia, where prices were no higher than in Irkutsk Province, they handed out a stipend of 20 kopeks. [Author's note.]

23 *Maidan* (sing.)—an institution combining aspects of the black market, gambling den, loan-sharking, hit squad, and other nefarious services.
24 In Irkutsk Province.
25 Semën Iakovlevich Nadson (1862–1887), Russian poet.
26 Probably the most popular card game in Imperial Russia.
27 During the seventeenth century a schism within the Russian Orthodox Church produced roughly two groups of believers, one that accepted the reforms being promulgated by the religious hierarchy and another that adhered to pre-reform practices. This latter came to be known as "Old Believers" and were persecuted by the Crown. To escape this persecution, large numbers fled to Siberia, where a thriving community of Old Believers was still in existence during Iakubovich's day. These Old Believer sectarians were colloquially known as *semeiskie*, a collective adjectival noun that derives from the words for "family" (*sem'ia*) and "seed" (*semia*).
28 "It's not true, but well devised."
29 A reference to growing tensions with Japan and other powers in northeast Asia.
30 From the word for tanner or leather-maker.
31 An informer.

Shelai Mine

1 Iakubovich's pseudonym for the Akatui mine in Transbaikalia.
2 This poem was censored from all editions of *World of the Outcasts* published prior to 1907. It first appeared separately from the book in a collection of poems Iakubovich published in 1898.
3 Ivan E. Razgil′deev oversaw the Kara mines during the 1850s. He was renowned for his cruelty.
4 In June 1893, the last prison in Kara was destroyed; there is no longer a single prisoner in the Kara region. Gold extraction has passed into private hands. [Author's note.]
5 Russian folklore associates cats with Satan.
6 Luchezarov's real-life prototype was a Captain Ivan Mikhailovich Arkhangel′skii.
7 A catch-all word referring to all Muslims. Iakubovich is averring that few of these prisoners understood Russian.
8 *Shestiglaznyi*— a probable corruption of *shestiglasnaia*, a type of local administrative council (*duma*) first established in 1785 and on which sat six representatives of various social estates. Through this term prisoners are commenting on Luchezarov's old-fashioned severity and watchfulness.
9 The author is reminded of a similar sobriquet for a prison warden in Dostoevskii's *Notes*, but it seems to him that this slight similarity merely proves the tenacity of nicknaming, customs, and even the pungency of witty ascription, and so he will retain it without fearing reproaches of imitating the great artist. [Author's note.]
10 Regarding prisoners' hostile, almost hateful, attitude toward doctors, which will be recounted more than once in the present essays, I would be remiss not to say that a certain part of this observation probably owes itself to random factors and purely local, happenstance reasons, like the personal characteristics of medical personnel in certain prisons during the period described. For example, Krasnoiarsk jail's elderly physician during the Eighties, the late Mazharov, is gladly known by me to have been warm and universally loved. He was not otherwise called "my own father" and "protector." Even the most wicked prisoners told with surprising affection numerous anecdotes, which traveled through the prison world, about this unusually gentle and kind man whom *katorga*'s wretched charges clearly deeply esteemed and loved, regardless of the fact that he was no longer young, was of high rank, and, of course, had in his time seen no small amount of the mare's varied artistry… But for all this, I fancy that the hostility towards medicine and its practitioners is sufficiently rooted in our dark folk—it is sufficient to recall the

cholera riots not so long ago. In the prisons I saw that there were, of course, good doctors and medics, but as a matter of principle they were cursed and unloved just the same. [Author's note.]

11 Sol'shtein. [Author's note.]

12 They call the "heap" the place where the slag or stones from the mining gallery are piled. [Author's note.]

13 Thus prisoners pronounce the word "pyrites"; "quartz" in their language is "*shkvarets,*" or more simply "*skvorets.*" [Author's note.]

14 City just west of the Urals, where a large transfer prison was located.

15 *Cheldon* was Siberian dialect for a vagabond or penal laborer.

16 There are only two offensive words in the prisoners' vocabulary that often form the bases for fights and even murders in prisons: one (bitch) means "spy," the other is too embarrassing to write—it is a man who takes on the role of a woman. [Author's note.]

17 One critic of the present book has found that in Ivan Nikolaevich's refusal there was a most serious mistake. Had there not been this mistake, Iukhorev [a character introduced in the next paragraph] wouldn't have been chosen headman and there wouldn't have been, in his opinion, such unpleasantness as the author describes in Book Two. But this opinion only shows that the esteemed critic didn't investigate the essence of the situation and failed to comprehend Nikolaevich's motives for refusing, which were not at all capricious or out of a desire for peace: for Ivan Nikolaevich, it was *morally impossible* to assume the rights and responsibilities of the headman of a criminal prison—the appointment would unavoidably be accompanied by all sorts of conflicts with the commandant, humiliation, compromises, etc. Not to mention that the commandant, of course, wouldn't have approved such a selection… But even granting the possibility—had Ivan Nikolaevich been elected and confirmed, what would this have led to? Only that the misunderstandings between him and the mare would have emerged significantly earlier, and he would have refused very early on to fulfil the position's responsibilities. The author previously thought all this was self-evident, but he now reasons that a clarification is not amiss. [Author's note.]

18 I.e., stand as a lookout.

19 Actually, this "economic theory" bears a strong similarity to that of economist John Maynard Keynes.

20 The mining administration was separate from the *katorga* administration.

21 Taras Grigor'evich Shevchenko (Taras Hryhorovych Shevchenko) (1814–1861), "Kavkaz" (The Caucasus). Ukrainian poet and painter Shevchenko was interested in depicting peasant themes. In 1847, Nicholas I exiled him to the Orenburg Siberian Corps for participation in the dissident group The Brotherhood of Sts. Cyril and Methodius. He returned from exile in 1857.

22 Lit., *My zavodskie ved'*. A *zavod* was a fortified industrial complex to which both peasants and convicts were assigned as laborers. Nerchinsk zavod was the most significant, but there were many others in Siberia.

23 Written by the poet G. Malyshev during the 1840s.

24 There's an untranslatable similarity here in the sound between "roof" (*krovlia*) and the adjective "blood" (*krovnyi*).

25 Popular variation on the poem "Uznik" (Prisoner), by Fëdor Nikolaevich Glinka (1786–1880).

26 Popular variation on the poem "Svidan'e" (Rendezvous), by Mikhail Iur'evich Lermontov (1814–1841).

27 Centigrade.

28 Popular shorthand term for Petersburg.

29 To this day I don't know if this is how the "barbarian" Razgil'deev died, but the story that he rotted alive and was demoted prior to death spread throughout Eastern Siberia. It's a pity no one's written a biography of Razgil'deev or gathered all the materials—letters, etc.—on his legend. With every decade that passes, the witnesses of that terrible period—the last of the old-timers, the "*bogoduly*"—die off, and it becomes still more difficult to do this. [Author's note.]

30 In Siberia, a birchbark bucket for holding milk is called a *tues*. [Author's note.]

31 A wedding song, significantly altered. [Author's note.]

32 The mining department's instructions strictly order in those cases when a charge has for some reason not detonated "to bore around" it, that is, to make another hole beside it; this is considered the most promising method. It would however be remiss not to acknowledge that this is quite dangerous, and prisoners often flatly refuse proximity boring. Another method is then tried: if possible, they pick out (if it cannot be completely extracted) the dud charge and insert a new one in the same hole. All the same, prisoners and foremen often die tragically in the mines. [Author's note.]

33 An allusion to a certain unnatural foul vice. [Author's note. Rakitin is apparently accusing Nogaitsev of bestiality.]

34 An allusion to syphilis, extreme cases of which cause the nose to disintegrate.

35 Tomsk is a city in what was then called Western Siberia. Barnaul is a city in Siberia's Altai region. Tara is a bit west of Tomsk. Biisk is a town in the Altai.

36 Thus prisoners pronounce the word "foreshaft," that is, the front part of the gallery where the ladders are. [Author's note.]

37 Corporal punishment of women was definitively abolished in spring 1893. [Author's note.]

38 *Ukazhivan'e za katorzhnymi dul'tsineiami...*

39 The Mordvins (or Mordva) are a Finno-Ugric-speaking minority in Russia.

40 A sedentary people from what is today Uzbekistan.

41 An administrative region covering what is today Buriatiia, east of Lake Baikal. Most Old Believer sects abjured a formal clerical caste.

42 Chinese tea entered Siberia through the border city of Kiakhta. Bandits preyed upon the caravans traveling from there to Irkutsk.

43 "A Russian."

44 However, I hasten to say that educational practice subsequently compelled me to make certain concessions to tradition. All my prisoner-students' letters bore names well familiar by their objects (*v* was known as *vagabond*, *w* as wolf, *d* as debauchee), and this arrangement helped many to succeed at their studies. [Author's note.]

45 A city some 430 miles northwest of Moscow.

46 Lit., *vandeiets*—an allusion to the peasants of France's Vendée region who rioted against landed nobles during the 1789 Revolution.

47 Ishim and Ialutorovsk were both in Tobol'sk Province.

48 Fifty lashes.

49 Mispronunciation of "Sakhalin Island," location of a large penal colony.

50 A mythical figure who, at the cuckoo's first call, led what was in fact the army of fugitives who escaped from Siberia's prisons every spring.

51 Salt production was a major industry in Perm.

52 A large percentage of vagabonds sought to disguise their past by assuming pseudonyms. The most widespread of these pseudonyms was "Nepomniashchii," which can be translated as: "I-Don't-Remember."

53 However, it should be mentioned that only in Western Siberia is the commonly used word "*cheldon*" applied to a peasant (just as "*varnak*" is applied to a penal laborer); in Transbaikalia, any peasant would be terribly offended if he is so called, and himself calls prisoners *cheldony*. But the latter, understandably, do not acknowledge this nickname. [Author's note.]

54 Meaning "Man-of-the-Road."

55 With very few exceptions, there were never any serfs east of the Urals.

56 A reference to the condition of most former serfs in the aftermath of the flawed emancipation arrangements of 1861.

57 An archaic and poetical reference to Russia.

58 In prisoner jargon, "chemist" means a demure person, a hypocrite, a toady. [Author's note.]

59 Residents of Siberia and Perm Province often figure disproportionately in the present essays, and this situation may cause the reader not to think well of such persons. Siberians, or, in the extreme, those sentenced by the court to Siberia, truly comprise a huge percentage among the residents of Nerchinsk *katorga*, but this is explained, I believe, for the most part because the large portion of healthy penal laborers travel from the Russian provinces to Sakhalin via the sea-route, whereas the weak and briefly-sentenced go almost exclusively to Siberia, and this is why the latter often enter the free command quickly. However, something is also left to the casuistry of a closed Siberian court hearing. [Author's note.]

60 There's an irreproducible similarity between the words for "student" (*uchenik*) and "teacher" (*uchitel´*).

61 Prison slang for a "miser."

62 Collective labor in which there are no individual quotas is called "bargain work." [Author's note.]

63 Archaic predecessor of modern Russian.

64 Near Kiakhta.

65 Concerning prisoners' ability to master grammar, readers shouldn't think on the basis of the purely happenstance examples in the foregoing and present essays that, in the majority of cases, they do so with difficulty. In my personal experience it could be said the ability of probably half the students was blunted. Taking into account prisoners' ages, regardless of their unusual and weakened perceptibility and poorer memory as compared to school-age children, I still think prisoners can directly impress us with their abilities. And I'm not talking about the outstanding ones in a familiar environment or those who've committed themselves to study for all those years. [Author's note.]

66 One of a series of large *katorga* prisons established in the early 1870s.

67 This could be a small village on the Lena River in Iakutiia, a village otherwise known as Uro.

68 Victor Hugo (1802–1885): *Quatrevingt-treize* (1874).

69 Priests.

70 "Prelestniki"—apparently a popular demotic tale.

71 Iakubovich is in error here: there was no Frankish king named Claudwig.

72 Iashka Pervanov's nickname, *Tarbagan*, means "Siberian marmot."

73 The southernmost region of European tsarist Russia, bordering the Black Sea and largely populated by Cossacks.

74 Eniseisk Province, east of Siberia's Enisei River, was a common destination for those exiled-to-settlement (*soslannye na poselenie*).

75 Siberian peasants traditionally left *mantuli* (dinner leftovers) and *savateiki* (small sweetcakes) on their windowsills for fugitives and vagabonds.

76 Lit., *kachestvo*—a prisoners' word for crime. [Author's note.]

77 Having deemed it possible to allow this or that prisoner into the free command, prison wardens in the Nerchinsk *katorga* administration are obliged to produce a preliminary report (a "present," in the prisoners' tongue). This goes on to be either denied or approved. [Author's note.]

78 Aleksei Vasil´evich Kol´tsov (1808–1842) was a Russian poet whose verse owed much to folk songs and tales. On Shevchenko, see previous note.

79 I.e., from around the Tobol River in Western Siberia.

80 Natives of the Volga region, the Cheremis people are today known as the Mari.

81 Luchezarov uses the formal "you" (*vy*) here.

82 Iakubovich actually received books from his sister Mariia Filippovna (1862–1922). The books he had in prison are held in the P. F. Iakubovich family archive and contain the watermark: "Allowed for reading in prison" (*K chteniiu v tiur´me dopushena*) and are signed: "Commandant of Akatui Prison I. Arkhangel´skii."

83 N. I. Kostomarov (1817–1885), Russian historian, ethnographer, writer; D. L. Mordovtsev (1830–1905), author of historical novels and stories.

84 Camille Flammarion (1842–1925), French astronomer, writer of scientific and popular works on astronomy, as well as science fiction novels.

85 "Bratia-razboiniki."

86 A town near the Lena River in southwestern Iakutiia to which penal laborers were assigned for gold mining.

87 "Komu na Rusi zhit´ khorosho," by N. A. Nekrasov.

88 I don't remember in detail Malakhov's first case for which he was exiled to settlement in Siberia. I know only that he was charged with raping a female neighbor; but Paramon crossed himself and swore (and his story persuaded me) that he was at that time slandered innocently, the sin resulting from his not conceding to this woman's husband in a dispute over a piece of land that he was convinced had passed into their hands. Bearing in mind his haughty disposition and passion for amending the truth, I will allow that false evidence could have been sworn against him. Malakhov recalled with great affection his first wife, whom, out of compassion, he did not bring with him, regardless of her readiness to go to Siberia. He had no communication with her, nor did he even know if she was alive or not, but I remember he would often, having awoken in a gloomy mood, say out loud that he'd seen his wife in a dream and begin recalling his former life in Russia with great bitterness. [Author's note.]

89 Georgian for "novice."

90 "On the mark."

91 The name of the demon central to this same story's plot.

92 Written in summer 1893. [Author's note.]

93 Apparently, a compendium of Russian literature.

94 *Susliki*—probably a metaphorical shorthand for "gopher holes."

95 Thomas Mayne Reid (1818–1883), an Irish-American adventure novelist, published *The Plant Hunters, or, Adventures Among the Himalaya Mountains* in 1858.

96 An obvious pun, meaning "Without opinions."

97 Petushkov can be translated as "little bird."

98 The real-life persons inspiring these characters were as follows: Petushkov—Petukhov; Bezymënnykh—Besprozvannyi; Voronkov—Voronov.

99 The Lezgins are a people native to Dagestan and Azerbaijan.

100 "Mother" was prison slang for "Tatar."

101 Unit of measurement equaling almost 12 liters.

102 "The (bad) time of Razgil´deev."

103 "Monakhov" comes from the word for "monk."

The Little Eagle of Fergana

1 Fergana is a city in eastern Uzbekistan.

2 A variation on the Turkic word for "Russian."

3 "To beg," in prisoners' jargon. [Author's note.] *Savateiki* were baked goods Siberian peasants commonly handed out to vagabonds from their windows-sills—hence these colloquialisms' origin.

4 Alternate spelling of Margilan, in what is today southeastern Uzbekistan.

5 Modern-day Almaty, in Kazakhstan.

6 In all probability this is explained by the great distance between the post offices and his homeland's inhabitants, living in some backwater village, but even more so, by their ignorance of the Russian language. Sometimes, having received a letter from even a son or a brother in *katorga*, an Uzbek or Sart cannot find not only someone able to write a response but even to recite the typically barbarically ungrammatical and illegible letter. Yet

prisoners were forbidden to write or receive letters in non-Russian languages. [Author's note.]

7 *Dumka.*

8 *Urgui* is a quite hearty and beautiful flower that blossoms in Transbaikalia from beneath the snow: five violet petals with a yellow bud in the middle. [Author's note.]

   V. I. Dal´ identifies *urgui* as *Anemone daurica*. However, Dal´ may have been mistaken. Given Iakubovich's description, this flower actually appears to be *Brunnera macrophylla*, which is popularly known in English as "Siberian bugloss" or "Heartleaf."

9 Iakubovich was very close to Usanbai. In his journal and in this book's 1896 publication (and subsequent editions) he says of Marazgali: "In describing Marazgali, I especially wanted for my own sake to preserve and record every minute detail of this kind man still in my memories…" A letter from Iakubovich to his wife's brother, S. F. Frank, tells of Marazgali's subsequent fate: "Of Marazgali, I may inform you (but only you—and in secret), that in actual fact he remained alive and left for a settlement somewhere, and that only 'artistic license' made it seem better to me that he should die…"

Solitude

1 Concerning fetters, the prison command generally exhibited no great consistency and more often followed its own moods. This is why in my essays (in the first as well as the second volume) prisoners appear now with chains, now without chains; at one time they even had to constantly wear manacles… [Author's note.]

2 "With a grain of salt."

3 A reference to the wives of men drafted into the military for standard twenty-five-year terms. Service terms were drastically reduced in 1874.

4 This and the previous quotation are from Nekrasov's poem "Who Lives Well in Rus´?"

5 Readers may find a summary of my views on this subject in "From the Author (*Postscriptum*)," at the conclusion of this book. [Author's note.]

6 One of a series of large prisons designated for those sentenced to *katorga*.

7 "Life" in *katorga* in fact lasts twenty years, but the compounded terms of prisoners who've been sentenced for escapes and other crimes committed in *katorga* are incomparably longer (twenty-five, thirty, even fifty years). [Author's note.]

8 Affectionate name for the popular writer Ivan Andreevich Krylov (1769–1844).

9 *Zhaba*, which facetiously looks like a contraction of *zhena* (wife) and *baba* (woman).

10 An Old Believer sect that practiced genital mutilation.

11 A Skoptsy formula referring to the severing and removal of the penis and testicles.

12 Variation of *chaldon*—a Siberian-born ethnic Russian.

13 A reference to Emel´ian Pugachev, the late eighteenth-century rebel leader who figures in Aleksandr Pushkin's novella *The Captain's Daughter*.

14 *Podduvala*—one of those lower-caste prisoners who worked as a servant for another.

15 Lit., *khokhol*, which means "top-knot" and was also a disparaging word signifying a Ukrainian, since they had traditionally worn top-knots.

16 In southeastern Russia, along the river Don.

17 Recidivists are assigned by a high court to probationary terms (always comparatively lengthy). [Author's note.]

18 A city in south-central European Russia.

19 The Chika is a river in Transbaikalia.

20 Tobacco was a folk remedy for scurvy.

21 Such reassignment was all the more likely given that fugitives typically disguised their identities.

22 A reference to a character in Ivan Ivanovich Panaev's (1812–1862) story "Akteon" (Acteon).

23 The region's supreme prison authority.

24 As Iakubovich surely intends the reader to understand, this phrase ironically mimics that used before emancipation against serfs who were administratively exiled by their owners to Siberia.

25 German D. Goppe (1836–1885), publisher and author whose *Khoroshii ton, sbornik pravil i sovetov na vse sluchai zhizni obshchestvennoi i semenoi* (Good Manners, A Collection of Rules and Advice for All Social and Family Situations) appeared in five editions between 1881 and 1910.

26 A reference to either Laïs of Corinth or Laïs of Hyccara, each a renowned courtesan of ancient Greece.

27 Excluding the stone wall, all Shelai Prison's buildings were wooden and, to tell the truth, had been hastily built irrespective of an enormous expenditure of money. A dignitary who visited us, after treading on a loose floorboard, said, reproachfully shaking his head: "But, you know, each board here cost a hundred rubles!…" [Author's note.]

28 A pseudonym, meaning "Little Elena of the zone."

29 In spring 1893, by decision of the State Council, the corporal punishment of females was definitively abolished. [Author's note.]

30 "N" is written using the Latin letter, and refers to the fictional narrator's patronymic: Nikolaevich.

31 From Shevchenko's poem "Kavkaz."

32 Words doubtlessly of French derivation are to be encountered in prison jargon. Hence, "*bumó*" (gossip, fictitious rumor, witticism) is, of course, derived from "*bon mot*"; and "*motia*" (portion, part) from "*moitié*," and so on. [Author's note.]

33 Original spelling of what is today the city of Khabarovsk, in the Russian Far East.

34 Kara, Zerentui, and Kadaia are each located east of Lake Baikal, near the present-day border with Mongolia and China.

35 Because of its concentration of industries along the Chinese border, as well as its large population of Cossacks, soldiers, and convicts, Transbaikalia District was distinguished from most of Russia's other administrative regions by having a military governor.

36 A town in Transbaikalia.

37 In Greek mythology, Poseidon's son Proteus is an old man of the sea who can change shape and predict the future.

38 A line from Lermontov's poem "I skuchno, i grustno" (Bored and Sad) (1837).

39 Line from Pushkin's poem "19 oktiabria" (19th of October) (1825).

40 In actuality, I was arrested in 1884, that is, nine years before the moment being written about (three of those years were spent under investigation, three in Kara, and very many in Akatui). [Author's note.]

41 Line from an untitled poem written by S. Ia. Nadson in 1882.

42 The rest of this paragraph was apparently censored.

43 Various Akatui Prison officials did what they could to improve conditions for Iakubovich so he could write *In the World of the Outcasts*, including allowing him to spend time in the prison infirmary.